THE CRUSADE OF DARKNESS

Giulio Leoni is a professor of Italian literature and history.
He lives in Rome with his family.

Shaun Whiteside's most recent translations from Italian
include *Venice is a Fish* by Tiziano Scarpa and *The Solitude
of Prime Numbers* by Paolo Giordano.

ALSO BY GIULIO LEONI

The Third Heaven Conspiracy
The Kingdom of Light

GIULIO LEONI

The Crusade of
Darkness

TRANSLATED FROM THE ITALIAN BY
Shaun Whiteside

VINTAGE BOOKS
London

Published by Vintage 2011

2 4 6 8 10 9 7 5 3 1

First published in Italy as *La Crociata delle Tenebre* in 2007 by Arnoldo Mondadori
Editore S.p.A, Milano. This edition published by arrangement with Piergiorgio
Nicolazzini Literary Agency.

First published in Great Britain in 2011 by
Vintage
Random House, 20 Vauxhall Bridge Road,
London SW1V 2SA

www.vintage-books.co.uk

Addresses for companies within The Random House Group Limited can be found at:
www.randomhouse.co.uk/offices.htm

The Random House Group Limited Reg. No. 954009

A CIP catalogue record for this book
is available from the British Library

ISBN 9780099549048

The Random House Group Limited supports the Forest
Stewardship Council (FSC), the leading international forest
certification organisation. All our titles that are printed on
Greenpeace approved FSC certified paper carry the FSC logo.
Our paper procurement policy can be found at
www.randomhouse.co.uk/environment

Typeset in AGaramond by Palimpsest Book Production Limited,
Falkirk, Stirlingshire

Printed and bound in Great Britain by
CPI Bookmarque, Croydon CR0 4TD

For Anna

She brought upon me so much heaviness,
With the affright that from her aspect came,
That I the hope relinquished of the height.

Dante, *Inferno I, 52–4*

CAST OF CHARACTERS

DANTE ALIGHIERI (c.1265–1321) – Florentine ambassador to Rome, poet and author of *The Divine Comedy;* occasionally referred to as Messer Durante, because his full name was Durante degli Alighieri

Some real persons, places and events are described in greater detail in the Glossary at the back of the book (see page 535).

NICO ANACLETO – the keeper of a tavern

BONIFACE VIII – Pope of the Roman Catholic Church, 1294–1303; born Benedetto Caetani

ANTONIO CAFFARO – Decurion of the Castle Guard and hangman; also known as 'Master Hemp'

GIACOMO COLONNA – a member of the powerful Colonna family, nicknamed Sciarra ('quarrel' in Calabrian)

CORAZZA UBALDINI DA SIGNA – another Florentine ambassador

DOMENICA – the old woman with whom Dante lodges, mother of the murdered girl, Ninfa

FIAMMA – the raven-haired daughter of Senator Spada

VANNI FUCCI – a Pistoian whom Dante wounded at the siege of Caprona

GIOTTO DI BONDONE – the Florentine painter and architect, who is painting mosaics for Boniface in the Vatican

MASTER GIUSEPPE – a tailor with a shop in the Theatre of Pompey

KANSBAR IBN TALIB – the ambassador of the Khan of Persia; also called 'the Persian' and 'the Mongol'

MARTINO DA VINEGIA – a sage and the legate of *La Serenissima* (the Republic of Venice)

MASO MINERBETTI – another Florentine ambassador

NICOLETTO – the landlord of Virgil's Inn

NINFA – a young Roman girl who has been murdered

PIETRA – a whore from Florence, and Dante's lover

MASTER PIETRO – one of the diggers who uncovers the coffin of Pope Joan

BROTHER RAIMONDO – a monk of the Dominican order, at the Curia

MANOELLO ROMANO – a Jewish rabbi and a doctor

SATURNIANO SPADA – a Roman senator, raised by Boniface to the rank of Administrator, first among the senators

Florence, 21st October, 1301, after midnight

BLOODY FLORENTINES! Great bladders bloated with the wind of envy, serpents nesting in the garden of the Empire. Craven cowards, rejecting all wisdom and honesty, persecuting the orphan and the widow, devoting themselves instead to the works of Satan – you who open your doors to the seven deadly sins, and shut them in the face of the just, who create exiles and aimless wanderers around all the lands of Italy, arrogant, gluttonous, mendacious . . . And now they wanted him to represent them.

With a furious gesture he thumped his fist down on his desk, making the little candle shake. The flame trembled and went out. And in the sudden darkness that had fallen in the room, the shades of the great men of the past with whom he was in discussion came still closer. Farinata, Tegghiaio Aldobrandi, Mosca Lamberti pressed down on his shoulders with their iron hands, whispering in his ear with voices that seemed to emerge from a stinking pond.

He narrowed his eyes to stare at the document spread

out on the table. He was alone, in that autumn night poisoned by the yellow fog that had enfolded the whole city and now filled the narrow streets around his house. His head echoed with their ghostly voices. Perhaps it was only the buzz of a nocturnal insect, but then the dead are said to announce their presence with a whisper.

He gripped his head in his hands. Soon the companion of his nights, that fiery blade embedded beneath his eye, would come back in search of him. He heard the distant footsteps that heralded its arrival, that pulse in his temples growing ever more intense. He sat back in his chair, rubbing the numbed muscles of his neck, then picked up the piece of paper that lay in front of him.

'Who goes if I stay? And who stays if I go?' he repeated silently to himself, running his eye over the short lines of the text. The Council's decision to send an embassy to Rome, to the court of Pope Boniface. The decree that he, Dante Alighieri, should be part of it.

He shook his head. Days, weeks – maybe months far from his home: that was what they were asking of him. A house that threatened to collapse, inundated as it was by problems and the contrary wind of fate. Towards a hostile lair, into the mouths of his enemies.

And why? To look after the interests of a gang of rich and fearful merchants, ready to give in on everything? Was he to be the one who put his seal on their accounting books?

He angrily screwed up the sheet and threw it on the ground. With a dull thud the lead seal of the Commune bounced on the floorboards and rolled away.

He was suddenly aware of a presence behind him, accompanied by a quivering light. One of the servants had entered silently. He seemed uncertain. He bent down to pick up the lantern, lighting it with the candle that he held in his hand. 'Master, there is someone here looking for you. He insisted on coming up to your room . . . even though the hour . . .' he added, looking towards the still-open door.

Dante saw a tall, slender outline slipping through the doorway, wrapped in a cloak that seemed to mingle with the shadows of the wall. The face too was hidden by a travelling mask, against the dust and filth of the streets, giving it an appearance at once grotesque and unsettling.

The new arrival had stopped in the doorway. It waited for the servant to leave, standing aside as if it feared being brushed by his body. Then a voice emerged from behind the fabric covering his mouth: 'Are you Dante the Florentine?'

The voice of a woman, young, firm, coloured by a faint inflection that Dante thought gave its origins as Campania, or perhaps the lands of the Capitanata. Her hair was gathered in a scarlet bonnet, closed at the throat by a golden pin, illuminated by a stone that gave off green reflections. Without waiting for his reply, the stranger took a few steps forward until she entered the circle of light. 'The son of Alighiero? Who was prior of the city?'

It was more a statement than a question. But because the poet, still disoriented, hesitated before replying, after a moment's silence she repeated: 'You are Messer Dante?' again asserting rather than questioning, in the same calm voice, as if indifferent to the reply that still did not come.

At last Dante stirred himself: 'Yes, *Madonna*. Yes, I am Dante the Florentine, at your service,' he replied, suddenly rising from his writing desk and courteously holding his hand out to her so that she would come still closer. Then, as if thinking again of his own words, he hastened to add: 'Florentine by birth, *Madonna*, and certainly not by habit.'

'Dante the poet, who wrote:

> *Love wept within my heart where he abides;*
> *Whereby, indeed, my soul was so dismayed,*
> *That then I, sighing, said within my thought:*
> *"Sure it must be my lady too shall die".'*

And then, without leaving him time to reply: 'So you are on intimate terms with death?'

The poet had listened dreamily to his lines being recited by that melodious voice, which warmed his heart again, prompting an avalanche of memories; and he wanted to cry out that yes, he was indeed their author. But he was unable to utter a single word, frozen as if every syllable had been transformed by regret for a love that once had been, into a poison that paralysed him now. And it was the sweetness of that voice that cast the spell.

The woman seemed to be waiting for a reply. Certainly, she was staring at him, her head slightly tilted towards her shoulder, as if assessing his reactions. But he could see nothing through the holes in the light cloth mask, only two dark and indecipherable patches. Then he saw her shivering slightly.

'So you are on intimate terms with death?' she repeated. 'They say you know the reasons behind things. The things that are because they are. And those that are not because they are not. They say you studied at the École des Beaux-Arts in Paris, that you uttered your lectures from memory, that you left the other sages who were opposed to you confused in their darkness. They say you know the science of the stars.'

Dante remained silent, spellbound by that hidden boy who had now assumed a definite form in his imagination. He saw in his mind a youthful face, but one with very marked features, as clear as those that the Romans had left in their ivory cameos. Perhaps surrounded by a crown of bright curls, which must surely have shone with the strength of those full lips that quivered beneath the fabric. As tall as the poet himself, holding herself upright without a trace of fear or shame, as if she was used to treating men as equals. But there was also a hint of modesty in the hands folded in her lap, as if she felt a strange deference towards him.

'Yes, I . . . indeed. Is that what they say?' he stammered, blushing. 'And who says that?' he added, as if to ease the flames that these words of praise had unleashed in his soul.

'Someone who told me of your infinite skill. I appeal to you, for a task dependent on your skill. Have you been asked to move to Rome?'

Dante's lips half-opened in surprise, as his eyes ran towards the sheet of paper on the desk. How could this woman know that? And who was she? Only now did he realise how unusual it was for a woman to be alone in the home of a married man, and the dangers this might involve. For a moment the hypothesis occurred to him that it might be a plot organised to damage him, that in the shadows behind her men might be crouching, ready to surprise him and drag him into a public scandal.

'The hour is beyond the depths of night, an unusual time for a decent woman to leave her own rooms. And dangerous for the times, and the place,' he began cautiously. But the stranger raised her right hand, bringing her index finger to her hidden lips, while her other hand rested on the poet's heart, almost as if she wished to interrupt his words. So he added only: 'Tell me what you wish.'

'You must come,' she said. Then, without giving him time to object: 'You are expected.'

'By whom?' the poet murmured.

Instead of replying, she put her hand under her cloak and drew out an object. It looked like a wooden cylinder, perhaps two spans in length. 'Here is a gift for you, the only one worthy to receive it. But it is only one part. The rest is hidden in Rome. It is waiting for you.'

Perplexed, Dante took the object that the woman held out to him. A kind of box, carved from an olive branch. He ran his fingers over its gleaming surface. There must be some way of opening it. The wood was covered with a series of very fine carvings, a scene populated by figures drawn with the gouge of a master. He brought the object to the candle flame, trying to see more clearly.

Beneath the quivering light the pictures seemed to come to life. A man and a woman, in old-style clothes, were standing on the banks of a brook. On the other side a mass of indistinct figures was crowding onto the banks, as if waiting for the couple to move to join them. But something prevented them from advancing, something other than the tranquil billows that separated them. The landscape too was different, the branches of a forest behind the couple, a desolate wasteland behind the crowd. Upon the whole scene seemed to lie the unquiet shadow of a curse: as if that river were not merely a stream, but the boundary between two kingdoms . . .

The man was holding something in his hand, something that looked like a little leafy branch. Dante looked up at the woman with an exclamation of surprise. He thought he had worked it out. The golden branch, the sign of the gods that opens the road to the depths below.

The two figures were Aeneas and the Cumaean Sybil, standing on the banks of the River Styx. And on the other side, the crowd of shadows waiting, the dead frantically awaiting the visit of the living. The lines that rose to their lips as if they had before their eyes the pages of the book:

Just in the gate and in the jaws of hell,
Revengeful Cares and sullen Sorrows dwell,
And pale Diseases, and repining Age,
Want, Fear and Famine's unresisted rage:
Here Toils, and Death, and Death's half-brother,
  Sleep
Forms terrible to view, their sentry keep.

How many times had he reread the sixth book of the *Aeneid*? He grasped the head of the cylinder, and after a moment's resistance the stopper gave, revealing something inside. It looked like something rolled up: he started shaking the cylinder, trying to make it slide out, with mounting excitement.

'Gently,' he heard the woman say as she lightly gripped his wrist. 'Cease your impatience.'

She delicately removed the container from his hands,

then plunged her long, slender fingers into the cavity, taking out the roll. With great care she unrolled part of it on the desk: it was covered with characters, lined up neatly in narrow parallel columns.

'Few have touched it, since its author finished writing it. More than twelve centuries ago.'

Dante felt short of breath. He had to lean against the desk, taking deep breaths to overcome the vice that had gripped his chest.

The roll of papyrus really seemed to have been dried up by the heat of the centuries, fragile and torn in some places. Woodworm had erased the text here and there, dragging it with them to oblivion. But Dante's eager mind closed each gap with the precise words, drawing them from his prodigious memory as if from an inexhaustible well.

He had stretched his hands towards the papyrus, but he remained motionless, not daring to touch it. Had Virgil's pen really left its trace on this frail piece of matting? Had his divine hands really touched it, and had his divine words settled upon it? In those distant, time-worn signs, could his voice really be heard? He found himself listening as if to pick up the echo that seemed to rise from the roll, like a spirit from the tomb that seeks to imprison it.

Gradually his senses returned to him, and with them the lucidity of the intellect. And with it doubt, which is the flame that revives thought, the base spectre of deception appearing to the mind once more.

'How can you say this . . .' he murmured, turning back towards the woman. She raised her hand, bringing her index finger to her lips once more.

'The work of the master, written with his own hand.'

'Why? Why me?'

'There's a task awaiting you. Accomplish it, this is the prize. Given in advance, as a pledge for the pact.' Then, quickly, she made for the door on nimble feet, disappearing among the shadows beyond.

Dante wanted to cry out, to attract the attention of the servants, to run after her towards the stairs down which her light tread faded. But he sat there petrified, his dilated pupils still filled with the papyrus roll on the table. Nothing seemed more important now. Then he managed to pick up a corner of it, and beneath his fingers the ancient papyrus rustled faintly, as if his touch really had awoken the voice concealed inside.

Now the pain in his temples exploded with fury, as if the gods wanted to punish him for his joy a moment before. He delicately gripped his treasure: was there the slightest chance that the woman had been telling the truth? That this papyrus really bore the mark of the great Virgil? And that the rest of his work was hidden in Rome? That it waited for him there?

He felt against his shoe the leaden weight of the seal

that he had thrown to the ground. How much more wretched was that other piece of writing, even though cloaked in the arrogance of power.

And yet perhaps that too was precious, he said to himself, picking it up from the floor and unfolding it as best he could. In a way that he would never have imagined.

2

5th November, at sunset, on the road to Rome

YET AGAIN, the rain came crashing down on the roof, accompanied by a crash of lightning somewhere nearby. Water had already started cascading inside, following the outline of the old straw-covered beams. The man shifted along the bench on which he was sitting, to avoid being caught by the jet, until he was touching his companion with his shoulder. His companion moved in turn, irritated by the proximity of the massive body looming over him.

'The Colonna family's people are in revolt. They've attacked the rock of Morlupo, and burned down the way-station at Fiano. And there's no trace of the troops who were supposed to be arriving from Rome,' the man murmured in his interlocutor's ear, as though afraid that this news, uttered in a louder voice, might make the situation worse. 'What is your decision?'

The other man came closer to the flames in the fire-place where he was trying to dry his clothes, drenched

from the rain that had accompanied his journey uninterruptedly for the last two days. It was dusk, but his body
was already aware of the signs of the terrible night ahead.
Shivers ran through him, his forehead burned with fever.
He stared at the fire as though searching it for an answer
rather than warmth, clenching his jaws to ease the ache
that had taken root in the back of his neck for several
hours.

'I don't know. Let me think.'

'Perhaps it would be better to wait . . .' a third man
whispered behind them. 'Or perhaps . . . go back?'

'You can't get back along this road, Messer Maso. The
Commune and its freedom depend on us. Nothing must
stop us. And nothing will stop us,' Dante said after a
moment. 'Ask the landlord if there's another route to the
Eternal City. And you, Corazza, ensure that the mules are
accommodated for the night, and fed. I . . . I need to rest.
For a moment,' he went on, wrapping himself tightly in
his cloak.

HE HAD been left alone. He closed his eyelids, motionless, waiting for the nausea and the sense of dizziness that
had taken hold of him to subside. Suddenly he was aware
of the presence of someone behind him. He turned his
head slightly and half-closed his eyes.

'Excuse me, Messer,' he heard a voice saying in the

THE CRUSADE OF DARKNESS

shadows, standing beside him. 'Are you the ambassadors of Florence?'

With a crash the log in the fireplace broke in two and rolled onto the brick base with a cloud of sparks. The man who had spoken wore the simple clothes of the people: a greyish jacket complemented by a hood raised to cover part of his head. Without giving him time to reply the man continued: 'And you are at their head, Messer Dante Alighieri. The poet. I heard you're looking for another route to Rome. I can help you.'

Dante had become watchful, as anger welled up in him, driving away his unease for a moment. This expedition was supposed to have been veiled in secrecy. And instead it seemed that everyone was aware of it, starting with their names. He glanced towards Maso Minerbetti, who was still intent on conversation with the landlord. He, the idiot, must have been the one who had been showing off around the place, probably with some servant-girl at the inn. Or else the other one, Corazza Ubaldini da Signa. The two men who had been imposed upon him as companions, more to keep an eye on him, he was sure of it, than to help him.

'What's the other route?'

The stranger slipped his hood back onto his shoulders. He was just a boy, with thick curly hair. Dante met his lively, open gaze. Still without the malice that comes with age. There was something about him that inspired trust.

'A few miles from here. Near the Rock of Turrita there's a landing place on the river. A relative of mine is the ferryman there. But he can take you all the way to Rome for a small consideration.'

Dante meditated on the offer for a moment. Certainly, it was possible. Since abandoning the Via Cassia to try and avoid the insurrection, they had seen the banks of the Tiber in the distance several times. 'We have some mules with us, and luggage.'

The boy shook his head. 'It's a small boat. There's only room for one of you. But we've got to leave straight away.'

Dante leaped to his feet. He closed his eyes tight to stop his head from spinning. This could be the opportunity that he was waiting for, to free himself from the others and get to Rome first. His eyes alone would see what awaited them there, his mind would have time to draw up a plan all by itself, without having to answer to the others about the fate of his city, which had been placed in his hands. Suddenly he felt better. He gripped the pot of wine that lay on a table next to him, and took a long swig. The liquid flowed down warmly within him, accentuating the sensation of unexpected well-being that this new possibility had granted him.

THE OTHERS had received the news of his solitary departure with suspicion, but also with relief. They could wait in safety for the waters to calm, with all their luggage and supplies. Besides, what could the poet do on his own? And the river was in spate, after the heavy rains of that autumn, and all kinds of things could happen . . .

It certainly wasn't goodwill that he had read in their faces as he took his leave.

The boy had witnessed his rapid preparations in silence, in a corner.

'Wouldn't it be better to wait for the dawn?' Dante asked him, seized by sudden doubt.

'It isn't safe to get from here to the river. And the ferry won't wait for us beyond midnight.'

'Why do you say it's waiting for us? How do they know we're going?'

But the boy had already made for the door without answering.

OUTSIDE THE storm seemed to have eased, turning into a fine, cold rain. Dante huddled in his travelling cloak, trying to shield from the rain the bag that he carried with him. The rest of the luggage would follow him, with the other two. But he wasn't concerned: everything precious that he owned was there with him, in that leather bag. Inside it he had put the credentials of the Commune of Florence, accrediting him as ambassador to the papal court, along with a small reserve of florins for the journey, the bundle of his most recent writings, from which he never parted, and – most importantly – the Virgil papyrus. Those papers that he constantly covered with words before erasing them again, always in search of the perfect expression that continually eluded him.

As soon as he had crossed the threshold, the boy had headed along a path through the grass, barely recognisable in the intermittent light of the lamps. He walked briskly ahead of Dante, turning from time to time to check that the poet was still following him, and gesturing him onwards. After a few steps all traces of human presence seemed to have disappeared. The landscape had suddenly turned harsh, bramble bushes lined the path, which seemed to lead towards a forest of tall trees. They passed the trees, as the ground beneath their feet seemed to sink. A branch bent in passing by the boy struck him in the face.

Dante stopped himself from cursing, noting that the boy had stopped and was looking cautiously ahead of him. He was looking for something in the darkness, his ears pricked. Then he brought a finger to his lips, gesturing to Dante to be quiet. The poet too peered intently but could see nothing threatening. There was only the faint sound of the rain-whipped branches.

At a new gesture from the boy they set off again down the now-precipitous path. They must have been close to the river. He had to grip the reeds to keep from falling, his pace slowed by the mud in which he had begun to sink.

'Will it be long now?' he asked the boy. But the boy, by way of reply, merely pointed straight ahead to where a gap opened up in the reed-bed. Then, a few footsteps further on, he stopped.

Dante caught up with him. In front of them, in the darkness, a huge snake of water, swollen with the rains, swirled and eddied turbulently from one shore to the other. He couldn't see the opposite bank.

'There it is,' the boy said. 'The Tiber. The ferry isn't far away. But we've got to get a move on – it's nearly midnight!'

At that moment the wind opened a gap between the clouds, letting the shimmer of a thin sickle-moon cast its feeble light on the muddy shore. Dante spotted a boat half-hidden by the reeds. He hurried after the boy, who was sliding down the steep ridge of the river bank. His shoes plunged into the icy water, and for a moment the squelch of his footsteps drowned out the roar of the turbid water.

'Climb aboard, Messere,' said the boy, after exchanging a glance of agreement with the man on the boat, who immediately pulled the barge-pole from the murky bottom, pointing it at the shore and starting to push to free the boat, which was already rocking unsteadily under his feet.

'Are you sure . . .' Dante murmured, suddenly uncertain. The sensation of being caught in a trap unsettled him once more. But before he could think again about what he was doing, with another powerful thrust of the pole the boat was several yards from the bank. Beneath the keel he felt the embrace of the current, which grasped the craft mightily, dragging it away from the shore.

'You've got to get to the city, Messer Alighieri. They are waiting for you.'

'But who are you?' the poet shouted at the boy, who was starting to disappear into the darkness. 'Who are you?' he yelled again. 'Who's waiting for me?'

'The ones who trust you,' he heard the boy saying in the distance, as his outline disappeared.

Dante turned towards the ferryman, who stood in the stern of the boat. The man stared straight over his head, correcting the course with sharp blows of the oar. The boat was about to reach the middle of the river, making straight for that series of swirls and wrinkles that revealed the line of the current in the moonlight.

'Do you know that boy?' asked Dante.

The man ignored his words, continuing to inflict nervous little twitches on the oar. Dante repeated the question in a louder voice, and this time he seemed to attract the other man's attention. The boatman raised a finger to his ear, shaking his head.

'Are you deaf?'

Again no reply. The man merely stared at him from the depths of the hood that covered his head, careless of the big drops of rain that had started falling again.

Rolled up in the bottom of the boat was a rough felt blanket. Dante unrolled it and hid underneath it in search of shelter.

From beneath that improvised refuge he could see the far-off shores that slid away at growing speed, now that the boat had reached the middle of the river. The rain had been joined by violent gusts of wind that slipped under the cloth, trying to tug it away. Among the reeds the last outposts of the forests could be seen, and trees that waved their branches in the night. Where the mud carried by the waves had formed sandy islets, thickets had grown, with conjoined branches, straddling the watery road with their bridges and triumphal arches.

This was the spectacle that Aeneas must have seen as he reached the shores of Latium, Dante thought, his imagination fired with Virgil's ancient verses.

SUDDENLY HE heard a chorus of distant howls that seemed to be moving along the shore. Made yet more fierce by the inclement weather, the wolves of the area must have woken up, and for some mysterious reason they were accompanying the boat's descent with silent footsteps.

Dante crossed himself. Above him the wind had parted the clouds: he raised his eyes towards the vault of heaven, scouring the east in search of some sign of dawn. But fever and the exertions of the journey must have confused his sense of time. The night was still black. High above shone the Hair of Berenice with its cold dust of stars. The Virgin rose on the distant horizon, as the luminous Twins sparkled in the middle of the sky, inflamed by the great yellow eye of Jupiter. He wished he could draw a good omen from this, but something in his soul prevented him. Those stars were cold, motionless, frozen by the same fever that shook his bones to the marrow.

They were mute, as if their power to leave their mark on the fate of men were in some way suspended. Perhaps it was the ceaseless howling that marked his journey with ill omen, calling to him that he could count on his own strength alone. He was alone, more alone than he had ever felt before.

At that moment the boat was shaken by a violent shock. As if to confirm his feelings, the poet saw the swollen carcase of a horse passing beside him, its hooves raised to the sky in a kind of macabre gallop. The whole surface of the water was dotted with a mass of detritus torn from the banks, descending with him towards the same destination.

3

D AWN HAD risen. Dante shook himself from his brief and troubled sleep and came out from beneath his makeshift shelter, breathing in deep lungfuls of the fresh morning air. The rain had stopped, making way for a cold light that sullied the landscape with a greyish halo. The man at the tiller was still in his position as if he were made of the same material as the boat. Without relaxing his grip on the oar, with one foot he pushed towards himself a goatskin that lay on the bottom of the boat. Dante brought his lips to it, after pulling out the cork stopper with his teeth and sniffing. Wine, he thought, darting a grateful glance at the man. Then he took a long swig.

He felt the liquor spilling down his throat, sharp and tepid. He felt as if his body too had just started to wake up, conquering its nocturnal torpor and the sharp pains that fever had stirred in all his bones.

He ran a hand over his brow. It seemed less hot than the night before, and the burning of his lips had eased as well.

He tried the wineskin again, to quench with a sip the sense of nausea that tormented him. Shivers still ran through him. He rose to his feet, careful not to stagger, struggling to relax his numbed muscles. Meanwhile he glanced around him, towards the banks of the river. The shadowy mass of vegetation was further away now, on either side of the boat. The river had grown wide, truly becoming the abode of the Tiberine god. And even the tangle of branches and foliage dragged from the shore, and carried away by the current for a moment, seemed as if it might be the submerged hair of the god, as he appeared to Aeneas when he saw him rising from the water.

Suddenly a big stone bridge appeared as if by magic from behind a river bank and slipped above their heads.

Now the signs of human presence were distinct. Broad open spaces appeared among the green of the scrubland, and cultivated fields and vines had replaced the reeds on the banks. Large shacks in the distance and some stone farmhouses entrenched themselves on the slopes, with thin filaments of smoke above their roofs.

Ahead of them the river took an L-shaped bend, disappearing from view. The boat took the curve, where the current seemed faster.

'Is Rome still far?' Dante asked.

The oarsman stretched out a hand, pointing in front of him. At that very moment the boat came out of the bend.

Dante opened his eyes wide and got to his feet. Ignoring the rocking of the boat, he stood where he was, still drowning in the splendour of what had appeared in front of him. The corners of a huge boundary of walls, lit by the light of dawn, stretched along the bank of the river as far as the eye could see, alternating with majestic towers and marble arches. It looked to him as if all the stones and bricks in the world had been aligned by a race of giants, who had used their strength to produce not a city, but an entire kingdom. Masses of banners and flags fluttered on the terraces, like flames stirred by the wind.

The boat continued to glide along the river. For a moment, the vision disappeared behind another bend, then the city revealed itself once more, as new details of its shape emerged.

They carried onwards, until they ran alongside the walls which at that point touched the water, looming above their heads. On the right bank the gigantic dark stone drum of the Castel Sant'Angelo appeared, breaking the vast horizon, like one of the four columns that hold up the celestial vaults.

And yet there was something unhealthy about the splendour of it all. From close to, the walls revealed all their decrepitude, studded as they were with cracks and occasional reconstructions made with salvaged materials. At one point particularly weakened by the rushing waters, which must have undermined the foundations, a mass of hastily accumulated marble blocks and soil could be seen. Broken shafts of columns, torn from who knows what temple of forgotten gods, had been piled up on the terraces, and the remains of delicately carved entablatures acted as makeshift jetties. A forest of climbing plants enfolded them in its clutches, as if after the violence of the barbarians it was now the countryside all around that was assailing the city.

Furthermore, the banners that flapped on the towers were only threadbare pieces of cloth that soared over deserted walkways. No one seemed to be guarding the fortresses.

For a moment he had the sense that he was heading towards a dead city. The river seemed to be the only living thing.

Around them, the number of boats had increased, and his pilot constantly had to manoeuvre the oar to avoid crashing into them. Low, wide barges, full of agricultural products, others loaded with tree-trunks or building stones, seemed to be waiting for a gap in the forest of triangular sails to unload their own cargoes.

The oarsman raised an arm, pointing to a broad staircase that descended towards the river, looming like a marble waterfall from the walls, which at that point withdrew from the shoreline. This must be the harbour, Dante said to himself, observing the frantic activity of men and carts on the shore and on the two great curved ramps that climbed towards the arches dug into the wall.

HE SET foot on land with a start. Just enough time to stretch out for his bag, and immediately the ferryman had pulled the boat away, using his pole as a lever against the river bed.

'How much do I owe you?' called the poet. But the other man was already looking back towards the middle of the river, losing himself in the forest of the other boats.

Dante tried to watch after him, puzzled by his strange behaviour. He barely avoided a cart being driven at him with great violence, bewildered by the sudden tumult of frantic shouts and movements in which he found himself plunged, after a night of silence and the initial impression of the experience of death.

He looked around, perplexed. There was something strange about this frenetic activity, something different from the ordinary confusion of a normal market. Cries and exclamations pursued one another. And fear. The same smell that he had been aware of on the battlefield, the impalpable smell that is kindled in the mind before it reaches the nose, and which inflames the teeth to bite, the legs to flee.

Everyone was shouting, pointing at something behind them. He turned once more towards the waters from which he had come: a few yards from the shore one of the boats was approaching, dragging something attached to one of the oars. A white, slimy mass, just under the surface of the water, as shapeless as one of the monsters said to live in the depths.

One of the people on the shore leaned forward and stretched out to grasp the white mass. Then, with the help of some others, he managed to drag it onto the wharf, where it lay inertly. Dante too stepped forward, concerned about what he was seeing.

The body of a woman lay on the road. She must have been immersed in the water for a long time. The fish had already begun to attack her face, making it almost unrecognisable, and the waters had washed it away until it looked like a boneless mass, distorted by its own weight and flattened to the ground like a deflated goatskin. Only its long black hair remained to prove the body's sex with any certainty. The crowd around them was filled with convulsive animation. Dante pushed his way through, until he was only a few feet from the body. Careless of the agitation around him, he knelt down to get a better view.

'Where is the drowned woman?' he heard someone shout behind him. Some soldiers were coming quickly forwards, forcing their way through the crowd with rough lance-blows to the backs of the curious. 'Send for the Red Hoods!'

'She didn't drown,' Dante said calmly. 'Look,' he added, pointing to the woman's torso.

It looked as if someone had traced a cross on the body. The water had washed away every trace of blood, and the belly of the unfortunate woman was marked solely by a faint greyish line. Only the hands and feet seemed strangely well preserved, as if submersion had had no effect on those parts of the poor corpse.

From beneath his cloak the poet drew the dagger that he carried hidden in a secret pocket of his robe, and with its tip he delicately lifted one flap of the wound. He gave a start, as a horrified murmur rose up among the crowd. The thoracic cavity was completely empty: only a few pointed ribs emerged brightly, drowned by the grey of the decomposed flesh. He went on lifting the flaps of the wound, running his blade along the body of the wretched woman. The belly too had been emptied of innards, and swarmed with tiny river fish. The murderer had gone beyond killing: he had inflicted perversions on the poor woman, butchering her like an animal.

The crowd around them had begun making the sign of the cross. Some knelt and prayed in a loud voice. The chief of the guards had carefully followed the poet's movements. His baffled eye moved from the corpse to Dante, as if unsure which of the two was more deserving of his attention.

'Who are you?' he asked after one last glance at the corpse.

The poet rose quickly to his feet and looked at him resolutely. 'My name is Dante Alighieri, a Florentine. Head of my city's embassy at the court of Boniface.'

The man seemed uncertain for a moment. He was tall and massively built, with a complexion so dark that he might have been mistaken for a Saracen, and black narrow eyes between two large ears adorned with gold rings.

He looked Dante up and down, lingering on his mud-splattered clothes and the simple travelling bag that the poet wore around his neck. Then he stretched out one hand, testing a corner of the poet's robe between his fingers. 'An ambassador. Florentine. Cheap clothes: your city must be a poor one, if it sends you as its representative all on your own, on foot and without a retinue. And yet I'd have said you lot were drowning in gold, judging by the arrogance of your merchants.'

'It isn't trade that gives the sign of a people, but its customs and its laws,' the poet replied coldly. 'And laws and customs do not go clad in gold. You should set your mind to avenging this wretched woman. Seek a man who is skilled with blades. But not a soldier – a cut as clean as this was not inflicted with a sword. Seek a surgeon, or a butcher.'

'They're often one and the same,' the officer stammered, leaning over the wound again to have a better look. 'I see what you mean, Messere. In your own country are you a sawbones, perhaps, or a tooth-puller?'

Dante clenched his jaws, holding back the reply that had leaped to his throat. Then he calmly shook his head. 'I am a member of the Guild of Apothecaries, if you're interested. And as for you, I imagine you are in charge of taxes,' he added poisonously.

The man stared at him, as a shadow crossed his face. Then he exploded unexpectedly into peals of laughter, which immediately spread to the other armed men. Some of the other members of the crowd started laughing too. Dante felt a sudden pang of shame at the wild hilarity that had broken out around the poor woman's corpse. He felt that another insult was being inflicted on her, perhaps even more ferocious than the one that had lacerated her flesh. The murderer had erased her life, but they were ignoring even her memory.

'I am Antonio Caffaro, the Decurion of the Castle Guard. And the tax that I impose is made of ropes, Ambassador,' he added, kicking away an onlooker who had got too close. 'Some people also call me the dance-master, because of all the people I've had dancing in the gallows-yard of the Castello. People who had the strange idea of violating the laws of His Holiness the Pope.'

'You're the hangman!'

'The executor of justice. Or Master Hemp, as the common people call me. When I'm not listening, of course.'

The officer burst out laughing again, very loudly. As

if this laughter were a signal, his armed men deployed their lances, roughly pushing away the surrounding onlookers. Then they picked up the corpse, after wrapping it roughly in a piece of sack-cloth, heading towards the steps that rose from the wharf along the bank of the river.

LEFT ON his own, Dante looked around him again. The landing place swarmed with porters busy loading and unloading the barges, beasts of burden yoked to the wheels of strange contraptions set up on the shore to lift the cargoes, piles of bundled merchandise. And everywhere there were rows of men in chains; lined up along the steep ramp that ran along the steps, they dragged themselves along slowly as they climbed and came back down again, beneath the lash of the guards. Every now and again one of the whips cracked against the skin of one of the men, without any apparent motive for choosing one or other of them for pain.

'Who are they?' the poet asked a man standing near him.

'They're from Palestrina. They rebelled against the Pope, and now they're in chains. The ones who weren't killed.'

Dante watched the long line of unfortunates, amongst whom there emerged from time to time the grey hair of an old man. Palestrina had been destroyed shortly before by Boniface's army, thus paying for its loyalty to Colonna, the Pope's rival. Razed to the ground like ancient Carthage, and – like it – scattered with salt so that even its memory would be lost over time.

With a shiver he turned once more to the stranger. 'Where can I find a place of lodging in this city?'

'Are you a pilgrim? Try the friars, at Santa Maria del Popolo,' the other man replied, after a brief glance at Dante's wet clothes and his shoes still covered with river mud.

'No, I'm looking for a house,' Dante replied, unable to hide his irritation at the man's smugness.

'Then try the Campo Marzio,' the other man replied with a shrug.

DANTE SET off up the staircase, to the top of the stone river bank. He found himself in a long, narrow street that stretched in either direction until it disappeared on the horizon, lined with an array of brick constructions that formed a second wall after the one level with the waters of the Tiber. He turned to glance once more at the opposite bank of the river. In the distance, the great bulk of the Castel Sant'Angelo blocked off completely the view of the Vatican basilica and its palaces, which could just be glimpsed behind it, peeping out from a forest of rooftops. He could also see one corner of the long, narrow bridge, which ended just in the lee of the rampart of the Castello.

He tried to take his mental bearings. Back in Florence, in the Franciscan Library of Santa Croce, before his departure, he had studied a map of the city. But that simple circle, surrounded by the drawing of a wall and dotted with pictures of churches, palaces and bridges, now revealed itself to be entirely useless, so far was it from reality. He must have been on a road parallel to the Via Lata, as the popes had renamed the old Via Flaminia. By following it, he should, he reflected, be able to reach the centre of the city.

He set off at a march. A sudden burst of sunlight, lukewarm and bright, had split the pall of clouds from which it had rained all night without interruption. He felt comforted, as if it was a good omen. His clothes were drying, and his feverish shivering had abated. A sense of languid torpor was taking hold of him. A little way on, the road widened slightly, running alongside the arcade of a little church. A toppled Roman statue rested against the colonnade, a figure of a woman with her head covered by a helmet.

'Minerva,' he said to himself, dragging himself under the portico and dropping to the ground. There, protected by the shadow, the light and the hubbub of carts and pedestrians in the street became a vague murmur, like the waves on a distant sea. No one seemed to pay him any heed as he slipped into sleep.

Only the ancient goddess seemed to watch him benevolently. Perhaps in her exile she would extend her protection to a poet far from home?

EVERY NIGHT the fever brought him dreams infested with nightmares. And in his dreams he thought he was still walking, along a road of broken rubble. The houses had disappeared, making way for bloody sand-dunes on which he clambered with ever greater effort. He felt exhausted, his eyes burned by a storm of flaming sparks. Around him, the sea of sand swarmed with poisonous snakes, which moved in a circle, in bundles bristling with mouths and scales, like bramble-bushes carried on the wind.

Further on, the desert seemed to be torn by a vast, circular abyss that barred his way, leaving the far side out of sight. A confused and indecipherable noise seemed to be rising from the depths, like the backwash of a storm-tossed sea.

Having reached the edge, he decided to lie down on the ground, to lean over the edge of the abyss to see what was hidden in the depths of that great stone gullet. He felt as if he was tumbling in, filled with horror. A huge mass of people teemed in the void, clutching the walls of the abyss like worms on a carcase, stretching their hands out towards him, emitting horrible screams in an incomprehensible language. From the very bottom a reddish glimmer rose to the mouth, as if a river of lava flowed in the depths.

Frozen with terror, he tried to escape the sight, covering his eyes with his hands. But his skin and bones seemed to be made of glass: nothing could erase the vision of those bodies seeking an impossible salvation from him. He didn't understand their voices, but for some inexplicable reason he was sure that each of them was crying out his own name, as if that cloud of desperate creatures consisted of men and women he had met on Earth, crying out to be recognised.

He was filled by a feeling of infinite compassion. He had to do something to help them, however huge the task. He lay down again on the rim of the abyss, stretching out his arms towards those nearest to him. In his dream he thought he could feel on his skin the cold of those fingers touching his, as the white faces, disfigured by horrible sores, came closer to him, and their twisted bodies, swollen or skeletal and starving, writhed below him like snakes.

The horror, which had been submerged by compassion, took hold of him once more: suddenly he understood all together the infinite cries that rose up towards him. Those creatures did not want to be saved; they were waiting for him, they were calling to him to join them. He felt the rock beneath his chest becoming fragile, the handholds that he was clutching crumbling and yielding beneath his weight. He cried out in desperation, as he began to slide into the huge mouth.

It was then that he felt a hand behind him grabbing him to hold him back. A hand that he gripped with all his strength. A strong, ancient hand. Paternal.

HE WOKE up with the sound of screams still ringing in his brain. The sun was already hiding behind the tall buildings on the street, but the coming and going of the people around him continued unabated, entirely indifferent to him. The Romans must have been used to the sight of homeless pilgrims, he said to himself. He hastily checked the bag on which he had rested his head while he was sleeping. Everything still seemed to be there, he recognised with a sigh of relief. He felt hungry, but the pain in his bones and the sensation of fever seemed fainter. He looked around, trying to get his bearings.

He was supposed to be meeting the others at the Florentine delegation. But something inside him told him it was better to keep his distance: the idea that they had been assigned to him as companions to keep an eye on him had not abandoned him since the first steps of their journey.

At the harbour they had told him to try at Campo Marzio. They had to be there, but the forest of towers and stone constructions that had taken root on the remains of the Roman monuments, with their barred doors and the big chains that blocked entry to the alleyways, did not seem to suggest any particular hospitality. He slipped into the flood of people, still looking curiously around. The towers followed on one from the other, sometimes clustered together like the hands of giants coming out of the earth to grasp the sky.

Having walked a short way, he suddenly emerged into a square, a kind of clearing in that stone forest. In front of him the imposing colonnade of an ancient temple, surmounted by a tympanum on which could still be seen the remains of the bronze bas-relief that had once adorned it. Heads and arms and legs of majestic proportions, clothed in robes that still seemed stirred by a divine breath.

He froze in astonishment, his nose in the air. Behind the temple a great dome rose towards the sky, one that could have contained the Baptistery of his city four or five times over.

'Never seen anything like this before, eh, stranger?' he heard someone asking beside him. He turned towards the man who had spoken, a peasant with a big basket of vegetables under his arm. He seemed happy with Dante's amazement, as if he felt he were in some sense responsible for this wonder.

'What is it?' Dante asked breathlessly.

'The church of St Mary and the Martyrs. But the sages also call it the Pantheon. Do you like it?'

HE WAS suddenly filled with a feeling of wretchedness, of impotent sadness. How had that wonder been constructed by creatures without divine Grace, far from Revelation? Violent, blinded by vice and greed, tempted only by worldly glory, without the sweet song of the Scriptures. And yet so majestic, so infinitely great. What a pathetic spectacle his own contemporaries were in comparison.

Before the puzzled eyes of the peasant he took from his bag the cylinder with his Virgil inside it, and brought it to his lips, kissing it. As for that big dome, who would ever be capable, nowadays, of bending the shapeless fluidity of language, of beating it with the illuminated power of poetry, until it bore a similar, terrible splendour?

He stirred himself, carefully returning the cylinder to the bag. 'Are there lodgings hereabouts?' he asked.

The man pointed to a building that led onto the left of the square, a big three-storey construction with a large wooden roof.

'Try over there, at old Athanasius' place. You'll find the Sun Inn there. It's famous among outsiders. Good wine and good food, and never more than three people to a bed.'

Dante shook his head. 'I need a room. On my own.'

The other man looked him ironically up and down. 'There's no lodging for gentlemen here. And none of the families who rule here,' he added, nodding towards the towers that jutted all around, 'receive tramps in their houses. You can try the other side of the river.'

'Which direction?'

'Straight ahead. Cross over at the Island Bridges. Maybe on the other side, around the Prati di Castello, some peasant or other might be willing to take you in.'

The poet set off along the way suggested. He passed by the drum of the Pantheon, once again confronting the forest of alleyways that resumed beyond the piazza. Several times he was forced to turn back and try a different route, constantly finding the road blocked off with chains or walls cobbled together by piles of masonry and fragments of marble, piled up to block his passage. He crossed a wide space still paved with the remains of big travertine paving stones, on which the raised foundations of lots of ruined temples still stood. He climbed onto one of these, trying to find his bearings: perhaps this was the old Forum, he said to himself, where the Caesars and the first martyrs had walked. But in that case he would have been able to see the Palatine Hill; while instead the texture of buildings continued uninterrupted on the other side, broken only here and there by new towers and new ruins.

He must have got lost, he thought, recognising a broken column that he was sure he had passed before. And then, all of a sudden, he found himself on the bank of the river. At that point the Tiber broadened, its agitated waters running alongside a little island similar in shape to a ship beached by the current. In the middle of the island a leaning obelisk further marked its resemblance to an ancient boat. He thought he actually noticed a huge marble face appearing from the waters near the downstream tip.

He crossed the first humpbacked bridge that arched towards the island, passed down the gap between a tower and what looked like a fortified monastery, then faced the second bridge, which reached the other bank of the river. At the top of the arch there were three men leaning indolently on the stone balustrade. They wore clothes that had once been vividly coloured, but now appeared faded and worn by time and dirt.

He had thought he spotted a look of accord running between them and immediately put himself on his guard. He felt his muscles contracting, while with a swift gesture his fingers brushed the dagger in the secret pocket of his coat, to be sure that the weapon was still there.

But perhaps they were only three layabouts, he said to himself, continuing nonchalantly towards them. When he had reached them, one of the three stretched out his leg to block his passage.

'Stop, stranger. You've forgotten the bridge toll,' he said in a coarse and grating accent.

'The toll? How much is that?' Dante replied cautiously.

It was possible that to cross a bridge you had to pay a sum of money. At the end of the ramp a little guard's tower protected access from the other shore, and perhaps there was some kind of border before you reached the district on the other side of the river. Except that these men, with their strange liveries, really were suspicious-looking toll collectors.

'That depends.'

'On what?'

'On your bag. Show us it.'

The other two had also come forward. Dante took a step back to regain his distance, but the men kept walking. 'No,' he snapped.

The man who had spoken took another step forward until he almost touched him. The poet could clearly smell the horrible breath that issued from his rotten mouth. Suddenly he was aware of a swift movement behind him. He jerked his head round, just in time to catch in the corner of his eye the presence of a fourth man who seemed to have appeared from nowhere. He was crouching behind Dante on all fours, like a dog hiding in his shadow.

Before he could realise the purpose of this strange behaviour, the poet felt a violent shove against his chest, which sent him tumbling backwards. He fell over the man crouching on all fours behind him and ended up on the ground, with his legs in the air.

With the speed of a wild animal, the crouching man grabbed him from behind with his legs, at waist height, while the other two men gripped his arms, pinning him down.

Dante recognised that he was lost, with no chance of reaching his dagger to defend himself. But a blade had appeared in the hands of the man who seemed to be the boss. He felt the fold of the metal touching his throat, while the now-familiar voice was heard once more, accompanied by the unbearable smell.

'Now you'll see what it means to rebel against the guardians of the bridge.'

Caught in that defenceless position, Dante saw from the corner of his eye one of the men stretching his hands out towards his bag and rummaging in it. He first took out the cylinder containing the papyrus and, having opened its top and quickly looked inside, threw it indifferently away. The container bounced on the cobbles, rolling towards the balustrade, accompanied by a desperate cry from the poet. He saw it come to rest, swaying back and forth on the edge of the bridge next to a crack in the balustrade. One more hand-breadth and his treasure would be swallowed by the waters.

Careless of the blade still pointing at his throat, Dante writhed with all his strength, although without managing to free himself from the grip that held him immobile. That grip had in fact become even more violent, while the man drew from Dante's bag his little purse of money, with a cry of triumph.

Suddenly he was aware of a change in his condition. The man with the knife had leaped to his feet, backing away from him. And the grip on his arm had gone too. The only one behind him was the man gripping him with his legs, but Dante felt him moving as if he in turn were trying to extract himself from this uncomfortable position to get back on his feet.

With a jerk the poet freed himself, throwing himself towards the cylinder, heedless of everything else. Only when he felt his fingers clutching the carved wood did he turn towards his assailants, while with his free hand he finally gripped his dagger.

The scene had changed completely. His assailants were lined up against the balustrade of the bridge, surrounded by a group of armed men threatening them with their pikes. Leaning lazily against the balustrade, a dark giant surveyed the scene.

Master Hemp seemed to recognise him. 'Messer Florentine Ambassador, apparently you should thank your lucky stars. And not just them,' he laughed, tapping his own chest with his thumb.

Then he motioned to his men, pointing to the four prisoners, who looked at him in terror. The soldiers swiftly reversed the direction of the lances, holding them near the blade, and began beating them brutally. Dante listened to their cries of pain and pleading, becoming increasingly faint until the four men were nothing but a bloody, weeping pile.

The guards went on beating the inert bodies. Dante had followed the work of justice with satisfaction. When, in the course of the beating, the man who had threatened him with his knife had rolled near his feet, he had taken advantage of the fact to give him a kick, still trembling within himself at the danger in which he had put Virgil's papyrus.

But now he was beginning to fear that the fury of the beaters would finally kill them. He held the Decurion's arm. 'Stop your men, or you will bring only four corpses to the cell.'

'To the cell? We reserve lodgings at the Castello for a quite different breed of men, Messer Florentine Ambassador. Perhaps in your prosperous city the Commune is rich enough to give bread even to your thieves. But here we follow other rules,' the man said, snapping his fingers at his men.

At this signal the soldiers lowered their lances and hurled themselves on the bodies, from which there still came a chorus of laments. They lifted them up, laughing loudly as they did so, and threw them one by one into the river, ignoring the faint pleas that some of them were still in a condition to utter.

Dante had followed the scene with horror. He dashed

to the balustrade just in time to see the wide circles in the water where their bodies had plunged in. After a few moments he saw a few black dots re-emerging downriver, only to be dragged away by the current.

The Decurion was leaning against it too. He glanced ironically at the poet, as if surprised by this unexpected pity.

'They're river rats, scoundrels. It's the second time for two of them. With a bit of luck, they'll live to see a third.'

One of the soldiers had bent down to pick up the bag and purse. He held it out to the Decurion, who weighed it in his hand. Then he loosened the laces, looking carefully inside.

'You are well supplied with gold, Messere. It isn't prudent to walk around our streets like this, without an escort.'

'This money belongs to the noble city of Florence, and it has been entrusted to me because of my office. Thank you for saving it. My Commune will reward you, should you ever pay us a visit.'

The Decurion had nodded in silence at his words. But rather than handing him the purse, he tipped its contents into the palm of his hand. He quickly counted the florins, then took away a good third of them, pouring them into a little bag fastened to his belt. Then he gave what was left to Dante. 'You have only paid for the light of the sun, Messere. Which will be able to continue shining down on you.'

'What do you mean? Is this the justice of the great city of Rome? The sun shines on us all, certainly not because of you!'

The man laughed. 'Wrong. Every morning the sun, in order to rise, asks permission from God our Father. Then, to rise over the seven hills, it asks permission from the Holy Father, Pope Boniface.'

He had come closer, stretching his hand out towards the poet. He tapped his chest with his index finger. 'But to cross this bridge it asks my permission. As you see, there is justice – and lots of it. But tell me, where were you going? The far side of the river is certainly not a place for men of your condition. Carters and pig-breeders. And Jews,' he added with a grimace.

'I'm looking for a place to stay.'

The Decurion glanced diffidently at him. 'Only rats hide in these parts. But you may have your reasons. You can try old Domenica's place, over there beside the tower,' he said, pointing to a construction of stone and wood that rose beside a big tower, just past the point where the bridge curved to the stony bank of the Tiber. 'The old woman hires out her house and her daughter to pilgrims. And I think she's got another one free at the moment – a room, I mean,' he added with a mischievous wink. 'Hurry up, it's nearly sunset. And the bell of the Campidoglio's about to ring the curfew. You could have another bad encounter. Or you could run into me,' he added, exploding once again into cruel laughter.

*

46

DANTE WENT down the steps. On the opposite shore the head of the bridge was watched over by a tall brick tower crowned by dilapidated crenellations. But around it, hunched like beggars, were shacks and cabins, and the long sheds of the stables. There were no people in the streets, unlike the excitement on the other shore. It was as if a curse or the plague afflicted this part of the city. He quickly approached the house to which he had been directed, and knocked on the little door that opened up into the courtyard. Next to it, under a shelter of branches, a fat sow grunted, suckling a litter of piglets. A strong smell of dung filled the air.

No one replied. He was tempted to turn back, when the door half-opened. A boy poked his head out. His face was pale, his eyes drenched with tears.

'Is this old Domenica's place?' the poet murmured, caught off-guard. 'They told me I might find lodging here . . . I need a room. My name is Dante Alighieri, a pilgrim, from the city of Florence.'

He didn't want to mention his post. Not immediately, at least. It was always wiser to be cautious. The boy went on crying and sniffing. He stepped aside without a word, inviting the poet inside.

The house was plunged in darkness. Even outside, the poet had noticed how all the windows were locked with wooden bars. Only the occasional rare blade of sunlight trickled through the chinks of the shutters. He followed the boy through a first little room immediately after the door. At the end he glimpsed a narrow stone staircase that must lead to the floor above. Next to it was a door, from which there seemed to come the quivering glow of a lit flame.

The boy motioned to the poet to follow him, heading towards the other room. In the doorway Dante stopped with surprise.

In the middle of the room there was a rough wooden table, surrounded by four lit candles in rough wooden candlesticks. And on the table, laid out motionlessly under a white cloth, was the body of a very young girl with long black hair loose around her pale face.

In the gap between her half-open eyelids he glimpsed a crescent of her eye, and her mouth too was open, her lips drawn back over a set of regular little teeth. It looked as if she had just finished uttering a word, or singing a song, and that death had frozen her like that, holding the last breath in her throat. That delicate face, even though frozen in agony, suddenly reminded him of the faces of those girls whose celestial voices accompanied the sacred ceremonies in the church choirs of his own city.

He crossed himself. Less than a day in St Peter's city, and death had already crossed his path twice. He went on studying the boy's face, wondering sadly why no one had thought to lay out the body before rigor mortis froze its features. He approached to bat away an insect that was hovering above the dead girl's face.

Lined up against the wall a small group of people was immersed in a funeral litany.

'She's my sister,' the boy said suddenly, behind him. At these words an old woman, her head half-hidden by a pall, looked up at him, interrupting her prayer. But then she immediately resumed it, plunging herself back into her grief. The others, too, after a momentary interest in the newcomer, returned to their litany.

'She's my sister,' the boy repeated with a sob. 'She was killed.'

Dante stared at him in surprise, then looked back at the dead girl. Those twisted features were not the result of carelessness, but the ravages of violence on that poor innocent body. And that half-open mouth had been stopped not mid-song, but in a cry of desperation.

'Who killed her?' he asked the boy in a whisper.

'A demon, Messer. He tore her flesh with his claws, before throwing her away like rubbish. Poor Ninfa,' he groaned again, disconsolately.

The poet's eye returned to the body, which until now he had observed only fleetingly, all his attention absorbed by the dramatic expression on her face. The thin cloth covered the corpse like a pitiful shroud, hiding it in a strangely confused way. He became aware of something unhealthy, as if . . .

Seized by an irresistible impulse to know, he approached the table and stretched out his hand. He stopped only for a moment and then, having overcome one final hesitation, resolutely lifted the cloth.

He felt his lips contracting with horror. The whole left side of the unfortunate girl seemed to have been mangled. The leg had been torn from its socket just below the knee, and a stump of femur still protruded from the tortured flesh, cleanly severed as if by a surgeon's blade. The arm barely reached the elbow, which ended in a frayed lump of blood and shapeless tissue. The knife had also penetrated the girl's side, and a long wound ran from her armpit to the start of her pelvis: that whole side seemed squashed, as if the lungs and other internal organs on the heart side were missing.

He dropped the shroud again. He felt a violent pain, as if that gesture dictated by curiosity had become another assault, and as if he himself were in some way the cause of the disfigurement that he had merely revealed.

The men and women present had not protested. It was as if that vision were itself enough to leave them paralysed with horror. Or perhaps they were used to the insolence of the powerful, and did not dare object to the actions of someone with the face of a nobleman. Only the boy moved, approaching to rearrange the shroud over the body.

'It really does look like the work of a demon,' Dante murmured. 'When did this outrage happen?'

'Three months have passed since the night my sister disappeared. She had gone out to . . . to . . .'

The boy had stopped, suddenly blushing. Dante looked around. The modesty of the house, the poverty of the furniture and this very ceremony clearly suggested the likely trade that had led this unfortunate girl to tempt death.

But she could not have been killed three months before. The body, although ravaged, showed no trace of decomposition. The flesh – what remained of it – although marked by a greenish pallor, seemed solid and firm around the bones. It wasn't possible.

So someone must have abducted her, held her in his claws for a long time, and only launched his attack at the very end.

'Where was the body found?'

'On the bank of the river, outside the gate beyond the Monte dei Cocci. Thrown in a ditch, as naked as a dog. Her poor clothes had disappeared too. The Red Hoods were about to put her in an unmarked grave, had it not been for an acquaintance of ours who happened to be passing.'

All around, the rhythmic chanting of the funeral litany continued unabated. But the poet's mind had begun frantically connecting all those details, trying to put them into a pattern. He tried to draw a syllogism from them, according to the teachings of the great Aristotle.

But then he suddenly stopped, abruptly waving those

fantasies away. He had come to Rome for other reasons, not to investigate yet another manifestation of human wickedness. And yet something kept him there, something stronger than his mission.

Meanwhile a sound of heavy footsteps coming from the doorway drowned out the prayers, and a group of soldiers burst in. Among them he recognised the Decurion: the man glanced at him ironically, then without a word came forward towards the coffin. He looked contemptuously at the corpse, then turned to the mother.

'I came to check that you weren't breaking the law, old woman. At night and without a candle, remember that. And let there be no trace of the corpse at dawn. And remember: for what you have paid, only my generosity allows you to bury her here, and not at the Muro Torto!'

Dante instinctively darted forward. He placed himself between the man and the coffin as if to protect it from further profanation. His hands were trembling. But the Decurion did not seem troubled by his gesture.

'So you followed my advice, Ambassador. You'll find it satisfactory here, once the house has been cleaned.'

'Why don't you look for the perpetrator of this outrage and take just revenge, rather than insulting these people, who are suffering the effects of a crime that you could have prevented?' the poet asked in disgust.

'The cellars of the Holy Spirit are full of the bodies of

the ones we find in the street, each time we do our night patrols. What's special about the girl?'

'Innocence. And this,' Dante replied, taking one corner of the shroud and lifting it to reveal the horror beneath. 'Don't you see the connection with the other butchered woman, at the river?'

The Decurion glanced distractedly at the body. 'Yes, I see. So?'

The poet hunched his shoulders. 'Don't you think it's strange?'

'These whores must have come up with a new way of attracting customers. It'll come from France, I'm pretty sure. Like all the other nonsense that the pilgrims bring here, along with scabies and the plague of heresy. And murder: the Red Hoods never worked so hard as they did during Holy Year. But luckily the Jubilee is over, and the murderers will have gone back home, with a holy blessing,' he concluded with a snigger.

'Were many prostitutes killed?'

'Who knows? Since Boniface was illuminated by the Holy Spirit, and put a twopenny tax on every shag, those good ladies vanished like mist in the sun. They've gone into hiding, and if one of them disappears, they're certainly not going to come and tell us. But enough of all this, or I'll think you've come to Florence for reasons that have nothing to do with politics.'

The man glanced threateningly around once more and,

after motioning with his head to his followers, made for the door, followed by his men.

THE ROOM had suddenly been plunged back into darkness. Dante was boiling with rage; he was ashamed at himself for not having stood up to the Decurion's arrogance, and was also disturbed by what he had guessed, and what he feared.

The others had followed the scene with their heads bowed, motionless, as if used to undergoing such harassment. And yet it seemed as if the Decurion's warning had been understood. One of the women approached the corpse and covered the girl's face with a fold of the shroud. Then, with a big darning needle, she began sewing up the flaps of the cloth with coarse stitches. As the fabric tightened around the girl's body, the nature of the outrage inflicted on her God-given form became increasingly apparent. The sense of order violated, God's design destroyed by a perverse hand.

The last stitch had finished tightening the cloth around the girl's head, after the mass of her hair had been gathered up in a fold of the fabric. It was then that her mother abandoned herself to a terrifying wail. She howled like a dog, louder than the wolves that had accompanied the poet's night-time journey on the river. Louder than any scream he had ever heard in his life. Not even at

Campaldino, not even among the laments of the soldiers being hacked to pieces, had Dante ever heard the voice of such pure and absolute pain.

Surrounded by the other women, who tried in vain to comfort her, the mother had got to her feet, her arms raised aloft, and thrown herself on the corpse for one last embrace.

The only two men present, the boy and an old man, approached in their turn, taking the corners of the improvised sack and lifting it. But that wretched weight seemed too much for them. Dante saw that the old man was staggering on his feet, threatening to fall. He instinctively stepped forward, taking a corner of the cloth and supporting the old man with one arm to help him regain his balance.

'Please, Messere, help us,' the boy said imploringly. 'The cemetery isn't far. Just outside the gate.'

Dante had a moment's uncertainty. Then he nodded, and took the body's weight at the feet.

The little cortege set off in silence, along a path that passed by the big tower and then proceeded amongst the shacks and vegetable patches parallel to the river bank, towards the walls that could be seen further off.

No one had a candle or a lantern. The sickle-moon above gave off just enough light to make out the harshness of the terrain. They all seemed anxious to proceed quickly, in that sad, unlit funeral. No cleric accompanied the corpse to its final rest, nor was there any oration in the clumsy Latin of the priests. The order from the authorities only stressed what a sad and ancient custom had decreed since time immemorial for women of this kind, who had died in the sin of lust. From time to time a few stifled sobs pierced the silence, otherwise broken only by quick footsteps on the cobblestones.

THE WALLS had got closer, and now appeared as a dark barrier that closed off the view of the horizon. They reached the barred door. No one was guarding it, as if no one was concerned about what happened in these parts.

But beside the great gate, a postern was open. A little gap, just big enough to let a person through with their head bent. They passed down the narrow passageway, struggling to carry their cargo to the other side, following the trace of the old Roman road.

This must be the Portuense, the poet thought. In spite of the pungent air, still filled with rain, his forehead was pearled with sweat. The effort was starting to become unbearable, his fingers clenched around the cloth contracted in a painful spasm. He felt the fabric escaping from beneath his fingers, and constantly had to renew his grip to ensure that their cargo did not slip away. For a moment he was worried that he wouldn't be able to do it and, panting, thought of asking for a rest. But the sight of the boy and the old man hobbling along with the strength of desperation led him to clench his teeth and keep going. He had been the prior of Florence, he had accompanied his companions at arms, his friends to the tomb. He wouldn't give in now.

Beneath the soles of his shoes he felt the road-bed getting harsher, as if the further they got from the gate, the worse the state of the road became. By the roadside, a boundary stone uprooted and thrown to the ground and a few bits of column testified to the old graves that had once been here. Modest graves, nothing like the solemn sepulchres that had been said to flank the Appian Way. Then the road began to run alongside an open space, surrounded by a low dry-stone wall. Little humps scattered without rhyme or reason gave the ground an unequivocal significance. A few crosses and not even a carved stone, no sign of pity. A graveyard of the poor, a thin veil of earth against the void.

Reaching a corner of the field, they stopped, leaving their burden on the ground. One of the women had brought a big wooden spoon. She handed it to the boy, who began to dig a hole in the ground with all his strength. A few hand-breadths, just enough to hide his sister's body from the light of day, certainly not to protect it on its long journey to the Day of Judgement, the poet thought.

They laid the body in the little ditch. The boy began

to cover it with the earth he had removed, while Dante and the old man pushed additional dust with their feet, piling it up against the grave. '*May the earth be light to you, as you were to the earth*,' the poet murmured between clenched teeth, crossing himself.

Meanwhile it became apparent that someone had joined them, emerging from the dark almost like a ghost. A thin man, covered by a black cloak and with a stiff, tall hat on his forehead. Sewn to his chest he bore the yellow wheel that distinguished him as a son of the people of Judah.

The man held a stone in his hands. He approached the tomb and set it down reverently close to the dead girl's head. Then he took a step back, and Dante heard him intoning a chant in a low voice.

The voice at first rose shrilly, as if a night bird had risen from the ditch to insult the unfortunate girl. But then the chant changed its tone, the incomprehensible sounds began to connect into a melody that evoked an ancient grief, marked by the *Amen* that provides comfort in the face of nothingness.

It was no longer a barbarian verse; now it seemed as if an angel had descended among them, to contend for the young woman's soul against the powers of darkness. The chant became a whisper, a groan, a cry of triumph. It glided over the stones and the graves, embracing that desperate place with its pity.

'That's Manoello Romano,' the boy murmured, noting the poet's surprise. 'He promised he would intone the *kaddish*. Even though they are infidels, I wanted at least one prayer to go with my sister to her place of rest.'

Dante nodded. But what God had this man invoked? he wondered. And if he was the same as the God of the Christian people, how could his majesty bend benevolently to the invocation of someone who had denied him in the Son? He thought of that shattered body that lay beneath the dust: did those sounds help her soul to rise, or did they chain her to the void, with a second injury?

AT THAT moment the chant came to an end with one final flourish. Manoello raised his face to heaven, remaining motionless with his arms open in supplication. Then, after a long pause, he turned and moved towards the poet, stopping a respectful distance away from him. He lowered his head and murmured deferentially: 'May I pay my respects to the prince of poets? The great Alighieri?'

Dante gave a start, disconcerted at having been recognised. How could this man know about him? But before he had time to reply, the other man went on.

'The elders of our people, in Florence, informed us that you were coming to Rome. You defended my people when you were prior. I awaited you eagerly. And when that boy told me your name, I read that as a sign of the will of God.'

Dante didn't answer. He was pleased, but also embarrassed. 'The obstinacy of your race and your faith condemns you to loneliness and suspicion. All I did was discern the truth in your belief, according to law and conscience.'

Manoello was about to reply, when the dead girl's mother dragged herself painfully over to them. The old woman seemed to be shaken by the torpor into which she had been plunged, and approached the poet, her eyes filled with tears. She looked at him as if she were seeing him for the first time only now. 'Messere, help me,' she said all of a sudden. 'I have heard that you are a just man. Punish the murderer.'

Dante stiffened. 'I'm the ambassador of Florence. I can't take care of you. It is a very high office that weighs upon my shoulders,' he exclaimed. He was about to leave, but something held him back.

'Who will mete out justice for me, if the men at the top don't look my way?' the woman went on pleading behind him, between her sobs. She wiped her eyes with a flap of her veil, and stared at the poor grave as if expecting more of an answer from it than from the men around her.

The poet felt uneasy. With that refusal he was putting himself on a par with the low soldiery that he had known – as useless as them. The old woman in tears, the little mute heart behind him: where had he seen that image before? Where had he read about it?

Then he remembered the legend of the Emperor Trajan. The Roman had stopped his army to help a widow imploring for his help. The plan of the emperor, his fate, had come to a halt among the forests of a hostile land. The gold eagles of the legions had been lowered, everything had stopped to wait.

'Very well, old woman. Your daughter will be avenged,' he said on impulse. Without yet knowing how, without knowing anything.

He felt the boy take his hand. 'You were looking for lodgings. Stay with us. There's a whole empty room now.'

THE BOY walked ahead of him on the way back, concerned that the poet might change his mind. Then, once they were back in the house, he guided him upstairs. The atmosphere up there seemed even grimmer than before. The boy opened a door, showing him a little room, little more than a passageway carved in the recesses of the wall. But there was a bed, a water jug and a tall chest beside the narrow window. He could use the chest as a desk, if necessary. He didn't need anything else.

Without thinking, he threw himself on the bed with his clothes on, after putting his bag in the chest. But first he had picked up the wooden cylinder. He took out the papyrus, which he unrolled slightly, delicately. He looked again at those faded signs, with no need to read the words. He knew everything by heart, and the sound of that ancient tongue came pouring into his head, line by line, as sweet as the song of the sirens. Again sleep slipped within him, as it had done under the temple portico. But this time he didn't dream.

4

WHEN HE awoke it was broad daylight. With trepidation, he picked up the papyrus that had slipped to the foot of the bed and put it back in its holder, then fell to his knees, feeling an intense pang in his stomach. Nature was rudely reminding that him he had eaten absolutely nothing for over twenty-four hours. He had no time: he had to go to the Curia, present his credentials and request an audience. And alone, before his other two companions arrived. He had chosen to enter the wolf's lair, and now any failure or triumph was his responsibility alone.

He picked up the decree of appointment and left the room, after carefully putting the other papers back in the chest. But first he tied up the papyrus cylinder with one of the belts of the bag and hung it around his neck, hidden under his clothes. He headed towards the landing, in search of someone who might be able to show him the way to the Vatican palaces.

On the stairs he bumped into the boy, who was coming up with a jug of water and a loaf. 'I thought you might be hungry, Messere,' the boy said.

Dante thanked him. Then he broke the bread and ate it quickly, standing there on the stairs. The boy stared at his every movement, curious at how swiftly Dante ate it, to the last crumb. Around them the house seemed deserted, without any of the sounds that animate the residences of the living in the morning. Perhaps the women were shut in their rooms, Dante thought, cultivating their own grief.

'To the Vatican,' the poet said at last, after taking a long sip of water. 'What is the quickest way?'

'Walk along the Tiber, heading upriver. At the gate, turn into the Via della Lungara, which runs along the edge, through the fields to the Castello. After a mile you will see ahead of you the walls of the Leonine City, and the roof of St Peter's. You can't go wrong.'

'The Leonine City?'

'Pope Leo's wall. The fortress where Boniface lives, protected by the lances of his soldiers. And by his hangman's rope,' the boy replied, spitting on the ground with a grimace. 'It encloses the Basilica of St Peter's and the tower of the Castello, and between them the palaces of Boniface and his gardens. It is there that he takes refuge, when there is a revolt and he abandons the Lateran.'

*

DANTE SET off at a brisk pace in the direction indicated. When he reached the gate of the Aurelian walls, which protected the district of Trastevere, he had to wait patiently in line for his turn to be let through, amongst the small crowd of peasants heading for the fields. The toll guards carefully looked through everyone's panniers and bags, in search of something to tax.

At last he was allowed through. A white road ran along the shore of the Tiber, passing by a dense line of water-powered mills and spinning wheels resting on stilts built on the river bed. In front of these, a flotilla of boats came and went with their cargoes, in the frenzied motion of a beehive. He saw a big pyramid covered with travertine slabs, some of which had slipped off and lay in fragments at its base. It must have been the ancient tomb of Romulus, one of the two pyramids in the city of which the pilgrims told fabulous tales. Further on lay the mass of the Castello and a long wall, high and well fortified, which stretched eastwards until it touched the distant hills. As he came closer, the poet made out its details, beginning with the height and the massive consistency of the fortress, more robust than the ancient Roman walls that surrounded Trastevere.

After two hundred yards he stopped to reflect. The fortress really seemed impregnable. On the terraces there were dozens of catapults ready to hurl their load of stones at an assailant. And just as many ballistas pointed through

the gaps in the crenellations that protected the communication trenches of the defenders against shots from below.
On the side of the river it would have been impossible to
attack without ending up in the hell that would have been
unleashed from the terraces of the Castello. And towards
the country, the land beyond the walls had been deliberately ravaged with ditches and earthworks, so as to make
the use of siege engines almost impossible.

He shook his head disconsolately. If ever in his dreams
he had hoped it would be possible to confront Boniface
as an equal, the sight of that insurmountable obstacle now
destroyed all hope. So, he said, continuing on his way.
The head of the serpent cannot be crushed in its lair. You
have to draw it out. With the patience of the soul, with
the ingenuity of the mind.

The high wall was interrupted by a gate reinforced by
stone buttresses. The gaps allowed a glimpse of the
internal fortifications, the guards' lodgings and the
murder-holes, behind which were doubtless hidden jars
of oil to be poured on any possible attackers. Lined up
in front of it were some pikesmen, decked out in the same
multicoloured liveries as the men who had accompanied
Master Hemp, on their chests the double azure wave on
a gules ground, which was the crest of the Pope's family
of origin.

The poet approached the man who seemed to occupy
the highest rank. 'I am Dante Alighieri, Florentine.

Ambassador of the free Commune. I must present my credentials to the Curia.'

The officer looked him suspiciously up and down. He too obviously found something strange about the man in his sober clothes, with no mark of his rank, on foot and unescorted. But there was something in the poet's resolute attitude that must have suggested caution. 'Very well, you may pass. Take yourself to the Curia, where you will find the seals room. Call in at the Basilica.'

The man pointed him to a little street on the right, between two tall, narrow huts. From that point the Leonine City looked no different from any other suburb: an intricate line of tufo buildings leaning against one another without any apparent order, often connected by aerial bridges onto which windows or little loggias opened. And set within the walls a certain number of towers – not tall, but massive in appearance, as though the entire zone were a parade ground rather than the walls of a sacred place.

But as soon as he had emerged into the next lane widening into the road, Dante found himself under the beginning of a long, straight portico whose brick vaults were supported by a string of precious marble columns. Some of these, having collapsed with the passing of time, had been replaced by quickly erected brick pillars, and at one point the vault too had collapsed, making any restoration pointless. Even so, he had the sudden sense of walking down an ancient triumphal road.

He began to walk: in front of him, obstructed by the narrow perspective of the colonnade, he managed only to guess the existence of a widening in the road, blocked off by a larger building of which he could see only a small part framed by the flight of columns and dominated by an imposing bell-tower.

When he had reached the square in front of the Basilica, he stopped for a moment and stared upwards. In front of him, beyond the big rectangle paved with grey stone, a large building loomed, perhaps wider than it was high, composed of two side blocks linked by a portico reached by a long stairway. Beyond the construction there rose the roof of the central nave of the Basilica.

The openings provided a glimpse of the internal courtyard. On the right there rose a commanding campanile, its walls hollowed by various levels of mullioned windows, and still further, high on the edge of the portico, a severe brick construction grew out of the side of the church. He assumed it must be the Curia, and that it was reached by the portico. Pushing his way through the crowd of pilgrims that thronged around the passageways, he entered the courtyard. There was a big kiosk in the middle of the vast square space, around which whirled a mass of clerics and laymen dragged into a kind of perpetual motion, coming and going between two orderly queues of pilgrims who entered and left the building through different gates.

The atrium was a hive of activity. The façade of the

Basilica, with its three portals, was completely hidden by scaffolding, on which half a dozen men could be seen at work. Big pieces of canvas had been tied to the structure as if to hide from people's eyes what was being done behind them. But here and there the patches of bright colour shone through the joints in the canvas. Dante approached curiously. He thought he recognised one of the outlines – a squat man busy yelling something at the others, with a basket of stones in his hands.

He walked to the foot of the scaffolding. 'Hey, Giotto, what have you got to shout about in the house of Peter?'

The man appeared at a gap in the structure. He looked down to see where the words were coming from, and then his face, with its marked features, lit up with a smile. 'Oh, Dante, you old bastard! Come up, till I do your eyes in with my pictures!'

Dante quickly gripped the pegs nailed to one of the poles and began to hoist himself up. As he climbed, the patches of colour in the mosaic assuming shape on the wall passed before his eyes: he saw the towers of a city, storm-tossed waves, the keel of a boat among the breaking waves of a roiling sea, faces and bodies bent by the wind.

The stone tiles gleamed in the light of the sun behind the scaffolding, which swayed dangerously under his movements, as if it might yield at any moment. Reaching the level where the men were working, Dante clutched one of the poles to be sure of maintaining his equilibrium, before embracing with his free hand the man who came running towards him.

He felt himself shaking violently, as the scaffolding lurched fearfully once more.

'My friend, it would be better if you didn't economise too much on the wood for your work. Now that you have access to Boniface's purse, you could afford something better, you filthy miser!' Dante laughed, letting go of the other man's hand and gripping the pole again.

'Boniface is as generous with his money as a hen's arsehole. I couldn't say my finances have changed for the better here in Rome. On the other hand my expenses have,' he said, nodding to the workers scattered around the scaffolding.

'Do you at least get to draw the beautiful women you wanted to do?'

The painter exploded into thunderous laughter. 'God, no! Just saints and apostles! I heard they've done a naked Eve up north,' he added, lowering his voice. 'Can you imagine, Dante? People walking about in wooden clogs, and they're ahead of us!'

'Or behind. Perhaps they're going back to the lesson of the ancient Romans.'

'Yeah . . . But if they'd at least let me do the wedding at Cana! I'd have filled it with pretty girls. And yet look! St Peter walking on the waters! Do you think that's possible?'

Dante leaned forward to look at the big scene on the walls. 'My friend, you're sticking your little stones upon the grave of the Prince of the Church. What would you have wanted to put there? And yet you also show him at a certain age, judging by the white that you've put in his beard. You could at least have surrounded him with matrons . . .'

'Ah, but at least they gave me a commission for a lovely temptation of St Jerome . . . Luckily there was someone left in Rome who was interested in women. But not much in the way of hard cash!'

'That's strange. In Florence they think Boniface has filled his coffers with income from the Jubilee. For a year all the merchants in the city have been coming here to trade.'

'He must have taken a lot, that's true. But the scoundrel keeps them well hidden. He wants to keep his family in Anagni rich. Or else he has something else in mind. What is certain is that not so much as a wave of that river of gold has been seen. What are you doing here, though?'

'Ambassador of our excellent populace, seeking peace with Boniface. I'm going to the Curia to ask for an audience. Is that the palace?' Dante asked, pointing to a construction beside the Basilica, whose great mass of reddish bricks loomed above the portico.

Giotto nodded, suddenly growing serious. 'To the Curia? Stay on your guard.'

'Why?'

The other man gestured vaguely. 'I heard your name mentioned the other day. They're waiting for you.'

Dante clenched his fists. 'Their spies in Florence! But it doesn't matter, it's better this way. Will we see each other again?'

'I've taken lodgings near the column, in Campo Marzio. Above the Angel Inn. They've got a decent wine there, and the landlord has brought in some pretty little peasant girls from the Alban hills, along with the barrels of white. Come and see me there one of these evenings. I'm always there. And besides, where else would I go?' he added, nodding with a grimace at a group of clerics who at that moment were coming out of the Basilica in a line, chanting psalms. 'After sunset the only people out there are cut-throats, the Pope's guard and the armed patrols of the families.'

'And how do they tell each other apart?' Dante asked with a hint of irony. Then he hugged his friend again and started to climb back down, trying not to lose his grip.

THE ENTRANCE to the Curia was guarded by a new group of armed men in the same gold and blue livery. They looked much more well groomed and efficient than the ones who guarded the gate. The blades of their pikes and the metal of their helmets gleamed in the sun, their belts

and leggings were clean and tidy. Dante had to repeat his
own name several times, show the decrees of the Commune,
explain in detail the reason for his visit, before persuading
two of them to accompany him along the stairs leading
to the upper floors.

One of the guards walked up the stairs ahead of him,
while the other followed him, brandishing his pike just
over his shoulders. The poet felt more like a prisoner than
a guest. And rather than waning, the impression became
more intense when he was introduced to a high-ceilinged
room, lit by a single narrow window at the end.

A wooden bench on a platform occupied almost the
whole of the back wall. Behind it, sitting on a wide-backed
chair, a cleric wrapped in the black and white of the
Dominican order studied him in silence. Dante approached
as the guards took up position on either side of the door.

'What do you want?' the man asked, interrupting his
silence.

'I'm Dante Alighieri, ambassador of the free city of
Florence. These are my credentials,' the poet declared,
showing the document for yet another time. He had held
out the parchment, but the other man showed no sign of
wanting to take it. He stayed motionless, his hands hidden
in the wide sleeves of his habit. The poet waited for a
moment, then dropped the document on the bench. The
lead seal landed with a crash, breaking the silence. 'I request
a personal audience with the Pope.'

The monk stayed in his impassive pose. He merely stretched his neck slightly, darting a glance at the document. 'We knew you were coming. Where are the others?'

A sudden fury took hold of the poet. For a moment he forgot where he was, with the armed guards at the door, the malign power of Boniface that seeped from every stone of the building. He took a step forward, climbing resolutely onto the platform. Now his eyes were level with the monk's. 'The others? They will come, sooner or later. But it's my word that translates the will of Florence, my judgement that decides whether to accept or reject. So arrange my audience, and let it be soon.'

Rather than replying, the other man had risen to his feet, with a threatening glint in his eyes. He opened his mouth to give an answer, while his gaze ran to the poet's shoulders. Dante suddenly turned round, fearing that the guards at the gate had moved towards him. In fact the two soldiers had remained in their place; a new figure had appeared between them. A tall, imposing man, in a sumptuous robe, its hems embroidered with purple. A layman, his wide brow furrowed with thin lines. His short hair, scattered with grey and cut very short, framed a face with marked features and a massive nose.

The newcomer rapidly crossed the room, brushing the stone floor with his cloak. Reaching the poet, he stared at him with his dark eyes, then his lips spread into a cordial smile. He spread his arms as if he wanted to press him to his chest. 'Messer Alighieri! So the news I was given by the palace guard was true. Be patient with Brother Raimondo: as a man of faith, he is more familiar with the Scriptures than with the voice of poetry.'

The monk had followed the scene with puzzlement. He cast another glance towards the poet, then at last picked up the parchment.

'Consign the file to the archive, Brother. As for the audience, I will attend to it personally,' said the newcomer. 'In five days, at the Patriarchate of St John. You will meet His Holiness. He too is anxious to improve relations between the Church and your city.'

'You may go,' the monk said crisply to Dante, lowering his eye before the newcomer. He carefully watched the documents being put back into a drawer, then affably addressed the poet again. 'Meanwhile, let the affairs of politics wait, and allow me to enjoy your unexpected company. If you have no other business that needs you elsewhere, allow Saturniano Spada, Roman senator, to go with you for a while.'

Dante bowed his head slightly as a gesture of greeting.

'So that we may exchange greeting and acquaintance: my little compared to your abundant,' the senator added. 'You, the prince of poets.'

Dante vaguely waved the thought away. 'I think you exaggerate the breadth of my knowledge. I'm just—'

'No, no!' the other man interrupted. 'I know who you are.

And the Curia knows it better than me. Much has been said about you over the last few days, when it became known that the Commune of Florence had invested you with the office of representing them.'

The poet did not reply immediately, busy as he was trying to interpret the meaning of these words.

The other man took advantage of the pause to resume. 'I have some friends in Florence who keep me informed about what is imagined, and then written, in your city. And few things have given me such delight for the mind and such bread for the spirit as certain of your compositions. Not to mention that extraordinary line of yours, *Love that converses with me in my mind!*'

The senator had stopped and was staring Dante intensely in the eyes, as if he wanted to read the next line of his poem there.

'Love that converses in the mind! Yes, that is the divine consistency of love, that conversation that God holds with our soul. And in which every word assumes the form of a sigh . . .'

'Your esteem flatters me,' Dante murmured cagily.

But the other man didn't seem to notice the frostiness of his reply. He went on staring at the poet admiringly. 'If the cares of government in Rome left me more time, all of your work would be carved in my memory, rather than just this modest homage.'

'The cares of government? I thought Pope Boniface

held the reins of the city tightly in his hands,' the poet remarked.

'His person, directly illuminated by the Spirit, is entirely absorbed in his first task, which is to reassert the universal subjection of the thrones to the Chair of St Peter. A venture that really calls for all his powers and the help of divine protection, given the reluctance of so many princes to bow their arrogant heads to his word. And not only the ruling dynasties, but sometimes the wretched councils dare to oppose his power, with the blind perfidy of a mad dog biting the hand that feeds it.'

'Was the town of Palestrina one of those mad dogs?' Dante hissed, thinking of the sad scene of the chained men in the port of Ripetta that suddenly reappeared before his eyes.

The senator shrugged, embarrassed. 'Sometimes the fear of the wolf arms the hand even of the good shepherd.'

Dante didn't reply. He stayed on his guard. In spite of the affable tone and the admiration demonstrated towards him, the man was still a servant of Boniface. And they could not really have met by chance. 'Are you part of the glorious Roman Senate?' he asked softly.

'Yes. My family has always provided members to that assembly. And the Pope's benevolence has raised me to the rank of Administrator, the first among the senators. A serious position that implies a range of tasks. Ensuring the security and order of the city, amongst other things. I am in charge of the men who fight crime and sin. A role once assigned to the Prefect in the Rome of our forefathers.'

'So the patrols I have seen at work depend on you,' the poet observed. 'So you will know about the terrible crimes that have been afflicting your people.'

The senator glanced at him uncertainly, as if he did not understand his words.

'The women who have been murdered recently,' Dante insisted.

'Ah, yes. The Decurion of police has informed me of these events. It is disgraceful, in fact, that the use of prostitutes should be maintained in the city of St Peter. It would appear that such weakness is not ineradicable from human customs, unfortunately. And fornication brings with it every other kind of depravity, all the way to crime itself.'

The senator seemed to want to dismiss the topic. 'But even though they are prostitutes, those women certainly did not deserve such an atrocious fate,' the poet insisted. 'And justice should compensate them in the only way our fragile state allows: by judging and punishing the guilty.'

'You place such importance on justice, Messer Alighieri? And yet it is only one of our many imperfections in the eye of God.'

'Justice is a community's greatest good, the end towards which all human action must tend. What would glory be, in fact, were it not tempered by its scales and its sword?'

'Do you think justice is an end, Messer Alighieri? Yet isn't it only a means of obtaining harmonious coexistence amongst people who obey a single power? And like the whip to the horse, must it not be used in wise doses, to avoid all excess? It is a precious coin to be spent judiciously. But let us move on from these subjects,' the senator replied affably. 'Is it true what they say about you, that you have begun a poem about the realm of the living and the dead?'

'Yes,' Dante replied. He wanted to bring the conversation back round to the murders, but he was flattered by the other man's interest. 'It's still in its early stages, and its form is not yet well defined in my imagination.'

'Do you have it with you?' the senator asked anxiously.

'Only a few pages,' the poet replied evasively.

A brief shadow of disappointment seemed to flicker across the other man's eyes. 'Of course I understand your reluctance. No author speaks about an uncompleted work. So the living and the dead . . . Perhaps there's something that might interest you, then,' he said, suddenly lightening up. 'Do you have time to keep me company? There's something I'd like to show you. Are you interested in the vestiges of our forefathers?'

'Certainly,' the poet replied. 'Their lesson must always take primacy among our thoughts. If the hearts and dispositions of our rulers were more influenced by the mastery of the ancients, freedom and justice would find a better refuge in our temples.'

The senator looked at him furtively. 'You have forgotten charity, Messer Alighieri. The Romans were great, but deprived of Grace as they were, they gave the world an order that was the child of human reason – superior, certainly, to the fierce order of the barbarians, and yet as hard and as harsh as that rule can be. They stopped on the threshold of perfection. Or at least that's what any good Christian should believe,' he enunciated slowly.

Dante looked away. He thought he heard an ambiguous tone in the other man's voice, as if his words concealed an allusion or a challenge. He felt he was undergoing some kind of test.

'Or don't you think that's so?' the senator urged him.

'The Romans were not illuminated by the Redemption, it's true,' the poet replied at last. 'But their Empire remains the child of a higher design, which the work of universal Redemption prepares and condones.'

'So the Roman Empire is the vehicle of the reign of God on Earth?' the senator asked again. He seemed pleased with this suggestion.

'No, but it opened the way to it.'

'I think you're right. But I was telling you about my researches. Not far away, in the fortresses of the Castello.

Digs have been under way for some time, in search of relics of the true tomb of the first Peter.'

'The Apostle? But doesn't his tomb lie beneath the Basilica? Isn't that where pilgrims come to plead for his blessing?'

The senator nodded. 'That's the tradition. And it is likely that it was in these parts that he officiated in the rites of the ancient Church. There was a necropolis there, which occupied almost the whole of the Vatican Hill, and our forefathers often took refuge amongst the tombs to take Communion.'

'Tombs from which they had nothing to fear, given their faith in the Resurrection and the second life.'

'Yes. But when the Apostle died, according to the presbyter Gaius, his body was buried on Via Cornelia, near the tomb of Romulus: that great pyramid that you must have seen near the Porto del Borgo. The very place where the Emperor Hadrian went on to build his mausoleum, the Castello.'

'And you think Peter's true tomb is there?'

'I'm sure of it. And I have received permission from His Holiness to dig there, in search of the true vestiges. I hoped I would find something to coincide with the great Jubilee: it would have been a worthy crowning of that admirable work. But the work proved to be longer and more difficult than predicted.'

As they spoke, they had come down the stairs of the

Curia and crossed the atrium of the Basilica once more. Having emerged into the square in front of it, the senator guided Dante to the left. Together they walked about three hundred yards, passing along the walls of the Borgo until they reached the shore of the Tiber again, then moved towards the fortress of the Castello, making their way through the brambles and reeds, and climbed from the shore to the lee of the wall.

'Come, it's here,' said the senator. Beside the fortress there was a large hole, surrounded by a palisade and guarded by a group of armed men. Above the opening, four solid crossed poles supported a pulley, from which hung a rope that sank into the depths. From the bottom there came a confused noise of human voices and digging tools.

'Raise the tackle!' ordered the senator.

From the bottom someone activated a hidden mechanism, and the pulley began to turn. A few moments passed, then from the abyss emerged a rudimentary wooden platform, suspended on the rope.

'Take your place, Messer Alighieri,' the senator exclaimed, walking nimbly ahead of him onto the platform, which immediately, at a call from him, began to descend towards the darkness. But first the man had taken a lit lantern from the hands of one of the guards.

The dig must have cut many ells into the earth, bringing to light the traces of a dense stratification of ruins that had built up on the river bank over the centuries. Here and there remains of bricks and fragments of marble appeared, and pieces of glorious statues, punctuated with rubble and thick tree-roots. The flickering lantern-light animated that shapeless matter as they descended, waking it from its sleep and turning it into a theatre of macabre shadows.

Dante thought he also spotted an accumulation of human remains at one point. Then the hoist stopped with a jolt. In front of them opened up a transverse tunnel that seemed to bend towards the river bed. The senator moved in that direction, walking ahead of the poet into a kind of little circular cave, whose irregular walls still bore the marks of digging tools. The whole space echoed with a confusion of exclamations. Suddenly they were surrounded by a group of workers pointing excitedly at something further on. The senator pushed his way through the little crowd, silencing them with an imperious gesture. Dante followed him curiously. Then all of a sudden he quickened his step in wonder at what he saw.

In the middle of the dig there rose a marble sarcophagus, its walls decorated with a complex haut-relief that ran along the four sides of the tomb.

The sepulchre, seen close up, looked even more splendid, carved from a single block of white marble. On the long sides were two reliefs showing scenes of feasting and battle: dozens of little figures engaged in dancing and combat. Above them, the cover in the form of a sloping roof, with four ritual masks at the corners, had been slightly dislodged from its seat.

Dante speeded up again, under the smug gaze of the senator, until he reached the sarcophagus. His fingers ran delicately over the carvings of the relief, like a blind man's fingers trying to interrogate the stone.

The senator stepped up beside him. He had gripped the edge of the cover and began pushing it to no avail. 'Maybe God has answered our prayers! Doesn't it look like a tomb fit for the Prince of Apostles? At last we will be able to prostrate ourselves before his true bones.'

The man's voice trembled with emotion and effort. Dante glanced dubiously at him, interrupting for a moment his examination of the reliefs. Saturniano Spada suddenly ceased his efforts and faced him again.

'Doesn't this stone talk to you as well? And yet they say you can read the voices of the dead!'

Dante gave a start at those words, which reminded him of the phrases with which the mysterious woman in Florence had greeted him. 'It is not the voice of death, but the voice of glory that shouts from this marble,' he said, having overcome his perplexity. 'I am sure the bones of some great man rest in there. Even if I knew it was the custom of the ancient Romans to arrange their sepulchres along the roads of the Empire. And I doubt that the head of a persecuted faith, executed in a street corner like a thief, might be entombed with such pomp. Unless . . . I've seen tombs of similar beauty, in Florence: and some of them were still used, over the following centuries, for new burials.'

'There, that's it! Perhaps one of the patricians, secretly converted, gave the Apostle the sarcophagus originally planned for him, just as Joseph of Arimathea offered Christ his family's sepulchre. Let's see,' he called to the workmen. 'Open it up!'

Dante suddenly gripped his arm. 'Wait. Perhaps we shouldn't disturb his rest, whoever he was in life. If God wanted him to wait patiently for the resurrection of the flesh, it would be a shame to drag him into the world that he abandoned.'

But Saturniano Spada seemed prey to uncontainable excitement. With a jerk he broke away from the poet's grip, as the workers crowded around the sarcophagus. One of the diggers inserted the tip of his iron pole into the gap beneath the cover and began to push with all his might, with help from the others. With a creak, the heavy slab shifted slightly, and then, with a more determined shove, it slipped again, opening a gap a hand-breath wide. The man stopped with a shout, dropping the iron bar, as his companions drew back suddenly with cries of fear.

A shaft of light had burst from the crack, faint and glimmering, as if a little flame stirred by the wind were burning inside the tomb. Ignoring the confusion, Dante had thrown himself forward, elbowing his way through to get a better view. He bent over the opening, but could make nothing out. His eyes were dazzled by the cold, bluish light that filled the cavity like a glowing fog. Still staring at the light, he reached for the iron bar that had fallen at the feet of the sarcophagus. As soon as his fingers felt the metal, he picked it up and put it back in the opening, starting to push the stone once more.

All alone, arching his back with all his might and using his knees as a lever, he began pushing like a lunatic, while the glow continued to spread and now bathed him too, turning him into a phosphorescent statue. At last the slab fell to earth with a crash, breaking one of the corner masks under its own weight.

Now the interior of the sarcophagus was no more than a vague cavity and its contents could finally be seen. Inside there was a second wooden sarcophagus, covered by a thick layer of dust, beneath which traces of colour could be seen, and at its feet a sealed ampulla from which the light was coming. Its brilliance seemed to be growing more intense. Dante gripped it and lifted it from the bottom.

He looked at the object with fascination. It was a cylindrical glass jar, perhaps a foot high, and rendered opaque by the corrosion of time, topped by a curious sculpture that looked like the muzzle of a dog wrapped in a kind of triangular bonnet, which seemed to be the sealed stopper. Through its thick sides a kind of dense liquid could be seen, half-filling the vessel. And that oily mass seemed to burn with a flameless light.

The movement of the jar produced a change of shadow in the wooden box, revealing the painting that decorated one of the ends of the sarcophagus; even though it was obscured by dust, Dante had the brief impression of a wonderful woman's face, a gently elongated oval, a strong but slender nose, two half-open green eyes. It seemed to be looking serenely straight ahead, as if just awoken from a long sleep, without fear or hope. The expression of someone studying death, or returning from the dead.

FOR A moment Dante felt he had seen that face before, in the distant past or perhaps in his dreams: but it was the source of light that attracted all his attention. How could that light have come intact through the abyss of time, still burning? Was there really such a thing as a *lux perpetua*, as wished for in the prayers for the dead? Close beside him, the senator's eyes ran from the painted image to the ampulla that Dante still clutched in his hand. Then his attitude concentrated on the painting: beneath the face there was a cartouche, and in it some words: *Virgo pulcherrima ex Anglia Johanna Pont. Max.* A most beautiful virgin, from England . . .

'Johanna . . . Joan . . . the female Pope,' the senator

stammered. Dante too had been staring at the words in disbelief. 'It can't be . . .'

Behind them the workmen seemed to have overcome their fear and crowded excitedly around. Certainly, no one was capable of understanding the Latin, but they had heard the senator's words, and some of them knew the legend. They stayed there, uncertain, exchanging worried glances. Some of them had fallen to their knees, others crossed themselves in horror, as if the devil had appeared among them. The luminous ampulla that the poet still held in his hand, and which had been the first source of puzzlement, now seemed to have been forgotten.

'We've got to know who's in the box,' Dante said suddenly, with great feeling. Any puzzlement, any scruples he might have had about the sleep of the dead had vanished. 'Give orders for it to be opened!'

Now it was the senator who proved to be hesitant. He seemed lost, all the certainty and enthusiasm of only a moment before had disappeared. 'We would need to inform the Tribunal of the Inquisition . . .'

He seemed to be about to add something, but then moved forward without waiting. Dante glanced towards the excavators, in search of help. But they stood numbly in position, muttering to one another. 'You help me, then,' he snapped at the senator, setting down the light-source at the foot of the box and bending forward to test the joints of the box.

The senator reacted to these words with a gesture of surprise. His features hardened.

'Please,' the poet added immediately, realising that in his excitement he had neglected to appreciate that he was no longer in his own city and had no power whatsoever.

'Very well, perhaps it really is better for the first news to reach the Holy Father through eyes that can see, and minds that can understand,' the other man said more gently, picking up an iron bar from the ground. He inserted it in the chink between the wooden box and its cover, before using it as a lever.

The box began to creak, splintering at the point where the force was applied, but it also resisted the assault. Dante joined the senator in gripping the iron bar and pushing. Slowly, creakingly, the lid began to lift. Then, with a dull crash, the hidden pegs that fixed it to the structure fell aside, and the whole panel suddenly turned over, falling to the ground.

A reclining body appeared, dressed in white robes that reflected the torchlight. The head bore a tall tiara, also white; the delicate little hands crossed on the chest seemed just to have been united in prayer, so elastic did the skin appear; still soft, too, the slender muscles of the fingers. The well-shaped nails still bore a faint shade of pink, almost a reminder of the gentleness with which the woman must have touched things during her own life. Because this plainly was a woman, the startled poet saw.

The face that emerged from the wimple like a flower from its calyx, crowned beneath the tiara by a cascade of still-soft blonde hair, was very like the image painted on the box. Only a suggestion of tightness in the features, where the bones of the skull pressed under the skin at the temples and in the cheekbones, indicated that these were remains of someone who had been portrayed in the splendour of her life.

An animated murmur had begun to spread among the workmen. The senator seemed to be becoming increasingly nervous. 'It really is the she-Pope . . .' he said, before abruptly ordering everyone to go back. Then, as if once the emotion had passed he had regained perfect control of himself, he turned to one of the diggers. 'Run, Mastro Pietro, tell the Inquisition to send their men. What has come to light requires all the attention and the prudence of the Church. And we will cover up these remains, Messer Alighieri. Too many people have seen them already.'

The man closed up the box with its lid. Then he prepared to wait. Beside him, Dante went on examining the details of the tomb. He was increasingly astonished: the remains of a wall that rose from the ground looked ancient, and must certainly have gone back to the time of the building of the ancient mausoleum of Hadrian, if not indeed to an even earlier era. And yet they must in some way have been part of the foundation of the big funeral drum that subsequent generations had turned into the Castel Sant'Angelo. For a moment he felt a sense of unease, at the thought of the vast mass of stone that lay heavily above his head. But if they really had been the funeral remains of Pope Joan – the greatest scandal to have struck the papacy throughout the whole of its history – why had they been buried here, of all places?

'Pope Joan . . .' the senator went on repeating, as if he too could not believe his eyes. 'Do you know about her? Do you think it's possible, Messer Alighieri?'

He too knew the story, having heard it told so many times, each time enriched by fresh details with which the morbid imagination of the people had finally transformed it into an extraordinary legend. Of how a girl from the far-off land of the Angles, celebrated for her beauty and learning, had been seized at a young age by an unhealthy desire to excel at the arts of the faith. And, not content with joining a female order, and hiding her figure beneath the false clothes of a young page, she had been taken in by the Franciscans. And there, thanks to her knowledge and to the occult arts, she had risen through the ranks, still hiding her own sex, until she reached Rome, where she was crowned Pope.

'But even if it were so,' Dante replied, 'how could she possibly have ended up here? For over a year she governed the fate of Christendom, but then, unable to conquer the call of the flesh to which her weak sex was prone, and falling in love with a nobleman who had discovered her true identity, she conceived of that forbidden love. And during a procession, between the Colosseum and the church of St John, she went into premature labour and gave birth to a child, on the public road, to the bewilderment of both people and prelates. And that same people, feeling betrayed, stoned her on the spot, killing her with savage fury. I knew that her body had been scattered, or buried at dead of night, at the very point where she was killed. But can she possibly be here, a few feet from the Cathedral of Peter, and buried with honours that were not even reserved for martyrs, but for ancient noblemen?'

'Perhaps the legend isn't true . . .'

'And how is it that her body wasn't torn apart by the people, and that it didn't rot, according to the demands of nature?'

The senator lowered his eyes. 'Perhaps her reputation for wickedness is undeserved . . . Perhaps she was in fact a paragon of virtue, if God in his majesty decided that her remains remained uncorrupted like those of the saints. Perhaps the tradition of her lustfulness is merely a slander passed on by those who wanted to erase the fact that a woman had legitimately followed in Peter's succession.'

Dante shook his head. 'If that were the case, the chair of the first bishop would have been shaken to its foundation . . .'

'That's right, Messer Alighieri. There were good reasons for all this to stay a secret.'

Meanwhile the entrance to the dig was full of excited chatter again. Some men in the habit of the Dominicans had appeared, accompanied by men armed with lances.

'The Inquisition is about to speak,' the senator said in a worried voice, as he went towards the newcomers.

The group of monks was led by a tall, thin man, so pale that he looked almost like a ghost. He listened, head bowed, to the brief account in which the senator informed him of the facts and then, after a quick glance at the poet, gave some abrupt orders to his companions. Immediately the monks headed for the wooden sarcophagus, sealing it with ropes that they had brought with them. Then, once their work was done, they lifted it onto their shoulders, moving swiftly towards the door, while one of them picked up the ampulla that continued to give off its strange luminescence, hiding it from view beneath his cowl. Meanwhile the soldiers kept away the employees, so agitated now that they seemed to be on the brink of rebellion.

'You!' barked the senator, turning to the assembled workmen. 'Go on digging. I want you to push your way further into the tunnel: if there is any more ancient testimony, I want it to be found at all cost!'

Then, turning to Dante, he added in a lower voice: 'Don't forget that, according to the legend, Joan had just given birth. And if the child was buried beside her, I don't want it to become another source of scandal.'

With the help of the men, the box was yoked to the winch and dragged outside. Here the little procession reassembled and, having hoisted the coffin back on the shoulders of the monks, it set off at a march towards the walls of the Leonine City and the nearby Basilica of St Peter.

Dante had followed the strange spectacle with interest, amid the mounting curiosity of the little crowd that watched, crammed together on the bank of the river and along the ramps of the Ponte dell'Angelo. The crowd walked quickly, growing in numbers, as if an invisible voice had run along the streets around the Borgo, announcing the wonderful discovery. Everyone who had come running seemed to be perfectly well informed about what had happened, and commented among themselves with shouts and exclamations, turning the event into a kind of marvellous story.

'The miracle! The miracle!' people were shouting everywhere. Many of them threw themselves onto their knees as the coffin passed, actually prostrating themselves on the ground as if witnessing an epiphany of Christ. They in turn were climbed upon by the people at the back, who trampled on them as they attempted to push their way forward and somehow touch the wood of the coffin, begging for grace and intercession.

The senator watched this influx of people with a concerned expression. Astonishment was turning into insubordination, and now all the people were climbing on top of each other to get a better view, barely kept at a distance by blows from the lancers, who struck the legs and heads of the most audacious.

'Pope Boniface has found his wife at last!' someone hidden behind the barrier of bodies suddenly yelled. 'Maybe he likes Joan better than the Holy Roman Church!'

'The last thing we needed was for the Roman people to find out about this,' the senator murmured. A sudden smile had appeared on his face at these words. He stared around at the enthusiastic faces that were gathering around. 'Ours is a generous people, Messer Alighieri. In it there still burns a trace, however faint, of its great forefathers. But it is easy to follow fairy-tales, to be carried away, even for a heresiarch.'

'But there are also some who seem enthusiastic about the find,' Dante replied.

The mocking voice had been heard again, alluding once more to Boniface's sexual voracity. These words seemed to have made their way around the throng, because a number of people had risen to their feet, and while some were still crowding around the coffin in search of comfort, others had started to answer back to the solitary voice, adding their mischief to his own.

The senator's smile broadened. 'Be mindful of the

memory of the ancients. Did not the people follow Caesar in his every venture, running to arms under his banners, and pouring their own blood into the lands of half the world? And yet it was that same people who insulted him in passing, calling him the *moechus calvus*!'

'Bald adulterer,' Dante nodded.

'Exactly so, Messer Alighieri. These are the people who invented jokes and japes, a people for whom nothing is too high and nothing too low. And these are the qualities required of those called by the gods to rule the world.'

'The world has changed a great deal since then. Other peoples have emerged in the North, and they have picked up the sword that your men dropped. The Franks, and the Teutons: it is upon their shoulders that the weight of the imperial eagle now rests.'

The senator shook his head. 'Believe me, Messer Alighieri: there is only one people with the strength to bring together the devastated lands of Christendom, and raise again the banner of the she-wolf, the ensign of peace and justice for centuries. Never has such a city as this been seen since then, never will another be seen. And if its splendour has been obscured for a short while, it was not for want of a guide to reawaken those gifts that cannot die.'

'Is Peter's throne not enough? It has never moved from his walls since the Apostle came within them. Another empire has arisen, heir to the ancient one. But it does not seem to have left amongst the common folk the mark that was expected . . .'

In the midst of a rising hubbub, the men of the Inquisition were struggling to leave, surrounded by an ever-growing crowd.

WITH A quick word of farewell, the senator had taken his leave.

'We will see each other again, Messer Alighieri,' he called to him as he disappeared towards the Hospital of the Holy Spirit, following the transport of the box. Dante was left alone, disturbed by the confusion that had been sparked amongst the rabble, who were still flooding into the area. He thought his only option was to return home, the way he had come.

This time he decided to avoid the zone with the mills, cutting through the tilled fields that insinuated themselves between the two layers of wall. But the web of paths between the various plots was more intricate than he had expected: he lost his way several times, and it was only at dusk that he found himself in front of the gate granting access to the triangle of walls that protected Trastevere.

He passed through just in time, before the entrance was closed off for the curfew. He was in the alleyway leading to the widow's house, when he met the Jew who had recited the prayer at the funeral. He was not wearing the simple clothes of the previous evening; instead he had on a long embroidered tunic, and a cloak decorated at the corners with tassels that waved in the wind. On his head was a white hat, as tall as a mitre. A yellow circle was pinned level with his heart.

The man was holding a cylinder of decorated wood, which reminded the poet for a moment of the container that protected Virgil's papyrus.

'My respects, Messer Manoello,' said the poet, running his eyes over his face. 'I was not aware of the post that you occupied.'

The other man replied with a polite bow. 'I am the rabbi of this community,' he said, pointing to a dome that could just be seen rising above the surrounding rooftops.

'Is it here that your people are confined?'

'Since the days of the reign of the Emperors, my people have found refuge on the other side of the Tiber. In those days we were not forced to live like recluses, and neither are we today. Even though since the Lateran Council it has become law to wear this mark,' he murmured, pointing to the yellow sign on his chest, 'and not to leave our houses during the hours of night. Along with all our other obligations, not so easy to bear,' he added sadly. 'Our customs and our faith force us to live close to one another, and this corner of the city has always been welcoming to us. But you — are you coming from the

Castello, by any chance?' he continued, looking behind the poet.

'Yes. I have just been there.'

'Then perhaps you know about the extraordinary discovery?'

'So stories travel in Rome just as they do in small towns,' Dante said, astonished. 'I happened to witness it.'

'And is it as they say? Has Pope Joan's body really been discovered?' the other man urged, strangely excited. 'And is her body intact, as if laid in the grave only yesterday?'

'That's how it looked to me. And I still don't know whether to believe my eyes.'

'The body really was sound in all respects?'

'Yes,' the poet replied. 'Or at least that was how it looked.'

Dante was even more surprised by the other man's curiosity. Perhaps it was a characteristic trait of the whole city, and the Jews took part in it as much as any other inhabitant. But he also seemed to read something more in Manoello's anxiety.

'Internally too? The innards had survived as well as the muscles?' Manoello continued to press. But then, as if he had read in the poet's face the confusion he had aroused, he stopped. 'Forgive me, Messer Alighieri. But it is my profession as a doctor that makes me anxious to know everything that seems to violate the natural laws that govern life and death. My religion does not clearly assert, as yours does, the resurrection of the body, or its preservation as proof of holiness. I would not wish to insult your faith by pressing my point.'

'And you haven't done, Messer Manoello. My mind too is confused, not least by the light that I saw illuminating the miracle.'

'A light? What light?' the rabbi asked again, insistently this time. 'No one mentioned a light . . .'

Dante briefly told him of the curious phenomenon that he had witnessed. 'And that ampulla, where is it now?' the other man asked.

'The monks of the Inquisition took it away, as they did the body. It's incredible, but everything suggests that the flame has been burning uninterruptedly since the time of the burial.'

Manoello had fallen silent. 'A light . . . that has been burning for centuries . . .' Dante heard him murmur.

'Do you have any idea what it might be?' Dante asked in turn, seized by a sudden idea. But, after a moment's silence, the other man shook his head. He seemed suddenly anxious to take his leave. Dante saw him glancing quickly towards the synagogue, and then with a rapid bow he walked away, pressing to his chest his wooden cylinder. Dante opened his mouth to ask him something else, but the man had already reached the corner of a building, vanishing beyond the intersection of alleyways that disappeared into the darkness.

The rabbi's words still echoed in his mind. He wondered if it was the hunger for occult wisdom that still floated around that cursed race. Or whether it was not only the air of mystery and reserve attached to their rights that won the Jews their reputation as custodians of incredible knowledge. He shook his head. If the people really had signed a pact with God, then they had also betrayed it by refusing to recognise the Son as the messiah. And it didn't seem possible to him that God should grant the gift of wisdom – the only one that linked the human apes to their Creator – to a group of rejects. And yet many people believed as much. He thought again of Brunetto Latini, his teacher during his youth in Florence. Of the way he spoke with enthusiasm of his experiences in Castile as ambassador to the court of King Alfonso, with the Jewish sages of the School of Toledo. And of the wonders of ancient thought that he had been able to discover thanks to them.

A smile came spontaneously to Dante's lips. What role might the languor in certain eyes have played in Brunetto's judgement, or the curly hair and olive skin of the boys bent over their illuminated codices? What strong shoulders, backs lithe as river-reeds that his hand had brushed, pretending to turn a page? If that man had not been a fine intellectual, and the great negotiator of peace between the Guelphs and the Ghibellines in his city, he would probably have ended up in the flames of the pyre, rather than buried with honour in Santa Maria Maggiore.

And now, where was his soul? Under a rain of fire, burning as his passions had been burned. Yes, perhaps Brunetto himself would be the ideal person to illustrate the horrors of sodomy, in Dante's own book. A sin made of violence and delicacy, love and desperation, of one who distorts the order of nature within his own body, and by way of compensation tries to ruin it in others. The readers of his teachings would have learned from it that the excellence of reason is not on its own enough to protect from sin. So he would put his master in hell, rather than one of the foul inverts who swarmed in the taverns of Florence.

His mind had returned to the papers that he had brought with him. His head felt heavy with weariness, but he was seized by fresh anxiety. He was neglecting the very thing that he hoped would bring him immortal glory, the work that would give a shape to the sky and the earth – a meaning to the peregrinations of men, that convulsive running that is a run towards death.

He frantically opened the box at the foot of the bed and took out a roll of faded parchment, sheets of paper recovered from old Commune files, and cleaned with lime so that they could be used again. Stolen almost stealthily from the rooms of the Council. He cursed his lack of means, which forced him to consign his lines to this vile material, then took out the wax tablets that he used to write the lines that love, justice or indignation dictated to his mind.

He had a sense that the papers were not in the precise order in which he had left them, as if the most recent events that he had been through had been somehow mixed in with his work. But perhaps this was only a mistaken impression caused by his weary mind, still prey to a whirl of images in which the day's events mingled together, producing other situations, other faces, other voices. And over everything the faint light of the moon coming coldly through the window. A bluish glimmer that fell upon the papers, upon his hands, everywhere.

5

8th November, shortly after dawn

H E OPENED his eyes, awoken by a ray of light striking his cheek. He immediately sat up, only to be frozen by the painful spasm that he felt in his back, preventing him from rising from the desk at which he had spent the night. He was stuck in mid-air, trapped by the pain.

He propped himself up on the desk with all his strength, trying to get his breath back. With a series of little movements he finally managed to stand. In a corner of the room there was a jug with a basin. He poured some water, before plunging in his hands and vigorously splashing his eyes and his face.

The cold water seemed to rejuvenate him. He was still repeating the operation when he heard a sound on the other side of the door. Someone with a heavy footstep was climbing the stairs, shouting something. The footsteps and the voice stopped outside the door, and then after a moment came imperious knocking.

'Messer Alighieri, open up!'

Dante opened the bolt. There was the Decurion, with his fists on his hips. 'Ambassador, Senator Spada requests your presence. He is waiting for you at the Campidoglio, for a ceremony. I have been ordered to accompany you.'

'A ceremony?' Dante asked, bewildered. 'And I've been asked to attend?'

'Saturniano Spada asked specifically for you,' the Decurion continued, sounding perplexed, as if he were not too convinced of his own mission.

Dante straightened his back and regained his composure. He quickly dried himself with a rag that lay by the basin, then arranged his night-crumpled clothes as best he could. A ceremony, and his presence was required. In the Campidoglio. He took a deep breath, exhilarated.

The senator would surely have organised an official welcome for him. Was that not the hill where the glory of the army was celebrated, but also that of knowledge and of art? Perhaps the laurel crown awaited him, that crown that the accursed Florentines still refused to award him. Riff-raff, but at least there were other cities where his merits were recognised. He would rise to the glory of Parnassus in the centre of the world, rather than his old den of vices.

'Let's go,' he announced. He was only bitter about the poverty of his clothes, and the scruffy beard that scraped beneath his fingers. But surely those great men would be able to understand and forgive the simplicity of the pilgrim, and the laurels would hide with their splendour all the poverty of the flesh.

OUTSIDE THE door a two-wheeled carriage awaited, pulled by a pair of tawny horses. Giving the poet just enough time to follow him, the Decurion jumped into the box, extracting a whinny of pain from the beasts with a switch of his whip.

The vehicle lurched forward, forcing Dante to clutch with all his strength at a handle on the side. Standing upright like an ancient charioteer, with a skilful tug on the reins the Decurion almost turned the carriage over, before hurtling towards the bank of the Tiber, heedless of the obstacles that appeared in front of him as they galloped down the narrow ramp leading to the Ponte dell'Isola.

Dante hunched back on his side of the carriage, trying to resist the bumps and jolts that continuously threatened to throw him to the ground. The Decurion fearlessly went on whipping the animals, accompanying the blows with loud and urgent cries. He seemed perfectly at ease, an amused light in his mocking gaze, which he occasionally darted at Dante from his lofty position.

Down below, the poet couldn't help feeling some admiration for the Decurion's adroitness: the charioteers who had fought below the walls of Troy, or those who had raced in the great circus of the Caesars, could not have been very different from him.

Given that Dante had to endure his company, however, he tried to take advantage of it. 'What news is there, of the crimes?'

'What crimes?' said the Decurion without turning around.

'The murdered women. At the port, and the daughter of that widow in Trastevere. Have you found any clues that might lead the guilty man to pay the penalty for murder?'

'Oh, them . . . Why do you care about them? They're in good company. Food for rats, like the others.'

'What others?' asked Dante.

The Decurion let a moment pass, busy slipping the wheels of the carriage through the narrow passage between two broken columns that protruded from the buildings along the street. Then, after crashing the axle several times against the stone and dragging away a cart leaning against a wall, once he was back on course he seemed to count quickly. 'Well, maybe ten of them, with the widow's daughter. Five in the last few months alone. The first last Christmas, towards the end of the Jubilee. They must have wanted to celebrate the end of the big procession,' he finished with a vulgar laugh.

'Ten murders . . . in just one year? Mutilated like the ones I've seen!' exclaimed the poet.

'Mutilated? Whatever. The whores were all gutted in the same way.'

'And you did nothing?' Dante insisted, shocked. 'How is it possible that the Holy City . . .'

'These are not matters of justice, Florentine. Justice intervenes only when a house is ransacked, or when the knives fly over a bottle of wine. When a cleric is insulted, or a merchant stripped and beaten. But the whores are already dead when they start their trade, and it is only a matter of time. Sooner or later they'll be killed by their pimps, or a dissatisfied customer, or else they fight among themselves. And because they're lost souls, no one pays them any heed. They come from somewhere, one day they disappear. Some of them the Red Hoods fish from the river, and what does it matter if they come out of the water drowned or cut to bits?'

A violent new jolt threatened to hurl Dante to the ground, preventing him from replying as he would have wished. Besides, his attention was focused on something that the Decurion had said. 'Did you say the bodies had been eviscerated? Like the one I saw at the port?'

'Yes . . . I think so. But you'd have to ask the Hoods, they're the ones with the job of stripping the corpses.'

The frenzy of their race seemed to have disappeared as if by magic. Oblivious to everything, for a few moments the poet's mind had begun to wander around something that was still obscure, but which he sensed just beyond the confines of his memory.

His thoughts were interrupted by a curse from the Decurion, followed by a new explosion of laughter. 'I have an idea, Florentine! What if the guilty man were one of our innkeepers, who wanted to serve them up in his dining room, stuffed like capons? They say that in Africa the pagans eat men on feast days. And Rome is full of Africans, like me! Haven't you seen my lovely face?' the man said with a grin, turning towards him and shaking his earrings.

'You do look like a Saracen, as a matter of fact. Were you an oarsman on a galley?'

'What do you mean, Florentine?' the other man replied, staring at him menacingly.

'In Florence, too, there are Saracens, men who were captured, who recanted and recovered their freedom.'

'My race is an ancient one here in Rome, even older than the family of Boniface the Pope!' the Decurion went on, irritated. 'But when the Saracens attacked Rome a few centuries ago, one of them must have left a little souvenir with one of my great-great-grandmothers. Basically I'm grateful, if you had any idea how many rogues I've persuaded to confess just by looking at them with my lovely face!'

Facing a new bottleneck, the Decurion concentrated on driving his horses again. Dante had resumed the thread of his deductions. Certainly, the Decurion's hypothesis was laughable, and yet he was sure that the horrible injury had a significance beyond mere wickedness.

Why would a murderer waste his time on an operation that was as horrible as it was meticulous, at the risk of leaving traces of his own work? Was his mind blinded by obscene perversion, or was there a reason for his action?

Might it be some sort of rite? A series of crimes that followed a rule?

With one last tug on the reins, the Decurion had halted the horses, which reared up whinnying. The carriage continued on for a few yards, pushing the foaming creatures on, before coming to a stop in a cloud of dust at the foot of a stone staircase that rose towards the sky.

Dante got out, still dazed from the ride. They were at the foot of a hill, on the flanks of which large and small buildings accumulated. He also glimpsed a little church, which seemed, incredibly, to rest on the roof of a building several storeys high and now almost a ruin. All the other buildings, on the other hand, were swarming with life. The cries of women and children came from countless windows, dense as an anthill, and sheets and rags of all sizes hung like banners from every opening. Only once had the poet seen a similar spectacle, when the Pisan fleet had come up the Arno with its festive flags, bringing home the Florentine crossbowmen from the Holy Land.

Perhaps this was how the Roman people celebrated its new triumphs. At the top of the steps, the corner of the façade of a large church could be seen. He thought it was the place towards which the Decurion was guiding him; but rather than heading towards the flight of steps, the man turned towards the left, slipping into the gap between two dwellings, and began to climb briskly on a path that ran along the side of the hill.

'Come on, Florentine!' the Decurion shouted, turning every now and again to check that Dante was still following him. This steep climb in turn became a fleet of stone steps, less imposing than the other. The poet was exhausted when at last they emerged at the top: in front of them spread a square with an irregular perimeter, and at the end of it a massive building of soft volcanic stone and brick, closed at the corners by solid great towers. A fifth tower rose from the tiled roof, with a little bell on the top.

Dante stopped, filling his eyes with what he saw. The Campidoglio! Once this had been the pinnacle of the world, the place of origin of the most majestic power that man had ever known. The remains of a few broken columns on the left still bore witness to the former patrons of the place, and the big church that he had glimpsed from below, and which dominated the whole side of the square with its great mass, seemed to preserve with its rough brick walls the same solemnity that had distinguished the ancient temples.

In front of the portal of the towered building, at the top of the short flight of steps that linked it to the square, someone was waiting for them. Dante recognised Senator Spada, wearing a long white robe, his shoulders covered by a sumptuous cloak embroidered in red, wrapped in a thousand folds around his left arm.

As soon as he spotted them, he moved, coming a few steps towards them. Then he extended his hand towards the poet, greeting him warmly as the Decurion withdrew discreetly into a corner.

'Come, Messer Alighieri! Before the audience that awaits you, I should like to introduce you to the beautiful things of this city, and its ceremonies. There is certainly one thing, in the senatorial palace, that I am sure will arouse your interest.'

'I'm sorry about my clothes, which fall short of the honour that you do me . . .'

'Oh, don't worry, Messer Alighieri,' the other man replied with nothing more than a rapid glance. 'As my guest, you won't need anything. You will be a discreet presence, and no one will notice.'

Dante was quick to hide his disappointment. He had surrendered too quickly to his dreams. Then he would have to talk about something else, he thought bitterly. But he immediately consoled himself: perhaps the Senate had assembled to discuss the marvellous discovery, and required his presence as an exceptional witness. Yes, that must be it.

Having passed through the doorway, he followed the senator down a long corridor, distinguished by large stone pillars topped by vaults. At the end he glimpsed one last arch, which led into an even larger room.

A distant murmur seemed to come from there, growing louder as the distance shrank. Every now and again Dante glanced at his companion, who was walking resolutely towards the hall. And he wondered anxiously what awaited him there.

The senator had spoken of ceremonies, and he still keenly hoped for that. But he would have expected some explanation from the senator, if that was really the purpose of his summons. Instead the man went on walking silently, merely darting him the occasional quick smile that did nothing to dispel his doubts.

When they were a few feet from the entrance, and the voices had become a clamour, Dante decided to confront him.

'What's going on?' he asked firmly. 'Perhaps it's better that I should know, if I'm to . . .'

'Oh, Messer Alighieri, trust me. You certainly won't regret the time you have spent in my company. Besides, even yesterday you contrived to witness something entirely unpredictable; today the spectacle, although different, will certainly be no less interesting!'

The vast rectangle of the Capitoline hall was full to bursting. Crowding onto the benches were all the grandees of the city, in a strange attitude of hilarity. Standing in the empty space at the end was a long row of men with their heads covered, each one holding a bundle. Dante was struck by the sight of them: the little crowd was dressed in an unusual, but respectable way. They looked neither like beggars nor tramps. And yet their humble, tremulous tone, their uneasy expressions suggested an exhaustion that the poet could not at first explain. It was only after a moment, when he noticed the yellow wheel on their chests, that he understood. 'Are they Jews?' he said to his companion. Before the other man could confirm, the first man in the line, who until that moment had had his back to Dante, turned so that he could recognise him. It was Manoello, in the ceremonial robes that the poet had seen him wearing before.

The senator merely nodded. 'Come with me, Messer Alighieri. Take your place among the dignitaries, and see how the city settles its scores with this evil breed.'

Guided by the senator, Dante sat down apart from the rest on an empty bench. The senator had climbed onto the central rostrum and, standing there, turned to the man who seemed to be the head of the group.

'Rabbi, have you brought your forfeit?' he said in a voice that was supposed to be solemn, but which could not conceal the hilarity that seemed to have taken hold of everyone.

The man in charge of the group bowed without replying, holding out towards the rostrum the bundle that he was clutching. The others had imitated his gesture, offering up their burdens.

'Open them.'

The rabbi loosened the flaps of the bundle. The light bounced off the objects that the man was carrying, some silver chalices and beakers.

'Is that all? With such a petty tribute all you are doing is confirming your people's rapacity.'

The man shrugged. 'It hasn't been a good year for trade. And the costs of the war that you imposed on us—' he tried to say by way of apology.

The senator cut him short with a crisp gesture of his hand. 'Fine. We will endure you for another year.'

Dante saw the rabbi closing his eyes and turning away, flexing his back slightly. The senator lifted one leg and delivered a powerful kick to the buttocks of the chief rabbi, pushing him away. As if his gesture had been the agreed signal, all of the little Jewish delegation began to slip away in an orderly fashion amongst the explosions of laughter and irreverent remarks of the senators, who kicked them as they passed.

The rabbi had come level with Dante. The poet hesitated for a moment, then beneath the resolute gaze of the senator he too raised his leg, just brushing the small of Manoello's back.

'You too, Messer Alighieri?' the rabbi murmured in a discreetly reproachful voice.

'Not for your learning, to which I bow. But for the arrogance and obstinacy of your race in denying the Annunciation of salvation: it is this that I punish with a blow to your backside,' the poet replied, overcoming his embarrassment with a twitch of his head.

The rabbi sighed, then drew himself up and straightened his hat, which had slid off under the blows.

The senator had followed the scene with a wry smile on his lips. He glanced after the rabbi's outline as it headed towards the stairs, then turned to look at Dante. 'I too find this man's wisdom remarkable, Messer Alighieri. Remarkable, and maybe dangerous.'

'Dangerous? Why? Knowledge and learning honour a man, and call God's indulgence on his sins. I am sure that in your judgement He will spare him the flames of hell, like our patriarchs, all of the wise ancients, who thoroughly immersed themselves in the investigation of His secrets.'

'So you don't think God is a jealous master, who mistrusts the servants that enter his vineyards?'

'On the contrary, did he not give those servants a number of talents so that they could make them bear fruit? And did he not praise and punish, according to whether it was done or not done? Knowing is a way of praying, for the soul of those who have not been granted the grace of faith in Revelation.'

The senator bit his lips thoughtfully. 'Perhaps you're right,' he said after a moment. 'So, if you were to imagine the condition of non-believers after death, would you save from the flames those who tried to know? But are simple souls not perhaps more guilty, those who were not touched by doubt of their own ignorance?'

Dante was about to reply, but the other man cut in.

'And yet we will have a way of talking about it. You want to honour me with your company? In a place less glorious, but certainly more discreet than this.'

'Where?'

'My private dwelling, on the Pincio. There's someone I would like you to meet. My guest is an illustrious visitor who has come from far-off lands.'

Noting the poet's puzzled expression, the senator waved his hand in the air as if to dismiss his reservations. 'The man I speak of, as you will see, is above all a man of studies, even if that is not the chief reason that he came to Rome. I should like you to see this man's nature. Come, I entreat you.'

Dante politely bowed his head in consent. He thought he had caught a certain emotion in the senator's voice, as if the man were particularly concerned to have the poet with him. Dante set off with him, walking reluctantly down the long corridor that led to the door. As they walked the senator went on benevolently greeting a large number of people, who stepped aside for him with a respect that bordered on fear, staring curiously at the poet. Dante walked in silence, cautiously, from time to time glancing at the man's noble profile. He thought of the monster Gerion, with its human face on the body of a dragon.

He sensed that Boniface's man must have been driven by motives as yet unrevealed, to wish to have his presence again. He thought once more of the curious circumstances of their first encounter. The man had appeared behind him, apparently by chance: but did anything really happen by chance in Boniface's city? The Decurion was at the poet's personal service – could he have informed the senator of his movements? And why? In Rome the post of Administrator had not been an elected role for decades, and had become a function bestowed directly by the popes upon their trusted men. Perhaps behind his ostentatious admiration for Dante lay a plan that concerned Dante in some way. A plan drawn by the hand of Boniface himself.

He decided to resist his curiosity, which would have led him to ask straight away the questions that troubled him. Since first arriving in the city he had realised that time ran differently within its ancient walls, and that words had to adapt to the rhythm of things. If Spada had received the task of fathoming Dante's intentions, before the formal audience with the Pope, then he wanted to be the first to find out.

THE DECURION was still waiting in the forecourt, chatting in a loud voice with some of the guardsmen. When he saw them he moved quickly towards them. 'Your carriage awaits you below, Senator,' he said obsequiously.

A little while later the poet found himself back in the vehicle. The Decurion deferentially held the reins out to Saturniano Spada and stood aside. The carriage began to run along the side of the hill, passing by the stairway of the Ara Pacis, before slipping into a narrow alley among the remains of what must once have been a big temple. Then it climbed to a long, straight road that headed north. The area looked almost unpopulated, but after about a mile a building came into view in the distance, vast beneath the sun that warmed its brick structure.

At last the carriage came to a halt in front of the semi-circle of an exedra so vast that it could have contained the whole of the new palace of priors that was currently being built in Florence.

'I wanted you to see in close-up the traces of past greatness. These are the Baths of Diocletian.'

Dante looked around, uneasily, running his eyes over the imposing ruins without stopping on any particular detail.

'You seem distracted, Messere,' the senator observed, watching him intently. The poet stopped biting his lower lip, then turned towards his interlocutor as if returning from a long journey. 'I'm wondering what's happening in Florence at the moment. What they're talking or deliberating about, what sermons are being delivered in our Temple.'

'You can't even forget your village amongst the most solemn relics of our forefathers? Your whole Temple, as you say, and with it a good few bridges and towers, and perhaps a bit of the Arno too, could be accommodated under these arches!' the other man snorted.

The poet had stopped, busy admiring the imposing ruins of the Baths. He took a few steps to the side, so that he could take in the whole arch of the exedra all at once, then his eye rose towards the dome of the *caldarium*, above the big brick pillars.

'What are you thinking about, Messer Alighieri?' asked the senator, who had not taken his eyes off him. The man studied him with the same greedy attention with which Dante observed the remains of ancient Rome, almost as if the poet were – like these ancient remnants – a source of wonder and curiosity to him.

'Of how changeable are the destinies of the world, and how Fortune lifts up and then casts down first one people and then another. And I was wondering whether it happened according to a plan, or whether it were not merely blind chance that defined the path of glory from one end of the world to the other.'

'I think the same rule holds for peoples as it does for families. The generations succeed one another, and some-times the children are wiser and more virtuous than the parents, so that the wealth and glory of the house grow, and fame shouts their name to the world. That was what happened to Caesar and Scipio, who were certainly greater than their forefathers had been. But sometimes the road goes downhill, and what happens afterwards barely attains the levels of just a few years before. As happened to Tiberius with Augustus, or Nero with Claudius.

Dante meditated in silence. Then, with a jerk of his head, he turned to his interlocutor. 'Or Boniface with regard to Celestine,' he murmured frostily.

The senator didn't react immediately. He seemed embarrassed by his companion's remark. 'If you wish,' he said, clenching his teeth. 'Many regret the pious hermit. Are you among them?'

'Better not to have paved the way for the Caetani, with his great refusal,' the poet replied drily. 'It certainly seems hard to believe that men capable of making things like these,' he continued after a brief pause, 'vanished into the night, leaving behind them only ruins and the immortal words of their poets.'

'It happened to other men too. It is said that the ruins of Thebes in Egypt, or Babylon, or Persepolis in Media, are just as imposing. And those people, after pushing their swords to the edges of the Earth, and crushing beneath their heels every enemy that crossed their paths, are also now little more than a memory, known only in the songs of their successors. At least the Romans held out longer than the others against the force that seems to try to drag down everything that attempts to raise our condition out of misery.'

'A misery sought by man himself, that day in Eden when our progenitors dared to challenge the will of God. Every vice to which the flesh is heir, every pain, is only the fruit of that first insult.'

'And yet it is pain that unleashes our frailty, Messer Alighieri. It is pain that moves our actions, that keeps us alive. Woe to him who dreams of freeing himself from weariness, and looks proudly at his fruits and says: See, I have sown well, and the crop that awaits me will be abundant and enduring, even for the years to come. It is that dream that undermines the power of nations, that sends them slowly towards the void in which they disappear one by one.'

'What do you mean?' asked Dante, puzzled.

'Sloth, lust and covetousness. The three beasts that devour man. And the peoples, however great they might be, are nothing but groups of men. And as such, they are born, grow, struggle to make lives for themselves, go in search of glory. And as such, at the evening of their days, they abandon themselves to dreaming. And they dream they own all the things they still lack. You see, Messer Alighieri, a moment comes in the history of kingdoms, in which sage civilisation abandons itself to the greatest dream of all, the removal of pain, of the toils of life. It is then that those peoples take the first step along the road to their defeat. That was what happened to the Egyptians, when Cleopatra abandoned herself to the love of Caesar, or to the Greeks, when on the heels of Alexander they came to know the lusts of the Orient.'

'But that is the fate of peoples unilluminated by Grace. And it is right that that which is entrusted to men should follow the blows of Fortune. But why should the throne of Peter, which was built by God himself, follow the same laws that govern the frail constructions of the pagans, at the risk of being brushed away by a gust of wind, like a nest built uneasily on a branch?' the poet went on sadly. 'Why should not Rome, chosen by Providence as a sword and herald of the new alliance, not have remained as a solid tower of its potency, a shield for the expansion of Christendom? If its legions were still guarding the very boundaries of the Earth, the raiders that sprang from the sands of Arabia would never have been able to take Jerusalem, that holiest of cities.'

'Rome paid the penalty for her weakness. You yourself have seen the wretchedness in which her descendants live. And yet all is not lost; a great plan is under way that will revive the fate of the city,' he added enigmatically. 'The enthusiasm that brought our eagles to Gaul and Africa is about to reawaken. But we will speak of this again when the time is right. Meanwhile, will you not admire the greatness of the work of Diocletian? Look, I will show you something you're not expecting!'

Still talking, Dante and the senator had walked around the whole semicircle of the outer exedra, and had opened one of the doors set into the wall. They found themselves in a high-ceilinged corridor, completely covered with big slabs of coloured marble, in which passageways decorated with columns opened up at regular intervals. 'Come, Messer Alighieri,' said the senator, making his way down one of the passageways.

Beyond the walls a large space opened up, covered by a barrel vault and surrounded by a massive wall with semicircular niches carved into it. In each of the niches a huge statue celebrated the feasts of the ancient gods and heroes. Most of them were damaged, and all that remained of some of them were legs that rose from the base like the macabre remains of a battle of Titans. But some of them were still intact: Dante had never seen such beauty of form, such majesty.

He thought again of the images that adorned his Florence, the Roman statues that still stood among the remains of the sarcophagi, around the Baptistery. The love with which they were studied by the stone-cutters of his city, the efforts they made to return to the ancient beauty after the barbarous interlude of the Goths. What would happen if artists studied these incredible forms once again? What pinnacles might art reach in the coming century?

Seized by admiration, his whole attention was concentrated on the statues. It was only after a moment that he realised what these statues were guarding: a huge basin of gleaming marble, more than one hundred and fifty yards long.

'This was the reservoir of ablutions, Messer Alighieri. So big that it could have held perhaps ten galleys. Oh, if the ships could only be transported to the Tiber, we could fit out a whole fleet right here . . . but look down there. Follow me.'

Dante walked towards the senator, his eyes lost in what he saw above him. They followed the edge of the big basin, and emerged on the other side through a new forest of columns. Here another room opened up, an octagonal one this time. Above their heads rose the dome that had already attracted his attention from outside: the large structure covered a new basin. 'Those who have studied this building assert that this was the ancient *tepidarium*, the place where the Romans could enjoy heated waters before passing to the *caldarium*, the room beyond those arches. There, from the open cracks in the floor, the steam produced by the boiler of the big underground heaters restored weary limbs, relaxing them for their next ventures.'

The senator stopped, to give Dante time to appreciate what he was describing.

'Note the wisdom of our forefathers,' he went on. 'The divine equilibrium with which the city thought of its citizens, first exciting their souls with the cruel spectacles of the circle, and then calming them with the gentleness of the reviving waters.'

'Yes. But it was blood that held everything in the balance. Was it really wise to turn men into beasts, and then try to calm them down? Was it not a tragic game that was being played with our nature? Thousands of martyrs paid with their lives for the need to enrich the lives of so many slothful people, before Grace descended to sweeten their habits.'

As THEY walked, they had come back towards the exit. The senator turned towards the carriage, but showed no sign of getting in. He seemed to be waiting for something. Every now and again he craned his neck towards the forest that stretched to the east, nervously tapping his foot on the ground.

'At last!' the poet heard him exclaim, as the sound of hoofs rang out in the distance. A unit of cavalrymen had emerged from the forest, half a dozen armed men who were heading towards them. 'They're my servants, they will escort you to my place of residence. From here on, past the Quirinal Hill, it isn't wise to move around on your own.'

The senator motioned to Dante to take his seat in the carriage, while the soldiers arranged themselves on either side of the vehicle after giving a respectful salute.

Then the little column set off, leaving the ruined Baths behind. They climbed a path that cut through the forest of unplanted trees and brambles, from time to time crossing an area that revealed the hand of man. Only the occasional charcoal-burner's shack interrupted the desolation.

Suddenly the poet felt the wheels of the carriage bouncing along a paved section of road: he leaned from the carriage and saw a long, straight line of basalt heading towards the north, where the mass of walls could be glimpsed on the horizon.

'We've crossed the Via Nomentana,' the senator explained, having followed his movements. 'Now we're going down into the valley.'

The carriage had begun descending the twists and turns that ran down the side of the hill, in a landscape increasingly rich with gorges and marshy vegetation. A brook raced at the lowest point, and someone had thrown large planks into the ford to help people across. The carriage now tottered shakily across them.

Beyond the ford, the land rose steeply. 'Nearly there,' said the senator. 'It was here on this plain, which extends as far as the walls, that Lucullus once had his gardens. It may even be in one of his villas that my family has always lived.'

At that point the hill had begun to level out. In the distance lay the great curve of the Aurelian walls, with their regular cadence of quadrangular towers, closing off the horizon, protecting with its embrace the building towards which they were headed.

The path stopped in front of an exedra, at whose centre the stone basin of a fountain issued forth its jet. White statues rose between the columns, a people in stone left there by the ancient landlords to guard their own properties. Behind that solemn entrance lay the rest of the building, a vast brick square, topped by sloping tiled roofs.

The senator's coach must have been noticed a long way off, because as they approached, Dante saw two rows of servants lined up beside the arch, craning their heads towards them. One of the men, wearing the livery of the house, came towards them first, and tugged on the horse's bit to halt its race.

'Is everything ready?' asked the senator, getting out of the coach and coming solicitously towards Dante. But the poet had already leaped to the ground and was looking around, fascinated by the magnificence of the place.

'As you have commanded. The oriental gentleman awaits you in the red hall.'

'Very well. Come, Messer Alighieri. I am keen for you to meet an extraordinary guest of mine,' said the senator, heading towards the inside of the building.

As soon as he had passed through the outer walls, Dante found himself in a wide courtyard, closed all round by a portico of slender marble columns. The space was decorated with lush lemon plants, their trunks twined with thorny rose branches, holding them in a multicoloured embrace. The atmosphere was permeated by a subtle perfume, profoundly different from the scent of dust and stables that predominated in the streets of the city. The poet followed the senator through a door in the end wall, entering a huge hall decorated with red and yellow marble that echoed the colours outside.

Here, too, large numbers of servants came out solicitously to meet the master of the house. A woman held a silver jug full of water. The senator gestured to Dante, inviting him to refresh his hands. Then he invited him to follow him further inside the building. After the first hall there was a second courtyard, this one too surrounded by a portico, with many rooms leading off it. The senator guided the poet towards one of them. 'Come, Messer Alighieri, we're there.'

They crossed the threshold. Inside there were low wooden chairs covered with cushions, and on one of them a man was sitting, busy reading a small codex.

Dante concentrated on the seated man. He wore sumptuous robes in the oriental style, his head covered by an abundance of silk wrapped in such a way as to make a large turban in the shape of a dome. He looked up at the senator, gave a hint of a polite smile, then turned back towards Dante, getting to his feet and respectfully bowing his head.

Dante returned his greeting. But his attention had been drawn, even before noticing the singular appearance of the man, by a low table scattered with some codices and half a dozen rolls of papyrus.

'This is Kansbar ibn Talib,' said the senator, indicating the man. But then, as if he had noticed Dante's curiosity about the manuscripts: 'Just a few volumes that I've picked up over the years,' he added, with seeming nonchalance. 'But some of them are the most precious ornaments of my house.'

The poet's eye ran from the man to the books as if he really couldn't decide where to satisfy his curiosity first. He instinctively took a step forward, stretching his hand out towards one of the codices. He brushed the back of the volume with his fingers, then quickly withdrew them, as if he had violated a treasure trove. Pulling himself together, he turned round to stare at the oriental gentleman.

The man had followed his movements with a glow of sympathy in his features, which were marked by a long black moustache that descended at the sides of his thin mouth until they almost brushed the collar of his robe.

'Messer Alighieri, the senator told me I would have the honour of meeting you,' he enunciated slowly. The tone of his voice denoted the effort of expressing himself correctly in a foreign language, which he pronounced with a curious Mediterranean accent, as if he had been taught to speak it by people from the kingdom of Naples.

'Perhaps the name of Kansbar is not as well known to you as it deserves to be,' said the senator. 'But you will soon be able to judge.'

Dante turned politely towards the other guest. The man

had set the little codex down on the table. 'The senator overstates his praise of me. I am only the humble voice of other people much more worthy than myself.'

'Kansbar is the ambassador of Ghazan Khan, the lord of the noble khanate of Persia. He has come to the court of Boniface to negotiate an alliance with the Church against the Turk, who is impoverishing both the Holy Land and the Mongol's Persian possessions.'

'An alliance with the Tartars, against Islam?' Dante said in disbelief.

'A big project that might change the history of our times. Look,' the senator replied, holding out his hand towards a book-roll on one of the library shelves.

He unrolled the parchment on the table. A mass of signs and colours lit up on the desktop. Pictures of rivers and mountains, trees and flowers and animals that the poet had never seen, the blue of the seas and the whiteness of the snow alternated with the ochre and yellow of the higher ground and the grey of the little walled towers. Fascinated, Dante leaned over to look. After a moment's hesitation he thought he recognised in the depiction the extreme tip of Europe, with the symbols of the great city of Constantinople, on the narrow stretch of water that was its tiny defence against assault from Asia. Further on, the coast of Palestine, with the walls of Acre, Tyre and Sidon. And at the centre the hundred towers of Holy Jerusalem. And then the yellow of the sand of the desert, and proud Damascus, and Baghdad in the flame of the equatorial sun, and Babylon with its hundred gates. And then, towards the edge of the page, Persepolis with its big stone lions.

Dante looked up again, his eyes full of wonder. Before he could say anything, the senator spoke again. 'Yes, Messer Alighieri. It's one of the pages of the great planisphere of Ptolemy, made by one of the geographical scholars of Alexandria. But it is not to display my treasures that I have shown it to you. But to show you in tangible form the suggestion of the Mongol,' he said, inviting the man to complete his speech.

'Ghazan Khan is fighting on the Persian border to free these lands from Arab invasion. He has a mighty army massed around the ruins of Persepolis, and every day they are joined by other units of the Golden Horde, pouring in from the north of the Russian steppes to join the venture here,' said Kansbar, pointing at the thin blue line that marked the course of the Euphrates. 'He proposes that the Frankish peoples from the west be ready to attack the Turk in Jerusalem. At the moment, other emissaries of his are in Constantinople to negotiate with the Roman Emperor about his descent from the north, beyond the Bosphorus.'

As he spoke, the oriental gentleman was marking out the guidelines for his future actions on the map with his finger. 'Gripped in the clutches of a triple-headed attack, the Turk's forces will be routed, and his fanatical greed will be swept away for ever. And peace will reign upon a quarter of the world.'

'Do you understand the great opportunity that's being offered to you, Messer Alighieri? A crusade, in short. But not a simple military expedition, from the surrounding horizon to the reconquest of Jerusalem. It is something that has already been attempted by kings and emperors. Richard of England and Frederick of Swabia, for all their heroism, could not attain their goal, because their divided forces were too small. But now—'

'Now I don't think the King of France will grant troops to Boniface,' Dante interrupted him.

'That much is certain. In his greedy short-sightedness, Philip the Fair will at first refuse. But when he learns from his spies that the great expedition is in motion, you will see his lilies joining the crosses on the battlefield. And with him the lion of England, and the black eagle of the empire. But this time it will be Rome that rules and dominates, in this work that fate and justice entrust to her. It is from here that the crusade will depart, here that it will return to crown its leaders on the Campidoglio. Glory, with her carriage and her horses, will return to light up the hills of the great city.'

Dante was still bent over the paper, his eye concentrating on the map. Then he looked up at the senator. 'So what they whispered even in Florence is true, that Boniface craves a new crusade.' His eyes suddenly narrowed. 'Even though the Pope has only injured the Roman lands so far, devastating Lazio, scheming in Tuscany. All Christian lands – far from what you now say is his goal.'

The senator shrugged. 'Nothing compared to the greatness of his true venture. The Rome of the Caesars was not always kind to its subjects, either. Even the champion in the arena, before making his leap, needs to be sure that the ground on which his feet will land is solid, that it will not yield. Bringing the patrimony of St Peter back to reason and respect is the necessary and preordained condition for the execution of the greatest project,' the other man replied.

'It could take thousands of men . . .'

'When the ships raise their sails, the Roman people will run to enlist like a single man,' the senator exclaimed, in an inspired voice.

'But the people don't even seem to know of the great design that you are preparing. The city is drowning in its ignorance and violence,' Dante objected.

A thin smile crept across the senator's lips. 'These are the building blocks with which empires are built. The men who fought the Carthaginians at Zama certainly hadn't come out of the Accademia. You will see, Messer Alighieri, if they are not up to their task!'

'But this venture will cost an incredible amount of money,' Dante argued. 'Fitting up dozens and perhaps hundreds of ships, the premium for the cavalry and pay for the infantrymen. All the carriages, tents and weapons, the horses and donkeys for transport . . . the cost of tolls, and the purchase of the favours of the populations whose lands will have to be crossed – not even the coffers of a great kingdom could cope with all that.'

The senator exchanged a rapid glance with Kansbar. 'Don't forget the Jubilee, just past. The generosity of the pilgrims who flowed into the city has filled the state coffers with coins from the four corners of the Empire. And if you take away the part necessary for the works of religion, the rest is guarded in the strongboxes at the Castel Sant'Angelo, ready to be spent in its entirety on this noble purpose. No, Messer Alighieri, if the wind of Providence blows in our favour, it certainly won't be money that's missing.'

So that was where Boniface's money that Giotto had mentioned was destined for, Dante said to himself, thinking again of his friend's words. He hesitated, thinking about the thousand things he wanted to ask.

The senator studied him carefully, as if trying to read his secret thoughts in the wrinkles on his face. 'Do I sense that you have some doubts about the venture?'

Dante bit his lips. 'The force that sustained the first crusades was not only the desire for conquest, or hatred for the pagans, or the wish to free the holy places. The deep faith that animated them was what led to victory, even more than iron and fire. Which God supports your allies?' he said, glancing towards the Persian.

Kansbar allowed himself to smile. 'The Mongol adores the gods of wind and water, and cares nothing for the faith of his subjects. As for me, like many in my country, I have opened my heart to the word of Zoroaster. It is in him that I trust, him that I abandon myself to, and I pray to the God of light that at the end of time he will free us from the weight of being.'

'Kansbar is a follower of the mighty Ahura Mazda, the God who has protected those people for millennia.'

'You speak of him as if he were a substance of the Trinity,' Dante observed darkly. 'But the Zoroastrian faith, with its belief that the world and the flesh are creations of darkness, is sister to many Gnostic heresies, and to the Bogomil Cathars! How can Boniface associate the Christian armies with someone who shares a belief that only a few years ago was swept away in Provence, amidst the most terrible devastation?'

A SUDDEN animation on the other side of the portico attracted his attention. A group of the senator's servants had thrown open the door, and now they were crowding around a horseman who had come galloping in, stopping with a tug of the bridle in the middle of the courtyard.

One of the men had gripped the animal's bit, and was trying with all his might to stop it from running, while beside him the rider was still spurring his horse on. The laughter that reached them suggested that the man must have been hugely enjoying himself with this improvised game, which threatened to knock the unfortunate man under the animal's hoofs. At last the horseman seemed to have had enough of his prank, and skilfully jumped from the saddle, running towards them.

Dante watched the man throw himself into the arms of the senator, exploding once more into cheerful laughter. Then, stepping back, he turned towards the other two, as if he had only just become aware of their presence. On his tanned face, still red from the sun and the wind of his race, thin drops of sweat pearled on his forehead, under the brim of a heavy travelling cap that hid his cheeks and fastened under his chin. The poet caught the dark flash of his eyes, two black wells under thin arched brows, curiously taking everyone in.

'You have guests, Father.'

The boy had spoken in a harmonious voice. He was wearing hunting clothes, a leather jerkin lined with fur, held in at the waist by a wide belt that emphasised his slender waist and long legs beneath leather hose, his feet in a pair of heavy boots with unusually long tips. He carelessly threw onto one of the stone chairs two rabbits, heavy with blood, that he gripped by the ears, then slipped from his shoulder the short bow that he wore around his neck. As he did so, the cord caught the crest of his cap and pulled it off.

A cascade of raven hair, so dark that it looked almost purple, fell on his shoulders and around his neck, glistening with sweat and tumbling in loops like a tangle of snakes. The boy brushed aside that vivid mass with a nervous gesture, before bursting once more into an explosion of silvery laughter that revealed a set of brilliantly white teeth.

'Gentlemen, allow me to introduce my daughter Fiamma,' said the senator, gripping the girl's hand and pulling her towards the two men who had risen respectfully to their feet.

Dante darted a swift glance at his companion to check whether he too had been taken by surprise. Then he looked again at the girl, who after a quick examination of the Persian had stopped in front of him and was looking at him with curiosity. Freed from the cap that had largely covered it, the face that he had mistaken for that of a youth now revealed itself in its true nature. The face of a woman in her early twenties, in all its splendour. The darkness of the eyes and hair was tempered by the red of the mouth, wide and full; the round line of the chin marked by a dimple under the lower lip, like the last sign of the hand of the God that must have moulded her, the poet thought.

The girl, still staring at him, began to loosen the laces that fastened the jerkin around her neck, as if driven by the desire to free her full, delicate bosom from that masculine outfit. She stood patiently and waited for the respects that her father's guests paid to her, bowing her head respectfully to them, then held out her right hand towards them in a gesture that did not seem to be addressed to anyone in particular, but which Dante imagined was meant primarily for him. For a moment he was tempted to take that hand and brush it with his lips, but he held back for fear of committing some indelicacy in his host's house. He did not know the customs of the city well enough; in his Florence, only a married woman could have dealt with adult men so confidently, and then only in the presence of her husband, while a girl of marriageable age would have stayed far from their eyes, the veils on her head indicating her status. And she would never have appeared in such clothing. His eyes involuntarily slipped to her legs, which he sensed were firm and full under the tight leather of her hose, and at last to her hips, barely covered by the hem of the short jerkin. Now, freeing himself from the trap into which his intellect had fallen, deceived by the superficial sight of the object, it struck him as impossible not to have recognised the true nature of the girl at first sight, so obvious and so delicious were the features of her sex.

He felt his face flaring up and turned his eyes hastily away, before looking quickly at her face again. He thought he caught a spark of irony in her ebony eyes, as if the girl had guessed his thoughts and was amused by them, rather than being shocked.

'I beg your pardon, gentlemen,' she said, taking a step back and turning towards the half-open door that was opening beneath the portico. 'I will come back in clothes more appropriate to my state, if my father allows me to enjoy your company later on.'

She picked up her bow and quiver and quickly passed through the door, disappearing from view. The senator had watched after her with an expression of affectionate reproach. 'She's just a tomboy, rebellious and fickle. Her soul constantly visited by dreams that pass through the ivory gate,' he said tenderly.

'If that's the case, it means that wisdom has tempered your eyes, making them so keen that they can penetrate beneath the surface of bodies. My coarser eyes see only admirable beauty that would make any man fall in love with her,' Dante murmured.

The senator sighed deeply. 'She is the apple of my eye,' he said, unable to conceal his pride any longer. 'But come. There is still much that I want to tell you as we wait for her to come back to us. You were asking how it's possible that people who follow such different faiths can bring to its conclusion the venture I was telling you about.'

Dante pulled himself out of the reflections that the sight of the girl had awoken in him, and turned back towards the Persian. 'You were telling me about your faith, Messer Kansbar. I thought all the lands to the east of Constantinople now fell under the faith of the schismatic Mohammed.'

The Persian shook his head firmly. 'Their troops have brought the crescent moon to Mesopotamia, imposing it with fire and iron. But beyond the sea of Basra, their impetus came to a standstill: in Persia the Khan rules, and he is preparing to fight the invader and his prophet for Babylon itself. My faith prospers in the shadow of his banners.'

'But the Cross is the sign of a life that is equally contrary to your convictions. How can you—' Dante suddenly broke off, distracted by the faint sound of footsteps behind him. The poet blinked a few times at the sight of the girl who had just entered the room. Fiamma had abandoned her hunting outfit, and now wore a long white tunic embroidered with scarlet, held in at the waist by a gilded belt formed by a series of little interwoven laurel leaves. On her head she wore a light silk bonnet that held her sweet profile like a caress, and with a strap at the neck that emphasised both her slenderness and her strength. The bonnet, open at the nape, let the coils of her hair slide down her back; no longer tangled now by the ardour of her gallop, but arranged in a neat braid, gathered in a gold hairnet whose links slipped gracefully over her shoulders, sparkling with each movement of her head.

The girl looked at everyone, aware of the admiration her entrance had provoked. 'I have given an order to prepare something to refresh your guests, Father,' she said, turning to the senator. Then she clapped her hands, and some servants appeared in the doorway, holding large bronze plates. Silently they arranged them on the low table in the middle of the room and then, as the others quickly disappeared, the servant holding a large amphora appeared behind them, ready to serve the wine.

Fiamma had taken her seat on one of the *triclinia*, stretching out gracefully, imitated by her father who motioned his guests to do likewise.

Dante went on studying the woman's manners with mounting astonishment. Fiamma was behaving as only a mature matron could have done in Florence. She had sat down without waiting for the men, and had even done so ahead of her own father – something inconceivable as far as good manners were concerned. She seemed to be the mistress of the house, and Saturniano's benevolent gaze, which still caressed her, bore witness to the truth of his surmise.

The girl told the cup-bearer to pour wine into the goblets that had already been set out and, without waiting, she lifted her own and brought it to her lip. She took a long sip, then smiled, running the tip of her tongue along her lips.

Dante went on staring at her with fascination. There was an unexpected grace in that childish gesture, as if the adult forms of her body still concealed the soul of a naughty child, ready for mockery and play. By contrast, he thought of the line that he had dedicated to Beatrice many years before: *She looks so gentle and so pure*, and the very different effect that this new vision provoked in his mind. No, he wouldn't have said that Fiamma was a symbol of gentleness, or of the moderation of customs that recalled the ancient virtues before the spirit of the age had plunged the world into decadence.

But then why did he notice in her the fascinating, subtle attraction of love? Almost angrily he swept the word from his mind, at the same time darting a covert glance at the senator. He feared that the man might have read his feelings on his face. But he was still staring at his daughter, heedless of the things going on around him.

And yet there was something familiar about it all, something that awoke a presence in his memory . . . Suddenly he realised what it was. Her haughtiness, her way of keeping her arms along her sides rather than folded in her lap. As if nothing in the world could touch her. Not the voice, distorted by the mask, but certainly the confident tone, the precision of speech, were those of the mysterious woman who had drawn him to Rome with the mirage of his Virgil.

'Your guests have come from far away, Father,' Fiamma said, pointing brazenly at Kansbar's exotic robes. 'At last we'll be able to listen to a tale of far-off lands. Tell us something you have seen or heard, Messere. A lovely story of unknown lands and mysterious beasts.'

Embarrassed, the Persian cleared his throat. 'Perhaps I could tell you something about my travelling adventures. But I fear they are not suited to the tender ears of a girl, since journeys dug from sand are so much more wretched in real life than dreamed in the pages of a book. But if you really want me to cheer the company with a tale, I will tell you the adventures of a great navigator from my part of the world. A man enwrapped in legend, who lived perhaps in Basra, in the days of the great Caliph Haroun, the rightly guided. His name was Sinbad, and seven times he is said to have faced the great Ocean, and seven times returned. Poorer and richer. Younger and older. Wiser and more reckless.'

'You have decided to speak in riddles, Mastro Kansbar?' said the senator.

'Let him speak, Father,' Fiamma interjected, hushing him with a gesture of her little hand. 'The great Aristotle teaches us that things are or are not, but perhaps in the far-off Orient the mind of men knows intermediate states, and the laws of our intellect do not apply there.'

'But what few books record is the story of his final voyage,' the Persian continued, after bowing in acknowledgement of the girl's observation. 'From that one he did not return.'

'Did he die in the venture?'

The Persian shook his head. 'After every voyage, boredom took hold of him again. And he was not distracted by the running of his household, or the sweet arms of the women who kept him company. So once again he went to Basra and fitted out a ship, and set sail towards the waters of the South, beyond the great circle that we call the Equator. Then for several days he faced the waves, under stars that no one had ever seen, sailing along the shores of the vast continent of Africa, all the way to the rock that marks the boundary between the two oceans. And there he saw the islands of ice that sail freely, and the big fish that has swum there since the dawn of time. On the shores he saw the traces of unknown peoples and marvellous beasts. Then, still spurred on by his anxiety, he set the tiller for the west, until he came within sight of an island that rose alone in the middle of the waves.'

'An island, in the middle of the western Ocean?' Fiamma asked curiously.

'Yes. The island shone in the distance with running waters and dense forests, sweetened by the song of birds with multicoloured plumage. Sinbad dropped anchor and disembarked alone, leaving his men in charge of the vessel. He plunged into the forest, meeting on his way happy people who, in an unfamiliar tongue, invited him to join him at their table to recover from the toils of the voyage. And drinking milk and honey, he learned that this was the blessed island where the storms and troubles of life are calmed for ever, and where the great spirits of humanity find refuge after death. A voluptuous girl offered him lotus leaves so that he would forget. And all traces of the anxiety that had accompanied him throughout his life disappeared, as if by magic.'

The Persian's voice fell silent on that final word. Dante waited for a few moments for the story to continue, but Kansbar merely stared at him in silence, as if waiting for their reactions. He opened his mouth, planning to ask what happened next, but Fiamma's silvery tones cut in before he could speak.

'And then? What happened?'

'The king of the island opened his own treasure to him, telling him to help himself. And Sinbad returned to Basra, laden with the greatest wealth that anyone could ever have dreamed of.'

'And then? And then?' the girl exclaimed again, clapping her hands in childish joy.

'He had attained the perfection of life, in being freed from desires. He stayed down there, contentedly, surrounded by gold and children. And history reveals nothing more about him.'

'What do you think, Alighieri? Should not the figure of this ancient hero be put forward for the admiration of our people?' the senator said. 'I don't think his obstinacy in wanting to know the land that surrounded him is any less than that of Alexander, who travelled the whole world in search of its borders. Or of the ancient Romans, who returned to those borders with armies to turn every inch of the world into an inch of their rule.'

Dante thought again of the story, his hands clasped under his chin, his lips pursed in a reflective attitude. He gave a start at his host's direct question.

'As I was listening to these wonderful tales, my imagination was visited by the shade of a great Greek, Ulysses of harsh Ithaca. And I wondered if a distant memory of his deeds might not have reached the ambassador's lands.'

'It is true, Messer Alighieri,' Fiamma cut in. 'I couldn't help thinking the same thing. Perhaps all seafaring peoples have the same heroes.'

'Or else every people is visited by the same dreams,' the senator remarked. 'In the Bible there's a big fish, which swallows Jonah.'

'Perhaps it's the same one that that man saw!' exclaimed Fiamma, in the same joyful voice that had so astonished the poet. For a moment he wondered if she wasn't making fun of all of them by pretending to be more naïve than she really was.

'So all stories told by different peoples are the same?' the senator insisted.

Dante shook his head. 'No, the differences are profound. It is the yearning for wealth that drives the oriental, and his itch for adventure is merely an execrable hunger for gold, which men can only acquire through the sweat of their brow. Every one of his actions is devoted to greed, and it is only on the scales of usury that he measures good and evil. A very different matter, though, is the indolence of the Greek.'

'You think so, Messer Alighieri? And yet Ulysses set off for Troy seized by the desire for booty.'

'It was his obedience to his king that brought him there. But he was able to turn that order into an opportunity for knowledge. And above all, his fate is profoundly different. In the end, Sinbad wanted the serene calm of the enjoyment of his accumulated wealth, in the city of Baghdad, the cradle of all kinds of splendour. Ulysses, on the other hand, returned to his humble palace, among his pigs and his dogs, undefeated in his soul. And he sought death on the sea.'

'How do you know that?'

'It's what I imagine. He had no wealth but his son and the company of his faithful wife. But for company at night he had the undying thirst for a job unfinished. I don't think he died as legend says, far from the sea in a land that did not know the art of navigation. No, Ulysses returned to the sea at last, towards the lands that lie beyond the Ocean of the dead.'

'But nothing lies beyond that watery abyss! Even the great Ptolemy shows only water on his maps, to the west of the Pillars of Hercules!'

Dante hesitated for a moment. 'It's not true. Beyond the waters there rises a very high mountain, the seat of our unsullied forefathers. There dwelt Adam and Eve, before the Fall. And I think unsullied people still live there.'

As he spoke, he had risen from his chair, taking a few nervous steps. 'You are blaspheming, Messer Alighieri,' the senator muttered, threatening him ironically with his finger. 'But luckily no ears of the Inquisition are hiding in my house. Unsullied people! So these would be people who escaped original sin, for whom the sacrifice of Jesus and the Redemption would be pointless?'

The senator had sounded shocked by the very idea. But the poet thought he sensed that he was basically satisfied with his opinions. The girl couldn't take her eyes off him, either. The senator too noticed her look of interest.

'You have aroused my daughter's curiosity. I think she wants to swap some opinions with you. With your permission, Messer Kansbar and I will take advantage of the moment to withdraw to another room. I want to take a better look at the papers you have brought us. And above all this new way of projecting the curve of the world onto a plane, discovered by the surveyors of Babylon,' he said to the girl with a smile and, holding out an arm to the ambassador, turned towards the door.

Dante was left alone with Fiamma. He felt the girl's eyes examining him. 'You're a strange man, Messer Alighieri. Come and sit next to me,' she said after a long moment of silence, holding her hand languidly out to him.

Dante bowed towards the hand that she held out to

him, kissing it devotedly. Then he immediately straightened, embarrassed. Perhaps a representative of the government of Florence should have been more reserved with a girl who was little more than a child, and who was too uninhibited in her manners to be a gentlewoman.

But there was something about her that disarmed him.

Not just her beauty, which glowed like the morning star beneath the thin fabrics that did nothing to hide her figure. The tone of her voice, certainly, which had its own secret and mysterious music. But above all her way of moving, that way of passing through a space as if she weren't part of it, making the air around her tremble. A luminous form, the like of which he had only ever seen once before, many years before in his own city . . .

'What are you thinking about, Messer Alighieri?' she asked him outright, with a playful smile on her lips. She seemed pleased by his confusion, with that arrogance that young people always have when they discover they have impressed one of their elders.

'Nothing,' he answered hastily. 'For a moment you reminded me of someone I knew in my earliest youth.'

'Someone who looked like me?'

'No . . . perhaps . . .' he murmured vaguely. But the girl went on staring at him with her indecipherable expression. She remained silent for a moment, then spoke again, melodiously enunciating the syllables:

All of my thoughts concerning Love discourse,
 And have in them so great variety,
 That one to wish his sway compelleth me,
 Another argues evil of his force;
One, hoping, sweetness doth to me impart,
 Another makes me oftentimes lament;
 Only in craving Pity they consent,
 Trembling with fear that is within my heart.

The girl had recited the lines in a single breath, like a consummate actress. As she reached the last line her voice grew faint, and faded to a sigh on the word *heart*, as if while reciting she really had felt within her soul all the sentiments that the verses expressed: the tempest of love that throws the lover's soul into a confusion of uncertainty and expectation.

Dante had listened open-mouthed, as a torrent of memories broke their banks and exploded in his mind. He wanted to thank her for her homage to his poetry.

'Did you write your great work for your lady, Messer Alighieri?' she said before he could speak.

'No . . . which . . .'

'The one you alluded to in your book,' she insisted, reaching her hand out towards the table and choosing a little codex. '*La Vita nuova,*' she said, showing him the frontispiece. She rapidly flicked through the pages, brushing the handwritten lines with her finger as if she were very familiar with their content, then stopped at a point towards the end. 'Here: *I hope to say of her what never was said of any woman.* What was it that you wanted to say about your Beatrice?'

'I don't know – I had some ideas in those days. But so much time has passed. Fate pushed my boat towards other shores,' the poet replied. 'The fate of the Commune has consumed all my efforts,' he replied evasively. He felt irritated by these questions, which took him back to a distant era. A time that he had pushed away, but which had taken part of his soul away as it fled.

The girl had sat down on one of the little chairs. She still held the book in her hands, as if preparing to open it again. 'Haven't you written anything as wonderful again?' she asked, after another brief pause. 'Are you no longer a poet?'

'I've written some rhymes . . . a few little things.'

'I knew it. Once you've drunk from the spring of Parnassus, it's no longer possible to stop, for the rest of your life. I know that very well. I write verses too.'

'You?' Dante asked. His curiosity was aroused. But he was also sceptical. Poetry was the art of men. Even though the occasional gentlewoman might beguile her time composing rhymes, like Marie d'Aquitaine. Or Sappho, as they said. But those were exceptions. Poetry never emerges from the convulsive stirring of the senses, but from the desire to rise, from the mind's yearning to comply with something it believes is superior. It was Plato who said that our soul craves more than anything to join the higher world of God; and for that reason poetry is the form with which the soul prepares for that ascent. Through woman, who inspires in man a desire for transfiguration. If she were the one inspired by love, rather than inspiring it, she would be like a flame stretching downwards. An absurdity.

'Yes, for a while. Do you want to hear some of my verses?' he heard her continuing, still sunk in his own reflections. Only now did he realise the intensity with which she was staring at him, from the shady corner where she sat. Her face looked different, more mature and timeless at the same time. An angel, like the ones who had walked the streets of Sodom, he thought with a hint of repugnance.

Then the girl began to talk. A cadence of syllables emerged from her mouth. Dante immediately recognised the unmistakeable rhythm of the Latin hexameter. Modelled on the sweet sensuality of Ovid, the poetry sang of the pain of a distant love, a return awaited. Puzzled, he followed the subject as it developed through the lines: they seemed to speak of the love of a woman for a son, a son who was strangely also her husband. He pricked up his ears, trying to understand precisely something that at first sight seemed to be an absurdity, or an extravagant obscenity.

But suddenly the language had changed, and now the

verses continued in Provençal. The poet immediately prepared to follow the new part, in that language that he understood equally well, but before he could be sure of what he was listening to, the language had changed again. The rhythm of the composition seemed to have returned to the hexameter, but at first he understood nothing of the new part. Then, still without grasping the meaning, he thought he recognised the sound of what he was listening to: at the lectures of the Franciscans, at Santa Croce, he had sometimes listened to one who had learned Greek in the east, and used quotations from the language to support his own arguments.

In the confusion of that strange metre, the admiration for a woman who seemed to know Greek grew quickly within him. But before he could express it, even with a gesture, he noticed that the language of the composition was changing once again.

This time the sounds that emerged from the girl's lips like water from a spring were really indecipherable. They recalled none of the languages of Empire, or the bristling one spoken by the Alemani, nor the equally harsh tongue of the Angles, which he had sometimes listened to in the markets of Florence. Nor was it the horrible barbarian idiom of the infidel pagans in Syria, nor the disjointed words of the Jews, perhaps the language most like the one spoken by the first men, but as remote from us as the cold stars in the fixed sky.

Disconcerted, he went on listening to the girl as she
recited her lines quite naturally, masking their incompre-
hensibility with the delicious harmony of the sounds. For
a moment Dante thought he was witnessing a reincarnation of the celestial tongue, as it must have been before
the arrogance of the tower of Babel forced God's furious
sword to break it into pieces.

By now he had lost all hope of understanding. But
the girl's dilated eyes, the gleam of tears that he saw
shining in them, made him sure that love must still be
the subject of the song. A desperate love, for something
unattainable.

Then all of a sudden the voice fell silent on one last
heart-rending note.

'What were you reciting?' the poet asked, unsettled.

The girl didn't reply. A shadow in her eyes gave him
the sense that Fiamma was wondering if he was capable
of understanding the response. 'A hymn,' she said at
last. 'Celebrating the splendour of the Mother of
Mankind.'

'You've written a song of praise to the Virgin?'

'She who as a virgin had a child, the mother of the
universe. Sovereign of all the elements, prime origin of
time, queen of the spirits,' Fiamma replied in an inspired
voice. 'She who governs with a nod of her head the luminous peaks of the celestial vault, the health-giving sea winds,
the desolate silences of the lower depths.'

The poet had recognised some features of the litany, mixed with other elements that he had never heard before. '*Regina maris* . . . certainly. Ruler of the three kingdoms?' he murmured, puzzled.

He waited for her to explain, but with a sudden shift of mood Fiamma suddenly exploded into unbridled laughter. She stared at something on the wall behind him. Then, as if she had been gripped by a new idea, she got to her feet and walked quickly to a little table with some writing implements lying on it. She returned with a bronze stylus in her hand.

Dante had watched after her with astonishment. The girl approached until she was almost touching him, then she suddenly brought the metal tip to his face, brushing it dangerously. 'Stop! Don't move!' she exclaimed.

Dante looked around in alarm.

'No, don't move your head!'

The girl, still gripping the stylus, was leaning against the wall. With the tip of the blade she began to carve at the layer of whitewash on the wall. 'I'm capturing your shadow,' she said, following the poet's profile with the tip. 'As this cuts stone.'

Having quickly finished the operation, she took a few steps back to stare at the trace she had left. On the wall there was now a carved white furrow delineating a resolute human profile. She seemed to reflect on the features of the face she had just outlined.

'What attracts you to a copy, if you have me to observe?' Dante asked. 'It's like being in Plato's cave and preferring the distorted image to the true idea!'

The girl suddenly turned towards him. 'Have you read those extraordinary pages? In that extraordinary language?'

Dante hesitated for a moment, embarrassed. 'No. I don't know Greek. But I've read it elsewhere . . .' he declared evasively. But she didn't seem to have been listening. She started tracing the sign with the tip. 'What an extraordinary language, Messere! The fathers of our religion assert that Hebrew is the language in which God originally spoke to the first and greatest men of our species. Perhaps that's true. But it's certainly in Greek that those great men talked to one another, penetrating the secrets of nature, setting down the steps of the staircase that was supposed to bring them to the heaven from which they had been banished.'

She broke off, stopping to contemplate the long scratch that ran along the wall. The nose straight and strong, the forehead high and spacious, the chin pronounced.

'It's just an outline, a vague shadow,' the poet insisted.

'Not so, Messer Alighieri. Your body bears the mutability and imprecision of a form sculpted by time, a sequence of expressions written on water. But in the geometrical essentiality of a contrast between light and shadow, the whole vastness of the book of your soul is reduced to its essential. This profile gives you to me, stripping you of your capacity for change.'

'That's what they say of Perseus, who defeated the Gorgon by looking upon her in the gleaming hollow of his shield. Do you fear that my gaze will freeze you, that you too will be able to contemplate me only in effigy?'

'Not fear, so much as the anxiety of penetrating your secret.'

Dante fell silent for a moment. Then he shook his head. 'My secret. No one can get so close to the depths.'

'You really believe that?' she smiled slyly. 'That there's an abyss in man so deep that a woman can't go there?'

It was only then that the poet realised that Senator Spada had come into the room unnoticed some time before, and stood listening with signs of vivid emotion on his face. He approached the girl, who was saying nothing now, but breathing quickly, and rested a hand on her head as if delivering a blessing. Then he turned back to the poet.

'You were listening, Messer Alighieri? I hope you have not been too importuned by my daughter's sweet petulance during our absence. It's her youthful impulsiveness, which in her sex often assumes the form of endless discourse,' the senator said.

Dante bowed respectfully to the girl, who had received the paternal observation with a smile of understanding. 'If I hadn't seen it with my own eyes, and heard it with my ears, I would share your opinion, Senator. But there are rare cases in which the graces of nature and the favour of God join in a single creature, upon whom alone the stars bestow the purpose of revealing the miracle of creation. And I believe your daughter is one of these. In her the weakness of her sex has been erased.'

While speaking, he had watched from the corner of his eye the effects of his praise on the girl. He was disappointed to notice that she seemed to have listened distractedly, her attention focused on something far away.

'So you appreciated her verses?'

Dante hesitated for a moment before replying. 'What your daughter showed me is something that few men in the whole of Christendom could do, perhaps no one. A masterful, mystical oration in all the major languages. And it makes me regret my little learning, which has excluded me from most of it. Particularly the latter part, written in a language that perhaps only the angels could understand.'

The senator leaned slightly forward in a sign of gratitude. 'The last language is not angelic, but is perhaps the one that, when spoken, most closely resembles it. It is Coptic.'

'Coptic?' Dante replied, puzzled.

'The language spoken by the ancient Egyptians, which survived in the lands of the Nile until the Mohammedan fury came to wipe it out. A few years ago some monks who had survived in those parts came to Rome, and I myself received them for the time of their stay, as they waited to continue on their journey to the lands of the

Byzantine Empire. And during that time I was able to learn something of their ancient tongue, the customs that they had passed down, the obscure knowledge they had preserved. The little I learned I taught to my daughter, an excellent pupil, as you have heard – better than her teacher.'

'What was your daughter singing?' Dante asked, with an unresolved doubt about what he had heard.

The senator briefly turned his eyes to the girl, as if inviting her to explain herself. But since she merely smiled, he went on, 'An ancient story. Perhaps the first of all stories. But have you given any thought to what I was talking to you about? The new crusade, the last and definitive one. Is your soul not excited by the idea of taking part?'

Dante stirred himself at this new direct question. 'Would you like me to ask my compatriots to contribute? The Commune of Florence—'

'Always that city on your lips!' the senator broke in. 'It is in other ways that your genius must help us, not by gathering together a handful of florins in your Tuscan lands.'

Dante wasn't sure he had understood. He saw father and daughter exchange a swift glance. 'Father, we will have his words, I'm sure of it. Entirely sure,' Fiamma said enigmatically.

'Yes, my daughter. I'm sure of it too,' he murmured, looking back at the poet. 'When he has seen and known everything.'

'Are you alluding to the crusade?' Dante asked. 'You're talking as if it were the simplest thing in the world. But the difficulties involved . . .'

'Preparations are much more advanced than you think. But so that Papa can calmly give the order to leave, the Patrimony of St Peter must first be calmed and subordinated.'

'So what happened at Palestrina was a stage on the road to Jerusalem?'

'That was a nest of ruffians and Ghibellines, Messer Alighieri. Where the Colonna family had entrenched them-selves, lording it around all the gates of the city. And Boniface did well to bring the town to reason. Unfortunately the unruliness of some great families is a source of some concern for His Holiness. But gradually they are being put down, and their fortresses eradicated. What remains is perhaps the greatest and strongest among them, and in the coming night its turn will come. I would like you to be there, Messer Alighieri. So that the great city of Florence can have an idea, through the eyes of her most illustrious citizen, of how order reigns in Rome. The man within the city walls best able to judge good and evil.'

What was Boniface's man trying to drag him into? Good and evil: Dante's instincts heard in this new request traces of a theme that continued to elude him. He agreed with a nod, waiting for the plan to reveal its hidden scheme.

*

8th November, towards evening, in the rooms of the Vatican Palace

A CLERIC stepped timidly forward, bowing to the ground. Boniface was sitting on his throne, his eye turned to the window that opened up onto the fields towards the Tiber. On the right, the imposing mass of the Castello and its fortresses blocked the view to the east, where the sun gilded the pinnacles of the distant Quirinal.

'Your Holiness, the inquisitor wishes to be received.'

The Pope leaped to his feet with a curt nod of the head. The cleric withdrew after a quick genuflection, to be replaced after a moment by the black and white form of the Dominican.

'What do you bring me from this man?' Boniface asked avidly, staring at a bundle of papers that the other man clutched in his fists.

'A poem. Which the Florentine seems to value more highly than his soul, given the attention with which he hides it and drags it behind him each time he moves.'

'A poem?' the Pope replied in disbelief. He seemed disappointed. 'I thought . . . I thought it would be something different . . . In Florence he fiercely opposed my will: I thought he was hatching some sort of plan to thwart us, to give voice to the wicked imperial doctrine that rejects our authority over the kingdoms of the Earth. A poem! A little poet has crossed our path!'

The muscles in his face had begun to distort with rage. 'But he is in our hands, and he will not leave them.'

The inquisitor held out his hand. 'It is a poem, it's true. But not the usual nonsense of the kind. There is something concealed in it.'

Boniface stared at him anxiously. 'What?'

'It escapes us. Still. He has something in mind.'

The Pope tore the papers from the man's hand and brought them up to his eyes. 'At least now he will stop,' he murmured, running through the first few lines of the text, struggling to focus his short-sighted eyes.

'It's just a copy, Your Holiness. I put seven of our scribes to work on it, to produce it in a single night. It's a good thing the man doesn't know we're in possession of it: he has a prodigious memory, and would be perfectly capable of rewriting the text at any moment, if we had taken it from him. This way, however, he won't suspect that we are aware of what he is doing, and we will be able to penetrate his consciousness without his knowledge.'

'Why such caution, if they are only verses?'

'Perhaps you ought to listen. Your wisdom, made famous by the light of the Almighty, can and will shed light on my concerns. It tells of a journey to the Underworld.'

'Another one!' Boniface exploded. He span round, furiously throwing the papers to the floor and walking back to the window. 'Why is the world plagued by lunatics who claim to know the future, the shape of the Earth, the reason and purpose of things, rather than entrusting themselves piously to the great arms of the Church, which orders and understands all things?' he shouted, as if he expected a reply from the lead roof of the Vatican basilica. 'And now they want to extend their tittle-tattle to the Beyond? As if the Kingdom of heaven and the caves of hell were not already clearly delineated in the Scriptures, with their light and their flames, without the need to draw additional maps of them? Just for playing with the things revealed, the Florentine would deserve the noose. And then he would know in his own flesh the fire that he imagines for others, I'm sure of it.'

The inquisitor bent patiently to pick up the pages and put them in order. Then he began to read the first paragraph. At first Boniface ostentatiously turned his back on him, then slowly turned, puzzled. He lingered by the window for another few moments, then approached his chair again and slumped silently into it. He half-closed his eyes, as the sound of his enemy's words began to fill the void of the room.

The monk read for over an hour, enunciating the verses in a colourless voice until he reached the final page:

And we, in company with the dusky waves,
Made entrance downward by a path uncouth.

A marsh it makes, which has the name of Styx,
This trustful brooklet, when it has descended
Down to the foot of the malign gray shores.

The inquisitor broke off. For a long moment the silence of the night seemed to swallow up the echo of the last words. Boniface suddenly opened his eyes. 'And?'

'The poem ends there, Your Holiness. Plainly it's only the first part of a much larger composition. Like the ruins of the ancients by which we are surrounded in the Eternal City, from beneath its surface of rubble and detritus torn from the ancients, something appears that represents a threat . . .'

'What? Apart from insults to the clergy, to which this man has already made us well accustomed.'

'Something still more perverse. This descent to the demons is only a mask for his recondite desire to summon them up among us!'

Boniface clenched his fists. 'Do you think that what is spread out on these tables is the root of a *grimorium*? A horrible invocation under the appearance of a journey?'

'I'm sure of it. You've seen who his guide is: the magus Virgil. Do I have to cut his hand off?'

Boniface hesitated for a moment, as if he were uncertain. Then his face lit up with a malicious light. 'No. Let him get on with it. If he really knows how to summon up demons, I don't want his art to be lost with his head.'

The inquisitor looked up at the Pope, perplexed. But the other man was looking out the window again, towards the far-off hills. 'Perhaps even the Black Arts, in certain circumstances, can be turned to the greater glory of God and his Church,' Boniface murmured. 'Especially now that my own city is pervaded by the insult of heresy. Grim meetings are held in hidden places, but the Evil One's claws have even penetrated my apartments!'

The inquisitor nodded. 'We too, Holy Father, have a sense that some members of the Curia have opened their ears to the voice of Satan. Like some members of the Senate, perhaps. Who they are is not yet known, but Senator Spada has his eye on the matter, and sooner or later he will find out.'

'Saturniano . . . sadly, God has sent few men of his stamp.'

6

9th November, towards sunset

THE SENATOR had arranged to meet him at sunset, at the Torre dell'Isola. While waiting for the appointed hour, Dante several times reread Virgil's precious book. He read, but he could just as easily have been blind, such was the precision with which the words rose to his lips, even before his eyes recognised them in the signs set out upon the page. He lingered for the hundredth time on one passage:

> *Ibant obscuri sola sub nocte per umbram*
> *perque domos Ditis vacuas et inania regna . . .'*

'Obscure they went, through dreary shades, that led along the waste dominions of the dead.' Yes, it could not be better expressed. That was what the hell of the ancients was like, an insubstantial and deserted realm, before the coming of Christ gave succour for ever to the pain of men, opening up the hope of a second life. A desolate land, where death found no meaning or redress. A forest of phantoms, in which souls, stripped of their bodies, no longer shone with purity, but wandered, confused, waiting senselessly in the darkness.

He lowered the codex and stared into the middle distance. That was the pain of the pagans, the loss of life. But his hell must be more terrible.

He had to show his readers the form of evil! There was no choice, at the cost of reducing the Creator to the rank of a sneering architect of torments, if he wanted his lesson to imprint itself on people's minds with the force of a hammer. He thought again of the Persian ambassador: certainly, if he had admitted the existence of a malevolent god to whom he could attribute every abomination, it would have been easy to weigh him down with even the strangest forms that lay beyond the grave, the most terrible punishments. Fountains of fire, burning paths like the ones he had read in the Arab's book, *The Vision of Mohammed*. But then he too was a pagan.

He shrugged and glanced out the window. The tenth hour had just passed, and the shadow of dusk was slipping across the walls of the building. At that very moment he heard in the distance the sound of bells, picked up immediately by other bells. The *patarina* on the tower of the Campidoglio was sounding the curfew, and the other bells of the city were falling into line.

Soon it would be night, it was time to set off. He wondered what it might be, this spectacle of justice that the senator had promised him.

HE REACHED the tower that dominated the island and went down by the Ponte Cestio. The whole of the island square, which extended between the tower of the bridge, the church and the monastery on the other side, swarmed with soldiers, gathered in groups around bundles of lances set up to form little pyramids. The whole space was lit only by the faint gleam of the moon, but that was enough to allow a glimpse of some big carriages that were lined up on the opposite bridge, already yoked to pairs of oxen.

There must have been at least a hundred men there, he judged, taking in the scene with his eyes. Too huge a number for the simple police operation to which the senator had alluded. The crowd seemed to be engaged in the first preparations for the action itself: whispered orders ran from one group to another, and officers harangued their men, waving their swords at something beyond the dark mass of the Palatine, which obstructed the view beyond the river. The Caetani Tower, which loomed massive in front of the monastery, seemed in the grip of frantic activity: lights passed repeatedly behind its loopholes, as if large numbers of men with torches were going up and down the staircases within.

No sooner had he left the parapets of the bridge than he found his passage blocked by two sentries who crossed their lances in front of his chest, brusquely commanding him to halt. Perplexed, Dante was about to respond to their mounting pressure when he was relieved to hear a familiar voice coming to his aid.

'Messer Alighieri. Just the man! We were waiting for you so that we could begin our display of justice. Please, go and join my unit.'

The senator had appeared in front of him. He had abandoned his ceremonial robes in favour of a light body armour consisting of strips of steel and a pair of shoulder plates in the same material, and a tabard of chain mail that reached his knees. Under one arm he gripped a classical-style helmet, a kind of stout iron cylinder with a narrow slit at eye level, and he clutched a two-handed sword in his right hand. He was closely followed by an officer of the papal troop, likewise covered in iron from head to toe, and holding a bullseye lantern. The man lifted the flap of the lamp to shine a ray of light on the poet's face, as if to see this stranger for himself, the man for whom the senator had been waiting.

The senator abruptly signalled to the sentries to withdraw, then he too stepped into the narrow beam of light. He passed his weapon to his subordinate, and with his free arm gripped the poet's shoulder, clutching it tightly.

'Tonight you will see how His Majesty Boniface treats the unruly in his Christian city. It might even teach you something about how to face the factions that are tearing your Florence apart.'

'Rome has always been the ruler of the peoples. She might be so again,' the poet replied crisply.

The officer, who had stayed a few feet behind, now approached, removing his helmet. Then, lest there be any doubt about his identity, he raised the lantern for a moment to illuminate his own face. Dante recognised the sinister features of Master Hemp, who flashed his yellow teeth in what was supposed to be a smile.

'Listen to the senator, Florentine! You'll learn more from a night of bloodshed than you will from all your books about the history of things.'

'So are you about to write a few fine chapters of that story?' the poet replied wryly, looking round and taking a closer look at the men lined up around him. Now, beneath the moon's faint light, more than an orderly army, it looked like a gang of cut-throats ready to be unleashed. The senator seemed to have guessed his thoughts, because he silenced the Decurion with a frosty glance, before turning affably back to him. 'Ignore the unruliness of my underlings, Messer Alighieri. They have been called upon to deal with the lowest part of mankind, and this impresses upon their minds a savage trait that might easily disturb a learned man. But it is upon this very class of man that empires rest, and the sword of justice is no less sharply honed than the scythe of a simple peasant. After the day of the eagles comes the night of the wolves, and this is one of those.'

'Where will the wolves go?'

'There is a town that is rising up against the holy will of Boniface like a bubo on a plague-ridden corpse. The fortress of the Frangipane, beyond the ruins of the ancient Forum. They have settled among the arches of the Colosseum, entrenching themselves there with their families and their soldiers. Their house has rejected every invitation to act reasonably, strong in the walls of their fortress which they hold to be impregnable. We have been trying for a long time to negotiate with them, promising that they would be able to maintain their fortress if they agreed to allow a guard of Boniface's men amongst them. They haughtily refused, strong in the remote protection that they believed their alliance with Colonna might grant them. But tonight they will know their just punishment, and their insolence will be brought low. The fortress will be returned to the dominion of the Roman Senate, and one more tile will join the others in our city's orderly mosaic.'

'The peace of Boniface?' said Dante, unable to keep a caustic tone out of his voice.

'The peace of Rome. Which was once the peace of the world, and will be once more.'

The poet shrugged. Around him the senator's men were picking up their weapons and lining up in groups, while the head of the column had already begun to cross the Ponte Fabricio, slipping between the four-sided herms that decorated its parapets. The carts, too, had set in motion and, stung by the switches of their drivers, the oxen pulled powerfully, waving their long-horned heads around, irritated by this unusual night-time work.

Dante recognised the outlines of two big ballistas, and the low, squat form of a battering ram, covered by a roof of solid oak boards. The senator had followed his eyes. 'The fortress is well protected, as I told you. The building is vast, and rivals even the Castello in scale. But, unlike that great construction, it is not surrounded by a rampart, and the large numbers of openings – even if they are walled up – provide a greater possibility of storming it. With the battering ram we will try to knock down one of the portals and burst into the amphitheatre. Once inside, the troops will be able to make the rebels see sense. Their whole family does not number more than three dozen, and they are hampered by the women and children who live with them.'

'There are women and children in the fortress? Aren't you going to give them shelter before you attack?' Dante asked, scandalised.

In the light of the torches that had now been lit, the various groups set off across the bridge. Dante and the senator were in the group at the head, which advanced along an alleyway next to the arches of the ancient Theatre of Marcellus. Once past the theatre, the column moved first towards the Campidoglio, lit up on high by the torches of the sentries guarding the seat of the Senate. Then, having reached the base of the Tarpeian Rock, a volcanic precipice that overhung the road, the troop passed the remains of a flight of steps leading to the Campidoglio and turned towards the Forum, the forest of whose columns (those still standing) could be glimpsed in the distance like the remains of a wood shaken by a storm.

A narrow paved street ran through the lowest point, cutting the mass of monuments in two. Many of the ancient buildings were reduced to a pile of ruins, in the midst of which little sheds and hovels had been erected. The mooing of the animals shut inside them, disturbed by the passing men, rose suddenly and mingled with the creak of the wheels of the carts and the regular steps of the soldiers.

They continued marching, with each step plunging further into that vast marble cemetery, closed off on the right by the Palatine Hill and gripped on the left by the mass, still standing, of the Basilica of Massentius, whose huge vaults obscured the sky.

When they were level with the basilica, Dante noticed beyond the walls, at the top of the Viminal Hill, a huge bonfire that seemed to be burning in the sky itself. Stunned, he stopped, still staring open-mouthed at the incredible spectacle. It looked as if an angel flying over their heads had lit a huge torch in the moonlit sky. The moon itself shone palely further down, and its light now seemed fainter than the other light that flickered on the horizon.

'Look, Messer Alighieri, the Tower of the Militia is giving the signal to attack,' said the senator, who had noticed his surprise. 'The Pope recently negotiated the purchase of this fortress from the Annibaldi, who were its rulers. Now that fortress too is in the hands of his troops, and an army will come from there to join us and back us up. But in fact they've already begun their attack. Look!'

Dante concentrated his eyes in the darkness. Behind the flames he could just see the dark outline of the tower: a huge square block on which two further massive floors rose up before the heights on which the flame was burning. So enormous that it really looked as if the sky had reached the earth at that point. It could not have been very different from the famous lighthouse of Alexandria, one of the Seven Wonders of the World that the great authors had written about. Around the tower rose a stout wall, from whose terraces issued a series of sputtering sparks that passed through the sky above their heads, before falling to earth beyond the Basilica of Massentius.

'The catapults in the fort are striking the Colosseum.'

'Are they trying to destroy the monument?' Dante enquired.

'Not even the whole artillery of Christianity could move a single block of that building, Messer Alighieri,' the senator replied, while continuing to exhort his men to advance with great sweeps of his hand. 'The trebuchets are hurling jars of flaming oil against the arches, in an attempt to disorient the defenders and keep them busy with the fires as we get to work with the battering ram down below. Our men are already posted on the Arch of Titus, ready to stop throwing as we arrive.'

At that moment the column came to a hesitant stop as the men crowded in on each other.

Dante saw Master Hemp running towards them. 'The bastards have blocked the street with a chain. The carts can't get through!'

'I was expecting something like that,' the senator replied calmly. 'Let's go and see. Where are the blacksmiths?'

The senator moved swiftly towards the head of the column, followed by the poet. A big metal chain had been stretched in a narrow passageway between two buildings. Beyond it could be seen the great curve of the Colosseum, with the projectiles from the trebuchets raining down on it. The fiery trails continued to fall; several of the arches had caught fire, and tall flames rose up, fed by the wind.

Behind him Dante saw two men running up holding long iron levers. They quickly inserted the metal bars into the links of the chain and began levering with all their

GIULIO LEONI

might. The iron slowly began to twist, until one of the rings yielded with a snap and the chain fell to the ground, freeing the way for the carts.

'Come on, now!' cried the senator, pointing ahead to the level ground in front of the ancient Julian Basilica, which appeared as a kind of terrace looking out over the valley of the Colosseum. 'Arrange the ballistas down there and start to fire at the walls.'

As the operators trained the siege engines, the rest of the column marched on, crowding behind the team of oxen that pulled the battering ram. Then, once the animals had been freed, the men pushed their way on towards the big arch, barred by the oaken portal, heedless of the stones and other projectiles that rained from above and bounced off the cover of the vehicle. Master Hemp was ahead of the rest and whipping up the orderlies with shouts and slaps on the back.

Having reached the gate, the men gripped the heavy trunk of the bronze head and began swinging it on the ropes from which it was suspended. As the battering ram gained velocity, its head came closer and closer to the panels of the door, until with a dull thud it struck its first blow, making the whole structure shake. A second blow followed immediately afterwards, and a loud crash announced that a crack had opened up in the barrier.

From up at the Julian Basilica, among the stumps of columns, the troops directed shouts of enthusiasm at the enemy, certain that their defences were about to yield. On an order from the senator, they started climbing down towards the boggy dip that surrounded the monument, swarming up the slope, guided by the flames that shone in the arches of that vast beacon.

Dante moved with the others, dragged along by the passion of the attack. He found himself coming down along the side of the hill, the damp earth coming away beneath his feet, threatening to drag him, hurtling, to his ruin. He struggled to keep his balance, then all of a sudden plunged up to his knees in putrid water, surrounded by dozens of men crowding towards the battering ram, splashing about under the weight of their armour. A great column of mud and water rose up a few feet away from him, sent up into the air by a big stone fired from the terraces of the Colosseum, followed by lots of others. A chorus of cries of pain hurt his ears; among all the blows that now followed in their dozens, a good few hit home, crushing into the mud the broken bodies of the more unfortunate assailants.

From the marsh in front of him a man emerged, completely covered in mud and panting as he tried to breathe, spitting out the slime that he had swallowed. But before he could recover, a second stone cut him down. Dante quickly darted to the side, trying to dodge the next blow, while a salvo of cries exploded on his right.

Dante looked up, his attention captured by the noise.

A group of horsemen was coming down the slope of the Caelian Hill, their swords in their hands. He sensed a wave of fear spreading among his companions. The group broke ranks and scattered to the left, through the reeds, trying to escape through the marshy ground.

The poet, too, instinctively moved to that side, hoping that the boggy ground might act as an obstacle to the attackers.

'Try to stay together!' he called to the nearest men. Meanwhile he had drawn his dagger from his secret pocket and was clutching it tightly. 'Wait for the horse to draw near and get underneath it. Strike it in the belly!'

'Get underneath, you idiots!' he yelled again to the vanishing shadows around him. He found himself alone, while the group of horsemen had reached the edge of the reeds and had spread out in search of the enemy. One of them must have spotted him, because he came resolutely towards him. Dante desperately looked around in search of the others, to form some kind of common defence, but saw no one. He crouched among the reeds, trying to make himself invisible, waiting. If the horse approached in a straight line, pursuing its course, he had to be ready to throw himself a few feet to the right, to avoid being knocked over and to find himself in an attacking position.

Dante floundered about in the undergrowth, weighed down by his drenched robes. Behind him, the thud of the animal's hooves was growing frighteningly louder, then all of a sudden the mass of the horse was above him.

He turned, just in time to glimpse the flash of an iron mace flying towards his head. With a jerk of his hips he avoided most of the impact, feeling only a pain in his back where one of the spikes had torn his flesh. He slid up against the flank of the horse, gripping the stirrup to stay upright. His pursuer, unbalanced by the energy of his failed blow, had turned to the other side.

The animal, stung by the spurs, was still trampling the mud. Its rider must have given it a tug on the reins to make it give a half-turn so that he could strike the poet again. The animal reared up with a wild whinny, before falling back into the bog, throwing up a cascade of mud. Its hooves had come down dangerously close to Dante's head, but, dragged down by its weight, the animal seemed for a moment to be hampered in the movement of its slender hooves, which appeared to be sinking ever deeper into the morass.

Dante darted sideways to avoid being run over, then sprang forward with his blade outstretched, striking the beast just behind the leather belts of the saddle. He pulled out the blade with a violent twist of the wrist, to enlarge the wound, then jumped forward again, trying to strike the horseman's thigh, which seemed to be unprotected. He stretched his arm out with all his might, but the second blow was less precise. The blade sank into the man's flesh, tearing the muscle and then scraping against the stirrup-strap. The animal's violent whinny, along with a human cry of pain, confirmed that he had hit his target, but his adversary was still standing over him, tugging frantically on the bridle to force the animal to turn towards the poet as he in turn tried to strike Dante with the mace.

Taking advantage of that moment, Dante inflicted a second blow to the horse's flank, his blade reaching a point between the belly and the joint of the back legs. A violent gush of hot blood rained down on him, telling him that he had struck the animal's artery.

With a whinny of pain, the animal reared up, waving its front legs as if seeking in the air the support that it now lacked on the ground.

Dante was almost under the animal's belly; from that position he managed to plunge his blade into a spot level with the rear hocks, extracting a new whinny of pain from the horse, while its rider tried to reach him with his mace. The steel spikes flashed again, catching his forehead. A stream of blood flowed into his eye, obstructing his vision on the left. He saw the imposing mass rearing up above him again: with the strength of desperation, he threw himself to the side again, falling on his back and dragging himself away, kicking frantically.

Again the horse lowered its hooves. But this time, no longer supported by its back legs, whose tendons had been severed by the blade, it fell to the ground, turning onto one side, its head raised to call for death in a terrified whinny.

The unseated horseman was stuck with one leg under the animal. He tried desperately to free himself from the weight, frantically pushing at the ground with his hands, which had dropped their weapons. Seeing that the rider was unarmed, Dante leaped up, ready to finish him off. He threw himself at the horseman, gripping his shoulders from behind, while with one hand he tore at the man's collar to expose his neck to the blade.

He saw the face of a dark-haired young man, his eyes wide with terror. He was still trying to escape Dante's grip, panting under the twofold weight of the horse that immobilised him and that of the poet, who had leaped onto his chest, crushing him with his knees. Dante felt the sting of fingernails on one cheek, and gripped the boy's neck harder, trying to suffocate him as he struggled desperately. He struck him hard on the nose with his elbow, drawing from him a cry of pain, then pointed the blade at his throat.

And stopped, frozen. In his mind, as in a dream, he suddenly saw again the very same scene that he had already seen on the plain of Campaldino, the same bestial fury, the same horror, the same sweet taste of blood in his mouth, the same fear in the eyes of an enemy, which turned into astonishment after the blow, the sudden pallor of God's design broken.

He loosened his grip, horrified by what he was about to do. He saw a flash of surprise lighting up the boy's eyes, then heard him panting as he tried to escape his grip. Dante let him slip away into the mud, after struggling to free himself from the weight of the horse.

The poet looked around, distraught. He had to escape this senseless war into which he had been thrown for no reason, a blind confrontation that did not belong to him. He tried to stand as tall as he could, to find his bearings in the middle of the reeds. But he couldn't see a thing. Then he suddenly became aware that the ground was trembling again, and a new dark mass appeared a hundred yards behind him. He began running desperately.

He felt lost, while the whinny of the second horse exploded behind him. He had already fallen and managed to get back on his feet twice, but the weight of his drenched robes now seemed too much for him. It was as if the hands of a thousand ghosts had emerged from the ground to hold him back. Blind fear took hold of him, misting his mind. He thought he could feel on his neck the violent breathing of the animal, his ears deafened by the noise of the hooves and the cries of the other men around him, crushed by this second attack.

He slipped again, ending up with his head under water. He re-emerged panting, spitting out the mud that had filled his mouth. The animal was on top of him, its flashing hooves ready to smash his skull. But before his assailant could run him through with his lance, a shadow that had come out of nowhere interposed itself.

Dante glimpsed a sword flashing through the air, followed by a scream of pain. Struck in the side, the horseman was unseated and fell beside him in a wave of mud. With a wild leap, his saviour was on top of the fallen man, tugging at his collar and slicing his defenceless throat with a clean blow. Then the stranger bent over him: Dante saw a cold face, with features that looked as if they had been carved from stone. The man gripped him by the arm and raised his sword, as if he too had decided to strike, but then, with a grimace of disgust, let him go. The poet saw him turning towards the Colosseum and disappearing into the shadows again.

He struggled back to his feet and began running wildly away. He realised that he had completely lost his bearings: he frantically wiped his eyes with his sleeve, trying to get rid of the mud that covered his face. In the faint moonlight he saw only dark shadows, some moving, others huge and motionless. Suddenly, in the dark mass in front of him, lights appeared, like stars after a cloud has passed. Down below, the arches of the Colosseum had been lit up as if someone had thrown up the doors of a furnace, revealing the flames inside.

'Over here!' he heard someone shouting beside him, invisible in the reeds. 'The Frangipane are coming out of the fortress, they're coming towards us!'

Dante headed straight for the lights, hoping he had made the right choice. From the arches a trembling forest of torches was approaching, the torches of the defenders, accompanied by the hiss of ballistas firing once more from above, which had resumed against their assailants.

Suddenly he was in the midst of nothingness. He found himself surrounded by shadows splashing in the mud, trying to escape towards the Arch of Constantine. Behind the monument rose the terraces of the foundation of the Julian Basilica, where the senator's men might still be in position. But the troop coming down from the arches of the Colosseum seemed to be heading precisely in that direction, apparently determined to cut off his route to safety.

His only option was to try on the other side, along the dip in which the marshland seemed eventually to turn into a stream, between the Palatine and the Caelian Hill. He threw himself in that direction, sinking into the mud and forcing his way through the reeds, heedless of the wounds that the sharp leaves were inflicting on his hands with every step he took.

He ran a hundred yards like that, until exhaustion and the pain in his side became unbearable. Then he was forced to stop, resting with his hands on his knees to get his breath back. He gritted his teeth, cursing the years that he felt crashing down on him with all their weight. Already thirty-six, more than halfway through his life. For how many years to come would he be able to grip a sword?

His lungs hurt, but gradually he felt his strength returning. He straightened and began to flee through the reeds once more. He thought that perhaps his flight would be easier if he turned off towards the first crag of the hill to his right, above the marshes. Clutching the tufts of reeds that had begun to thin out, he hoisted himself onto solid ground and went on climbing until he was halfway up. Above his head he thought he could just make out the avant-corps of a turreted building, perhaps a monastery or an abbey. He was unsure whether to approach it any further, since he didn't know whether it was inhabited, or by whom. He decided to keep a certain distance from the curved wall of what might have been the apse of a church, or the base of a truncated tower, and after reaching a kind of gap found himself in the middle of fields full of rows of vines, lined up neatly against their cane supports.

From that point the land starting falling again, losing itself down below in the darkness of night, softened only by the light from a half-moon. He stopped again, pricking up his ears to catch any sound which might indicate that his pursuers were on his heels. But nothing broke the silence, only the far-off cry of a night-bird.

He concentrated, trying to call to mind everything he remembered about the city. Where was he now? If he wanted to get back to his lodgings, he would above all have to return to human habitation. What he had seen of Rome had taught him that an enormous area of the city was practically uninhabited, while the bulk of the buildings were concentrated along the river. So he would have to move towards the Tiber. But where was the river?

He listened again, in the hope of catching the murmur of the waves, but again found himself surrounded by silence. He was concerned to discover that he had lost all sense of direction. If he turned back, towards the Colosseum, he would probably be able to reconstruct from memory the path he had taken from the island. But he hadn't the slightest idea of the outcome of the battle: turning towards the amphitheatre, he risked finding himself in the middle of that conflict once again and, as an outsider, involved in a war that he didn't understand and which left him utterly indifferent.

So he decided to carry blindly on: the only thing he was sure about now was that he was still within the circle of the Aurelian walls. However far away they might be, if he kept straight on, sooner or later he would come upon either the river or the walls. From there he would only have to climb back along the walls, walking along the *pomerium* of the city from gate to gate until he reached a recognisable place. Perhaps it wouldn't take all night, he said to himself, thinking with dismay of the huge circle of walls that had appeared before him as he had entered the city.

The ground beneath his feet began to slope steeply again. Several times he felt the rain-damp ground yielding beneath his weight, threatening to send him plunging far below.

He continued stubbornly on, trying to keep to the straight path that he had imposed upon himself. But deep inside he was beginning to feel uncomfortable: the panorama around him was becoming increasingly desolate. All traces of cultivation had disappeared now, making way for barren undergrowth from which clusters of tall trees rose here and there – pines, judging by their crowns, which seemed to float in the sky like dark clouds.

He walked along what seemed to be a path of beaten earth and finally glimpsed in the distance, in the middle of the plain at the foot of the hill, a regular outline that suggested a large building.

He suddenly stopped, frightened. If this were a fortress, as the height of the walls suggested, it was a castle so imposing as to rival the Castel Sant'Angelo. But in Florence no one had mentioned anything of the kind, and yet whoever owned this fort would have rivalled Boniface himself in his rule of Rome.

Strangely he didn't see any light, or any sign of life on what must have been the terraces of the outer walls. They seemed to have been abandoned, with no sign of any human presence, or any gates to provide access. He hesitated a moment longer, then moved resolutely in that direction, in search of someone from whom he could ask the way.

After a few hundred yards he found himself below what he had taken in the darkness to be a rampart. In fact it was a kind of gloomy enclosure, a long wall carved with niches and topped by a portico supported by a large number of slender marble columns.

If this was a fortress, he said to himself, only a god of beauty could have conferred such grace on a castle. Part of the wall had collapsed, opening up a passageway through which he slipped inside.

Beyond the outer walls barren space opened up, blocked at the end by a new large construction topped by a dome. He stopped again, disoriented. The ground all around was white with headstones and crosses, most of them leaning at an angle or completely uprooted. He began to move cautiously around that unexpected cemetery, stepping over ancient piles of earth that were now almost indistinguishable. So this must have been a church, if so many tombs had been housed in its grounds; the headstones stretched in all directions, as far as the eye could see, all the way up to the internal construction. But why had so magnificent a temple been abandoned and allowed to fall into ruin, along with its cargo of sepulchres?

His curiosity aroused, he continued walking across the ravaged graves until he reached one of the big vaults, interspersed with tall columns that led to the interior of the building.

He found himself in a huge hall, walled with marble, at the end of which a series of openings fanned out into large inner rooms that were lost in darkness. He went on walking. Under his shoes he felt the loose tiles of ancient mosaics coming away with every step he took. He stepped inside a new space that resembled a basilica. He looked up: part of the ceiling had fallen, and large pieces of the masonry lay broken on the ground. Through the opening the moonbeam came in like a blade, powerfully sculpting the corners of the big pillars that had once held up the vault. He looked to his right, where a new room opened up. Here it looked as if a boat had been washed up, its keel lying in the middle of the space. He walked towards it, realising that what he had at first mistaken for a boat was in fact a huge block of red rock, carved to support a vast bowl. He thought of the baptismal fonts of his own Baptistery, and how imposing they had always seemed to him. But if this was a font, only a Titan could have carved it. Only a god would have had the courage to use it.

The silence around him was broken only by the muffled sound of his footsteps. But he gradually became aware of a distant murmur of voices, accompanied by barely audible music, a fluting melody that seemed to float above a rhythm of little metallic beats. He pricked up his ears, trying to work out where it was coming from. But the sounds seemed to drift around him as if they were issuing from the very walls of the basilica.

For a moment he thought that he might, by entering the building, have unleashed some dark magic. Perhaps it was the memory of the ancient rites held in that place that was making itself manifest, as was said to happen in blood-drenched battlegrounds if a traveller came upon them at night. He instinctively crossed himself, hoping that the sign of the true God might dispel the demons' wails. He felt his forehead pearling with a cold sweat, and was seized by the desire to escape that impalpable menace, just as he had fled the menace of the swords a short time before.

The sign of the cross really seemed to have silenced the sounds, he realised with relief. But immediately the incomprehensible words and chants resumed, even louder than before. As if the invocation of Christ and his help had reinforced the rage behind them.

As he glanced around, gripped once more by terror, he thought that this time the sounds, more distinct now, originated not in the air around him, but in one of the large portals leading onto other rooms in the building. The opening was illuminated, as if an intense flame were burning beyond it. Stirring himself, he moved in that direction and found himself in yet another room, at the centre of which stood a second colossal stone basin, identical to the one he had already encountered.

He stopped suddenly, slipping silently into the shadow of an alcove in the wall. He felt his lips parting in astonishment. On the opposite side of the room, surrounded by dozens of torches that lit the marble surface till it dazzled, the statue of a woman seated on a throne almost entirely filled a circular niche carved into the wall.

The figure sat upright, holding in her lap a child wrapped in a cloak, upon which the chisel of an extraordinary craftsman had carved an infinite series of tiny marks, turning the stone into drapery as delicate as silk.

Dante looked up in search of the figure's face. But the head of the statue was covered by a black veil, which hid it down to the shoulders.

He had no time to wonder about this peculiarity – far from every form of the Virgin cult with which he was familiar. Standing in front of the statue a haggard woman, also veiled, stood motionless, her arms raised to the sky in a sign of invocation. And kneeling at her feet some dozens of men and women prostrated themselves, beating their chests irregularly with their closed fists, and waving with their other hand a little instrument that was the source of the metallic clink he had heard in the distance. Lined up against the wall some flautists were busy drawing from their instruments the sweet melody that he had heard from afar, as if they wished to take the metallic din of the sistra to some nobler harmony, supporting the veiled woman's mute supplication.

Dante retreated still further into the shadows. These strangers did not seem at all threatening, but he wanted to gain a better understanding before showing himself and asking help to return to the city.

At that moment the veiled woman turned her back on the statue. Then she began to sing. Dante could not understand the meaning of her song, modulated in a language unknown to him. The woman seemed to be obsessively repeating a single phrase, in which the sound of each vowel returned at intervals, wailed with an intensity that seemed, strangely, to be trying to express the most extreme joy along with the darkest pain. Then all of a sudden her words became comprehensible. Now the woman was speaking Latin.

'In the name of the Father unknown to all. In the name of Truth, the Mother of all, whom the world knows as She who destroys and grants rebirth. In the name of Her who adds life to life. Come and be purified!'

At that command the kneeling figures looked as if they had been whipped. Still waving around their instruments, which now filled the air with a swift hum, they rose to their feet and crowded around the woman who had been declaiming. She ran quickly to the basin, plunged in her hand in the form of a cup and withdrew it full of water. With that liquid she began to sprinkle the foreheads of the people who crowded around her, and who received her gesture with cries of ecstatic joy.

Those furthest away from the priestess thronged forward, trying to open up a passageway so that they too might receive this liquid, to which they plainly attributed miraculous power. Some threw themselves on the woman's fingers, licking them like dogs, and then frantically splashed over their faces the few drops that they had managed to win.

Others, obstructed by the crowd, covered the faces of their more fortunate companions with kisses, trying to catch on their lips at least a miraculous droplet.

From his hiding place, Dante watched this unexpected ritual with mounting perplexity. It was some kind of baptism, apparently, which the participants received with a rash devotion like that which inspired many sects of fanatics who travelled the territory of the Empire. Since the millennium had passed, with its freight of legends and superstitions, countless groups and sects had preached the coming of the Day of Judgement and a new baptism. Almost all of them had strayed into heresy, or else been brought penitently back under the great wings of the Church. But what sect would allow women as priests? And how could such a weird ritual flourish in the city of Peter? Perhaps, he thought angrily, this was the best proof of the misdeeds of Boniface, simoniac and corrupt, the bad shepherd who had turned Rome into a sewer?

He didn't know what to do. Meanwhile the water ceremony seemed to be coming to an end. Having received the ablution, the faithful had once again lined up in the empty space in front of the basin, as if waiting for something. As her final act the priestess plunged her hand into the basin once more, then lifted it aloft above her own head, opening her fingers and sprinkling the veil with water.

She remained motionless like that, as the wet fabric moulded itself over her face like a mask. In the light of the moon, Dante clearly saw the woman's mouth opening, as if she too were trying sensually to drink the liquid through the fabric, before turning her gaze back to the assembled throng.

'Virgin mother, daughter of your son!' the priestess suddenly cried once more. 'Now the spirit of the true God is present among us. Let the *Nymphon* descend upon you, and your souls join those of the heavenly angels who sit at the table of the true God!'

The priestess had picked up a cup from the stone altar, and collected some more water from the basin, raising it aloft. Meanwhile, at her side, two initiates lit with their torches something contained in a series of little plates arranged along the perimeter of the room. Suddenly, from some of the little braziers, filaments of bluish smoke began to rise, filled with a sharp perfume that reached as far as the poet's hiding place.

Then, as if in response to a signal, a new agitation began to stir the participants. First slowly, and then with mounting frenzy, men and women drew towards one another, stroking each other with their hands in a kind of strange dance, before sliding to the ground in a confused embrace. A murmur of groans and sighs, of ecstatic cries and shouts rose from the bodies, which were now shedding their clothes to couple shamelessly on the bare stone, while the noise of the sistra grew louder, as if they were being shaken by a storm.

DANTE HAD watched the scene in front of his eyes with disbelief. The sinful arousal that had taken hold of him when the bodies had first tangled themselves in that erotic dance had gradually made way for a feeling of disgust.

It was no longer the exaltation of freedom and the senses; this seething mass of flesh was now nothing but a symbol of abjection, in which the act of copulation – which God had given as the final end of the knowledge of souls and as his seal – was transformed into an obscene refusal of Creation itself and its order. The same attraction that he had felt before, when the beautiful forms of the bodies had disclosed themselves, had turned to horror and a desire to flee, as if those arms and legs, writhing in an exploration and a celebration of the clay from which we are made, were merely a perverse search for pleasure in every inch of the body that God built as a temple for the soul.

Overcoming the paralysis that had until that moment held him frozen, he flung himself back, reaching the adjoining hall and then hastily retracing his steps.

As he fled, he wasn't sure that he had gone the right way. He found himself in the huge courtyard, but at a different spot from the one at which he had come in. The white mass of graves lay on the other side, which meant that the gap that had granted him access was on that side as well. He started running towards the marble stones, driven by the infernal wind of lust that he still felt around him. In his clothes he still wore the smell of those bodies: in his hair and his hands he smelled the strange concoction that had burned in the hall.

He had reached the edge of the cemetery, when beneath the moon he glimpsed a dark outline that had suddenly appeared among the graves. He immediately stopped running, and came to a standstill a few yards from the shadow. The man, who had his back to the moon, was completely unrecognisable, as if he were wrapped in a black cap from head to foot.

'Who are you?' the poet cried in alarm. 'Go back, in the name of God, if you are a shade risen from the realms of death!'

Rather than replying, the outline took one step towards him, then another.

'Stop, demon!' Dante cried again, his voice choked with terror. He had drawn his dagger from his hidden pocket, and pointed it at the creature that was still approaching, trying to give himself courage. But the figure kept on walking silently towards him.

Dante turned and began to run. Ahead of him he thought he could see a pathway free of tombs, through which he might be able to get away. He dashed in that direction, towards an area of whitish land – perhaps the surviving remains of the ancient floor. Swirls of mist rose up on that side, partly hiding the surrounding land. He blessed the help that nature had offered for his escape, and in a few bounds reached that point. But when he got there his feet became aware of a soft and yielding sensation, rather than the solid surface he was expecting.

'Stop, Messer Alighieri!' he heard a familiar voice shouting behind him, but in the excitement of the moment he didn't recognise it. 'Stop. For the love of God!' the shadow cried again, while Dante felt himself sinking up to his ankles into something viscous. He stopped, trying to free himself from that white quagmire. And as he struggled to lift his feet, unsure which direction to move in, he felt a strong grip clutching him by an arm and pulling him back. He tried to fight, to escape from the grip, but the vice around his arm felt as if it were made of iron. 'Go back, before it's too late,' the man said. The powerful grip around his arm belonged to a living creature, and was certainly not the impalpable clutch of a ghost. Reassured, he turned towards the man, trying to make out his face beneath the hood that hid it almost entirely from view.

'Messer Martino!' he exclaimed in astonishment, recognising the man at last. The deep voice with which the man went on urging him to turn back was perfectly familiar to him. Completely wrapped in a dark hood, Martino da Vinegia continued to pull him backwards, with a distressed light in his eyes.

'You have gone down into the quicklime hole!' the man cried, tugging on his arm once more. Horrified, Dante lowered his eyes towards the ground that he was still walking on. Now the white that from a distance he had mistaken for paving appeared in all its terrifying reality: it was nothing other than a hole full of quicklime, left there to burn itself out, still boiling further on, giving off swirls of smoke – the fumes that from afar he had mistaken for mist. Still visible in the pool of boiling material were the remains of headstones that had been thrown there, which emerged from the surface like wreckage from a shipwreck.

Dazed, he took a few more steps back, while Martino went on guiding him by the arm. 'Be quick, Messer Alighieri! Over here, you must bathe in water.'

His companion had pushed him over to a basin full of water. The man quickly drew some water with a cloak, then poured it on the poet's feet, rapidly repeating the operation. The sudden cold at his extremities acted as a spur for Dante, who was beginning to shake off the effects of the perfume that he had inhaled in the basilica. He felt his mind becoming alert once more, after the agitation of the previous moments.

And now the strangeness of the encounter appeared to him in all its breadth. Martino da Vinegia, the old sage, the legate of *La Serenissima*, whom he had known during the tumultuous days of his time as prior in Florence. The man who had, in his youth, been companion to the great Emperor Frederick, who knew the secrets of both West and East. Just as imposing as Dante remembered, with his long mane of hair hanging down his back, still black as if in defiance of the ravages of time, which seemed to have no power over him.

'What are you doing here, Martino?' he asked animatedly.

'I walked out, to learn,' the other man said vaguely. 'But let us get away from here. There's an inn not far away. We will wake the landlord, you need to rest and dry yourself, after this adventure, or you risk catching a mortal illness.'

Martino had made as if to move, but Dante resolutely held him back. 'You're not trying to make me believe that it was your passion for studies that brought you here!'

'These are the remains of the Baths of Antoninus, and it is here that the Romans built their biggest kiln for the making of quicklime. They boil up the marble remains of the building, after pulling up the paving stones and breaking up the statues that once decorated it. Then they let it burn itself out in that great basin from which I have just rescued you. Perhaps that was once the pool in which the last senators swam before the Empire fell. There is a rumour in Venice that the quicklime found here is of extraordinary quality, the only one that can provide the resistance required to support the enormous weight of the great domes. And the Republic likes to know everything that might be useful to it . . .'

The Venetian remained impassive. Dante would have liked to reply, but he felt numb and decided to wait. 'Let us go where you say, then.'

Martino started walking resolutely off, as if he knew the way even in the dark. Every so often he turned to check that the poet was keeping up with him, then he started walking again across the uncultivated land.

In the distance, half-invisible in the shadow, a long, uneven wall rose from the ground, resting on a chain of arches. Above the arches a blind wall rose towards the sky, decorated by half-columns set into the building. Many of the arches had collapsed, and big gaps opened up in the construction, which looked abandoned. At first Dante thought of the remains of an imposing aqueduct, and then, when he had approached one of the gaps, he noticed that beyond the wall there was a flight of steps, and beyond that a long open space, a kind of grassy ring at the end of two stone monoliths.

'The Circus . . .' he murmured to himself. He set off walking with a dash, still following the Venetian, who seemed to be following a precise set of bearings, going back along the side of the building. At its end, on which some houses had been built, there was a small tower.

Dante was exhausted, and he was on the point of collapsing when they reached the building. The Venetian knocked at a barred door, with a sequence of blows that sounded to the poet like a prearranged signal. After a few moments he saw a light flashing through the chink of the door, then it opened and a man appeared with a lit candle. The stranger glanced quickly at the Venetian, then stopped suspiciously to examine the poet's features. But he immediately stepped aside at a gesture from Martino.

'This is Virgil's Inn, Messer Alighieri. It is kept by a compatriot of mine who came to Rome years ago, drawn by the sanctity that can be breathed among these walls. He was a particularly religious man,' he added, unable to conceal a mocking smile.

The man guided him towards the burning fire. As the exhausted poet slid onto a bench, the man started poking the embers, still holding the candle. Soon a flame crackled in the mouth of blackened stone. Dante relaxed; the heat of the fire was slowly dissolving his unease. And along with the solidity of his body, his mind too seemed to be getting its energy back.

He turned towards Martino, who had been watching him in silence, sipping wine from a goblet brought by the landlord's wife. The old man held the receptacle out to the poet.

'Virgil?' Dante asked, after taking a long sip. 'Is that the landlord's name? A strangely noble one for such humble employment.'

'No, Messer Alighieri. The man is called Nicoletto. But

he gave the great poet's name to his business because it stands beside the tower where, according to tradition, the magician performed one of his spells. Right next to this place,' the other man replied, gesturing with his thumb towards a point behind him. 'It is said that in that tower dwelt the Emperor's daughter, with whom Virgil was hopelessly in love. And that in attempting to scale the tower to be with her, he was stuck there for a whole night, before being revealed at dawn, to the great merriment of the people. Or at least that is the story told here in Rome.'

'The whole of Rome seems to be a place of mockery. Of both the humble and the wise,' the poet murmured, staring into his companion's eyes. 'Of God.'

He waited for the old man to reveal what he really thought. Dante was sure that the story of the secret of the quicklime was a hoax, and that Martino too had witnessed the lewd assembly. The poet wondered what had really brought him to that place. But the old man seemed unwilling to catch his allusion.

'Rome is still the centre of the world in every respect. Even if it is reduced to a pile of ruins, within those ruins the spirit of times of greatness still dwells – times in which men spoke as equals with the gods. And if the crusade that you know about succeeds, that time could really return.'

'The crusade? So you know about it too?'

'Perhaps the same destiny that sent you here during

these days has called you to bear witness to the greatest event of your lifetime.'

'It is not destiny, but the Commune of Florence that sent me here. It is to her that I am accountable.'

Martino exhaled deeply. 'It appears that you do not grasp the changing times, Messer Alighieri. In France, Philip has the cardinals in his grip, and the whole of the Church beyond the Alps is ready to support him and pay him tribute. His eyes have seen the riches of the Temple, and soon he will unfurl his sails against it. The Turk is spreading across Asia: after Jerusalem and Acre, Byzantium is next in the line of fire. The German lands are subdued by the high-handedness of the barons and Emperor Albert, who is concerned only with ensuring wealth and land for his family. In Italy the old freedom won at Legnano has disintegrated, beneath the blows of Boniface. And here you are worrying between your four walls about whether Cerchi or Donati should be in charge,' he murmured ironically. 'The new century will overwhelm you, and what you think is a second Rome will return to being what it was: a den of rogues. The big city walls that you have started to build will not encircle a glorious people, but only a mass of hovels surrounded by scrub. In Spain, in England, in France, the new kings are blowing their trumpets, and when they sound, great armies will rush to enlist, in search of adventure. But if you ring the bells in Florence, who do you think will come running? Apart from old women and fat merchants in search of shelter?'

Dante had turned red. 'The freedom of the Commune is the citizen's first desire!' he shouted. 'It is instinct that will free us and make us worthy of the benevolent eye of God. Of what worth is the conquest of the world, if you lose dominion over your own house?'

Martino shook his head. 'You'll see. You'll understand,' he went on, after a moment of silence. 'When you too have had experience of the world. Now you are like one of those wonderful creatures of which travellers in Africa tell. Of whom it is said that they are born with their heads on backwards and live their lives like that. Expert in what is happening behind them, but entirely ignorant of what awaits them on the road ahead. Capable, perhaps, of fleeing the cunning serpent, but destined to be torn to pieces by the proud lion. Of what worth are virtue and doctrine if you do not use them to guess the future? Foresight is wisdom! Look around you, at these proud ruins. Why do you think the giants who were capable of building them vanished like dust in the wind?'

Dante looked around. Then he suddenly raised his head. 'In my own little city of Florence there are men currently at work who have no cause to envy them,' he replied haughtily. 'I have seen the projects of the great Arnolfo, for the future Cathedral. A church that will outdo all the others in Tuscany!'

'Yes, perhaps. But just look at the dome of the Pantheon. Who among your architects could have built anything like it? Who among them has even guessed the secret of that great mass suspended for centuries between heaven and earth, without falling to the ground?'

'I don't know . . .' Dante murmured. 'In his design, Arnolfo has designed a dome to crown his work. Certainly not as majestic as the Pantheon . . .'

'And certainly not like the ones that the Greeks built in Byzantium. But when their city falls into the hands of the infidels, their science too will be lost. I have had the good fortune to see them, Messer Alighieri, in the course of my travels. But I fear that no one will admire their like in our own century.'

'And is that why you're interested in slaked lime? To build domes? Don't you understand that only the death of Boniface can restore the hope of freedom? And instead you are working together on the crusade, a venture which, if it really emerged from Senator Spada's dreams, would only reinforce his power? Boniface must be brought down!'

Perhaps it was the warmth of the wine, which was starting to go to his head, that made him speak so openly. He would have to be more cautious, he said to himself. But the Venetian did not seem shocked.

'Boniface is like an old mule. Thick-skinned, standing solid on his hooves. And the four legs of his power are ownership of the Castello, absolute control of the College of Cardinals, his lands in the fiefdom of Anagni, and his secret support of the Templars, who see him as a barrier to the greed of Philip the Fair. If you manage to strike just one of these, he will start kicking out like one of hell's Furies; only by crippling all four legs at once will you lay him low.'

'That's like saying that only the hand of God can free Italy from this plague. Leaving aside the other sources of his power, the Castello on its own would resist any attack. I have examined it close up: not even the magic black powder of China, of which Marco Polo and Friar Bacon speak, would be enough to shake its foundations. But the Pope is old, it is enough to wait for nature's work to take its course. Perhaps his successor will be a just man; God cannot allow his Church to remain unstable.'

The old man shook his head. 'The King of France is already plotting to have one of his own men elected. Loyal to his orders. It is said that a new seat for the Church is already waiting in the North, beyond the borders of Italy. He is working to gain control of the College of Cardinals: some he has already bought, others he is terrorising, others he will kill. Time is working for him.'

'Taking the Church away from Rome? Where the Apostle Peter himself built it? You are raving. And how do you know such things?' the poet suddenly added, seized by sudden doubt.

The old man smiled. 'The Venetian Republic is not only skilled in seamanship, or in the building of galleys. The security of a state that is strong on the treacherous waves, but weak on terra firma, can be guaranteed only by accurate foreknowledge of the acts of its rivals.'

'You have flooded the Empire with spies!'

'Informers. Highly efficient ones.'

'And you are one of them? Is that why you're in Rome?'

Martino smiled again. 'That too. That's the official business that they know about in *La Serenissima*. But every man conceals within himself several motives for action. Let's take you, Messer Alighieri. You are here as the Florentine ambassador,' he said, giving him a sideways glance, 'but that is not the cord that moves your soul. You are in search of something – something that might move you even more than the fortunes of your city. And, like you, I too am looking for something.'

'What might that be?'

'Knowledge, Messer Alighieri. Like you. This is the flame that consumes us. But come, I will give an order for Nicoletto to lend us his room, upstairs. Let us dedicate the remaining hours of the night to sleep, and tomorrow his carriage will bring you back to the island, and to your lodgings.'

Dante wanted to add something, but the old man's firm gaze testified that he had nothing further to say. 'Let's go and rest,' said the Venetian. The landlord had appeared beside them and was waiting with a candle in his hand.

7

10th November, late morning

DANTE WOKE up in broad daylight. He felt restored, but the fury of the night of battle and what had followed it still whirled around in his mind. He turned round in bed, towards the side where Martino had lain the previous night, but saw no one. He left the room, and at the bottom of the stairs bumped into the landlord, who was busy decanting a bottle of wine.

'Has Messer Martino already woken?'

'Some time ago. Messer Martino does not sleep longer than two hours. He asked me to pass on his greetings. He says you will see each other again.'

'Has he left?' Dante murmured in surprise.

'At dawn. Would you like to eat something?' the man replied, interrupting his work. He held out some bread and boiled eggs to the poet, who quickly devoured them. Then, when he had satisfied his pangs of hunger, Dante asked the landlord for directions to bring him back to his lodgings.

'That's easy, Messere. You walk along the walls of the Circus and go down towards the river bank. Keep to the left-hand side: there was a battle, last night, over by the Colosseum, and it would be unwise to get too close. There are still some stragglers wandering around thereabouts.'

Suddenly Dante was submerged in memories of the previous night's events, with all the distress they brought with them. 'Do you know the outcome of the battle?' he asked anxiously.

'They say the Frangipane surrendered to Boniface. Their fortress has passed to the Caetani.'

'And what was the fate of its defenders?'

The landlord shrugged, but did not reply. However, the expression that had appeared on his face was telling. Who knew how many other unfortunates had joined the lines of fettered men at the port of Ripetta.

Dante wanted to pay him, but the man strangely refused to accept the coin that he held out to him. So he said goodbye and turned towards the door.

At that moment his eye fell on a sacred image that hung above the door. A small painted panel showing the Virgin enthroned, with the Son in her lap. Without any artistic grace, like many that he had seen in the humble houses of the peasants, back in his own lands.

His mind ran to the statue he had seen at the baths, and the lewd ceremony that had been offered up to her. But like the veil that hid the eyes of the statue, in this new image too there was something strange and distorted in terms of the Christian tradition. On her head, the Virgin did not wear the traditional crown of the *Regina Coeli*, the Queen of Heaven: her brow was adorned with a disc bordered with sickles that looked peculiarly like horns.

'Where did you get this painting?' the poet asked. Nicoletto's eyes went to the spot he was pointing to, then looked immediately and indifferently away. 'The Virgin? It was given to me by a stranger who couldn't pay for his night's lodgings. Maybe two years ago.'

Dante came closer to get a better look. The panel looked old, and in several places the paint had come away, revealing the wood beneath. But as for the workmanship, he had to change his mind. Seen close to, the features looked extremely delicate and suggestive – not at all inferior, except in size, to the great altarpieces that adorned the churches of Tuscany. Only the clothes and the strange headgear made it different, giving it a mysterious and distant appearance.

He turned back to Nicoletto. The inn was not far from the place where the assembly had been held. If that ritual was repeated at regular intervals, as everything suggested, it was very likely that the man was not unaware of it. And perhaps that picture hanging on the wall was not a random gift, but proof that he too was somehow involved. But the man's closed attitude did not give much hope that he was willing to reveal anything else.

In Florence, Dante could have forced him to reveal what he knew. But here, he said bitterly to himself, he was as helpless as a flea. He clenched his fists and shook his head. In the end, what did the things he had witnessed have to do with him? Who knew what other infamies were concealed among the ruins, as if the walls, when they collapsed to the ground, had dragged with them the boundaries between good and evil.

He passed through the doorway, walking in the direction in which the man had pointed him.

HIS WALK was strangely solitary, all the way to the river. Only every now and again did he encounter small units of armed men, who fortunately did not deem him worthy of attention. When he came in sight of the widow's house he stopped in alarm: outside the door there was a group of soldiers who seemed to be waiting for him. He took another few cautious steps, then was relieved to spot among them the figure of the senator. Saturniano Spada had recognised him too. With a cry of joy the senator came towards him with open arms.

'Messer Alighieri! We were worried about you, after you disappeared in the battle. My men saw you making off, but we had no idea where you had ended up. So I decided to come and wait for you at your place of lodging.'

'I was close to death last night. I had no idea a police

operation could be so bloody. If it hadn't been for a man who came to my rescue . . .'

'Yes, so I was told, but for now let us forget any distress that might have occurred. It isn't military matters that bring me here. The Pope has ordered an examination of the body found in the grave, and I have requested the assistance of some men of wisdom, as well as faith. I want to have the comfort of your wisdom in such a delicate matter: you witnessed the discovery, and you know everything already. So you, of course, even more than the others. And Manoello the Jew, a doctor. And the Khan's ambassador, an expert in the science of the stars and the mysteries,' said the senator, indicating the two men who were waiting among the soldiers.

'So the race of Judah is not always despised at the court of Boniface,' the poet replied wearily, meeting the rabbi's eyes.

'No one doubts his competence in the medical arts, which he knows better than any cardinal. It is only his foolish obstinacy in a reviled faith that makes him the object of just derision. And as for the Persian, even though he too worships other gods, he has been useful in adding his oriental knowledge to that of the inquisitors,' the senator replied with a wry smile.

THEY SET off along the Lungara to the Hospital of the Holy Spirit. They passed through the door, then began walking down the long nave that constituted the first wing of the building, beyond the big octagonal dome that broke up the continuity of the internal colonnade. Along the walls, among the arches that marked the perimeter, the beds of the ill crowded together, full of sick and desperate humanity.

Dante walked quickly. He protected his face with the veil of his cap, trying to block out the stench that lay heavily among them. The whole space was full of bodies, amongst which moved the monks of the Holy Spirit, who had been entrusted with the task of running the hospital after its original patrons, the imperial Teutons, had abandoned it. Groans and wails rose up from the heaps of rags piled up haphazardly on the invalids, gurgling like bubbles from a muddy pool. Some of them sat numbly, clutching their knees with their arms as if trying to reassure themselves that they still had a body; others lay motionless, pale, with the mask of death already stamped on their straggle-bearded faces.

The monks crowded silently among the long rows of beds, trying their best to revive those still capable of reacting. Looking around, the poet noticed some of them who had gripped the four corners of a filthy sheet, lifting the corpse contained within it to drag it away. He shook his head in silence.

'You are reflecting on human miseries, Messer Alighieri?' asked the senator, who had not failed to notice his gesture.

'Yes, on the frailty of the little ship that receives our

spirit, and how the slightest storm is enough to capsize her, leaving us as wreckage on the shore.'

'It seems impossible that these men should be the heirs of the great ones who built the colossal walls that still mark the city. Walls that seem to say: here, amongst these streets, the gods once walked.'

'There is something unhealthy about our century. As if body and spirit lost the divine harmony that once gladdened both. Is it not said of the Patriarchs that they lived for many years in the best of health? And that they then peacefully laid down their heads as their final dawn rose? Today, on the other hand, it seems increasingly that the body expires before the soul does, and is turned into a prison of pain. And we join our Creator in a state of fury and excitement, rather than one of light. It would be better for them had they never been born!' Dante exclaimed with impotent rage. 'Better for all of them!'

The senator gave him a sidelong glance. 'Careful, Messer Alighieri. Do not repeat those syllogisms in the place we are about to go to, within the hearing of the Inquisition. Your words sound dangerously close to those of the heretic Marcione, the apostate bishop, expelled from the Church!'

'Many of those words are not unfounded. But it is in refusing the hope that Christ has brought among us that their sin lies, and that is the root of their misfortunes.'

*

WHILE WALKING, they had passed the octagonal space that separated the two wings of the building. In the middle stood a little stone altar, before which a monk, assisted by two of his companions, was busy officiating at holy mass for the little group that crowded around its base. They seemed to be in a slightly better state than the others. Their clothes were torn, their faces haggard, but at least they seemed to be able to stay on their feet.

'These men aren't sick,' the senator said, anticipating Dante's questions, 'they are pilgrims waiting to go to the Holy Land. The hospital also looks after poor travellers without a roof over their heads, refreshing them of their vow on the way.'

All around lay piles of clumsily tied luggage and heaps of bundles. In one corner, a donkey weighed down by a heavy burden waited meekly, its ears lowered. At that moment the monk had raised the chalice, while a mumbled prayer rose up in response to his gesture. Dante stopped for a moment and crossed himself. He looked at these people with an intense expression, full of pity.

'What are you thinking about, Messer Alighieri?' the senator asked him.

'About the force that drives them. To leave their own house, their own homeland. For an uncertain fate, with the prospect of a destination that many of them will see only in the distance, like Moses the King. Sleeping on the cold stone, going up and down other people's stairways, waiting for a scrap of bread that lets them continue on their way. I think that is the worst of misfortunes. And they have sought their fate, thus paying a higher price for the faith that inspires them. I believe that after martyrdom, few things could be greater or sadder.'

The poet pulled himself together and continued to walk along the nave. Here the stench was even stronger, if such a thing was possible. The sick-beds were slightly further apart than in the other wing, and the monks walked among them in smaller numbers. Some lay abandoned under their sheets, but most of them were sitting on their beds, completely covered with bandages, like corpses that had just awoken on the Day of Judgement.

Dante went on walking, pressing himself with revulsion to the side of his companions.

'Who are these?' he asked, pointing to one of the beds, on each of which two invalids lay. As they approached, one of the two had risen on his elbows, and seemed to be staring at them through the gap in the bandages that covered his face.

'They are suspected of leprosy. They are brought here before being confined outside the city walls.'

As they passed the bed the man cried out, 'Tuscan! Stop, I recognise you!'

Startled, Dante came to a halt. In the man's excitement, his bandages had slipped from his face, revealing his features. The poet froze with horror. The sickness had almost completely eroded his lips, reducing his mouth to a dark and irregular cavern, from which some splinters of teeth still poked like yellow worms. A swollen lid completely obscured one of his eyes, but in the other, wide with the effort to see, an ebony-black pupil still gleamed.

'You are Dante Alighieri! And you will recognise me, if you can!' he gurgled in a voice that seemed to issue directly from his throat.

Dante took a step towards him and stopped some distance away. There was something in the man's ravaged features that stirred an ancient memory. But he couldn't trace that mask back to anyone he knew. Then, all of a sudden, it came to him. The poet clenched his fists as rage welled up in him. 'Vanni Fucci!' he cried. 'You've changed since I wounded you at the siege of Caprona!'

In a second the terrible scenes of that ancient battle passed before his eyes. When the Florentine army, with its allies the Guelphs of Pistoia, had laid siege to the Ghibelline fortress of Caprona. After the Ghibellines had surrendered, on the understanding that their lives would be spared, they had passed in mortal terror between the two wings of the Florentines, who had observed their oath. But further on the Florentines' Pistoian allies had been waiting for them, and under Vanni's leadership they had slaughtered the Ghibellines, dragging the Guelph army into shame. Bastard Pistoians, thieves and rogues.

The man stared at him undaunted with his one eye, in

which all his old self-importance seemed to be concentrated. 'You are a thief,' Dante said frostily. 'You emptied the sacristy of San Jacopo. And had another man sentenced in your place.'

The other man exploded with laughter that gurgled in his ruined throat. 'In Pistoia they are still looking for the vestments and the holy vessels. They were useful to me for a while – gold soon runs out.'

'You'll end up in hell. Leaving aside your bestiality.'

Again Vanni Fucci abandoned himself to his laughter. 'I'm already there, my friend. Your prophecy is useless. But now let me read the future to you!'

The Pistoian raised his bandaged hand and pointed it at the poet. 'The Black side will win, and it will crush you and your men. I escaped of my own free will, and not even God's fury can stop me. But you will leave your houses pursued by fire. You will never see Florence again.'

Dante touched wood, then picked up a little lamp that burned by the bed and flung it hard at the invalid. 'Shut up, damned soul!' he cried, held back violently by the senator, who had gripped him by a sleeve. 'And it's burning now, since Hades seems to be taking its time receiving you!'

The lamp had hit the man full in the chest. The oil poured over him, drenching the bandages in which he was wrapped. The wick, caught up in a fold of fabric, set fire to the liquid. Vanni Fucci started convulsively beating his hand against the flame, trying to put it out. He crushed the flames between his fingers, still laughing, as if the fire could do nothing to his ulcerated flesh.

The senator and Manoello had witnessed the scene with astonishment. Dante turned towards Saturniano, who was still holding him back, shouting furiously, 'You give shelter even to brigands like this? Even his own city, a den of wickedness, sentenced him to the noose!'

Saturniano stepped aside, still gripping the poet by the arm. 'Since the Jubilee was proclaimed last year, the influx of pilgrims has been uncontrollable. Most of them are good Christians in search of absolution and indulgences. But in the midst of them the dregs of the whole Empire have poured into the city. The guards at the gates do what they can, but the crowds are too great, corruption is inevitable. They bring money, and all the whores, wine-sellers and innkeepers in the city are ready to throw open their doors to them, except that then they go running to the Castello to complain if one of these rabble rapes their wives, runs off with their money-boxes or cuts their children's throats. They hide among the ruins, which are turned into makeshift lodgings, forming gangs according to their nationalities: the Lombards in St John, Tuscans under the arches of the Nerva aqueduct, Germans behind the fields of Castello. And then Frenchmen and people from Puglia, with their brazen wives. But luckily the rains have already begun, and it is to be hoped that sooner or later the Tiber will break its banks, sweeping the whole mob out of the sewers where they have holed up. But I would never have expected you to know one of them personally!'

'It's impossible to forget that ugly face once you've seen it,' Dante replied flatly, turning around once more to look at Vanni Fucci. The Pistoian, for his part, arrogantly returned his gaze, from the depths of his ravaged face, surrounded by the sparks of the still-burning bandages.

'Ignore his ill-omened words. It is nothing but the impotent moans of oxen at the doors of the slaughterhouse.'

'It is not his prophecy that I fear. But the sight of him has reminded me of the many people who are threatening my home and the freedom of Florence.'

Meanwhile they had reached the door that opened onto the wall at the end of the corridor. 'Follow me,' the senator said. 'This leads to the hospital chapel, where the corpse of the girl found in the grave has been brought.'

Beyond the corridor there stood a little church, plunged into darkness. In front of the altar, a low balustrade surrounded the entrance of the underground crypt. With the senator still walking ahead of him, Dante descended a short flight of steps to find himself in a damp, low-ceilinged little space. Here too the proximity of the river announced its presence in the green stains that seeped from the cracks between the pavestones, and in the dark patches on the walls.

In the middle of the crypt stood a stone altar, supported

by what looked like two gryphons, carved in the fashion of the barbarians. Immediately in front of it, on four trestles, lay the wooden sarcophagus, surrounded by a forest of iron torches that illuminated the area with a bright patch of yellow light.

Around the box crowded half a dozen monks, in the black and white habits of the Dominicans and the grey of the Franciscans, swapping muttered comments. Noticing their entrance, the man who seemed to be their head abruptly stood back and headed towards them. Dante had a sense that he had moved not in order to welcome them, but on the contrary, to obstruct their passage to the corpse. Recognising the senator, the man immediately stepped aside with an obsequious gesture. But he went on staring suspiciously at the others.

'Fear not, Brother,' the senator reassured him, still walking towards the sarcophagus. 'I warned you that some scholars would be coming with me.'

'Your will be done,' the other man murmured, sounding unconvinced.

'Which would be the will of Boniface,' Saturniano slapped him down. 'So what have you found out about the body? Is it really that of the . . . she-Pope? The robes covering her, are they really the robes of a pope?'

The senator had hesitated for a moment, before uttering a word, as if he was worried by the very idea of mentioning that ancient scandal.

The inquisitor shrugged. 'They would seem to be. If her vestments were anything to go by. But too many times in the past the holy robes have been worn by fakes and antipopes!'

'And yet it could really be her . . . For centuries people have talked about her, and how she was buried on the road between St Peter's and St John . . .' the senator continued.

'But that's not possible. No woman has ever sat on Peter's throne. It's a trick. The fruit of the diabolical minds of our enemies. A simulacrum, a statue. It isn't a real corpse, I'm sure of that. It's what we all think.'

Dante had listened in silence, struck by the fury with which the inquisitor railed at the very possibility that this might really be the body of a woman. 'Have you studied it carefully?' he asked thoughtfully. 'With all the care of the medical arts?'

He too had bent over the coffin, looking again at the cause of such upheaval. For a moment his mind had returned to his city, assuming the duties of prior. Then he instinctively became aware of the chill that had descended at his words, and suddenly glanced towards the inquisitor. The man was staring at him contemptuously, and giving no sign of answering. The other monks had also interrupted their confabulation and were watching him uneasily.

'This is Dante Alighieri, a Florentine, a poet and his

city's ambassador at our court,' said the senator, coming to stand next to him as if to protect him with his authority.

The monk listened impassively. Strengthened by these words, Dante bent over the body once again. Now, in the bright light, the wonder that he had felt on the first occasion intensified. Certainly it could have been a wax statue, built with sublime craftsmanship. It couldn't possibly be a real corpse – nothing could have survived for so many centuries and been preserved in that form. For a moment he thought of the image of dissolution that he had seen in the hospital. It was the fate of the flesh, the fate that the body inherits.

He stretched out his hand until he touched the pearly face, then pressed one finger to her cheek, drawing it back immediately, perplexed. He had become aware of an unexpected sensation: the texture of the skin seemed to have responded to his pressure with unexpected elasticity, as if he had really touched a living body.

He looked again at the others, with an expression of surprise on his face. 'We too have been surprised,' the inquisitor said coldly. 'Whoever it was who played this joke knows very well what he is doing. He must have used tanned skin to make the exposed parts. Even the fingers seem to flex, as if this were a living body. But there are a good number of craftsmen here in Rome who could do the same. I've already ordered my men to arrest them and bring them to the Hall of Office for interrogation. Soon we will know who it was!'

Following the monk's suggestions, Dante took one of the hands, lifting it from the chest where it had lain crossed. The hand responded to his gesture with a fluid movement, and with scarcely more resistance than a real body would have shown. It must have been a kind of jointed doll, like the ones the best Florentine craftsmen made for the daughters of the great patrician families. The fingers, too, bent under pressure: truly, whoever had built it must have been a master of his art. Seized by sudden curiosity, he delicately lifted one of the eyelids, revealing a wonderful blue eye, perfectly delineated. If it was a trick, the glazier who had blown it had managed to instil within the material all the veins that nature gives to real eyes.

'What do you think, Messer Alighieri?' he heard the senator saying behind him.

Dante turned towards him. 'I couldn't give a judgement. Undoubtedly, what we see is extraordinarily similar to a real body, only recently claimed by the clutches of death. One would need to see what is hidden beneath the vestments to be certain. But I fear that this is a genuine human body.'

'You fear? Why such caution? If this really were the body of the she-Pope, and God's will had preserved it for our century to wonder at, should we not welcome this manifestation of his will as a new miracle, and give it the same devotion with which we pay homage to the other remains of saints and martyrs?'

Dante pressed his lips together. From the first instant he hadn't stopped thinking, not about the miraculous body, but about the picture painted on the sarcophagus. But he didn't want to reveal his suspicions before he was quite sure. So he made only a vague gesture with his hands. 'I was referring to the upheaval that something like this, once attested, could unleash throughout the whole of Christendom. But as I said, we would have to examine it in its entirety, beneath the vestments, and beneath the surface.'

'What do you mean, Florentine?' the inquisitor brusquely interjected. 'Under the surface?'

'There is only one way to be absolutely sure about the matter, and that is to discover whether the body also contains its internal organs, precisely according to the order of nature.'

'You want to take it to pieces? That's an execrable act, forbidden by the laws of nature and God! Let no man study what God has concealed! What do you want to know about the admirable composition of fluids and organs that sustains the spiritual flux, for the time that God decrees?'

'In Bologna I saw the tables of the anatomists on which the medical students study. Tables set up in secret, and bodies stolen from the battlefields. And what upsets you about that? If, as you seem sure, it is a doll, a miserable simulacrum, what offence could be done to it by the blade of a surgeon?' the poet replied sharply.

The other man uttered a furious denial and then, feeling the senator's eye upon him, lowered his head. 'Fine, let us summon a sawbones!'

'Maestro Manoello, the doctor, is with us,' the senator replied, gesturing to the man, who had stayed aside from the others, to come closer.'

'A Jew? You want to let a member of the cursed race be party to a possible scandal?' the inquisitor cried in horror, pointing his finger at the yellow wheel.

'Manoello is, above all, a doctor. It is his skill that we need. And he respects our laws; we have instructed him to be silent about what he sees, and I am sure that he will honour his word. Not least because if he doesn't do so, he knows that revenge will fall upon his people, in a proportion of one hundred to one. Think, Brother: a Christian sawbones would be much less trustworthy. If he spoke, we would be able to injure him, and his family. Perhaps his friends too. With a Jew, his whole race will be subject to our revenge, which will be further fired by the rage of Boniface.'

Manoello had witnessed the swift exchange. He remained motionless, under the contemptuous gaze of the inquisitor. But the senator's words seemed to have got through to the friar. He nodded his head a few times, and then said, 'Perhaps there is truth in what you say. Then proceed, let us see what is hidden within!'

Manoello set down on the ground the bag that he had been clutching tightly under his arm, opened it and began to take out a series of instruments that Dante had never seen before. Some looked like compasses, others the dividers used in the strange science of geometry. There was an infinite number of blades of various sizes, which the doctor began to line up meticulously on the edge of the coffin. Then he turned to Dante.

'Will you help me in this task, Messer Alighieri?'

A shiver ran down the poet's spine. In Bologna, as he had revealed, he had spent many nights over the tables of Mondino dei Liuzzi, studying the secrets of the body. And then, later, on the field of Campaldino, he had seen limbs severed by swords, and guts spilled on the ground, where the blood gurgled among the death-rattles. But that had been in the silence of the *Studium*, or amidst the hurly-burly of the battlefield: two opposite states from which consciousness is absent, silenced by too much smugness or too much despair. Now he would have to engage in a task that everything within him revolted against. He summoned all his courage, stepping up to the coffin and touching the unfamiliar instruments.

Manoello had followed his movements, perhaps guessing his thoughts. 'Are you horrified by the idea of knowing how our bodies are made?'

'No. But I'm not sure that tampering with a corpse is quite admissible. I do, however, think that the Inquisition is allowing it only because it is convinced that this is merely a fake.'

'Fine. We'll see in a moment,' the doctor replied, picking up one of the knives and testing its blade on the skin of his index finger. He brought it to the strings that held the clothes around the body and started cutting delicately, beginning at the bonnet and the throat-band that held the long and shapely neck. Then he slowly began to free the shoulders from the robes.

As he proceeded with his task, the body appeared in all its nakedness. Dante bit his lips, trying to suppress the sensations that were taking hold of him. The woman, in spite of the centuries that had passed since her death, seemed to have preserved almost intact the figure that, during her lifetime, must have led her to victory in wars of love. Her breasts, still full and buxom, with light-pink areolas, were erect, as if they had just been drawn from the kisses of her lover. Horror and lust fought over his mind. He sighed deeply, while beside him Manoello's hand, clutching its scalpel, approached the body. Without thinking, the poet darted out his hand, gripped the hand of the Jew and held it back from completing the gesture it had just begun.

Manoello stopped. Dante hesitated, his hand still gripping the other man's wrist. He shook his head mechanically. 'Why do harm to this splendour . . .' he murmured. Manoello delicately removed his hand from the poet's grip and went on lifting the clothes away, revealing the creature's belly. Dante's teeth snapped shut, biting his lips until they bled. Just below the sternum the woman's perfect forms seemed strangely altered. The body looked crushed, as if some diabolical hand had pressed furiously down on it, and it was crossed by a long vertical fissure from the navel to the pubic bone. She looked like an empty, crumpled chrysalis.

'You see?' the inquisitor beamed. 'It's nothing but a puppet!'

The body really did look like a rag doll and, as with those children's playthings, someone had made only the head and hands to perfection, leaving the rest of the body a kind of bag full of sawdust. With time, a gash had opened up and the stuffing had disappeared.

Manoello approached the tip of his knife and delicately lifted one of the flaps of the long gash, revealing the internal cavity. The blade sank in, and encountered a whitish obstacle that ran below the opening. Manoello suddenly withdrew his hand and looked around.

'It isn't a puppet. Someone has removed the guts and the internal organs from this body, but left the bones intact. This is the backbone, these are the ribs,' he declared.

With a furious grimace, the inquisitor bent over the corpse again, then suddenly straightened. 'It is fake!' he cried. 'These bones are fake!'

The doctor silently brought the blade to the vertebrae,

inserting it into a gap between the bones, which were still surrounded by brownish filaments. Then he delicately prised them apart, testing the response to pressure. The vertebrae parted slightly. The man shook his head. 'This is no fake.'

The inquisitor was frothing with rage. He turned towards the soldiers who were following the scene from a certain distance. For a moment Dante was sure that he was about to order them to intervene. As quick as lightning, a whole series of hypotheses flashed through his mind about what might happen now. If the Inquisition really did try to erase any trace of what it considered to be an insult to the majesty of the papacy, then all of those present could find themselves at serious risk. He turned towards the senator, in search of reassurance, but he too seemed unsettled, his face deathly pale.

All the poet's muscles were tense, while his mind wavered between the idea of flight and that of attempting armed resistance. But what was to be done, given the disparity between their forces?

Luckily the inquisitor did not give the order that Dante feared. Ignoring the others, he turned to the senator with a grim expression. 'This disgrace must return to the darkness from which it came. I told you your venture was a risky one, but I certainly didn't imagine what perfidies it might lead to. Now all of this must be kept completely silent, and no one must even dare to speak of what has been found. I will order my men to ensure that this . . .

body is buried again in the Vatican caves, so that it disappears from the world for ever. And you will see to it with the utmost energy that any whispers about it are stifled at birth. The Church has no need of scandals at such a difficult moment as this. Perhaps you would have been better advised not to bring a stranger and an infidel among us. But now the damage is done: it is your responsibility, as the Administrator of the city, not to make it irreparable.'

The man had spoken, ostentatiously turning his back on Dante and Manoello as if they were unworthy of his consideration. But the poet was sure that he had not lost sight of them for a moment from the corner of his eye, intent on catching their reactions.

Manoello had remained impassive, apparently indifferent to the agitation that had been unleashed. Dante, on the other hand, having overcome his first fears, felt rage mounting within him. Ignoring the furtive expression with which the senator invited him to be prudent, he stepped resolutely forward until he touched the inquisitor's chest.

'If I am the foreigner who disturbs you, I agree that I belong to a different nation. But I remind you here that, for the Roman and universal Church, there are no strangers, beneath the heaven that God has placed above our heads. From the first sermon of Paul to the nations, every people illuminated by Grace is a child of the same father. And besides, what does it matter who knows a secret, if it concerns the Catholics?'

The inquisitor looked him up and down. Then, after a long moment of silence, in which he had seemed to weigh up his answer, he hissed: 'Your hunger for logic does not seem out of place, Messer Alighieri. It is true, there are no strangers in the benevolent eye of the Church. But there are occasions when even the universal Church is forced to come down to the world, and this is one of those. In which even the glory of a divine order is limited by the mud of the world. And from the bottom of that mud I tell you, Messer Alighieri, that if so much as a single word about what you have seen leaves this room, you will know the fury of the arm of God.'

'You forget whom you are talking to,' Dante replied, red-faced. 'To the man who represents the authority of the free city of Florence. I myself am Florence! If I considered this news to be useful to the safety of the Commune, how could I hide it from those who have placed their trust in me by sending me here to represent them?'

'Messer Alighieri . . .' he heard the senator murmuring softly behind him. But the poet ignored him and continued. 'You are asking me to put the interests of Boniface before those of my homeland!'

'Messer Alighieri . . .' the senator pleaded. 'Calm yourself, I am sure the Brother did not intend to disrespect you. No one wants to restrict your freedom of action as ambassador of a friendly city subject to the Holy Roman Church. But you too will surely agree that an event such as this, if it suddenly entered the public domain, would have the effect of a river in flood, without the banks that the moderation of higher spirits provides as refuge for simpler minds. In other words . . .'

'In other words, Boniface wants to be the one who decides whether and when the secret will be revealed?'

The monk replied with a haughty shrug. Dante opened his mouth wide, his lips drawn back over his teeth in fury, and was about to insist. But he suddenly stopped.

The inquisitor had moved, heading towards the door, passing close to the wooden lid of the sarcophagus, which rested against the wall. The poet's eye fell on the painted image of the relic. When the coffin had been moved, the layer of earth had slipped away, and the features of the ancient face were now perfectly visible.

A memory passed through his mind, suddenly eclipsing everything else. It was impossible . . . And yet he could have sworn he knew that face! But before he could study it again he was swept away with the others.

THEY WERE outside again. Above his head the clouds had closed to form a dense cover, and a soft rain had started falling once more. As the senator walked away, leaving them on their own, Dante looked the rabbi in the eye. The man seemed uneasy.

'So, Mastro Manoello, what do you think about what we have seen?' the poet asked, inviting him to speak. When they were studying the corpse he had spotted something in the rabbi's attitude that had attracted his attention. As if, behind the doctor's certainty that he was in the presence of genuine human remains, there lay a shadow, something unsaid that Manoello wished to keep veiled.

'Don't you think this *mirabilium* might be proof of the favour of God, granted to a single being that the orders of nature had condemned to decay? A proof of the sanctity of the woman Joan, as is already being shouted around the streets of Rome?' Dante suggested.

'She is dead, but she has not corrupted,' Manoello agreed. 'As if she had returned to her original condition, that inert lump of mud, a golem waiting for the life-giving word of God. Or else . . .'

'A *golem*? What is that?' Dante interrupted, struck by this unfamiliar word.

The rabbi hesitated for a moment. 'An ancient tradition of ours. Things that might sound blasphemous to a Christian ear. Beyond the threshold of heresy.' He huddled into his robes as if he had suddenly felt an icy wind. He had moved slightly, as if he wanted to leave.

'Explain yourself,' Dante insisted, without giving any sign of letting him go. 'You said: Or else . . . what did you mean? Isn't what we have seen a body halted for some arcane reason on its path to corruption?'

The man stared into his face for a long time. For a moment Dante thought he was searching it for the signs of the just man, which according to the Scriptures God prints upon man so that his works may be known. 'Come on, Mastro Manoello,' he encouraged him. 'Even though I do not share your religion, I will not reveal your secrets to the Inquisition. I hold Caiaphas responsible for the death of Christ, and certainly not your people.'

'In the Talmud, where the deeds of the ancient rabbis are recorded,' Manoello began, overcoming his uncertainty, 'it is written of the rabbis Rava, Hanina and Oshaya that in the first days of the exodus they created living bodies with the magic arts. Calves, to assuage their people's hunger and to worship the Most Holy One in an appropriate way. And . . . men.'

'Men?'

'Yes, men. Or rather, living forms, apes of true creation. Brought to life by using the magic arts to steal the power of God's word.'

Dante waited a few moments in silence before the man continued. 'But these are legends like the ones that all pagan peoples pass on, for wonder or instruction,' he finally snapped, disappointed. 'Like the Greek tale of Deucalion and Pyrrha, sole survivors of the flood, like Noah the patriarch. Tales for children, like the stones that those two threw behind their backs, giving life to a new generation after the preceding one had been destroyed by the wrath of Jehovah.'

'The Greek tales, certainly. But not what is written in the Book of Creation.'

Dante listened carefully. In Florence he had heard about a mysterious piece of text of the Jews, held by Cabalists to be even more sacred than the Torah itself. It had been his master Brunetto Latini, newly returned from Spain, who had whispered to him about it, like someone referring to forbidden things. Something connected to the magical powers of the Hebrew alphabet, the power of sounds and Scripture, which echoed with the very power of God. But the poet had not paid too much attention to it, convinced that this was only one of many *grimoria* that circulated in secret amongst many magical sects. A book of spells and formulas, only good for deceiving the dim-witted and throwing open the door of hell to false prophets. He would never have imagined that a man as well versed in the natural sciences as Manoello could have believed in it.

But on his companion's face he saw the signs of great tension. 'Do you really think it's possible to instil life in an inanimate body?' he asked suddenly. 'And that what we have seen is thus not something that has strangely survived death, but in fact a form preparing to receive the breath of life?'

'Yes, Messer Alighieri. That is what I fear: perhaps the woman found in the grave is still waiting to live, once she has received all the organs that she still lacks.'

'That's impossible!'

'It's said that it has already been done, in Jerusalem, and that Titus brought back one of those bodies from the city, along with the treasure of the Temple.'

Dante bit his lip. Basically, what Manoello was saying confirmed his suspicions. For a moment he thought of confiding in the rabbi, but then decided against it. First he had to check what he had guessed. And besides, if his intuition proved correct, how could he rule out the possibility that the hand of the Jew lay behind the spectacle? Perhaps the allusions to the secret book were only a trick to throw him off the track. However highly he esteemed this man, he felt he had to stay on his guard.

'In the woman's grave there was an ampulla of luminous liquid,' Dante said suddenly.

He was struck by Manoello's reaction. The man had given a start. He approached the poet quickly, until he was almost touching him, as if he wanted to be sure of what he had heard. 'A light? Are you sure?'

'Yes, I saw it with my own eyes.'

'And where is it now?' Manoello urged him excitedly.

'It was confiscated by the Inquisition when the body was taken away.'

'But the others – the others saw it too?' Manoello

insisted. He seemed to be desperately seeking confirmation of the poet's words.

'I myself am not sure of the reality of what I saw. At the moment when the sarcophagus was opened it seemed to give off a bluish light. It came from an ampulla, and it lit the inside of the sarcophagus.'

'Are you sure it was already lit when the grave was opened?'

'Very much so. But the word you used is imprecise. The ampulla didn't seem to have been lit: it gave off a cold light, like a milky shadow. It didn't look so much like a lantern as a . . . you know the light of fireflies on summer nights? Or the luminescence that rises to the surface of the waves at particular times of year, which sailors speak of?'

The rabbi had been listening carefully, nervously rubbing his long beard. Dante studied him thoroughly, trying to read an answer on his face.

'Do you know what I'm talking about?'

'Perhaps . . . There's a legend that is handed down among my people, the lamps of Solomon . . .'

'Tell me.'

'It is said that the great King Solomon lit two eternal lamps to watch over the Ark of the Covenant, behind the curtain of the *Sancta Sanctorum*. Lamps that required neither oil nor wax, and that remained lit for centuries, until the destruction of the Temple at the hands of the Babylonians. A secret that had been given to the King in secret writings dating back to the Egyptian captivity.'

'Was it the Egyptians who discovered the secret?'

'The magic of their priests was powerful. My people learned much from them, beginning with our legislator. Some say, in fact, that they listened to their words even more than they listened to the word of God.'

'And where did those wonderful lamps end up?'

'It is said that the Babylonian conquerors took them with them, to give them to Nebuchadnezzar.'

'So their secret reached the East . . .' Dante remarked thoughtfully. 'Before coming to Rome and giving life to a miracle . . .'

'Is that how you explain it, Messer Alighieri? The hand of God in that grave?'

Dante let a long moment pass. 'No. And I suspect you have a different view of things as well.'

'Yes.'

'What is it?' the poet insisted.

'Something that even the ancients knew. A secret jealously guarded by the first of those who ventured into the mysteries of nature: the *spongia lucis* . . .'

'The Lucifer stone?' Dante cried. 'The stone that Satan had on his forehead, and which hastened his fall! I've always thought it was a legend. It was talked about at the Apothecaries' Guild. But like something crazy, a dream without a substance!'

'No, it really exists! It is a salt, produced by the distillation of urea. For some mysterious reason it seems to attract light, which it then emits for a very long time, burning silently like a cold and flameless fire.'

'So it's not a miracle, but knowledge that lies behind the ampulla that was found in the sarcophagus. Not the glory of God, but the hand of man . . .' Dante murmured thoughtfully. 'That's what you think, too.'

'Yes. Someone who wants us to believe in a miracle. And to spread it around.'

8

11th November, morning

H E HAD spent the whole night locked in his room with the pages of his poem. Every now and again he had added a few words before rubbing them furiously out, before they could come together to form so much as a single line. The ghosts of the previous night still stirred in his mind and, even more than that, the tangle of concupiscent bodies.

He tried to shake off the thought, but the whiteness of those limbs kept obsessively returning. Among them he sometimes caught sight of Fiamma's face, and the shape of her body that he had glimpsed under her hunting clothes turned into those of the women who had been coupling in that basement in that triumph of lust. He suddenly slammed shut his writing panels and put all the papers back in the drawer. He had to think about his diplomatic duties and prepare his speech. All the hopes of Florence rested on his words.

His eye fell on the sleeve of his cloak, threadbare at

the hem. The velvet border, too, did not appear to be in the best condition, and his hose were torn and mud-stained. He lingered for a moment on the image of his face in a little mirror on the wall: several days of beard on his hollow cheeks, eyes shrunk with exhaustion, lids as heavy as if he were in a fever.

Where his face was concerned, a few hours of rest and some work with a razor might have helped; but he couldn't present himself to Boniface in those clothes, which would embarrass not only him, but the whole Commune of Florence.

He looked around: in the little room there wasn't so much as a clothes-drawer to give him hope, but perhaps in the rest of the house he could find some male clothes that he might ask to borrow. He went to the doorway and called to the landlady's young son. A few moments later Dante saw him coming up the stairs.

'Do you need something, Messere?'

Dante quickly explained the situation. As he spoke, he saw the face of the young man, who was studying him with a critical expression. 'Your clothes are actually very different from the ones the others wear in the courts that go to the Patriarchate of St John. Ours is a poor household, there is nothing here that could be of use to you. But I know a very good tailor, close to the market square. In a few days he could provide you with everything you need. Mastro Giuseppe – his shop's inside the theatre.'

'A theatre? There's a theatre in Rome?'

'That's what the wise men call it, one day Mastro Manoello told me it was the Theatre of Pompey. He must have been a great actor in his day, given the size of his house.'

'The Theatre of Pompey . . . Where Caesar was killed. Now it's a tailor's shop . . .' the poet murmured to himself. '*Sic transit gloria mundi.*'

'What?'

'A few days . . . I need something straight away.'

'Mastro Giuseppe also has a second-hand clothes shop. I'm sure he could be useful to you.'

THEY CROSSED the first Island Bridge together and then, close to the steps to the second, they were forced to stop and wait for a body of armed men to enter the tower that provided access to it. On the tabards that covered their armour Dante noticed the coat of arms of the Caetani family. The boy, too, stood still and stared at them, a furious expression on his face.

'The Pope's men,' the poet observed. 'The island seems to be firmly in the hands of Boniface.'

The boy spat on the ground. 'He's taking over everything, one piece after another. At one time the tower belonged to the Pierleoni. It is said that they were Jews, before they converted. Then the Pope bought it, or rather he forced them to give it up for a small amount of money. Like the one that belonged to the Annibaldi, up towards the Caelian Hill. He turned that one into a fortress as well. And that other one up by Trajan's Market. There was already a castle there that belonged to his family, but he did a lot of work to reinforce it even more.'

Dante was trying to follow the boy's words, but the place names were still obscure to him. The only certain thing was that the Pope seemed determined to spread his fortresses across the territory of the city as quickly as possible, and was chiefly interested in the towers. As if he wanted to stretch a network from their summits, to clench his fist around the whole of Rome.

'By now there are only a few families that dare to stand up to him, now that he's managed to banish the Colonna,' the boy interrupted his thoughts. By this time the militia had come in, and with a dull thud the heavy oak gate had been barred behind the soldiers. Passage across the bridge was possible again, and the men, donkeys and carts that had been crowding around the little space in front of the church were starting to move again, amidst a confusion of cries and curses and the sound of loud braying.

At last Dante and his companion also managed to cross to the other shore. The final arch of the bridge straddled the mass of wooden shacks that crowded onto the river bank, most of them built on tall struts in an attempt to escape the floods, and ended up behind the remains of an old wall, in which a series of arches had been filled with volcanic ashlars, turning them into the foundations of the buildings that rose up above them. Dante thought they must be the remains of an old city wall, or perhaps an aqueduct. But some traces of the Empire had by now almost disappeared, crushed by the new demands of the modern city.

A SPIDER's web of alleyways just a few feet across snaked among buildings that looked as if they had gone up at random, without any logical rules except the desire to exploit the foundations of something that already existed. In the narrow, dark façades, stubs of columns and valuable sculpted entablatures poked out of the masonry here and there, some of them serving as cornerstones to reinforce the floors above. But most were scattered apparently at random, as if the people who had used them hadn't even bothered trying to remove the remains from the place where time or the barbarians had left them. It even looked as if they had decided to build on top of them, as the great Homer said of Odysseus that he had built his palace around the tree from which he had carved his nuptial bed.

Guided by the young man, the poet slipped beneath the low arches of an overhead bridge that passed above the alleyway, connecting two buildings that leaned away from each other like a pair of drunks. In the darkness by the foot of the arch, Dante glimpsed an arm stretching towards him. He made out a hand, well shaped, but whose fingers seemed to have been eaten away by a kind of leprosy that had left it horribly disfigured.

After a moment's puzzlement he realised that the hand belonged to a marble statue, which had also been drowned in the masonry. It looked as if this ancient inhabitant of the city had been trapped in a mudslide and was trying desperately to reach the light of day, to the indifference of passers-by. He thought he heard its cry of desperation ringing in his ears, the cry of a whole city suffocating in the landslide of time.

His companion passed by the obstacle without paying it any attention, and turned into the alleyway on the right, just past a narrow crossroads that followed the underpass. The whole of the narrow street was obstructed by the benches of people selling cloth, which protruded from the shop doorways like chariots preparing to go into battle. Rudimentary curtains had been strung from one side of the street to the other, to protect both the sellers and the crowd of buyers from the pelting rain that fell icily from the sky from time to time.

'Here we are, Messer Alighieri,' the young man exclaimed, pointing ahead of them. At that point the street bent in a wide curve, the end of which disappeared beyond the walls of the nearest building. A sequence of big arches punctuated the whole street, with a further confusion of other buildings on top of it. Only at one point was the forest of buildings interrupted, to make way for the beginning of a marble stairway, still intact, that seemed to climb to the sky before suddenly breaking off at the top of the building. Dante stopped open-mouthed at the foot of that inexplicable staircase.

The steps were made of huge blocks of white marble, over which the passing centuries appeared to have no power: they were still as solid and smooth as they had been when the great Romans had climbed them to go . . . where? What could be bigger than what he had seen already?

'Have we reached the Theatre of Pompey?' he asked suddenly.

'Of course, and this is Mastro Giuseppe's shop,' the young man replied without stopping, pointing to one of the arches further along. But Dante had frozen, and was staring with fascination at the stones around him. The flight of steps. Perhaps these were the very steps that had once led to the ancient Curia, on whose stairway the conspirators had waited for Caesar. Perhaps this white marble had once drunk the precious blood of the first of the Caesars, the man called by Providence to Earth to open the way for the great Empire of the Christians.

He felt his head spinning, as a dull roar thundered in his ears. Summoning his courage, he approached the arcade, trying to touch with his hands the base of the lowest step.

Heedless of the boy's calls, he had started to hoist himself up with all his strength. He too wanted to climb that flight of steps, reach its top and see what Caesar's eyes had seen in their last gleam of light.

He went on struggling to reach his goal, as the effort took his breath away. But something held him back, dragging him by the hem of his robe. He tried to break free, kicking out furiously, but then stopped when he recognised the boy's anxious voice.

'Stop, Messer Alighieri, for the love of God. You've gone mad! This is the fortress of the Marozzi. It's full of armed guards!'

Dante looked up towards the top of the steps. On the line of the horizon he thought he could make out a series of dark outlines, which his tired eyes could not get in focus. The shapes were becoming agitated, lining up in an increasingly dense group. Then all of a sudden he made out the cross-bows that were being aimed at him, and instinctively slipped back as a dart hissed just a few inches over his head, tearing through a curtain and lodging itself in one of the stalls.

'Come back down, please!' he heard the boy's voice imploring. Dante loosened the grip with which he had clutched the first step and fell back into the street below. He found himself in a chaos of people screaming as they fled, crowding among the stalls, trampling over each other and overturning piles of clothes onto the ground, amidst the cries of the salesmen who were already sheltering inside their shops. He threw himself to the ground, back to the wall, as another few darts crossed the narrow space. The boy was stretched out next to him, and from that sheltered position cautiously observed what was happening above their heads.

'The Marozzi are in dispute with the Renzi, on the other side of the street,' the boy explained breathlessly. 'They protect all the shops on this side of the street, and leave the opposite side to the others. But lately the Renzi are trying to take control of the second-hand clothes trade, and a battle has broken out between the two families. Seeing you there, the Marozzi must have thought you were trying to attack their house!'

'And the Commune allows this? The Pope, with his armies! Why does he not intervene to quell these skirmishes? They are the leprosy that is ruining our cities.'

'The Commune commands the hills, and the Pope has eyes only for its possessions. But here in the Campo Marzio there is only one king: the River Tiber, until he decides to forgive his people and stop destroying their lives. The Tiber alone receives the prayers of the people who live here. But for now let us go – follow me.'

The boy moved along the wall, stealing along with his head lowered in an attempt to remain out of range of the crossbowmen. Dante followed him, he too keeping his head down, and often resting his hands on the ground to give himself the necessary propulsion to keep pace. Around him, all those who had not yet fled were wandering cautiously among the overturned benches – a small, frightened crowd moving on all fours, barely daring to lift its head from time to time. The poet bit his lips with rage as he slipped forward, encumbered by his long robes: so this was what the Quirites – the burgesses of ancient Rome – were reduced to, a pack of terrified dogs, and he himself along with them.

Impulsively he rose to his feet, careless of the risk. He couldn't create this spectacle of himself for another moment, cost what it might. No one would dare to strike the ambassador of Florence. Standing in the middle of the street, he smoothed down his muddy robes as best he could, then calmly moved towards the boy, who had already reached the last arch and was giving him worried gestures. Step by step, to the astonishment of the others, the poet covered the stretch of road that separated him from his goal, clenching his fists.

At each moment he feared the painful sensation of a dart in his back. But luckily the rage at the top of the hill seemed to have calmed. Still standing fully upright, he stopped in front of the boy. He said only, 'Here I am.'

From the back of the shop a little bald, yellowish man was staring at him with a mixture of perplexity and admiration. Dante scurried towards him, but took care not to step outside the arch.

'Welcome, Messere!' the man cried enthusiastically, looking from Dante to the boy.

'Mastro Giuseppe,' the boy said, 'I have brought an important man to visit your shop, Messer Dante Alighieri, poet and ambassador of the free Commune of Florence. He needs ceremonial clothes for the papal audience.'

The little man glanced critically at the poet. It was obvious that what he saw didn't tally with his idea of an ambassador. But the young man had also said the visitor was a poet, and perhaps that might explain the wretched appearance of the man who stood frowning in front of him.

'You've chosen the best shop for your requirements, Messere!' he announced cheerfully. 'Here I have the best clothes in Christendom, all at your disposal. Wools that come directly from far-off Anglia, and brocade from Lombardy, cotton from Flanders! And take a look at this cloth,' he added, climbing like a cat onto one of the shelves that spilled over with a jumble of fabrics, and coming back down with a roll of cloth under his arm. 'Fifty ells of Genovese cloth, taken directly from a galley attacked by Pisans off Civitavecchia. Smell its perfume,' he went on, bringing the roll close to the poet's face. 'Sniff, don't you smell in the weave the perfume from the hands of the women who wove it? I can make you the most sumptuous of robes, worthy of a king! Trust me, and I will make you more handsome than the fair Philip of France.'

Dante recoiled with revulsion. Rather than the hands of sensual women, the cloth gave off a strong smell of mildew, but he refrained from saying as much. He cleared his throat. 'Mastro Giuseppe, I have no time to enjoy your skill. The audience is tomorrow, so I need something suitable that you already have in your shop. Besides . . . the Commune provides no funding for luxury, not even for its senior magistrates, so . . .'

A shadow crossed the little man's face immediately dissipated by a small smile. 'Are you short of money? Don't worry, Mastro Giuseppe is a friend to everyone, to the night and the pilgrim. I have just what you need. Over here.'

Still moving like a cat, the little man brought Dante into the depths of the shop. Here the shelves were filled not with rolls of fabric, but with ready-made robes, some in big wicker baskets, others piled haphazardly on the shelves. The man started fishing around quickly in the pile, picking up items of clothing and putting them back down again. When he discovered something that seemed to match his ideas, he set it aside to continue his hunt.

At last he seemed satisfied, and returned to the poet clutching an armful of clothes.

'I've got everything you need. So, you said an audience with Pope Boniface. You will be among the senators, the College of Cardinals and the senior prelates of the Curia. If you were a pilgrim, you could turn up in your habit and with your pilgrim's staff, or even barefoot, in the Franciscan way. But as an ambassador you need to look good, because the man is his city. And clothes make the man, and according to that syllogism, your clothes will say what Florence is like.'

As he was still thinking about the other man's daring Aristotelianism, Dante felt something settling on his shoulder.

'Above all, you will need a loose shirt, with a nice collar that puffs out to frame your chin. And reaching down to your knees, with strings to tie your hose firmly. Nothing humiliates a man like having to bend down in public to pull up his stockings. And in front of the Pope! No, you absolutely need one of these, and with strings, not with those newfangled buttons that have been coming in from France for some time. Strings, Messer Alighieri!'

Dante picked up the garment, examining it critically. It looked worn in places, with some sticky brownish stains. 'Oh, don't worry about its appearance!' the tailor quickly cut in, reading his puzzled expression. 'The man who wore it didn't die of horrible diseases or anything, just the privations of a long journey. And the stains will be invisible under the rest! So the shirt, and then the cloak, tight around the waist, as it's supposed to be. Observe the embroidery in gold thread. A marvel, the man who wore it came from Puglia, even if you look really closely you can't see the repair that I've done where the knife went in. And the boots, magnificently tanned Lombardy leather. The man who wore them can't have travelled many miles before he ended up at the Hospital of the Holy Spirit. The friars only send me the very best clothes.'

'Are you trying to turn me into a compendium of corpses?' the poet stammered, attempting to free himself from the clothes in which the man was submerging him.

'Oh no, your fine form needs to be seen in a quite different light,' the tailor replied blandly, who didn't quite understand the word *compendium*, but who had grasped the allusion to corpses very well. 'You are simply magnificent, and I haven't yet shown you the best! Wait, look at yourself in the mirror, I've got a wonderful one in the Venetian style.'

The man had run away for a moment, and immediately reappeared holding a little shining circle in a brass frame. He set it down a certain distance away from the poet. 'Look at yourself, you look like a figure in a painting. And now this cap!'

Dante felt a stiff object being placed between his hands. A kind of blue cone bordered with greyish fur, from which there hung two big wings of transparent veil. 'A cap in the German style. The most precious possession of a knight about to embark for the Holy Land. An object that would have been envied and desired by every infidel Turk, had the poor fellow ever got there. It looks as if it was made for you!'

Dante turned over the cap, which was stained with sweat inside. But at least there didn't seem to be any traces of blood – its former owner's head didn't seem to have been cracked inside it. 'How many cats did you kill to get this fur lining?' Dante asked caustically.

'Cats? You offend me, I said it comes from Germany. There are no cats there, it's too cold. It's genuine forest beaver! But I've left the best till last!'

Again the man disappeared and returned, holding a piece of blue cloth that seemed to be in better condition than the rest. 'And this is for the final touch, a cloak to enfold and enhance your overall appearance. Genuine French cloth, I can fix on the borders in a few hours, just in time for your appointment. Look at the embroidery, genuine Florentine lilies!'

Dante brought his eyes to the ornaments. They were little lozenges, slightly raised from the fabric. 'They aren't lilies,' he remarked.

'That's true, but forget the effect of the eye! You are a Florentine, aren't you? And from a distance everyone will think they're seeing lilies, on your clothes! I told you that clothes made the man, but the man makes the clothes too. Not even Boniface will notice the difference, as you bow solemnly before him. And your stockings will stay upright like a unit of halberdiers, allowing you to set out your arguments with all the confidence you need. And when you take off your cap, the evil will slip elegantly all the way to the ground, telling the world that you yourself are not miserly, and neither is your city!'

'Forget the cloak,' said Dante resolutely. As for the rest,

the cut was quite different from the Florentine style. But perhaps not too much so, and these clothes were certainly in a better condition than the ones he was wearing. 'How much do you want for all this?'

'If I were to ask you for the right price, it would be twenty Roman scudi. But for so illustrious a customer fifteen will suffice, along with the glory of having served you.'

'How much is that in Tuscan money?'

The tailor lost himself in a laborious mental calculation, with his fingers flying around in the air, touching now his nose, now his lips. At last he gave his reply: 'Two silver popolini, and I guarantee that I will take no commission on the exchange.'

Dante rummaged in the bag that hung by his side, while the boy rolled the clothes into a bundle and, having tied it with a cord, hoisted it onto his shoulder. Then, together, they headed for the door, while the tailor bowed low.

9

12th November, morning, at the Lateran

FROM A distance Dante recognised his two companions who were waiting for him on the steps of the basilica, in front of the big brick façade lit by the large windows that corresponded to the five entrances.

Maso immediately came over breathlessly to meet him. 'Messer Alighieri, at last. Have you prepared your speech? Because you will be speaking, won't you?' he said nervously.

The poet replied only with a nod of affirmation, then passed through the largest of the doors, entering the big central nave, lit by the light that shone intensely through the side windows. He stopped for a moment, startled by the great quantity of bronze and gold decorating the walls. In spite of the devastations that the basilica had suffered in the course of its history, including the earthquake that had almost completely destroyed it, for a moment he had a sense that all the treasures of the Earth had been brought under the huge trusses of the roof, to pay respect to the power and majesty of the Church.

At the end, in the middle of the marble-covered apse that closed off the nave after the longitudinal transept, there shone the carved stone throne on which the Pontiff sat during religious ceremonies. Even empty, the chair created a sense of reverence, Dante said to himself, something close to fear.

As he walked in that direction, lost in contemplation of all that beauty, he still heard in his ears the confused murmur of his companions, immersed in introductions.

About halfway down the church, on the right of the nave, an arch opened up, leading to a staircase. That must have been the entrance to the Patriarchate where they were awaited, he thought, taking a deep breath and preparing to go up.

The stairs stopped on the upper storey of the building that flanked the basilica. Dante continued walking slowly straight towards the end of the corridor, where a monumental door opened onto the audience hall. He kept looking ahead as he walked along his set route, with lines of armed men on either side. But as he did so he glanced to right and left, taking in all the signs of imperial pomp that embellished the walls of the palace. Frescoes and precious tapestries succeeded one another without a break, alternating scenes from sacred history with feasts from imperial Rome, as if to give visual emphasis to the idea that the power of Rome and the power of the Church were united for ever.

In the apses that opened up on either side, the magnificence of the pure-gold mosaics dazzled the eye.

On the rostrum at the end, sitting on the stone throne, Boniface sat motionlessly waiting, dressed in solemn robes and with his mitre on his head. Standing in a circle around him was the College of Cardinals, flooding the room with scarlet. On either side stood the deacons and clerks of the Curia offices, many of them holding the big registers of audiences and petitions. Further on, the Roman senators, with their flowing robes, seemed to confirm with their presence the very idea that the whole of Rome was clenched in the Pope's fist.

Dante walked the final stretch, trying not to alter the rhythm of the pace that he had imposed upon himself. He barely glanced at the unsettling figures of monks half-hidden by the throne, with the black and white habits of the Dominican order. He didn't recognise any faces, because they kept them hidden under their hoods, but he had no doubt about their function: they must be the members of the Inquisition. Dangerous, given that they were so close to the Pope's ears.

Behind him he felt the increasingly irritating presence of the two other ambassadors, who were clutching onto him as if in search of protection. He felt like a shepherd leading a herd of stragglers, who had already given in to the wolf. Meanwhile he kept his eyes on the imposing man – that face whose cheeks were now flaccid with age, but whose eyes glowed like two burning coals. It was as if the whole of his vital flame were now reduced to that terrible gaze, and Boniface's capacity to dissolve and to bind, symbolised by the keys in his fist, lay precisely in that gaze, and that he evaluated with those eyes everything that walked upon the Earth.

Dante felt that gaze passing through him like a knife, and going down inside him in search of his secrets.

And yet, when he reached the foot of the raised rostrum, he saw a smile suddenly illuminating those listless features, and the old man's face lit up as if it had suddenly been flooded with life. His eyelids, too, seemed less heavy. Dante saw him stretching towards him his imposing hand, with its ring.

He had reached this point without ever really thinking what he was going to do. He only knew that he would need all his spirits when he found himself before the great enemy.

And now he could look him in the face, stripped of the evil that was said to devour him. Perhaps close to death. And at the same time all the more dangerous, because he was now far removed from the weaknesses of the flesh that a vital body can harbour. An empty husk, but more solid than the marble of his monuments, with which he was now covering the whole of Italy, while the original unravelled.

A deacon came down swiftly towards Dante as if to bar

his way. Having reached a step, the man stopped, turning and genuflecting, while his face invited the poet to do the same. Then he heard his name and those of his companions being announced in a loud voice.

Boniface had received the homage impassively, merely turning his head slightly towards one of the monks by his side. The man seemed to murmur a few words, which the Pope received with a moue of distaste, before turning his eyes back to the poet.

'So, Messer Alighieri. What news have you brought me from Florence, our beloved daughter? Does that peace that has always been in our vows and in our prayers finally reign between your walls? We have spared no efforts to ensure that your citizens are united in harmony, and we expect as much diligence from those chosen by heaven to sustain the Commune.'

Dante took a deep breath. 'Peace is the supreme gift of heaven. And frail humankind is not always capable of defeating the evil plan of discord. The people of Florence and their government are doing everything they can to comply with your wishes, which are those of any man of goodwill.'

'And yet the same people who say they want the common good have not hesitated in putting to death two of your fellow-citizens with the false accusation of conspiring on our behalf. As if the advantage and the will of the Church differed in so much as an atom from the advantage and the will of the least little sheep in the Christian herd. *Extra Ecclesiam nulla salus! Contra Ecclesiam perditio est!* Boniface retorted. 'Outside the Church there is no salvation.'

'The two men who were sentenced lost their lives for plotting against the Commune, and after a fair and proper trial. Not their loyalty to the Church, but their hatred of Florence: that was what brought them death,' the poet replied firmly.

Boniface had tightened his lips, which withdrew into the toothless cavity of his mouth, stressing the features of old age that had immediately struck the poet. But his eyes still burned with fury. 'And not even the Cardinal of Acquasparta, a man of great probity whom we invited to make peace between your factions, was given a better welcome,' he hissed. 'Why, Messer Alighieri? Why does your city treat us with such overweening pride, not even lowering its head when it hears the honest words of holy men? Why did you refuse the support of men and arms that we ourself requested in our own defence?'

'Because the men you asked for would have weakened our already scanty defences so that the devastation of Lazio might be pursued with even greater intensity. Without purpose, without usefulness, without glory for the city of Florence.'

'Do not impoverish your intellect, Messer Alighieri. The Holy Roman Church aims at the universal salvation of all souls, through the wise regulation of the lives of bodies.

And you are rendering yourself bestial to defend a wretched city that differs only from a thousand others because you were born there? As if the origin of the physical body had anything to do with the immortal soul, and were not in fact the daughter of the Spirit, regardless of the sky beneath which it was received into the flesh! What does it matter to you if a few stretches of wall have been saved by this one or that one? The very body of Christ is wrapped in the poisonous coils of the French snake, the Emperor is a coward from whom it would be pointless to expect any help. So kiss the hand that I extend to you,' Boniface hissed. 'I won't extend it again.'

Rather than bowing towards the big ring that the other man offered him, Dante ostentatiously stepped back. Red in the face, Boniface waited only a moment, then withdrew the hand in annoyance, while a scandalous murmur spread among the assembly. A storm of emotions passed across his ravaged face, then the Pope suddenly resumed his icy pose. 'The audience is over. You will find out from the Camerlengo if and when it will have consequences. In the meantime do not leave Rome.'

Dante bowed his head slightly and took two steps back, trampling over the feet of Maso Minerbetti, who had remained motionless, paralysed with bewilderment.

'What have you done . . .' Dante heard him murmuring in his ear.

'The right thing.'

The deacon who had introduced him quickly joined Dante, guiding him towards the door. Behind him, as if trying to repair the outrage that had taken place beneath those sacred vaults, he heard the chorus of novices loudly intoning a psalm, drowning out the hubbub of voices with the sound of angels.

OUTSIDE, IN the Lateran Square, Corazza Ubaldini swooped on him, while Maso Minerbetti tried helplessly to make peace.

'You did that on purpose. You wanted the mission to fail, to put your insane ideas of rebellion into practice. But the Commune will be told of your effrontery! You are a traitor, you and your whole damned family!'

Dante had started down the steps, his head sunk into his shoulders, his eyes fixed on the ground. Corazza's hysterical cries whirled around him, although the poet seemed to pay them little attention. Exasperated, the other man gripped him by his robes, shaking him furiously.

Dante carried on striding down the stairs, the other man following after him. All of a sudden he felt his impediment vanishing.

He looked to the side and saw the Decurion, who had grabbed Corazza and was now shaking him unceremoniously. 'Florentine, do you need help? Since you've been here all you do is tumble into the claws of scoundrels.'

Maso stepped nervously forward, trying to explain the situation.

'So they're friends of yours?' the Decurion chuckled, showing no sign of letting go of Corazza's collar. Then, after lifting him into the air, he suddenly dropped him so that he landed painfully on his buttocks. 'Fine. But stay away from my Florentine friend. He's under Roman protection.'

While the other two Florentines walked away, mystified, the Decurion yelled an incomprehensible insult after them, then indolently approached the poet. He yawned noisily, and then engaged in a prolonged scratch of his genital organs. 'They tell me you're a poet, Messer Florentine Ambassador,' he said once he was satisfied.

Dante looked at him in annoyance and said nothing.

'And what have you written, to be so famous?'

'Things that are unlikely to have come to your attention,' he replied brusquely. 'I thank you for your help, but it wasn't necessary. And you shouldn't dare to insult my city's legates, however idiotic they might be.'

The Decurion took off his cap, then bowed until he touched the ground with his hand, in a pose of mocking respect. Dante muttered a quiet curse to himself.

But perhaps the appearance of this man could be useful to him. 'Once more I bring to your attention the scandal of the murdered women, who have received neither justice nor revenge,' he said firmly.

'What do you care about those whores? They all end

up like that sooner or later. That lot were just in a hurry to find out who was going to finish them off. They generally take a few years longer than that, but sooner or later they end up at the Muro Torto, and goodnight.'

'The Muro Torto?' the poet reflected. He had heard that expression before, he remembered. At the widow's house on the night of the funeral, with the lights turned out.

'Yes, outside the Porta Flaminia. At the graveyard of undesirables. Actors, thieves, prostitutes. Strangers, and do-gooders.'

'Who are the do-gooders?'

'Are you making fun of me? They'll ruin you just because you're a poet. I'm one too.'

'You too?' said Dante, unable to conceal the sarcasm in his voice.

'Of course. Or do you think it's only in Florence that they know how to write in rhyme? In Rome, every year during carnival, the poets hold a contest to find the best innovator. And I'm one of the ones who do better every time, and if I were a priest or a cardinal, rather than a soldier, I'd have won more than once.'

'Really?' Dante said incredulously. 'And what do you write?'

'Write? That skill's not for me. That's for lawyers and apothecaries. I write in my mind, and recite my thoughts out loud.'

'And how does the competition work?'

'The master gives you a starting verse, and everyone in turn follows in rhyme. And the one who keeps going the longest wins. I'm one of the best, Messer Poet.'

'Oh, really,' Dante replied frostily. He opened his mouth to get back to the subject of the murders, but the other man stopped him. 'Don't you think? Try and get me started. Give me a line to get my blood going!'

Dante flashed him a look. Then he said quickly: '*Love that on gentle heart doth swiftly seize.*'

'*My wife likes it as often as you please, The tradesman's entrance, though, is quite a squeeze!* So what do you think of that little ditty?' he giggled contentedly, giving the poet a dig in the ribs.

Dante took a deep breath. Then he clenched his fists. 'When this business is over, wherever fate decrees that our paths shall cross, I will tell you in full my opinion of your craft.'

'So my art does not meet with your favour, Messer Ambassador. For heaven's sake, it's better to be appreciated in Rome and ignored elsewhere.'

'I'm sure you'll do very well here. Could we get back to my question?'

'Which one?'

'The murdered women!' the poet replied, exasperated.

'Oh, them. You're always thinking about women, Messere. Okay, then. What do you want to know?'

'What have you done to find the guilty man?'

'Nothing.'

'What do you mean nothing? Aren't you supposed to impose justice? Senator Spada gave you the task of doing so, after all!'

The man yawned ostentatiously again. Then, with the attitude of someone finally summoning all his strength to confront someone annoying, he said, 'Anyone who kills like that must surely be afflicted with some diabolical perversion. Sooner or later he will kill again, and sooner or later he will get too close to my claws. Then I'll get him, like a hawk with a rabbit.'

'So you're waiting for the guilty man to hand himself over to you?' the poet observed bitterly. 'And instead you've got to try and find something that links the murders. The bodies, for example. There's something strange about them . . .'

'Why are you so bothered about it, Messer Ambassador? Rome's a big place, it wasn't built in a day, you know. It takes its time,' the other man replied, openly scratching himself again. 'And if anyone does know anything it's not me or my men.'

'Who is it, then?'

'Maybe the people who collect the corpses, the Red Hoods. The confraternity that takes care of the burial of people who die abandoned, or in the waters of the Tiber. Come, let's go and find them, if you're so keen on the idea. Prepare yourself, it's a long way to the river.

Everyone ends up in the river in this city. Sooner or later.'

THE MAN moved, after giving his men rapid orders to go on patrolling the square. Dante followed him in silence, choking back the bile that had filled his mouth. A terrible bitter smell rose to his mouth from his stomach, and once again he was aware of a circle of fire at his temples. But in spite of the weariness that would normally lead him to seek shelter at his lodgings, he walked quickly, trying not to be left behind.

He followed the man on the cart, and once again he was dragged up a hill and then back down again across parts of town that he had never seen before.

At last they reached the river bank, and from there they started following its course southwards. They crossed the Ponte Cestio and the Tiber Island, then continued on towards another bridge that could be glimpsed in the distance, towards Via Ostiense. On they went from there, among wooden shacks and cabins, interrupted here and there by watermills and pontoons fixed to long poles that protruded from the muddy river bottom. The Monte dei Cocci rose in the distance, its great mass blocking off the view to the south towards the solitary spur of the Aventine, crowned at the top by its churches with their turreted bell-towers.

'We're nearly there,' the Decurion said eventually, pointing to a low brick building that stood next to a small church in the lee of the shore. A dilapidated bridge stretched over the water of the river, with a long, narrow boat moored to it. In front of the building rested two handcarts topped by a sort of big wicker basket that reminded Dante of the vehicles with which greengrocers transported their wares from the field to the markets of Florence. A group of men was wandering about in front of the church, wearing long caps that had once been scarlet, but which were now, through carelessness and dirt, reduced to a vague brown colour.

An altercation must have been under way, because the group appeared very agitated, and coarse insults were heard through the damp air.

'These scoundrels are fighting over the clothes of some drowned man,' the Decurion whispered. Then, louder: 'Brothers, we need to talk to the head of your confraternity.'

At the sight of the soldier the Hoods had immediately plunged into guilty silence. One of them stepped forward with a mellifluous smile. 'Master Hemp, what brings you among the brothers of the good death?'

'Not what you're hoping, rogue. A lot of time will pass before you get your claws on my carcase. Take me to Titta di Nicola, if he isn't too drunk at this time of the morning.'

Stepping back obsequiously, the man walked through

the door ahead of them, after glancing suspiciously at Dante's face. The poet ignored him, paying attention instead to what he saw around him. The interior of the confraternity's base was more like a rag-and-bone man's storeroom than a church, filled as it was with haphazard piles of clothes and random shoes, reduced to little more than rags. At the end of the building, where the nature of the construction would have led one to expect the altar, stood a rough desk of old wooden planks. On it, his elbows resting heavily on top of it, a fat man slumbered, flabby from drink.

At the sight of the Decurion he too gave a worried start, but immediately set his lips in a smile of welcome. But his eyes, half-hidden by the fat folds of his heavy eyelids, were as cold as those of a fish.

'What can I do for the city's judicial authority?' he said hastily.

'The occasional stroke of work is what you ought to do. But first pay your dues to the Castello: Saturday's a while back, and the coffers are wailing like a stomach that's been empty for three days.'

The man looked disappointed. 'But you had your money just the other week . . .' he tried to object.

The Decurion stretched across the table, clutching him by the throat with the iron grip of his gloved hand. His massive fingers just managed to grip the fleshy mass, as the man drew his head back between his shoulders in terror, like an old tortoise. 'I've had seven of them thrown off the bridge,' he hissed.

'But we've only pulled in four . . .' the other man replied with a gulp.

'Your fault if you let them get away. Boniface pays two Roman soldi for every one recovered. And then there were the ones in the boat that capsized at the island, that makes at least ten. And anyway you owe me. But then you'll go and draw your jugful. This man is a great lord, a poet and the Florentine ambassador,' he said, changing his tone. Dante thought he caught a hint of sarcasm, but said nothing, merely clenching his fists and muttering an oath. 'He wants to know what happened to the murdered women, the ones who were found with their bellies sliced open.'

'Oh, them. They're all at the Muro Torto. Apart from Domenica's daughter, who lives on the other side of the river, the one who delivered the corpse. You saw her, you were at the mortuary as well.'

'What condition was she in when you found her?' Dante cut in.

'As the Decurion says, with her belly open and gutted like a pike.'

'All of them?'

'All of them without exception.'

'Where were they found?'

The man half-closed his eyes, counting mentally. 'Two in the river – the others in the fields around . . .'

'Others?'

'Of course, she's the tenth since last year.'

'Ten?' Dante nodded. Then he stared into the middle distance as if following a sudden thought. 'And what condition were their bodies in?'

The other man shrugged. 'What does it matter? They all seemed to have had their guts removed, I told you, some of them were actually butchered.'

'How many?' the poet insisted 'How many of them were incomplete?'

'The stuff you expect me to remember!' the head of the confraternity snorted. 'Maybe three or four. But why are you asking? Are you making fun of me?'

'Ten . . .' the poet murmured to himself. Then, turning back towards the Decurion: 'Have no illusions. The murderer isn't going to go away, not before he's struck once more. Just wait for the eleventh victim. Do you know if any more of these poor wretches have disappeared? They had clothes when you found them? Was there anything left?'

'Do you think I keep a record of whores?' the other man exploded with laughter. 'And as for the clothes, if there were any, they were so old and torn that they weren't worth a quattrino. Not even the effort of taking them off.'

Meanwhile a hooded man had come running in. Ignoring the others, he ran towards the desk, crashing into it and shouting excitedly, 'To the river! They've seen a body between the mills by the broken bridge!'

'Then run and get it, you animals! Before the rapids carry it beyond Monte Testaccio! Once it gets past Magliana, it'll head on out to sea!'

'The people from the Buon Riposo are down there already – they've put the boat out and they're going like lightning.'

'Those bastards, they know it's our land from the island to the Testaccio!' the other man cried excitedly. He had leaped to his feet, running to the door and leaving Dante and the Decurion speechless. Dante glanced quizzically at his companion, and got only a shrug in reply.

'The Hoods aren't the only ones who see to the burial of the poor. They're the oldest, and they enjoy Boniface's favour. But since the Jubilee increased the number of sudden deaths, other confraternities have jumped in. Come with us, Ambassador, we'll have a laugh.'

Outside, the group of Red Hoods was crowding onto the jetty. Some, guided by the master, had already got into the dinghy, while the others tried to untie it from its moorings. When everyone was on board, the master knelt at the prow, and the others started rowing furiously against the current, heading towards the middle of the river. Dante followed the Decurion onto the pier, from where he could see the course of the river all the way to the mass of the Tiber Island.

The men remained energetically upright as they slipped rapidly towards what seemed to be their destination. The whole of the Tiber was dotted with boats, some with multi-coloured sails: only in the middle of the river, just beyond the remains of the arches of an old Roman bridge, there was an empty space from which the crafts seemed to be deliberately keeping clear. There was only a single thin, dark line, low in the water, that revealed the existence of a boat.

'There it is,' said the Decurion, pointing with his finger. The two boats were rapidly approaching one another. The Red Hoods, who were favoured by the current, pushed their oars with all their might, encouraged by the shouts from the master, which bounced like stones on the surface of the water. The other boat had stopped, and its occupants seemed to be busy pushing at something beside them with their long oars. Dante saw one of the rowers diving into the water, probably with a view to tying the corpse with a rope. But while he was still intent on his work, the Red Hood boat was upon him.

The two boats collided furiously. The poet saw a number of figures plunging into the river, and then the oars rising up like the wings of two big aquatic birds preparing to take flight.

With a tremendous crash that could be heard even at that distance, the oars struck one another and the bodies of the oarsmen, amidst a chorus of shouts and curses. Caught in a furious struggle, the men in the two factions grabbed one another, careless of the rocking of the little decks under their feet, and leaped from one boat to the other, impelled by their rage. The boats seemed half-empty one moment, and an instant later so full that they threatened to sink. Meanwhile the river seethed with the furious blows of the men who had fallen into the water and were trying to get back onto the boats, obstructed by those with greater luck or skill who were still on board.

The battle continued relentlessly, as if what was at stake was the governance of a whole country rather than the wretched clothes of a drowned man. Meanwhile on both banks of the river, drawn by the hubbub, a growing crowd of onlookers was swarming, yelling encouragement to the combatants. They seemed galvanised by the presence of so many spectators, supporting their just cause, and went on fighting with double the energy. At the bow of one of the boats the master of the Hoods, momentarily isolated from his men, whirled his oar like a club, trying to keep his approaching adversaries at bay.

'Things are looking bad for the Hoods,' declared the Decurion, who had not taken his eyes off the scene for a moment, a smile of amusement playing on his lips.

Dante couldn't make out what was happening as confidently as his companion could. But he was sure that one of the two boats was in difficulty, abandoned by most of its occupants, who had now fallen into the water. He distinctly heard the cries of triumph on the other boat, encouraged by the support of their partisans on the shore, who were now abandoning themselves to scenes of jubilation, describing to each other the feats of their various champions and the probable fate of the losers. Then, while the others desperately struggled to get back on board, the other boat began to drift away, pulling behind it a kind of dark bundle, barely recognisable on the surface of the water.

'That means I'll have to head off and see the men of the Buon Riposo,' the Decurion murmured seraphically, taking his eyes off the scene.

'If this rabble had put as much energy into rowing the Christian galleys, the Turk wouldn't be in charge of Jerusalem right now,' Dante replied grimly.

'River boatmen, Ambassador. Don't you have them in your own city?'

Dante bit his lips. No, it was no different. That kind of leprosy seemed to have afflicted the whole of Italy. Without the bit and bridle of stable government, left to their own devices and the search for some quick money, the entire dregs of humanity were on the same road to hell – a river in full flood that was dragging everything along with it. And not even the walls of the noble castles could hold it back. Not even the citadel of knowledge was immune to the universal business of buying and selling. Not even laws were safe now, not even the money of the various nations. Counterfeiters were adulterating the florin, Gianni Schicchi was faking wills. No, it was no different. The only difference was the method employed: in Florence it was the trade in fabrics that had supplied the road to degradation, in Rome the theft of corpses.

A fresh outbreak of distant cries drew his attention. The winners' boat slipped along the banks, amongst ovations from its supporters, oars held high to greet the sky. As if they had returned from some glorious accomplishment, while in fact they brought nothing but proof of their own turpitude. Dante thought bitterly about that wretched corpse floating along tied to the stern. He hoped its immortal soul was far away by now, sheltered by the great wings of God. That it should see none of this, he said to himself once more, half-closing his eyes.

Then he said suddenly, 'I want to go to this Muro Torto, to the cemetery.'

'And why do you want to go there?' the Decurion asked.

'Isn't that where the murdered women were buried? I want to find out about them.'

'Why?' the other man urged. 'They were worth nothing

alive, and they're just rotting flesh by now. What is there to know?'

'I would like the chance to examine them. Talk to the guardian of the graveyard.'

The Decurion exploded with laughter. 'The guardian of the cemetery? There's no guardian down there. There isn't anything to guard, Florentine!'

'Show me the way and I'll get there on my own.'

The other man snorted ostentatiously, annoyed by the poet's stubbornness. Then he put his hands against his sides in a gesture of surrender. 'I'll take you there: you have to get across the whole of the Campo Marzio, and then leave by the Porta di Francia, into the countryside. The whole of the Via Lata, all the way to the Chiesa del Popolo. Those are not roads to walk alone, Florentine. Let's take a carriage to Trajan's Market. But first we will go up the river with one of the Red Hood boats, till we get to the Temple of Vesta. And there we'll find a cart, at Trajan's Market.'

THE BOAT dropped them off on the shore, past the island. From there they climbed to a circular temple, then the Decurion set off briskly towards the Campidoglio. But having reached the Tarpeian Rock, rather than turning right, the Decurion turned left, slipping into a hollow, along a path that led down to the Forum. Beside them, the whiteness of the columns of the ancient temples shone under the midday sun. Dante looked up, drawn by the massive arches that towered over their heads, with the senatorial palace looming over them. From that perspective it looked as if the building was emerging from the very mass of the hill, as if the ancients had not built those arches, but carved them from the very rock of the hill. He wished he had the senator with him, or at least a man of culture like Manoello, to ask them what it was. He tried to ask the Decurion, but he only gave Dante a distracted look.

'Old stuff, Rome's full of it. Why are you interested?'

'Because it's by the root that you recognise the plant, and what comes before marks the fate of what comes after,' he replied, still looking upwards as he trod the rough ground. He felt the Decurion's hand gripping him by the elbow, saving him from a hole that was bigger than the others.

'If, rather than looking backwards or upwards, people looked ahead, the world would be much better,' his companion laughed. Dante, red in the face, began to elaborate a fine riposte in Ciceronian Latin, to put the Decurion in his place, but then thought it would be pointless. 'We are dwarfs on the shoulders of giants,' he merely mumbled, as if to himself. 'In the words of the great philosopher, Bernard of Chartres.'

At that moment he saw the Decurion approaching a

laurel bush and starting to unlace his breeches. Dante turned away in embarrassment as the other man urinated with repeated grunts of satisfaction. Then he heard the man bounding back to join him, adjusting his clothes.

'But even on the shoulders of giants, we can't see that far . . .' the poet murmured sadly.

'Giants? You mean the ancients? There are giants even today: in the Castello guard there are two who are more than seven feet tall.'

Dante merely nodded, still walking down the hill. They had almost drawn level with a simple construction that stood next to a triumphal arch decorated at the top with a battlement from which some banners flew. It must have been a sentry post, put there to keep an eye on that great pile of ruins that was all time had left of the ancient Forum of the Caesars. Above his head he could make out the dark outlines of several men, resting lazily amongst the battlements. He was about to ask who they were when the Decurion jumped in ahead of him, pointing to the square building that had previously attracted his attention.

'This used to be the Curia, the senatorial assembly hall,' the man said triumphantly, proud to be able to demonstrate his knowledge. Dante stopped, enthralled by what he saw: the damage to the perimeter wall, the big holes that opened up in the roof, the brambles that had surrounded the whole building and held it in a green embrace. So this was the place where the decisions had been made over the fate of Rome! He shook his head and continued on his way. Then, after a tight bend, his mouth opened with astonishment: down below, where the path led to the level ground at the base of the hill, a huge column rose towards the sky, almost as tall as the summit of the hill behind him. It looked almost as if the people who had erected it had been trying to rival the natural landscape, attempting to get so high that they matched the soaring lines of the earth. Next to this one an orderly series of columns, smaller but no less majestic, marked the precise perimeter of a piazza that stopped against the remains of a basilica, most of which was still standing. And behind it all, a big semicircle several storeys high stretched out against the flank of the hill, pierced by a large number of holes that seemed to go straight into the rock.

'Here are the markets!' the Decurion exclaimed. 'And here are the carters!'

Around the big column stood a mass of shacks, leaning chaotically against the construction like so many beggars, and in the maze of alleyways that led among the build-ings there were large numbers of carts, some of them full of the most diverse merchandise, others empty, waiting to receive a load of some kind. The loud noise of whinnying and braying, along with the sharp smell of dung, filled the air, even where the two men were standing.

The Decurion, after making a swift choice, approached a little two-wheeled cart, with an elegant bay horse attached to it. Its master was busy feeding it from a feeding bag tied to the axles.

At the sight of the Decurion the man gave a start. Dante couldn't make out what Caffaro had whispered to him, but the man's contrite reaction was a clear indication that Master Hemp was well known in these parts. The man quickly leaped onto the seat, gesturing to the others to do the same.

'Come, Florentine. I've found the right man. And it won't cost us a thing, since the man was just going to pick up a fare from over by the Porta di Francia.'

The cart set off quickly, bouncing on the cobbles. The driver seemed anxious to go as fast as he could. The vehicle left the column behind it, and turned right as if it wanted to climb the hill in front of them. But having taken only a few steps, it turned left again and skirted a big building that blocked their way to the north. Once past the building, another left turn brought them back to what must have been the old Via Lata.

From that point the road continued straight on to the horizon, running through the houses like a blow from a sword. The carter spurred his horse to full speed, charging unrestrainedly amongst the people who got in its path, and the cart forced its way through amidst loud cries. They quickly passed a second column, as imposing as the one at the markets, and then suddenly the buildings began to thin out, while ahead of them a great stone cylinder appeared, surmounted by a grassy cone, on which new turrets and banners could be seen. Its shape recalled that of the Castel Sant'Angelo, although it was slightly smaller. But everything looked ruined, the battlements were broken, and various broken stumps of column lay scattered below its terraces.

'The fortress of the Colonna family,' the Decurion said. 'But it was pretty well destroyed after the last rebellion. The emperors' tombs were in there once, and even Nero seems to have been buried there.'

The cart passed this ruin, too, continuing straight on its way. Now, at the end, the poet could clearly see the double arch of the gate that marked the terminus, and the high city walls. They reached the gate and the Decurion, without getting out of the cart, announced himself to the guards. It was nearly curfew, and the large gates had already been barred shut. Only two little passages on either side of the building were still open. After a quick discussion one of the gates was opened, and the wheels of the vehicle briefly ran over the big stones that paved the Via Flaminia. But Dante immediately became aware of the rattle of rough ground beneath him, when the vehicle turned right to travel along the city walls.

The new road climbed amongst uncultivated fields, ditches and bramble bushes, crossing a desolate panorama made even sadder by the setting sun. The horse had started panting with effort, and whinnied and shook its head in irritation, in spite of the whiplashes and exhortations of its driver.

In front of them there lay a bleak plot of land, without any vegetation but sparse shrubs and bushes. The ground was scattered with a large number of little bulges, some barely perceptible, others large and raised. Here and there were open graves, from which torn rags protruded, and vague shapes that had once been human bodies.

Wandering among the burial mounds were figures wrapped in rags not very different from the shrouds that they were gathering, and which they carried with them wrapped in dreadful bundles. An unbearable stench of putrefaction floated around the whole area.

'Florentine, do we really have to get any closer?' said the Decurion, twisting his nose with a grimace. The poet too was struggling to overcome his revulsion. He had undone the veil of his cap and held it tightly over his nose, trying to shield himself.

'Where are they buried?' he asked, his voice muffled by the veil. He looked around, unsettled by his bleak surroundings.

With a shrug the Decurion looked around too, then raised an arm towards one of the shades that were wandering around nearby, ordering it, with an imperious gesture, to come closer.

'The whores' grave! Where is it?'

The figure pointed to a spot some way off, where the ravaged ground was rent by a deep trench. Dante was first to head in that direction. As he grew closer, the stench of corpses became more and more intense.

Having reached the edge of the grave he stopped, trying in vain to get his breath back. The miasma took his breath away, and he thought he was about to faint. Summoning all his strength he leaned towards the hole: piled up at the bottom of it were half a dozen corpses, half-naked but for a few rags.

'Here they are,' the Decurion said behind him. 'They weren't much better when they were alive, but now they really are filthy. And what are these piles of bones supposed to tell you?'

'Why were these poor wretches not consigned to the earth?' Dante asked, shocked.

'They're coming in all the time. There's no point covering up the grave until it's full. So get a move on, and find what you're looking for – the stench is going to make me throw up.'

The poet clenched his hands with rage, holding back the curses that had risen to his lips. Then he jumped in, landing next to one of the bodies. For a moment he feared that he wouldn't be able to withstand the fumes. A violent fit of retching ran through him, forcing him to kneel and empty his belly.

'What's up, Florentine? Weak stomach?' the Decurion mocked.

Dante was about to give up and come back into the open when, amidst his spasms, he suddenly noticed something. One of the bodies bore the same tear that he had seen on the drowned woman in Ripetta and on the woman's daughter.

His mind totally immersed in this discovery, he seemed no longer to notice the atrocious smell. He approached the other bodies: they too bore the mark of the same terrible wound. And all of them had the same empty cavern in their bellies, where their intestines had been contained in life.

For a moment he wondered whether that lack might be due to rats, crows or any of the other animals that accompany death; but here too the cut was quite resolute, the edges of the wound as clean as only a sharp knife could have inflicted.

Just to be sure, he had to control himself and shift some of them from their position. As a result he noticed one detail that had escaped him during the paroxysms of the first few moments. The bodies were in an advanced state of decomposition, plunged in a pool of rainwater in which the fluids of corruption mingled with mud. But the process seemed strangely unequal, as if – for some mysterious reason – nature had decided to safeguard individual parts of those wretched remains.

Here a leg, there an arm, in a third corpse both feet and hands appeared intact, different from the rest of their bodies, as if a desperate will to live survived within them. It was as if those poor women had fought death to the last, a castle yielding to the attacking army first one tower, then a rampart, then a gate. Until the surviving forces take refuge in the last redoubt and go on defending it to the end.

He was disturbed above all by one of them, whose face had survived in this strange manner: a face whose skin still stretched over the delicate bones, the lips still fleshy, even in the pallor of death. The eyes, too, seemed to flicker beneath the half-open lids as if death had not claimed them.

He found himself thinking of the strange and indecipherable contrast with the face of Pope Joan; it was as if nature had tried to replicate, with much less force, what the miracle and the protection of the sarcophagus had done with the usurper of St Peter's throne. Who knew whether, with such a wait of centuries, even these poor wretches might not have achieved the same simulacrum of immortality . . .

'Have you finished, Florentine? And what did you find?'

Dante stirred himself at the Decurion's shout. He struggled out of the grave, ignoring the hand that the other man held out to him. Then, after one last pitying glance, he turned to leave, with a sign of relief from his companion.

'Well? Was it really necessary to endure such filth?'

'My suspicions have been confirmed. These women were killed by a single hand, and certainly for a single reason. It was a sort of ritual, I'm sure of it.'

As they left the cemetery Dante thought furiously, trying to put together all the tiles of the mosaic that he had at his disposal. And always he reached the same conclusion. Someone had been trying to replicate, in flesh and blood, a page of the Gospels. Someone who hated the word of the Lord so much that he wanted to deride it in this terrible way.

'Let's get back, Florentine,' the Decurion said impatiently behind him.

The poet nodded. 'And please drop me off somewhere near that great temple, the Pantheon.'

'The rotunda? It's right on our way.'

12th November, late afternoon

DANTE CROSSED the Pantheon square, which was filled as usual with salesmen's stalls. Every now and again chilly rain was falling, momentarily dispersing the crowd that sought refuge under the temple colonnade, dragging with them their carts loaded with goods.

The Florentine legation could not be far away. He asked directions from a man whose face seemed more trustworthy than the rest of the scavengers wandering around.

The man pointed him towards a narrow street that turned off on the right. 'Your compatriots don't have a church,' he explained politely, 'not like the Teutones and the Lombards. But I know that the Florentines are somewhere around the Piazza Navona. You could try over there.'

'Navona? Meaning "big ship"?'

'Yes, you'll recognise it easily. You can't go wrong.'

Dante followed his directions. After a hundred yards the street opened up into a big oblong square surrounded on both of its long sides by a wall of buildings of various heights. He looked around. The place actually did look like the hull of a big ship. That must have been the origin of that unusual name, he said to himself as he tried to work out where he wanted to go. He asked a few more passers-by, receiving only shrugs or expressions of indifference, then at last a woman with a jug on her head, who was going to draw water, pointed him to an alleyway that could just be seen between two houses.

'At the end there, Messere. That's the Florentine square.'

At the end of the alley there was a small open space, and opening out onto it was a three-storey house with a lily clumsily carved into its façade. He headed towards the door, which was framed by two piles of merchandise.

The narrow corridor was full of chests and bales of wool. Some porters were trying to put these great hills into some sort of order, heaping them up on top of one another in piles that reached the ceiling. Dante pushed his way down the narrow passageway that was still free, and approached a well-dressed man who seemed to be busy testing the quality of a piece of silk between his fingers.

'Is this the Florentine legation?' he asked. The other man went on with what he was doing, barely glancing at Dante.

'The Florentine legation? The wool warehouse, you mean. But I know you,' he exclaimed a moment later, staring at him with greater attention. 'Aren't you Messer Durante, of the Alighieri family?'

Dante nodded.

'Of course, I've seen you in Florence!' the other man said, returning to his task. 'You're on the Council, on the White side! Are you in Rome to sell or buy?'

The poet shrugged, trying in turn to recognise the man. It seemed to be a face that he'd seen before, but in the faint light the name escaped him. Or perhaps his memory was tricking him: only a few years before, when Florence lived closed away within its circle of ancient walls, before the tide of bastards and adventurers had poured in from the countryside to ruin the place, he could have named almost every one of his adult fellow-citizens. Selling or buying! That was the mark branded on the forehead of every damned Florentine, like the ones on the bales of rags all around him. Not the lily, not St John – a pile of rags was what they should have built on the new towers that were going up all over the place, making it the standard of the divided city!

'What I have come here to negotiate – your freedom – can't be bought and can't be sold.'

'Freedom? Was it the Cloth Merchants' Guild that sent you here?' the man asked. 'So now they've decided to send someone for the taxes. Every time we get here we find the prices have gone up! Only last month it was two *carlini* and yesterday they demanded three from me at the gate. If it goes on like that, there'll be no point coming all the way to Rome. If we could persuade Pisa, at least we'd be able to use its port, and send cargoes of wool straight to the Kingdom of Naples. So what are we doing with Pisa? What decision has your side made?'

'Maso Minerbetti, and Corazza da Signa. Do you happen to know where the other two ambassadors are staying?'

The other man didn't seem to have understood the question. He went on mechanically rubbing the piece of silk. Then he turned his head towards a staircase that could be seen at the end of the corridor. 'There are two people from the Commune on the first floor. They've requisitioned the best rooms, with God knows what sort of papers. I expect they're the ones you're looking for.'

Dante turned without a word and headed in the direction the man had indicated. When he was halfway up the stairs he bumped into one of the men he was looking for. 'Messer Alighieri!' Corazza cried. 'At last you've deigned to show your face. We didn't know where to go looking for you.'

'I found you.'

'The Commune wants us to stay together, at the embassy! We're not animals, to live like wolves. Especially after what's happened.'

The poet gave him a poisonous glare and opened his mouth to reply. Then, at the last minute, he held back the sarcastic joke that had risen to his lips. 'Is Messer Maso with you?' was all he asked.

'He's upstairs, he's anxious too. Come on, hurry up.'

The other man turned and started climbing the stairs quickly, turning around every two or three steps as if worrying that the poet might disappear again.

On the upper floor the staircase ended in a wide room with brick walls hung with little tapestries showing scenes from the Holy Story. The furniture, too, was in a poor state: a big bed with a baldaquin and its curtain, and a couple of wardrobes lined up against the walls. At the end of the room there was also a small sloping table and a clerk's bench, on which he saw some papers. Taking a rapid glance around, Dante recognised the bag containing his personal effects, which he had left at the inn on the last night of his journey.

As Maso Minerbetti was rising from his bed, the poet bent over his luggage to check that its contents were all still there. At least next time he would be able to present himself before Boniface in his robes, and not dressed as a clown, he thought with relief. That's if there was a next time.

'Good job too!' he heard Maso exclaiming behind him. 'We have to write a report for the Priory . . . We were waiting for you, as a man of letters . . .'

'Even if there isn't much to write,' Corazza interjected wickedly.

'Yes – it didn't go as might have been hoped . . .' the other man tried to say in a more conciliatory tone.

'What on earth were you hoping, Minerbetti? Hercules would have had a better reception in the hall of Cacus than the one Boniface gave us. I came from my city to negotiate, not to genuflect.'

'Why do you say "I", Messer Alighieri, as if you were the only one involved in this mission?' Corazza replied spitefully. 'Florence came here as a party of three, so that our word and opinion would be threefold. And threefold our judgement and our assessment. And instead you silenced us, claiming a primacy that no one granted you.'

'Three is a perfect number, as the threefold nature of the divinity testifies. But if two of them are scoundrels, even the Trinity is reduced to one.'

Corazza had turned crimson. The poet saw him clenching his little fists until they turned white, as saliva spattered from his lips. Minerbetti too looked offended. 'Blasphemer!' he gurgled.

Perhaps he had exaggerated, Dante thought, in order to express his thoughts. Both of them had powerful friends in Florence, on his side and also on the other. What was the point of extending the list of his enemies, which was already overflowing with names? He waved vaguely with his hand as if to cast the event behind him. Minerbetti hurried to pick up the olive branch. 'We have to try and get a new audience. You will always do the talking, of course. But this time try to be less harsh – the Commune is in dire straits, we need this gesture of peace. We have had some news from the city . . .'

He looked anxious not to intensify the disagreement. And besides, back in Florence, there would be time for revenge, Dante thought he read in the man's black eyes.

'What news have we had from our homeland?' the poet interrupted him.

'Messer Pino del Monte, the merchant who arrived just yesterday. He tells us there has been a battle, near the market. The men of Messer Corso attacked the procession of priors as they were heading towards San Piero monastery. They were repelled, but all night the city was shaken by fires and mayhem. The French knights of Charles de Valois only intervened right at the end, and restored peace, but

GIULIO LEONI

the mood is still heated. By now only the Pope, with his authority, could bring the Blacks back to reason without loss of blood.'

Dante had listened grimly to the news, biting his lips between his teeth. 'All right then,' he snapped when the other man had finished. 'Boniface is shut up in the Vatican. I will go there and ask for a new meeting. We will go together. But I alone will speak.' He picked up his bag and made as if to move towards the door.

'Where are you going now?' Minerbetti stepped in front of him, blocking his way. 'Stay with us, at the legation. We've got to agree on your speech. There's room here, the bed is big, there's even room for all three of us.'

Dante glanced towards the bed and exploded with sarcastic laughter. 'It isn't that I don't want to appreciate the hospitality of Florence, Messer Maso. But other tasks keep me from it. My writings, which are waiting in my lodgings. And other things too . . . I'll let you know the outcome of the request.'

'Other commitments?' Corazza snorted. 'You're the ambassador of the Commune! What other commitments would you put before this one?'

'A commitment to justice.'

'What justice?' Corazza called out behind him when Dante was already on the stairs. 'What justice?'

*

297

HE CROSSED the bridge to the island, and then headed along the Lungara towards the walls of the Vatican. By the time he reached the gate by the pyramid it was sunset. For the last stretch, past the Hospital of the Holy Spirit and beyond, he had quickened his pace so that he didn't miss the curfew.

But when he was close to the gate he found himself passing through crowds of pilgrims who were wandering about, apparently aimlessly.

'The gates of the Vatican have been closed. You can't get through,' one of them said when he asked for an explanation of this unusual situation.

He went on walking, pushing his way through the people crowding by the gate. When he got to the front, the big gate was barred, exactly as he had been told.

He stopped and stared into the sky, while around him the little crowd wandered disappointedly away. After a few minutes, as if by magic, he found himself so utterly alone that he thought he could actually hear the murmuring waves of the Tiber.

Someone must have lit the fires on the towers, because the walls had begun to turn pink, as if the towers themselves were torches that lit up the coming night. Perhaps they were signals, he said to himself, addressed to some distant unit. Or perhaps they were a clue to something secret that was happening inside the walls. Among the terraces he glimpsed the shadows of the sentries coming and going indifferently. He was seized by a powerful desire to know what was going on. And he was also seized with rage at being excluded from it.

He felt his foot touching something. He picked up the big rock and went over to the door, beginning to knock at the panels with all his might. At the third blow he noticed that something was happening. High above his head a frantic commotion had broken out. The shadows had fallen into convulsive motion, almost a dance, and cries of alarm and curses and shouts ran all along the walls. He thought he could see faces peering over the edge to look at what was going on.

'Open this damned door, I'm the ambassador of Florence!' he cried, taking a few steps back to gauge the effect of his order. 'I have to see Boniface.'

His shout had been followed by a moment's silence. Other faces joined the first ones, amongst the battlements. Then a shrill voice came down from above. 'The Borgo's closed, no one's coming in tonight, by orders of His Holiness. Be off, or it will be all the worse for you!'

'I'm the ambassador of Florence. I order you to open up!'

'Give him the Good Friday service,' he heard the same voice say, this time to someone standing nearby on the terraces. Another moment passed, and then Dante saw three figures scrambling over the pediment of the gate. The three men turned their backs on him and then, as though participating in a single ceremony, unlaced their breeches and bared their buttocks, swaying ostentatiously from side to side. 'Put these three moons in your horoscope, Ambassador,' the voice called again, amongst the bursts of laughter of the other men at the top of the wall. 'And don't look too hard, they'll freeze you worse than the gaze of Medusa!'

Immediately after this he heard a clatter. Someone must have operated the tower latrines, because on either side of the gate he saw two cascades of dung flowing down the wall, like two malodorous tongues stretching towards him. He leaped back to escape them.

'Damned scoundrels! Thieving Romans!' he cried as he retreated, foaming with fury amidst the laughter and insults.

'What's up, Florentine? You look like a poisoned dog,' he heard a voice ring out behind him.

'You again, Master Hemp,' the poet shouted back furiously. 'You seem to be everywhere in this damned city!'

The Decurion followed Dante's gaze, still turned towards the terraces from which the mockery came. 'The walls of the Borgo? But this isn't the whole of Rome, it's just the seat on which popes and cardinals rest their arses. Come with me: I want to offer you dinner at Anacleto's tavern. And there you will see the Rome of the sensible folk, the ones who obey me. We could even discuss those dead people of yours, seeing as you're so fond of them. And I'll tell you who's really in charge in this city.'

The poet cursed again, unleashing a fresh tempest of

laughter, accompanied by a new discharge of dung, then turned around, setting off in the direction in which the other man was pointing him: a narrow alleyway between dry-stone walls that turned towards the countryside.

They passed by the remains of what looked like a circular temple, supported by the slender shapes of little columns refined with capitals carved with figures of animals. The gaps between the columns had been plugged in some previous age with brick walls, so as to turn the ancient temple into a Christian church. But now even that function had been abandoned, and the building looked like nothing but a dilapidated hay-barn.

He stopped for a minute to study the building, thinking about how in Florence, too, the signs of the Christian God had supplanted the ancient gods, installing themselves there too among their walls and banishing their shades. He dismissed with a shiver the memory of the legend of how the rage of the god Mars had struck his city when his statue was removed from the Ponte Vecchio to make way for the statue of John the Baptist.

Since that day it was as if the gates of the temple of war had been opened, and the city had not known more than a day of peace. What had Rome known then, where not a single god, but the whole of Olympus, had been ousted by the Nazarene? There too he had seen the sure signs of the revenge of the ancients, the wounds on its vast body inflicted by civil war. And yet the city seemed to resist, as if it were precisely in that constant destruction of men and stones that the strength that held it together was born, a place where no one was so strong as to prevail or so weak as to lose.

At a turn in the alley Dante suddenly found himself facing the door of a tavern, with a group of layabouts standing around outside it.

Anacleto's tavern opened up on the ground floor of a building that must once have been imposing, supported at its base by rows of arches that had now been walled up. Many other storeys rose up on that base, with the signs of the wooden floors still apparent in the holes for the floorboards that appeared in regular rows along the wall. The floors themselves had collapsed, leaving only a wall as desolate as a stage-set, in which the old windows opened like blind eyes.

It stood next to a stretch of aqueduct that was still in operation. Some time ago someone had dug a hole in the main conduit, inserting into it a tube made with a series of connecting terracotta cylinders, to open up a passage at the bottom for the precious liquid. From this makeshift tube a flood of gurgling water poured into a big stone basin that resembled a carved conch shell. Overflowing from there, it disappeared into the ground.

Dante walked cautiously past the puddle of mud, trying not to sully the hem of his robe, following the Decurion who was heading resolutely towards the inn, heedless of the mud and the little group of women busy drawing water from the fountain. The man must have been well known in the area, the poet thought, judging by the glances and giggles that welcomed his appearance. Master Hemp seemed flattered, and his chest swelled inside his jacket with the insignia of the pontifical keys.

THE REGULAR customers were drawn from the common people, wearing the simple clothes of workmen, apparently waiting to be called for work for the day. Some were drinking from rough earthenware cups, but most seemed to be immersed in a lively discussion, often interrupted and suffocated by shouts and explosions of laughter, which made it almost incomprehensible.

But Dante quickly worked out that an argument was going on about the finding of the body of Pope Joan.

It seemed to him that the crowd was divided into two factions: the ones outside the tavern maintained that the remains were authentic, and countered their invisible interlocutors inside with arguments embellished with richly imagined details.

'Wouldn't a woman's fine arse sit better on that throne!' one of them cried from outside, provoking, with an obscene gesture, a chorus of laughter on the part of his supporters. 'At least it would be fairer to air our own arses when that scoundrel Boniface goes in procession to St John!'

'What the hell are you on about?' shrieked one of the men inside, coming out with a knife in his hand. 'The Pope has to be a man, and his balls have to be clearly seen when he's enthroned in St Peter's!'

'What do we care about all these men, dressed as women, who keep all the convent novices for themselves? Why can't one of them come along to lead us? What about Maria and Marta, the two whores up by the Ponte Mollo? Don't you think they could chant the mass better than any number of cardinals? And while they've got their mouths open to perform the service, perhaps they could perform a little service for us at the same time!'

'That would be fine for pimps like you,' yelled the man who had just come out, waving his knife under his interlocutor's nose.

In an instant the other man had unsheathed his knife, a long blade that reminded Dante of a cross between an agricultural implement and a knight's little dagger. 'This goes for the whores too, if they free us from those bastard priests,' he yelled, darting a blow at his adversary. The other man had parried the lunge by leaping sideways, before hurling himself forward, trying to land a blow himself.

Imitating him, the first man had also thrown himself to one side. Carried by his own impetus, the assailant lost balance, slipping clumsily to the ground, to the scornful cries of the onlookers. With a sudden leap, the man turned onto his back like a cat, with a fierce gleam in his eyes. He seemed about to stand back up when his adversary's hand came down towards him to help him back to his feet.

'Richetto, you've made me dizzy with all that crap you come out with. If I'm going to open up your belly, I want to do it for Maria's lovely eyes, and not for someone who wants to be Pope. I don't care who it is, as long as they've got plenty of money.'

'Long live money!' the rabble cried in unison. Then, as if someone had given a signal, the whole crowd plunged inside the inn, singing the praises of Pope Joan, back from the grave.

Dante heard a confused sound of fighting coming from inside, gradually fading away as the regulars dragged themselves out, bruised and covered with cuts. In short, the supporters of the she-Pope seemed to have won the battle and taken the position by storm. As he walked away he caught the lines of a ribald song that someone was singing at the top of his voice:

> Down in the pub in the Vatican
> Boniface stands with his cock in his hand
> Calling out, 'Hey, what can I do?
> I want a shag just as much as you . . .'

Behind him the Decurion had exploded in vulgar laughter.

'I imagine these singers are your companions in verse,'

said Dante. 'In those competitions you were telling me about.'

'Oh, yes, some of the best! But let's go in, I'm starving.'

Inside the door, marked with the insignia of an oak-branch, a low, wide room opened up, permeated with smoke and the heavy smell of fatty cooking. At first glance it didn't look all that different from any tavern in his own city. The same background noise of the regulars, not softened here by the harmonious Tuscan speech, but mixed in with harsh sounds of the most vulgar kind, in which the poet could occasionally make out the liquid flow of French speech and the guttural bursts of German. The same greasy surfaces designed to receive food and regulars. The same hearth in a corner, with a copper pot boiling away on it, and spits large and small being turned by little boys crouching beside the flame. The most obvious difference was the greater use of stone and marble in the furniture, as if in this city even benches and tables were made as a challenge to the centuries.

The walls still bore traces of ancient frescoes, of which there remained flecks of bright colour, yellow and red, and surviving fragments of drawing: lines of naked bodies, male and female, depicted – as far as one could tell – during a kind of lovers' assignation. At one point, where the fresco was better-preserved, behind the representation of a laurel bush a couple were engaged in unmistakeable acts, depicted in a resolutely realistic fashion.

Beneath that display of genitals, the indifferent regulars were busy knocking back wine from earthenware cups, or spooning soup from wooden bowls, helping themselves with slices of black bread that each of them had beside his plate.

There was one particularly original detail: a whole wall was punctuated by a long series of tall marble staircases, lined up below a kind of gutter, it too carved from marble. On its surface, at regular intervals, a series of round holes opened up, some of which now held tubs of various sizes. After a moment's puzzlement, Dante gave a start as he recognised where they were.

'Mastro Antonio! Have you brought me to eat in a latrine?'

'Oh, those!' the Decurion replied. 'They belonged to our grandfathers. Still perfectly efficient, much more so than those filthy holes up at the Castello. But don't worry, Ambassador: Nico only allows his best regulars to use them, to relieve themselves if they need to, after enjoying his services. He certainly doesn't want them shitting all over the place – that would be the end of the good name of his kitchen.'

Dante opened his mouth to answer, but at that moment one of the regulars had got up from the table to approach one of the seats. The man was preparing to lift his short tunic over his hips, when in a flash a fat man was on top of him, gripping him by the collar. Ignoring the unfortunate fellow's half-open breeches, he gave him a great kick in the behind and then pushed him violently to the door, continuing to repeat the operation until the man had disappeared outside.

'What did I tell you? There are rules,' the Decurion observed approvingly. The huge man had turned to come back inside, looking haughtily at the other regulars. Then he noticed the two newcomers, and a self-satisfied smile spread across his face.

'Master Hemp! It's about time you did me the pleasure. And you're not alone – have you brought a strange knight to appreciate my cooking?' he exclaimed, eyeing Dante and his robes suspiciously.

'Ambassador from Florence, no less. Don't make me look stupid in front of such an important person,' the Decurion growled, stretching out more comfortably on the bench. 'Bring the best.'

'For you, nothing but.'

The landlord bowed respectfully and hurried towards the fire. After a few moments Dante saw him coming back holding a big tin plate, with a large roast capon steaming on it. A boy who was following him set a jug of wine down on the table.

The Decurion swept the cups away with an arm to make room for the plate, and unceremoniously grabbed the jug, taking a long swig. Then he held the receptacle out to the poet, inviting him to do the same. Dante politely refused the offer, and reached out his hand towards one of the cups.

'I see you take your time in Florence, Ambassador,' said the other man, wiping his lips with the back of his hand. Then he decided to pour the wine. 'Look at this capon. Have you ever seen such a big one?'

Dante cleared his throat. 'Do you think these creatures are all that different from one another in the various lands of the Empire?'

'I don't know. They speak of marvels in the northern lands. And they speak of marvels beyond the sea, and of the silks of India. But they must be talking nonsense, because in the end everyone wants to come to Rome. They come here with the excuse of the Jubilee and the tombs of the saints, of vows and reparations. And then they fill the streets with their rags, in search of the charity of God. If my men didn't scatter them around the countryside with their sticks, you'd find them picking your pockets even in your bed. As for me, I've never been beyond Mentana. Tell me about your own travels.'

'No, you tell me what you promised me. Who rules in Rome, and how,' said Dante, still staring at his plate. The smell emanating from it was undoubtedly appetising – it must have been stuffed with olives and capers, judging by the aroma.

'Right,' said the Decurion. He had taken his knife from his belt. He plunged it into the animal and started carving.

'Rome is like this capon. At the top of it all the juicy breast, and these are the towers and the Castello, in the hands of the Pope. And then the two wings, which keep it up when it's in search of rich pickings – they're Colonna and Orsini, each with his feathers to defend himself. And the whole animal stands on its legs, which are the Roman Senate and people organised according to their trades.'

As he made his way through his illustration, the Decurion carved up the parts of the animal, removing them from one another with the tip of his knife. He gripped it and turned it over, revealing its spine. 'And then there's the *Romana Fraternitas*, the society of the pious rectors of the churches. Confraternities, the Templars and the Teutons. And then the various orders of monks, Franciscans and Dominicans above all. They are entrenched in their monasteries, and each of them requests and arms militias, when necessary.'

The Decurion slipped one of the pieces of meat onto his knife and brought it to his mouth, chewing it carefully. 'Yes, Mastro Anacleto has done his duty. And then there's the Castello militia, in the hands of Senator Spada, my own master.'

'Spada is the senator of the Commune. Which means that he is answerable to the people, if I understand correctly.'

The Decurion swallowed quickly, then pierced another piece of meat, slipping it onto a slice of bread that he held out to the poet. 'That might have happened in the days of the ancient Romans. They say there once was a Senate in government. Did you know that?'

Dante nodded with a snort. 'But for a while now the Senate has been nothing but a parade of haughty names, as empty as an eggshell once the chick has fled. The mob watches and celebrates, and picks up the alms thrown from the windows of the Campidoglio.'

'But there still is a Senate. I've seen it myself, at the ceremony of the Jews!'

'Yes, they call each other senators as a joke. There must be about eighty of them, but apart from the glory of escorting the Pope when he goes in procession, they don't matter a damned thing. There's only one important senator, the Administrator, the one who's appointed by the Pope. He's the only one in government, Saturniano Spada. As long as he remains faithful to Boniface, or until Boniface kicks the bucket.' Dante drummed his fingers on the table, ignoring his companion's invitations to try the food.

'I forgot the best bit, Ambassador,' the Decurion said suddenly.

'What's that?'

'The best part is this,' the man went on, plunging his knife into the lower part of the animal and cutting away the triangle between the thighs. 'The Cardinal's mouthful, as we call it here. That's me, with my troop. More solid than the Castello and the senator. More solid even than the Pope.'

'Why?'

'Popes and senators come and go. If one of them dies, you make another. But whoever appears at that window, making himself Pope, *urbi et orbi*, to the city and the world, will need three things: the help of the Lord himself, money to keep the plebs happy and, if that's not enough, the work of the hangman. Incense, money and the rope: that's what keeps Rome going. That's how it's always been and always will be.'

Dante had followed this carefully, trying to find in the signs of this comical cartography of power the trace of a deeper truth. Master Hemp seemed most familiar with the lower end of Roman society, just as the senator claimed to know its summits. Meanwhile his hunger pangs were becoming more and more intense; overcoming his repugnance of the place, he took a piece of capon and brought it to his mouth.

The flavour was truly delicious, he thought. Or perhaps it was only his body, which, defeated by hunger and weariness, was freeing itself from the chains of the spirit.

He relaxed as he felt his stomach finally swelling again, creating a pleasant sense of fullness throughout his whole body. Even his violent headache seemed to have eased. He looked around, curious about what was going on around him.

The tables had gradually filled with regulars, busy drinking mugs of cheap wine even worse than what he and his companion had been served. His attention was particularly drawn by a table not far away, from which came an agitated chorus of shouts and laughter. Unlike the others, the group thronging around the table didn't seem by its clothes to be made up of artisans on the way back from their shops. On the contrary, their clothes were rather refined, albeit demeaned by the vulgarity and less-than-urban cut of their doublets, so short that they barely covered their privates. They seemed to be involved in a kind of pagan ritual, celebrated by the passing of wine from one mouth to the other, according to a rule that the poet was unable to work out. Rather than going round in a circle, the jar skipped turns or stopped in the hands of someone who drank a huge amount from it, to the hilarity and rage of the others. But even when they were foaming with desire, they respected the unknown rule. Every now and again one of the men leaped to his feet, inspired by the liquid he had swallowed, and ran to relieve himself in one of the stone holes, with his head thrown back to keep an eye on what was happening behind him.

'Who are they?' Dante asked, nodding towards the spectacle. 'What are they doing?'

'They're the local fops. They're playing *passatella*.'

'*Passatella*?'

'They're draining Mastro Nico's barrels. The Drawer of

Straws has nominated the Master and the Under, and now the drinking has begun. That one over there,' said the Decurion, pointing to one of the regulars who was sitting in a corner, motionless and grim-faced, 'is the Fool, who never gets to drink.'

The jar continued to pass from hand to hand, dragged along by the requests and pleas of the drinkers, each time deliberately skipping the man identified as the Fool, to the scornful laughter of the others.

The grotesque ritual reminded him of something he must have read somewhere. 'But this is the *Regnum vini*, the ceremony Horace talks about,' he exclaimed, suddenly recognising what was going on. 'A noble custom, reduced to a shameful parody . . .'

The Decurion cut in, gripping him by the wrist. 'Look, Florentine! The Fool's had enough.'

A knife had appeared in the silent man's hand, as he rose from the bench and stretched out his hand to grab the jar. The Master, who was clutching the receptacle at that moment, must have been waiting for just that move, so that he could draw it back in a flash. The man's hand grabbed at empty air, before falling back down on the wooden surface. Straight away, another regular, the one that the Decurion had called the Under, planted the tip of the knife between his fingers, brushing his skin, to cries of encouragement from the others.

With a roar the Fool turned towards his assailant.

'I think we should try and sort out this row . . .' Dante exclaimed, starting to rise from his seat.

But the Decurion slapped him back down. 'Hold it there, Florentine.'

'But aren't you the enforcer of justice?'

'This is why they play *passatella*. The good bit's coming up.'

The Fool and his challenger had started exchanging shouts whose meaning escaped the poet, but which must have been particularly insulting, given their hate-filled looks and the laughter that was breaking out among the spectators.

The room had cleared around them. Then, in unison, the two contenders sat back down facing one another, resting their left hands on the table with fingers spread, knives raised ready to strike.

'Your go, Mr Under!' roared the Fool. The other man spat ostentatiously on the table, and then in a flash he brought the knife down, planting it precisely between the little finger and the ring finger of his own hand, then repeating the operation for all the other fingers, a good three times. Dante saw the knife flashing swiftly: to the sound of shouting, the blade darted like the head of a snake, hard for the eye to follow. But the clicks on the wood and the cuts inflicted by the knife-point were there to prove the dangerous reality of what was happening.

When the Under had finished a second run he stopped triumphantly, shouting defiantly at his adversary, who then proceeded to launch into an attack on his own hand, trying to repeat the operation in a rhythm even faster than the other man. It must have been the speed of the act that decided who won, Dante thought, as he tried in vain once more to catch the lightning-fast movements of the blade.

A cry of pain followed by an explosion of laughter interrupted the flashing of the blade. The Fool had missed a blow, nailing one of his own fingers to the table. He cursed, bringing his injured hand to his mouth, in an attempt to stem the blood that had started flowing, while the Under leaped to his feet to receive the applause of the others. The other fops immediately surrounded him exultantly, grabbed him and lifted him onto their shoulders, carrying him around the tables in noisy triumph, to the tune of a ribald song.

Dante withdrew into his corner, to avoid being struck by the man's legs.

'Florentine, doesn't this seem worthy of the ancient heroes?' the Decurion said, his eyes glued to the scene.

'A sign of the times and their decadence. Mould on ancient temples, like the buildings you've built on magnificent ruins.'

'Yes, magnificent buildings, certainly. Have you made your pilgrimage to the seven churches, and seen the wonders of the city?'

'I have seen more wonders than I could ever have expected,' Dante murmured thoughtfully. 'But one in particular struck me with its strangeness. Why does the great circle of the wall enclose mostly unpopulated land, and why are people and buildings concentrated mostly in the bend of the river, where the ground is lower and exposed to flooding, rather than settling on the hills as the first masters of the city did? Rome seems to be chaos, as the Scripture says of the earth and the waters before the word of God came to divide and order it. But how does the Pope divide and order, if everything exceeds both order and measure?'

The Decurion laughed loudly. 'I like you, Florentine. You don't understand a thing, like most people from the North. But at least you try, and you deserve an explanation. And besides, you're a poet, so I'll explain it in an allegory. Rome is like a big toilet.'

'A toilet? You mean a latrine? Like this one? Didn't you say a moment ago that it was a capon?'

'That's the Rome of the priests and nobles. But a different rule applies to these beggars. This riff-raff, that Aeneas kicked about, to free the hills of their presence and make a bit of room. And wasn't Latrinus the first king? So let me explain, and you'll see whether or not there's any order involved. Everything goes downwards in this city. Princes, with their servants and families, entrench themselves on the hills, and the common people want to join them there. But cling as they might to the volcanic rock, back down they tumble, because it's in the simple man's nature to seek the level plain. And it's also in their nature to seek protection from the enemy in the shadow of those who seem stronger. So gradually they all ended up slipping into the Campo Marzio, in the shadow of the Castello. Because they imagine that, between the floods of the Tiber and the sword of the enemy, there's more to be feared from the latter than the former. Since the days of the barbarian invaders, the people have always run to put themselves under the protection of the walls of the Leonine City, at the first gust of wind. And then they've ended up clinging to its walls like fleas on a dog's neck. And the pilgrims, after the guides have fleeced them good and proper around the basilicas, end up down by Peter's tomb. And all this slipping and sliding ends up in the sewers at the Ponte dell'Angelo, the big cesspit where everything flows together.'

'Does that mean there are no guilds in Rome? No one to defend the people, to divide them up into districts and administer their needs and desires?'

The Decurion looked perplexed. 'Guilds? I suppose so, or at least there are different trades. And they're divided up into districts, too. Take the pimps, they never leave the area around Campo dei Fiori, on pain of losing a hand. The whores are beside them, while the perverts walk around quite openly under the arches of the aqueduct at Porta Maggiore. The pickpockets are based around the Corso, towards Via del Ponte, but then they're divided into four regions around the bigger basilicas. Twopenny scoundrels, by and large; but beware of the ones around Santa Maria, they're robbers and they won't be satisfied with your money-bags. The True Witnesses are behind the Cancelleria and by the Tribunale di Giustizia. Housebreakers stay between the columns of the Forum, rustlers in St John's meadows, where they wait for the herds coming through the Porta Asinara, when they come back from the Appian pastures. The Jews in Trastevere, but you've met them already, while Patarines and schismatics hide over towards the island, near the Temple of Vesta. Counterfeiters behind Via del Banco, beside Boniface's Mint: that's where they make the finest *carlini* in the world, better than the real ones. Card-players and acrobats are divided on either side of the Piazza Navona, while down at the Pantheon arches there are fortune-tellers and astrologers, and around Augustus' mausoleum the knife-wielders and the men dressed as women, who don't associate with the perverts over at the aqueduct.'

Dante had listened in puzzlement. 'And that's it?' he tried to say.

'Why not! There are other artists, but they have no fixed abode. The people who adulterate wine with water, and the poisoners, you'll find them in every tavern. Highwaymen mostly at the Via Lata, while the pilgrim-fleecers are based at the Agro Romano. Some venture as far as the gates, maybe disguised as excisemen, but the

border guards take care of them, because they don't want
their jobs stolen out from under their noses.'

'And are there many people like this?' Dante asked, shocked.

'A fair number, a clutch of each.'

'A *clutch*?'

'Yes, you know, a group, a gang – what would you say?'

'A *bolgia*, we would say in Florence. A madhouse.'

'Fine, then, a madhouse.'

When they left, the rain had started falling, cold and
insistent.

10

13th November, morning

THE WIDOW'S young son had appeared at the door. He
seemed worried about something, waiting for the
poet to address him. The poet looked up from the papers
in which he was immersed.

'The Senator Administrator is downstairs. He's asking
for you!'

'Senator Spada?' Dante murmured, getting up and
straightening his robes. 'Send him up straight away.'

'He wants you to go down. He's on horseback,' the boy
replied, in the embarrassed voice of someone conveying
an order rather than a request. Dante looked around for
his cap and cloak, and having quickly put them on he
headed towards the stairs.

The senator was waiting for him at the door, astride a
magnificently barded beast. He was holding a second animal
by the reins, it too of the most excellent quality. The poet
looked round, puzzled by the absence of the usual cortege
that he had by now learned to associate with this man.

'I would like you to be my guest again today, Messer Alighieri,' said Saturniano Spada, turning affably towards him. 'But first I would like to go and check how the preparations for the construction of the fleet are going. Will you come with me?' he added, holding the reins of the second horse.

Dante concealed his surprise. 'I will be happy to come with you,' was all he said as he jumped into the saddle. 'Where are the ships moored? I'm curious to learn your techniques.'

'We aren't right by the shipyard. I intend to inspect how far along they are with the collection of the wood they need. Towards the north, in the forests up from the city. Come, I'll show you an area that I'm sure you won't know.'

The senator spurred his horse, heading towards the Lungara, which led to the Borgo Leonino. But when they were within sight of the walls, having passed another pyramid, rather than heading towards the gate he turned to the left, skirting the ramparts. The two men rode along the city walls across uncultivated fields and marshes, then turned towards the north-east, where they followed the course of the Tiber for a few miles. The arches of a bridge could be glimpsed in the distance, and the bulk of a church isolated in the countryside.

'Here we are at the Ponte Mollo,' the senator said, pointing to the distant arches. 'And this is the Church of St Valentine. It's here that I ordered them to bring the wood cut on the hills. At this point the river is wide, and flows smoothly: it will be easy to bring the trunks to their destination from here.'

On the banks, a few hundred yards downriver from the bridge, lay huge piles of tree-trunks that looked ready to be entrusted to the current. Only some solid pegs fixed into the ground kept them in position. Some men were busy reinforcing the pegs with ropes, while others were unloading more freshly cut trunks from carts. Dante noticed that the men talked to each other in a foreign language, in which he thought he recognised the harsh sounds of German.

He looked up towards the bare slopes of the hills not far away. 'Have you stripped your lands completely of their forests?' he asked, astonished at what he saw.

The senator proudly followed his motions. 'The expedition to the Holy Land has so far been hampered not by a lack of men, because we have many of those, nor by the steadfast attitude of their minds, which is made of iron. No, the problem lies with the Venetian merchants, and the iniquity of the Genoese pirates. People who, for the sake of their own sides and their own various interests, have always been grudging with the only element that the venture lacks: boats to cross the sea.'

Dante went on staring in perplexity at the enormous tree-trunks. He bit his lower lip, under the senator's attentive gaze.

'You're not sure they'll be enough?'

'It's certainly the biggest collection of wood for ships that I've ever seen. Not even the Arsenal in Venice has as much. But . . .'

'But . . .'

'It takes more than wood to build a ship. It takes the knowledge of ship-builders, the skill of axe-masters, of caulkers, of rope-layers, of sail-makers. And to sail them you need helmsmen and strong men, paid men and galley-slaves. Resources that don't grow on hillsides like your trees. Where are you going to find them? To move two hundred galleys . . . And on what scale are you going to build them, if all the resources of *La Serenissima* aren't enough to construct twenty at the same time?'

The senator looked at him haughtily. 'You forget, Messer Alighieri, that you are at the Centre of the World. And that Rome has sailed the sea for hundreds of years – a sea that was ours and will be ours once again. We certainly aren't short of shipyards. And it's there that the trunks will be transported along the current. It's a method our ances-tors used, and which survives in the great rivers of the North, in France and Germany. And it's from there that I have brought the men you see, certainly more skilled at this task than our carpenters.'

As Dante strolled wonderingly around the vast piles of tree-trunks, the senator left him to confer with his employees. A little while later the poet saw him coming back with a smug expression on his face.

'Everything is going according to plan. We can set off again, to be at my villa before midday.'

They mounted their horses once more, and the senator headed towards the bridge that he had called the Ponte Mollo. It must have been the old Milvian Bridge, still in operation on its imposing stone feet since the days of Empire. They passed the tower built to guard the arches on the right-hand side of the river, then entered the span of the bridge, where a wooden floor made of planks had replaced the first arch, which had collapsed in ancient times. The last arch on the opposite side had been remade in wood as well, a sign that in its long history the bridge must have been reduced only to its three central arches. Perhaps that was why the Romans had called it Mollo – the Springy Bridge – Dante thought as his horse's hooves drummed on its planks.

THEY RETURNED via the Porta Flaminia. Dante kept pace with the senator's horse, taking in everything that he saw. Then his guide started to climb the tight bends that led to the hill overlooking the square just past the gate, and after a short ride he recognised the walls of the senator's house in the distance.

Meanwhile he tried to draw a map of the city in his mind. Rome was more or less the shape of an irregular circle, but its size made it difficult to place the various areas of the city in a regular pattern.

As soon as they had passed through the outer wall and handed the horses over to a servant who had come hurrying to meet them, the senator led him inside the building, through a long series of rooms, until he stopped in front of a closed door.

'Come, Messer Alighieri. There's something I want to show you. It will interest you,' said the senator, pointing to the door. He took a big iron key from his belt, inserted it into the keyhole and turned it. Then he pushed open the heavy oak panel, reinforced with strips of iron, and went in, beckoning the poet to follow him.

On the other side of the door a little windowless room opened up. The only light came from an iron circle hanging from the ceiling on a chain, with half a dozen lit candles in it. Other candles were fixed in torch-holders that protruded from the wall, like the arms of mute slaves, and a box full of yet more candles lay open on the floor. Visible traces of wax all over the stone floor and the smoke-stained vault suggested that the light in this room burned at all times. The frescoes on the walls were also covered with a brownish patina, which dimmed their once-dazzling colour: the red and yellow could still be seen, and the ochre of the ground, with which an unknown hand had traced the episodes of a story that Dante recognised immediately: a throne-room resplendent with amphorae and columns, a couple sitting on the throne and a naked young man approaching them. Then a couple setting off at night on a troubled sea, and the ship heading towards a cliff on which rose a city with a hundred towers. And a thousand ships sailing in their wake, and an army surrounding the walls, and duels and heroes victorious and defeated. The gods handing weapons to the heroes, taking part in the game of life and death with an inexplicable smile on their distant faces. And then the great horse outside the gate of the city, and the flames rising up among the walls, and the furious slaughter carried out by the victors, the weeping of the defeated, the flight of the survivors.

The story of the ancient city of Troy, unfolding before his eyes. In a corner of the last painting, a vigorous man was coming down towards the beach, carrying an old man on his back and holding in his hand the hand of a child, while a woman with her eyes lit by the flames departed with a sad farewell wave.

Deeply moved, Dante approached that last figure, holding out a hand to stroke its face. 'Yes, Messer Alighieri. That is Aeneas, the hero sung of by the great Virgil. Perhaps the master who drew this story immortalised his story too, in another part of the house. But if he did so, the work has been lost. However, that isn't what I wanted to show you.'

Lined up against the walls were two big shelves full of thick codices, most of them bound between wooden panels. They were of various sizes, some quite small, but most quite large and written on parchment. Dante opened his eyes wide in fascination. In that room there must have been at least two hundred books, a vast number for a private individual. Only in the royal courts were there said to be comparable numbers. Or in the cells of the most famous monasteries.

The senator watched Dante out of the corner of his eye to see what his reaction would be. 'I knew you'd be struck by my little secret. These books are the companions to the ones you saw the other day.'

In response to an invitation from the senator, the poet walked over to one of the shelves and gently took down a codex. Then he crouched down, resting the codex on his knees and opening it at the first page. After a moment he looked up, excitedly staring at the other man.

'It's Arnaldo Daniello – the best writer in his language . . .'

'Along with all the writings of the French versifiers,' said the senator, coming to stand beside the books. He stretched out a hand and took down another one, more slender than the first. He opened it at the first page and began to read out loud. '*In the book of my memory there is a section before which there is little to read. In that section, which bears the heading* Incipit vita nova, *I find the words that I intend to copy into this little book, or, if not all of them, at least their gist.* Do you recognise these words?'

Dante had flushed to his roots. Then he got his breath back and raised his head. 'It's a great honour to me that this book should be kept alongside works by authors much greater than myself.'

'I think this is the place it deserves. With the very best verses of our century, but not only with them. Here is the greatest work of Aristotle, and here the greatest by Plato, which have come here on a ship from Byzantium. Sadly I am precluded from any profound understanding of these works in their original voice; but it is from these pages that my daughter learned that extraordinary language.'

'Here you have all the knowledge of Christendom,' said Dante with a note of sadness in his voice.

His abrupt change of mood had not gone unnoticed by his companion. 'Does the sight of so much knowledge trouble you, Messer Alighieri? Rather than enjoying its riches, you seem to be frightened of them.'

Dante shook his head. 'Who will ever be capable of matching those minds in our own century? Who will ever be able to read in his lifetime all that those great men have left us?'

'It's true,' the senator agreed, casting his eye over the volumes. 'Leaving wisdom aside, our memories are no longer equal to the great minds of the past. Oh, those happy times, when Plato and Aristotle could discuss their theses, drawing in the air the shapes of their arguments without the support of the written word – just drawing from the treasures of their knowledge, still present in the book of their memory.'

Dante nodded. 'The only knowledge is that which

remains carved in the mind. Like the wayfarer's knapsack, which never leaves him on his peregrinations.'

'Perhaps it's true what they say about the god Thoth.'

For a moment a puzzled expression appeared on the poet's face. Not wishing to confess his own ignorance, he waited for a few seconds for the senator to explain himself. But the man went on staring at the shelf, lost in thought. Then he stirred, and seemed to notice Dante's embarrassment.

'The god of the Egyptians who is said to have taught men the art of writing, so that none of their thoughts will ever be lost. A secret art learned from his magical consort Seshat, the ruler of papyruses . . .'

Dante listened with great interest.

'. . . the god of swiftness, of agility, of the word and of intuition. The god who plays with men, who heals and deceives them . . .'

'It sounds as if you're referring to the Greek god Hermes under a different name.'

The other man turned towards him and broke off. 'A fair observation. But he isn't the only god that the secret religion of the Nile has given us. Perhaps the whole Greek pantheon is only a derivation of that mysterious religion, and only our ignorance prevents us from seeing clearly that Greek splendour is the daughter to Egyptian obscurity. Just as they say that Alexander the Great was the son not of his father Philip, but of the pharaoh Nektanebo.

And that that in itself was the root of his greatness, entirely disproportionate to the gifts that might have been passed down to him from a Macedonian highlander.'

'But that's just a legend . . .'

'Of course, it probably is. But it's also a true allegory, which reveals how the Greeks themselves, who gave voice to it, were aware that all their knowledge came from beyond the sea, along with the very form of their own gods. Something that Plato himself clearly admitted in his fables, when he spoke of how the sage Solon drew upon Egyptian sources for his innovations. And not just them, Messer Alighieri. Others too have drawn on those sources, others who then worshipped a single god, like the Jew Moses, or like—'

The senator suddenly broke off, pursing his lips as if he regretted that last observation.

'Like who, Senator Spada?' Dante broke in.

'But I was telling you about the god Thoth,' the other man continued, ignoring the last question. 'The god appeared to the pharaoh Thamus, offering him as a gift the new art of writing. And Thamus rejected the gift, convinced that the possibility of putting wisdom on paper, rather than in the mind, would mean the beginning of decadence for mankind.'

Dante nodded. 'Now none of us can do without writing. But you are right about the rest, perhaps our minds are no longer capable of retaining everything we need. That's why I'm thinking of a great compendium of knowledge, a kind of feast of minds that divides amongst men of goodwill the angelic bread of knowledge.'

'Some great intellects are still capable of it – your own, for example. Don't you know the entire *Aeneid* by heart?'

'Yes,' Dante replied, with a hint of pride in his voice. 'But it wasn't difficult, such are the sweetness and harmony of the Mantuan's verse that his words are carved in my mind like a hot seal in soft wax. It would have been hard to tear them away, so bound am I by love to his work.'

Dante's last words were received with a gleam in the senator's eye. 'So you love them as much as that?'

'It was his words that made me what I am.'

The senator nodded with a suggestion of triumph in his expression. Then he moved towards a low piece of furniture by the end wall, which the poet had failed to notice in the emotion of the situation. With a dramatic gesture he opened the lock that held it shut and revealed its contents: a series of carved wooden cylinders, like the one that the mysterious woman had given him in Florence.

Dante darted forward, trembling uncontrollably. He leaned over the chest, pushing the senator out of the way as he did so, and plunged a hand inside, gripping one of the cylinders. Only after bringing it close to his face and carefully studying its carvings did he seem to grasp his own movements. Red in the face, he leaned towards the senator and apologised. But he gave no sign of putting the cylinder back, and his fingers seemed paralysed by the container, which he was gripping tightly. 'And the thing – the thing you sent me? Was it your daughter . . . was it she?'

'Yes,' the senator replied proudly. 'Although I don't know which of us had the idea first, so great is our admiration of your works. The mastery of language and metre, which, for me, turns Tuscans into princes, and certainly the greatest of the moderns. But above all your devotion to Beatrice, and the intensity with which you celebrate her: that must have pierced Fiamma's heart.'

Dante had listened to this praise with his head lowered, rejecting it with what might have been excessively ostentatious modesty. But inside he was burning with that reference to the man's daughter. So Fiamma had been touched by his lines of love. And how often words bound by a rhyme, by their sensual sound, can melt a woman's heart more than an image can. Perhaps . . . 'And what do you expect from me?' he asked suddenly.

'I ask you to sing our venture. As Homer sang the deeds of Achilles and Odysseus, and Virgil those of the pious Aeneas. Only your pen could be a match for them.'

'You are putting a weight on my shoulders that threatens to crush me.'

'Come on, Messer Alighieri,' said a deep voice behind him.

Dante suddenly turned round to see Martino da Vinegia and the Persian ambassador, Kansbar ibn Talib. They must have been there for some time, after coming in as silently as ghosts. He stared into the Venetian's eyes, disconcerted by his presence in that place. But before he could utter so much as a word, the senator continued. 'With Guittone of Arezzo dead, and Guinizelli, and your friend Cavalcanti, who in Italy could take on such a task today, if not you? Don't you agree, Messer Martino?'

The senator looked from Dante to the old man. Spada must have sensed the poet's alarm, because he immediately added, 'Messer Martino brings with him the help and patronage of *La Serenissima*: he is a man of courage and learning, and the Republic did well to put its trust in him. But perhaps you have already had occasion to meet him, when he was on his diplomatic mission in Florence . . .'

Both Martino and the poet nodded. Then the old man looked away and stared into the distance. 'If we were at the court of Palermo, and the great Emperor Frederick were still the leader of the world, perhaps at his school someone could have been found who was up to the task. But half a century has passed since then, and you alone have lit that poetic light that first illuminated our lands. And I'm sure that if he came back to life, he would be the first to choose you among his closest followers. The senator did well in asking you to provide this work.'

Dante turned towards him. 'But it isn't Frederick whose venture this exploit is, it's Pope Boniface. Which means that my song would have to celebrate the very hand that is putting the freedom of Florence in jeopardy,' he replied curtly.

The three men glanced quickly at one another. 'There is a saying that I am sure you know: *a great flame follows a little spark*,' the senator said. 'Perhaps Boniface and his money and his ambition really are behind the project. But when the great machine is set in motion, it will matter little who provided the initial impulse. Just as the splendour of your celestial vaults, and their eternal and perfect orbits, shows no trace other than the allegorical of the invisible motor that governs it.'

'But a crusade needs a flaming banner in front of its forces!' Dante replied. 'And that can only be a deep faith in the justice of the deed. But if the hand that urges on the exploit is a simoniac hand . . .'

The senator shook his head. 'The force of Christianity grows dim wherever heresy is born and spreads. The Church's capacity to speak to the heart seems extinct. Oh, of course, it goes on persuading men, but that was surely not its strength at the beginning. It reached the hearts of nobles and patricians, and Virgil himself – if what they say is true – was one of its secret initiates. But today only the people follow it, sustained by their bestial ignorance more than by the strength of doctrine; it has returned to its original condition as a slave religion, and is destined to plunge into the darkness of oblivion.'

Dante was perplexed. 'If that is what you think, what is the point of launching a crusade?'

The senator stretched out on his bench, as if listening to a secret voice speaking inside him. Then, with his eyes half-closed, he continued, 'When Israel fled from Egypt, it was the hand of God that parted the Red Sea to allow their exodus. And it was certainly their childish faith in the Scriptures and the prophets that persuaded a people to go down to the sea bed, amongst the monsters that laid it waste with their terrifying convulsions, between walls of seething water. They followed the orders of Moses, but it was Aaron's rod behind them that spurred them on their way and dispelled their extreme doubts. Only the force of the sword can win back the heart of the best people for the Word. That's why it's important for the crusade to succeed.'

Dante was about to reply when he was interrupted by the entrance of the same servant who had welcomed them at the door. The man approached the senator and murmured something in his ear. The senator dismissed him with a gesture, then turned back towards the poet.

'The third guest I was waiting for has arrived, Messer Alighieri. He might surprise you,' he added with an ironic expression.

Manoello had appeared in the doorway. Once again the rabbi was dressed in the ceremonial robes he had been wearing at the Campidoglio, as if he too had come straight from there. Dante hadn't been able to hide his astonishment. 'I told you you'd be surprised,' the senator said.

'I thought your relations with the people of Israel were less friendly,' was all Dante said, mastering his reaction. Then he turned towards the rabbi, bowing slightly by way of greeting. Manoello replied respectfully, turning to greet all the others in a single gesture. 'Messer Manoello certainly doesn't enjoy the favour of the city,' the senator said, walking towards him. 'But in my home different rules apply, rules that are perhaps less respectful of the law. Here men are qualified by their learning and their knowledge: and in this area race and religion count for little.'

'The faith of each one of us is hardly a secondary part of our knowledge,' Dante quickly objected.

'If you wish. But, as I said, the venture for which we are preparing is a noble one. He is a representative of the people who is very well acquainted with the lands in which it will be played out, and whose help will be indispensable to us if we are to bring it to a successful conclusion.'

Puzzled, Dante went on staring at everyone there. In that library, that storehouse of wisdom, lay the living testimony of how human knowledge was by no means enough, if one were unequivocally to penetrate the secrets of God and produce a common image of them. Three cultures, the fruit of different traditions, and three different and mutually hostile traditions. And now they were supposed to be collaborating on a common venture? He choked back the fundamental objection that had risen into his throat. But there was something simpler and more immediate that stirred his curiosity.

'But even if your efforts attained their goal, and the Islamic fury was crushed and quelled in the Arabian deserts, how are you going to reach an agreement between the victors for the possession of Jerusalem? A city that is equally craved by different peoples. Isn't there a risk that the dispute will immediately reignite amongst them, frustrating the success of the venture? Even in the days of King Richard, the Christians certainly didn't demonstrate solidarity and agreement amongst themselves. And then they were competing only for a banner, or a castle. But now, when those who meet on the banks of the Jordan will not only be the French, Teutons or Venetians, but people who have come from every corner of the Earth, what pact could be extracted from them? Divided by race, by language, by heritage, how much time will pass before they raise their swords, still wet with the blood of the infidels, against each other?'

'You are right, Messer Alighieri. But this time there will be one difference, if we can leave aside the simple possession of Jerusalem, in the knowledge that its walls and towers are nothing but a mass of rocks, and that its paths have been walked by illustrious men, but not by messengers from God.'

'What do you mean?' Dante asked, perplexed.

'The senator is probably referring to an ancient wisdom,' Martino said suddenly, getting to his feet and walking over to a little table in one corner. On it lay a rectangular object that Dante had failed to notice, so enthralled was he by the library. 'I have brought something from Venice. But perhaps it's a lucky chance that you are here too, so that you can provide your judgement.'

Martino reached out his hand towards the little box. He opened the wooden lock with a small golden key that he wore around his neck and lifted the lid. The interior was meticulously lined with heavy felt.

He reached in and delicately lifted out an object that lay inside it.

It was a codex, held between two boards of painted wood. Holding it on the tips of his fingers, as if he feared to profane something sacred, he showed it to the others. The upper board was almost entirely filled with a gilded shield, with a black eagle depicted inside it, wings unfolded and claws stretched, its beak open as if it were about to devour its prey.

'A gift for you,' said the old man, turning to the senator. 'In Venice the richness of your library is well known. And since it includes the most ancient books, many of them outside the canon, my government thought this book might be the right seal for our alliance, given what you are about to undertake. And I too think it is the best place to receive it.'

'That's the coat of arms of Frederick, the great Emperor!' Dante exclaimed, his eye drawn by the shield. Frederick II of Swabia, the man who had stunned the world only a few decades before with his wisdom and courage, and whose name was still talked about from one end of the Empire to the other. A poet, a legislator, an implacable rival of the Church. The man who, perhaps more than anyone else in the modern age, had approached the greatness of the ancients. 'Is it from your library?'

Martino stared him in the eye, remaining silent for a long time. 'Yes,' he said at last.

At this exchange, Dante could resist no longer. He stretched out his fingers and touched the codex. Perhaps those pages contained the Emperor's sweet verses of love, the metres and rhythms of the sweet Sicilian tongue that had given birth to modern poetry. And to which he too owed his beginnings as a poet, in Florence. But he suddenly paused. 'How did it come to be in the hands of Venice? His relations with your city were not always cordial. It's said that you wouldn't even have one of your goldsmiths make his crown!'

'That's true, Messer Alighieri. The Emperor's rashness in the northern lands, and his long alliance with the tyrant Ezzelino, was often seen as a source of danger, and made relations uneasy, as often happens between friends who don't fully understand one another. But after his election to the imperial throne, Frederick was always generous with the privileges he bestowed on *La Serenissima*. And in exchange he had our respect and secret favour every time he found himself in difficulties. As in the case of this book, which was saved from destruction by our agents, after the fall of Vittoria.'

'Fall . . . Vittoria?' asked Kansbar, unsure about what he had just heard.

Old Martino turned towards him, still holding the codex beneath their eyes. 'Vittoria is the name that the Emperor gave to his fortified camp, which he had built near Parma when he placed that city under siege. Thrown up in only a few days, made of wood and canvas, but in his dreams made of stone and marble – that was where he planned to put his northern court, mirroring the splendour of Palermo. I have seen the plans for this new capital; and if fate had favoured Frederick, today a new Rome would stand in the heart of the Po Valley, as powerful and luminous on the River Po as Rome is on the Tiber.'

'But the Guelphs of Parma shattered all the Emperor's dreams in a single day. Having defeated his forces, they destroyed Vittoria and made off with all its tents as well as the imperial treasure,' the senator said, concluding his story.

'And this book was among his treasures,' said Martino. 'It was the one that he considered the most precious of all.'

'The tables of Fibonacci, the Pisan? Or Guido Bonatti's treatise on the mechanics of heaven?' Dante asked anxiously.

'Or the book about the dark art of alchemy, which he was said to have learned in Jerusalem during his crusade?'

A thin smile appeared on the old man's lips. 'An even greater work than that,' he replied, shaking his head. 'And one that only a few people can say they have really read. Because only one copy exists, and this is it.'

He lifted the painted panel, showing the frontispiece of the codex.

Dante and the Persian leaned towards the book that the senator held out to them. Manoello had also craned his neck in curiosity. Martino delicately turned the first page, to reveal the *incipit* to their eager eyes. Dante read a few words, written in thin characters like the Caroline script in use at the time, but traced with a nervous dash that made them strangely different from those of an ordinary copyist. 'But is this . . .' he murmured after a moment, disconcerted.

A tense silence had filled the room. It was the poet who broke it. 'I've always believed it was a legend.'

'It isn't, as you can see. This is the book on which perhaps the sharpest minds of the age have exercised themselves.'

'Or the darkest.'

A wry smile appeared on the Venetian's lips. 'Abu Tahir, Averroës, Michael Scotus, King Alfonso of Castile. Theirs are the voices that echo through these pages. Are these the men who would have spoken from the darkness?'

'Their great spirits were certainly the brightest. And their minds plumbed every question faced by the men of our time. But there is a deeper darkness, a blindness of the soul that sometimes obscures even the greatest spirits,' Dante replied, resolutely pulling the codex from the man's hands. He quickly scanned some other pages, as if to assure himself further of the nature of what was written there. Then he suddenly closed it, as if what he had read was burning his hands. 'The darkness of those who deny the Word and its incarnation. This book mocks Christ, and before him the prophet Moses. And it compares them to the schismatic Mohammed, turning them into three street robbers.'

'Is it perhaps its title, *The Three Impostors*, that disturbs you, Messer Alighieri?' Martino cut in. 'And if I were to tell you the true identity of its author, whom I saw writing these pages with my own eyes? A man whom you have several times claimed to respect.'

Dante half-closed his eyes. He knew what the Venetian was preparing to reveal. 'Him?'

The other man moved his head, just slightly, but enough. 'It was upon these pages that the Emperor Frederick poured out his convictions.'

'*The Three Impostors* – the book in which is said to be contained all the blasphemy of the century . . .' Dante murmured with disbelief. 'It was written by Frederick himself! By the man who stunned the world. But who was also the hammer of the world . . .'

Martino had picked up the book. But rather than offer it to the senator, he put it back into Dante's hands. He seemed to be trying to defy his reluctance. 'Don't you feel the desire to read it?' he asked silkily. Hesitantly, the poet took the book. The marks seemed to dance beneath his eyes, as if a hidden force were trying to make them incomprehensible. He rubbed his eyelids with his free hand, then bent over the text once more.

'*However much everyone might wish to know the truth, only a few men are allowed to reach its depths. Because even if within knowledge of the truth there lies perfect happiness of the soul, many obstacles interpose themselves along that path, which is longer and more arduous than life itself. And among the greatest of these are the three Gorgons: Steno, violence, Euriale, deception, and Medusa, ghastly superstition – the youngest and most terrible of the three . . .*' the poet began to read. He enunciated the syllables firmly, out loud, as was his custom even when he was shut in his room.

Silence had fallen around him. He stopped speaking and looked up. Through his voice, the old sovereign's voice seemed to come back from the dead, bringing darkness with it. '*And three too are the impostors who plague man's freedom, falsifying the truth and bending his brow to the earth, the brow that is born to rise to the sky: Moses the hypocrite, Christ the bastard and Mohammed the thief . . .*'

The poet snapped the codex shut and threw it on the table, with a snap of the boards.

'Go on reading, Messer Alighieri,' Martino urged. 'There aren't many pages, but the knowledge condensed within them is worth every drop of their ink.'

The old man's voice echoed musically in his ears, no different from the voice that had whispered in the ears of Eve. Dante was distinctly aware of it, but couldn't overcome his desire to obey it. As he went on reading, he felt his soul disintegrating beneath the blows of that perfect prose, in which syllogisms followed on from one another with a cast-iron, invincible precision. They were not new arguments; in fact he had heard them set out many times at the Franciscan school in Santa Croce, always refuted by the theology teachers as cheap and sinful versions of ancient heresies.

But in this text, for the first time he saw them ordered and arranged by a fiendish and superior mind: not the superficial babble of the illiterate, or the mocking words that Guido Cavalcanti had often hurled against him, in their Florentine disputes, spiced with jokes and derision about the habits of monks and priests. That book went striding along a road which, horrified, he had refused to walk, closing his eyes and taking refuge every time in the solid rock of faith, the sole hope of salvation. That book, on the other hand, called to men to be men, to claim their birthrights; it roared like a proud lion.

Dante looked up from the codex. He was shaking violently, as if all his nerves had been jarred by what he had seen. The others had watched on in silence, and looked at him, waiting for his reaction. But a lump in his throat stopped him. He felt his teeth chattering, as if a sudden chill had invaded the room.

'I don't know . . . I don't . . .' he finally managed to say. 'This piece of writing unsettles the mind . . .'

The senator raised a finger. 'Every time a door opens onto the unknown, our senses grow fragile. We respect your anxiety, the same that has been felt by many illustrious men when the Truth appears.'

'The Truth?' Dante said in a strangled voice. He wanted to reply, but his voice died in his throat, as if it had been thrown in chains by what he had just read. He lay back on his seat, stretching out his legs and resting his chin on his hands. He was trying to impose some sort of order on the chaotic thoughts that crowded into his mind. Meanwhile he observed the faces of his three interlocutors through half-closed lids. And their enigmatic expressions, the eagerness with which they seemed to be awaiting his judgement about something that undermined the very foundations of every faith.

Three men who were prey to distorted ideas, and who wanted him to join them in a venture born solely of pride and a craving for power.

'But there will be time to talk about it again,' the senator interrupted him once more. 'Messer Kansbar has discovered that you are adept in the science of the heavens.

And he too has something that is sure to interest you. So show us what you said you were going to.'

Kansbar picked something up from the foot of his bench. It looked like a little leather bag, tied at the mouth with a cord. He loosened the string and took out an object wrapped in scarlet cloth. Then he took off the cloth as well. A cube appeared, perhaps each side a foot or so long, of gleaming ebony. One of the faces bore a big brass circle, and on one side a little handle protruded, it too made of metal.

The Persian delicately pushed the box towards the poet, inviting him with a nod to take a closer look at it. Dante leaned forward.

The metal circle was carved with a dense network of tiny characters, and pivoted in the middle were a series of needles of different lengths. The poet counted seven of them, then looked up and cleared his throat with embarrassment.

'It's Greek . . . I don't understand.'

Kansbar gave a little understanding smile. Dante felt irritated by his benevolence, but decided to accept his momentary state of inferiority. 'What is it?' was all he said.

Instead of replying, the other man gripped the handle with his hand and turned it firmly. The needles immediately started rotating around the face at different speeds, stopping in positions that formed an irregular radial pattern on the circle.

Dante followed its movements with curiosity, unable to understand.

'When was it that you drew destinies from the stars, Messer Alighieri?'

'Just before my departure from Florence,' the poet replied, puzzled.

'It took you a lot of work, I should imagine.'

'The celestial movements are perfect, but complex. Deferents and epicycles require the greatest attention, and error lurks within every measurement, ready to disturb even the most accurate calculation. Hours, a whole night,' the poet concluded.

'You remember, at least in its broad outline, the table of angular position?'

'Of course,' Dante replied, narrowing his eyes. He scoured his memory for that ill-omened result, which came back to him in all its malign splendour. 'The Moon was moving into Capricorn, the sun was in Libra conjoined with Venus. And Mars, in treacherous Scorpio. The heavens seemed to break down into a forest of contradictions, far from favourable to the meditative work for which I was preparing myself.'

Kansbar listened to him, approving each of his statements in turn. The astral chart, in the poet's reconstruction, wasn't just a cold geometrical exposition: it was becoming a tale of destinies and emotion. Life.

'And yet, study the position of the pointers. Those Greek

characters that escape you indicate their meaning. A wonderful crown, that begins here,' said the Persian, pointing with his fingernail to one of the dividing lines on the outer rim of the circle. 'This is the spring equinox, followed by the twelve signs of the Zodiac. This one is the pointer of the sun,' he went on, running a finger along one of the needles. 'Here. In the last degrees of Libra. And the Moon, on the cusp of Capricorn. And Mars, in the twenty-eighth degree of Scorpio.'

Dante opened his eyes wide. 'That's impossible . . .' he murmured. He couldn't believe his own eyes. This pagan must surely have been enchanting him with some kind of magic.

Kansbar sensed his incredulity. 'Do you think it's a co-incidence? Would you like to have irrefutable proof?'

'Give it to me, if you can.'

'I'd like to make the machine reveal the stars of Caesar, or of the Emperor Frederick.'

'But they are known, and you could have them pre-arranged in the position of the pointers. Somehow,' Dante replied doubtfully.

'Yours, then?'

'Mine?'

'Of course. I don't know your date of birth, and neither does anyone else in the whole of Rome.'

*

DANTE HESITATED. To reveal his stars would be to give the pagan the key to his soul. At least for the part that the sky had imprinted directly upon the wax of his soul. But the temptation was too great, after what he had seen. 'I was born at midnight on the twenty-ninth of May, in the year of our Lord 1265.'

Kansbar moved something on the side of the machine. Then he operated the handle again, and immediately the various pointers started rotating, stopping in a new fan of positions.

'A brilliant spectacle celebrated your birth, Messer Alighieri,' the Persian exclaimed, after carefully examining the result. 'As if the heavens had summoned all their luminaries to shine on the night of your arrival in the world. Here, on the cusp of Taurus, glorious Jupiter, melancholy Saturn and swift Mercury came together that night, in a conjunction that gave light to the whole quadrant. But it is sad to think that so much light was not watched over by signs of good fortune. Because Jupiter in the quadrature with the ascendant marks the whole of your life with a shadow – a shadow that will go with you always, targeting you with his beams. But by strewing obstacles in your path, fate is somehow helping you: Venus in Cancer will mark your loves with torment. But March in glorious Leo is your strength. You will shield yourself against the blows of misfortune.'

The poet held his hand out towards the machine,

grabbing it from the Persian's hands. Then he carefully studied what the other man had shown him. The details of the dial were still not entirely clear to him, but what he had understood was enough to astonish him. Its astral theme was there in front of his eyes, calculated with inconceivable speed.

He handed the mechanism back to Kansbar. His eyes ran from the Persian's face to the machine, still wondering which was more extraordinary, the machine or the man in charge of it.

'Who built this marvel?' he asked at last. 'I can almost believe the things they say about your land, that there are spirits down there that dwell among the stones of the desert, whispering the secrets of nature into the ears of men!'

'It was not my people that made it. Many centuries ago the Greeks in all their greatness developed its design. I found only their story in the library in Baghdad. An ancient papyrus, brought there by the Caliph after the sack of Alexandria.'

'What does the story say?' Dante asked anxiously.

'On the island that you call Rhodes, at the time when the first Caesar was bringing his eagles around the world, there lived the maker of this machine. He made three copies before he died, and joined the stars that he had studied with such passion. This one went to Alexandria, one was dispatched to Athens and disappeared into the sea.

The third reached Rome, and was given to the College of Augurs.'

'But no chronicles record this wonder . . .'

'The Augurs were priests, and guarded their knowledge jealously. More than one of them foresaw its destruction – because the machine made it possible even for the people to calculate the movements of the heavens, and because it demonstrated that all their certainties were based on a false principle.'

'False? But the machine gives a precise position of the stars, confirming their undying order!'

'Precisely for that reason. What do you know of the movements of the heavens, Messer Alighieri?'

'The teachings of the great Aristotle, completed in the work of Ptolemy of Alexandria.'

'That the Earth lies motionless at the centre of the created universe, and the stars crown it in a necklace of heavenly epicycles?'

'Precisely, since the first gesture of God, in a certain and immutable way.'

'That isn't how the heavens turn the bodies. Have you ever investigated the meaning of nature, its perceptible phenomena?'

'I've heard lectures in physics and metaphysics . . .' Dante replied cautiously.

'But those are the words of sages, sometimes veiled with the blanket of their prejudices. Observing its perceptible manifestations, have you never discerned its deepest laws, its ultimate law, in fact?'

'Which is?'

'That nature in its every action takes the shortest path. And because nature is the mirror of God, his determination too is reflected in that glass.'

Dante hesitated. There was something in the man's words – that suggestion of identifying nature with God, creation with the Creator – that sounded dangerously close to heresy. 'God loves simplicity?' was all he could answer.

'Yes. Don't you say, in your religion, that the simple will inherit the Earth? That same principle applies in the celestial plan. But Aristotle and Ptolemy did not choose the simplest path. Their intellects, which so loved differences, went down a blind alley. While the straight path was taken by others. Even the Emperor, in his proud folly, guessed the truth. I am speaking of the great Nero.'

'Nero, the one who burned Rome? Are you making him a champion of knowledge?' Dante replied, disconcerted.

'The will of God follows mysterious paths. As if his infinite spirit were content with mockery,' Kansbar replied.

'Don't be too severe on the old Emperor. Did you know that the Roman people still paid homage to his grave until just over a century ago?' Saturniano broke in.

'You are blaspheming! The first persecutor of the Christians, the man who passed the death-sentence on Peter, whose grave you are still seeking!'

The senator raised his hand in surrender. 'Perhaps you will change your minds. But we are still listening to our friend's story,' he went on, nodding to the Persian.

'Preserved in Alexandria were many testimonies to knowledge and Roman history, you would be amazed, Messer Alighieri,' Kansbar went on. 'They were brought to Baghdad after the conquest of the city by the Caliph's armies. And the sages who lived there studied them intensely, and treasured it. A treasure that has come all the way down to us. The machine that I have shown you also owes its perfection to the principle that animates it, very different from the one that Aristotle and Ptolemy believed, and which you believe as well. I will prove it to you, if what I learned in Mesopotamia is true. And I would like you to witness it. And perhaps Messer Martino, too, who has in his long life explored all the seven sciences, will want to be with us.'

'Where?' Dante asked.

'Here, in Rome. I told you that the Augurs hid the machine from the people, but they certainly couldn't conceal it from their Emperor. And he used it to boost his pomp and his power, as you can read in the travel chronicles of Hermes of Alexandria, who visited Rome seventy years after the start of your era. One of the few books that escaped the burning of the library. Tomorrow, if you like, you too will know it.'

Dante was puzzled. His mind was still unsettled by what he had seen. But more than anything he was troubled about what he had read in Frederick's book. The insult that the Emperor delivered to all his convictions. And yet he couldn't react, the worm of doubt was already at work inside him, eating away at a myriad of cracks within his consciousness until they opened up an abyss. He stammered something, confused.

'Stay and be my guest for tonight, Messer Alighieri. I have already requested that you be given a cubicle, where you will be able to rest. And if you like, you can go on reading the pages of that book.'

Dante hesitated for a few moments, then nodded. His hand had moved involuntarily towards the codex. The senator followed his movement with a gleam of mischief in his eyes.

A SERVANT had led him along a corridor to an internal courtyard and from there to one of the cubicles that opened up beneath the portico. A sudden weariness had fallen upon him, and every part of his body painfully clamoured to abandon itself to sleep.

But the book that he still clutched in his hand seemed to burn under his fingers. The servant had prepared a lit candle for him before withdrawing. He sat down on the bed, with the codex resting unopened on his knees, then furiously opened it, returning to the page that he had read in the presence of the others.

In the flickering light of the candle, which seemed to transform each single letter into the scratching of a demon, he began to read out loud. And the Emperor's words began to flow into his mind first like the smooth gurgle of a stream, and then suddenly with the deafening thunder of an irresistible cascade, which swept everything away in front of it. An ear-splitting roar in which a thousand voices seemed to commingle, screaming into his ears a truth against which he had always fought, but which shone in front of him now with the power of the light that had shone on the brow of Satan. And among those thousand voices he made out, mocking and triumphant, the voice of Guido Cavalcanti. 'God doesn't exist, Dante. And you know it too!'

Did he know it too? Had he always known it?

He had stopped reading, snapping the codex shut. But around him he was still aware of a distant hum of words. Someone in the building was reciting something too. He thought he recognised the same sounds he had heard on Fiamma's lips. He leaped to his feet and went to the door of the room: on the other side of the courtyard he saw a white figure slipping among the columns and darting behind a corner. The voice had broken off, too.

In the shadow he thought he could still make out the figure, which seemed to be waiting. He took a few steps beyond the threshold, towards the patch of white that flickered in the shadow of the portico on the other side.

He had just reached the middle of the courtyard, and was walking around the *impluvium* when he clearly heard the sound of silvery laughter, along with a quick rattle like quick footsteps on a metal surface.

The white patch had moved quickly along the colonnade before stopping again. Dante quickened his pace, trying to catch up with it. Again he heard the laughter exploding in the darkness: he was sure it was a woman.

The image of Fiamma flashed before his eyes: it must be hers, that slender arm that he now saw protruding from behind the column, waving back and forth like a silent call. Without thinking he hurled himself towards the portico, dragged by an irresistible impulse. The woman, too, had started running away, slipping and hiding among the columns as if trying to keep an obstacle between her and her pursuer at all times. As she did so, her laughter rang out, frantic now, broken every now and again only by the effort of running.

The space that separated him from the woman was getting shorter. With one last leap the poet was behind her, and reached his arms out towards her. But before he could grasp her, Fiamma suddenly turned and froze.

Pulled along by his own momentum, he stopped just a few feet from her panting body. He felt her breath on his face, filled with a distant scent of flowers.

'What do you want from me, Messer Alighieri?' she breathed into his face. Her eyes sparkled with a guile that disturbed him. Behind her girlish features, Fiamma's face betrayed a hidden lust that filled him with uncontainable arousal.

He pulled himself together. This girl was his host's daughter, under his roof. He had to get away from here as soon as possible. If anyone surprised him in that situation, his honour would be lost. And perhaps he would pay for his weakness with his life, to the senator's righteous rage.

But suddenly Fiamma held out a hand and stroked his cheek. He felt her fingers brushing his face, giving him a jolt as if it were red-hot iron. He slipped to his knees, his arms wrapped around Fiamma's legs. With a smile, the girl bent her face towards him. Dante stretched forward in search of her lips, but her fingers pushed him firmly away.

Unsettled, he got up, his ears still ringing with the crystalline laughter of the girl, who still kept him at a distance with her hand. Then Fiamma suddenly grew serious.

'What you want is forbidden to me,' she whispered. 'What I too might wish for,' she added with a sigh that filled the air with her celestial perfume once more.

Dante didn't understand. But he lowered his head in a sign of respect.

'I will do it . . .' he murmured. 'Whatever you ask.'

'Anything? You have a major task ahead of you.'

'I will write – the crusade, its songs. I will do it!' the

poet replied animatedly, guessing what Fiamma was about to say.

But the girl smiled again. 'Maybe your voice will be called to celebrate something even greater,' she said enigmatically.

'Greater?'

'Promise you'll be with me at that moment. That you won't abandon me,' she went on without answering his question. She seemed suddenly sad. She held her hand out towards the poet, then abruptly turned and vanished through a doorway in a corner.

DANTE SLOWLY went back to his room and fell on his bed. The terrible book was still beside him; it seemed to be calling to him.

II

14th November, in Senator Spada's villa

THE SUN was already high in the sky when Dante woke up. The noises of the day rang out inside the building: the quick footsteps of the servants, the muffled sound of people busy going about their work in the big villa, a sharp smell of smoke and freshly baked bread in the air.

He had slept longer than he wanted to, he said to himself, sitting up on the bed. Someone must have come in while he was asleep, because he saw clean clothes laid out neatly beside his bed.

He quickly got dressed and went out in search of the other inhabitants of the house. Outside he bumped into Martino and Kansbar, who seemed to be waiting for him. For a moment he thought they hadn't even been to bed, and that theirs were the voices that he had heard in the darkness, in counterpoint to the voice of the senator's daughter. They both seemed to be perfectly awake, and ready to move.

'I was waiting for you, Messer Alighieri. Senator Spada

sends you his regards, and asks you to forgive his absence. Important commitments called him away before dawn to the Senators' Palace,' the Persian said indifferently.

'And Fiamma?' the poet asked cautiously.

'The senator's daughter has left the house as well. You know about her passion for hunting. She was heading to a hunt over by Via Nomentana. If you like, there's a carriage ready to take us to our destination.'

'Where's that?' asked Dante.

'You'll see. It's something you can't imagine.'

Puzzled, the poet moved after them, following them along the labyrinth of rooms that the two men seemed to know perfectly.

A cart was waiting outside the villa, with a servant on the coachman's seat. They climbed aboard, and immediately the vehicle set off. This time Dante recognised the route that he had taken before, coming down from the Campidoglio. They rode alongside the Baths of Diocletian, then carried on down towards the Campo Marzio, on the straight road leading along the ridge of the Quirinal. But before taking their final descent, which would have led them in the direction of the Forum, the cart turned left, running alongside a new peak, beyond which the upper edge of the Colosseum jutted above the jagged line of the horizon. They passed by a new block of ruins, almost as imposing as the ones they had seen before.

'What are these walls?' Dante asked eventually.

'The remains of another baths, the one built by Emperor Trajan. We should be there soon.'

THE THREE men were strolling about on the left-hand edge of the Baths. At the foot of the Oppian Hill there was a path of beaten earth that climbed past vines and vegetable gardens fenced with small dry-stone walls. In places the climb was so steep that it even challenged the donkeys, which could be seen moving around here and there, loaded with barrels.

Dante had already had to clutch several times at the scrub around them, to avoid slipping back. In front of him the Persian and old Martino were climbing quickly, as if driven by inexhaustible energy.

'Come on, Messer Alighieri!' the Venetian urged him, turning towards the poet with an indecipherable expression. 'Soon you'll be able to see something that will amply repay your efforts.'

For a moment Dante thought he was mocking him, and redoubled his efforts to keep up. In front of them, beyond the crest of the hill, he could see the ruins of Trajan's Baths, which dominated the whole of the boggy valley between the Caelian Hill and the Palatine. Big arches and spurs of reddish wall loomed towards the sky, surrounded by towers and shacks erected behind the ancient building. Here, too, the Roman remains reminded Dante of the carcase of a big marine animal, on whose remains a new life of lichen and parasites had flourished over the centuries.

'Is that where we're heading?' the poet asked breathlessly.

'Those?' Martino replied, pointing to the walls. 'No, they're in the hands of the Milesians, who built their fortresses there. It wouldn't be wise to approach, like that, without an invitation. No, not up there. But down below – that's where we're heading,' he added, continuing enigmatically on his way.

They climbed on up the twisting path, and then the Venetian turned resolutely towards the right, leaving the path and stepping among the laurel and bramble bushes that dotted the hill.

They walked on for another hundred yards until they reached what looked like a compact wall of volcanic rock.

'Here we are,' Kansbar declared, turning to the poet. 'Now you will have proof of your false science.'

Dante took a better look at what the old man was pointing to. It was not, in fact, a natural wall, but the still-compact remains of a building made of big square blocks. Blocks that seemed to have fused with one another over the centuries, with the work of water and wind. In the joints between the stones there were thorny climbing plants, giving the whole area the appearance of a rocky outcrop. In fact, taking a closer look, Dante could discern the outline of an arch, still partly hidden by a large pile of earth and other detritus that had built up in front of it. Other big clumps of earth and roots hung down from above, hiding the summit.

'This place was buried, like the rest of the hill,' Martino said. 'The heavy autumn rains carried some of the surface away at the top, revealing the traces of things hidden underneath. The rumour spread, and reached all the way to me.'

'Things hidden underneath? What do you mean?'

With a big sweep of his hand, Martino took in the panorama around them. 'Strange as it may seem, what we have just climbed isn't one of the hills of Rome, but the magnificent remains of a building that our forefathers wanted to hide from sight, to erase even the memory of the outrages committed here. This is one of the entrances to the palace of Nero, the ill-famed Domus Aurea that was the triumph of his pride and also the cause of his fall.'

In disbelief, Dante looked up, observing what the other man was pointing out to him. To his right the mass of the Colosseum rose towards the sky, obscuring from view the hill on the other side. But what lay under his feet could be no less majestic, he thought. If what Martino had said was true, and it struck him as impossible, that palace would have had to be so big that it would contain a whole city. And how could it possibly have disappeared from view? Not even Titans could have piled up so much earth as to bury it, as the old man claimed. In Florence, when the flat ground had been laid over the ruined towers

of the Uberti fortress to make way for the new palace of
the Commune, it had taken months of work and hundreds
of mules just to excavate the rubble. How was it possible?

'You mean the whole palace was hidden beneath the
earth?'

Martino glanced at him ironically. 'I don't think you
fully understand, Messer Alighieri. The whole hill is
nothing but the ruined husk of the house of Emperor
Nero. I have brought you here to give you proof. And
more than that, to enter with you into its most extraordinary secret.'

'What's that?' Dante asked anxiously. The Persian, beside
them, stepped forward as well.

'You'll see. Let's light the torches that we've brought
with us. From here on their light will be all we have to
guide us.'

Dante mechanically loosened the ties of the bundles,
and took out a bundle of resinous branches. Then, with
rapid blows of the steel on the firestone, he lit the dry
filaments of the tinder, and soon succeeded in lighting the
first torch. A swirl of aromatic smoke rose from the crack-
ling flame. 'I'm ready,' he said, passing it to the old man
after using it to light his own.

They passed through the narrow entrance, pushing their
way among roots and piles of soil. Beyond the arch there
was a kind of large cave, with walls more than twenty feet
high, which plunged into the depths of the hill, disappearing

into the darkness. A pool of stagnant water obstructed their passage. Dante went in up to his ankles, walking on without worrying about the mud and the cold, so great was his curiosity. He raised his torch as high as he could, but the smoky flame showed him only a confusion of shadows. Above his head, the passage must have been closed by a barrel vault along the whole of its length.

Clear traces of paint and the remains of pieces of coloured marble testified that this space must once have been richly decorated. The end of the passageway, only a few feet away, was more regular. Leaving the pool of water, he felt beneath his feet the solid surface of big stone slabs, a floor that was also decorated with uninterrupted multicoloured lozenges.

As they walked on, the drawings on the wall could be seen more clearly. Monstrous, horrific shapes seemed to be reaching out towards them. Creatures that were half-animal and half-human, monsters repellent to nature.

What mind could have conceived this lewd spectacle for its own pleasure? the poet wondered. Nero had really cultivated within his own soul a ferocity that went beyond his criminal behaviour, but that extended to the complete rejection of any kind of moderation. It was folly that had built these rooms, just as fear had given shape to the Labyrinth of Crete in ancient times. That was to hide from view the shame of Pasiphae, but what could these corridors have hidden?

There was one more obstacle in front of them. A large column had fallen over, breaking and dragging with it part of the entablature above. The mass of rubble completely blocked a big square opening, lined with pilasters of carved marble.

Kansbar went and stood below the obstacle, still studying a map and talking to himself. 'Here, this must be the place,' he exclaimed, unable to hide his emotion.

The Persian threw himself on the ruins, beginning to climb the detritus, clutching with his hands and using his elbows and knees as if he were being chased by flames. He no longer seemed to be concerned about his companions, whether they were following him or not, such was the determination with which he hoisted himself upwards.

After a moment Martino began to do the same, demonstrating once again his extraordinary physical condition. Dante moved too, gripping a marble edge of the column and carefully propelling himself upwards.

He climbed, trying to avoid the slipping fragments that were constantly coming away under his weight, threatening to send him plummeting below. His fingers bled with his struggle against the stone splinters and the fragments of brick, but he continued to climb anyway, following the figures of the other two, who had now reached the opening and were passing through it to disappear onto the other side.

At last it was his turn to reach their destination: with

one final effort he gripped a slab that seemed to be solidly fixed in place, and hoisted himself up until his head poked into the passageway.

Then he stopped, stunned, breathless with his exertion and wide-eyed at what he saw before him.

Below him a huge hall opened up, its walls lost in the shadow. The only illumination was a beam of sunlight that came in through a circular window in the top, like the eye that provided light for the Pantheon church. But it was enough to leave him utterly dumbfounded. He breathlessly struggled to the end of the narrow passageway, and then slipped to the other side with no regard for his own safety, trying only to get to the ground as quickly as possible. With one last leap he dropped to the foot of the rubble, ignoring the pain of the jolt.

He was beside the perimeter wall of a wide empty space, an octagon whose sides were carved with deep niches, so as to make it look almost as if the huge dome were suspended above their heads by some secret force. The room was as big as the Baptistery in Florence, Dante thought in amazement, slightly smaller than the Pantheon, but its decorated dome was not dissimilar. Beneath his feet, by the light coming in through the ceiling, shone the remains of a marble floor that must once have dazzled the eye.

In the middle of the hall stood a block of stone, perhaps the base of a throne, the poet thought. And in fact the

GIULIO LEONI

whole room looked like an imperial audience hall, if one imagined how it must have looked when every foot of the walls was covered with precious marble and gleaming stones. And as for the dome . . .

He looked up, trying to make out the details, in the shadow behind the ray of light. Only then did he notice something that had escaped him until that moment: fragments seemed to hang from the vault as if ancient lamps were still hanging up there from the days when they had bathed Nero's triumphs in light. He studied them with greater circumspection – those things must have been hanging up there for centuries, and could come down on their heads at any moment, if their footsteps had had the slightest effect on whatever it was that held them up.

But what could it be? He turned towards his companions, planning to draw their attention to what he had discovered. They too were looking up, with their eyes fixed on the vault.

'So, Messer Alighieri!' he heard the Persian say. 'Look how Caesar's craftsmen were able to translate into an extraordinary work of art the teachings of the machine that you have had the opportunity to study!'

Ignoring the possible danger, Kansbar had run towards the middle of the hall, climbing onto the marble plinth. From there he raised his arm to point above his head. 'Behold, the true motion of the stars!'

Impelled by the man's shouts, and forgetting all his

fears, Dante too moved towards the middle. Now he could see that the vault above his head didn't look like stone, as he had imagined. It looked as if it was built from a huge scaffolding made of boards of various lengths, connected by panels that were also made of wood: it was this alternation of voids and volumes, and the shadows that the structure cast on the ceiling, that had given him the erroneous perception of being in a kind of copy of the Pantheon dome.

'Quick, let's light all the torches!' shouted Kansbar, highly excited.

Dante too was in a state of mounting exhilaration. With Martino's help, he drew from their bags all the torches they had at their disposal, and quickly lit them one after the other from Martino's torch. A tremulous light spread through the whole of the vast space, at last allowing him to see the arrangement of globes of different sizes that hung above their heads.

For a moment he felt as if he were paralysed. A huge diagram of the heavens had been painted at the top of the dome. In the days when this machinery had been made, the globes of the various heavenly bodies must have been covered by a precious mosaic, of which only a few fragments remained, but enough to allow their nature to be deciphered in allegorical terms. The god Mars, and Venus, and swift Mercury. The Moon with her silvery face, and majestic Jupiter, and far-off Saturn, with its extreme and sad, slow orbit. Behind them, on semicircular panels that had by now disappeared almost entirely, a phantasmagoria of pieces of mounted glass must have represented the more distant stars.

But where was the light-giving Sun? One would have expected a gilded sphere, inserted in the third position that Ptolemy assigned to it in the hierarchy of the spheres. But in its place was a dark body, connected to the Moon by what looked like a kind of metal arm.

'Do you recognise the extreme precision of this representation?' he heard the Persian asking him, turning to face him.

'It's extraordinary . . . but it seems to me that you're neglecting the first of the luminaries, and the order of the heavens doesn't seem to me to respect the word of Aristotle—' But before he could finish his objection, his eye fell involuntarily on the block of marble that marked the middle of the room, and on that of the complex machine orbiting up above.

Suddenly he understood.

'This . . . is the sun?'

'Yes, Messer Alighieri. Now you see! Nero, in all his pride, assigned to his throne and to himself the place that is, in Creation, attributed by the eternal law to the Sun: the centre! On that throne he sat, a new Sun, to enjoy the homage of the stars and the planets. Thus usurping, with his vainglory, the centre of the universe.'

'That's impossible!'

'And yet you see it before you. It is this presupposition that makes possible the precise functioning of the machine that I showed you. And this work is confirmation of it.'

Dante was disconcerted. 'But the ancients, who also formulated such hypotheses, admitted it only as a geometrical possibility! This, on the other hand, is meaningless, relegating the seat of man – God's chosen creature – to the rank of a peripheral satellite of an immaterial mass of flame. This diagram denies the Scripture, which clearly assigns primogeniture to the Earth in the order of Creation, and to the two luminaries the sole function of serving it!'

'Your Book . . . of course,' Kansbar replied. 'But if today you can see the evolution of this model, all your doubts will be dispelled by the crystalline evidence of its soundness.'

Dante was still standing stock-still, gazing at the ceiling. He went on stubbornly shaking his head. 'All of this once moved, like the real heavens?'

'Certainly, according to the stories.'

'But who could have set it in motion? It would have taken a huge force, like the power of God that moves the real heavens!'

'You're forgetting the hundreds of slaves whose strength the Emperor was able to rely on, hidden in the rooms set back beyond the walls of the hall. Or even—'

The Persian had suddenly broken off. He seemed to be listening for something. 'Don't you remember the big tubs of water that we encountered?'

'You said they were the old cisterns of the Baths!'

'Exactly so. But that means there must have been a branch of the aqueduct somewhere around. Can't you hear a distant gurgling?'

Dante too pricked up his ears. In the absolute silence that had fallen in the hall, once the echo of their voices had subsided, he really did think he could hear a distant rush of water.

Martino nodded agreement, pointing to a spot beneath their feet. 'It must be here, the old piping.'

'If the vault was activated by hydraulic force, as I have seen in the marvellous fountains of Baghdad, there must be a mechanism linked to a mill wheel somewhere nearby. Perhaps in one of the niches that open up in the wall,' said Kansbar. 'Let's see if we can find something.'

Dante and the other two headed off along the perimeter, exploring the great cave with the light of their torches. A shout from Martino grabbed their attention.

'Come over here, I've found something!'

Dante hurried towards the spot, followed by the Persian. Martino was standing against the wall, and held his torch lowered towards something that emerged from the floor. It looked like a pair of levers, of metal corroded by rust, which poked out from the wall. Kansbar took a step forward, too, energetically testing the second lever without any greater success.

The two men exchanged a discouraged glance. 'It looks as if the machine has fallen into disrepair,' Martino said. 'After so much time it would have been crazy to hope—'

'Wait,' Dante interrupted. 'If the mechanism is anything like the one that connects the force of the water to the millstone, its workings will be similar as well. There are two gear-wheels that activate the movement: perhaps those two levers have to be activated simultaneously, if the command is to have its effect. Push that iron bar towards me, and I will do the opposite, until the two bars are aligned.'

The poet bent with all his strength over one of the levers, while the other did the same. For a long moment it seemed as if nothing was happening, then slowly the iron bars began to yield, running along their hidden conduits, while a thin powder of rust and bricks slipped slowly to the ground, accompanied by a distant creak. Fragments rained from above, forcing the poet to shield himself with his arm, followed by the loud crash of something heavy and dangerous. Before looking back up, he saw by his feet part of the starry panel, which had shattered into a thousand pieces, sprinkling the floor with splinters of coloured glass.

The whole vault had suddenly begun to turn, in a

crescendo of screeches and creaks. The bigger globes span according to their orbits, scattering around them a powder of fragments that passed through the ray of sunlight as they fell to earth, resplendent as meteorites.

For a moment Dante felt as if he was back in the hills of Florence, when on high summer nights the skies glittered with a rain of light. But his mind immediately returned to the cave, summoned by Kansbar's voice. The Persian was overjoyed.

He raised an arm towards the vault. 'Look! That's how the imperial *mechanici* translated into action the ideas of Pythagoras, Heraclides, Hipparchus! See the perfection of the geometry of the heavens that springs from it, and how the various bodies relate to one another in space with order and simplicity, without resorting to the infinite adjustments that Ptolemy was forced to introduce into his system.'

Dante's eyes followed the spots where the old man was pointing. His convictions were starting to yield, even though he still clutched at them with all his might. And yet it was his eyes that denied them, even before his reason did. He looked away, confused.

At that moment a crash more violent than the others called his attention upwards. The machine of the heavens had leaned to one side, although it went on turning, propelled by the force of the underground water. He saw some of the globes breaking against the stone surface of the vault, and then with another chain of almighty crashes the whole structure came away from the surface, spinning freely to the ground.

In unison, the three men threw themselves into one of the niches, just in time to avoid being crushed by the mass that smashed a few feet away from them, throwing up a storm of dust.

The echo of the crash filled the hall and the labyrinth of rooms with its great roar, only gradually fading away. Kansbar was the first to emerge from his shelter and walk around the rubble. 'No one will ever see this marvel again. We were the last men on Earth to do so,' he exclaimed with gleaming eyes.

'Perhaps we shouldn't have,' the poet murmured. 'Where is God now?'

'In the light,' the Persian replied, pointing to the ray of sunlight that still illuminated the base of the ancient throne.

'In the darkness,' Martino replied, pointing to the sequence of gloomy rooms that could be glimpsed beyond one of the niches.

THEY WENT back along their way to the entrance. Once they were there, almost without exchanging a word, they parted.

Dante slowly returned to his lodgings, crossing the maze of streets to the river almost without noticing the mass of people swarming past him. He walked lost in thought, trying to do battle within himself against what he had seen, to send it back to the dark realm from which nightmares come.

He wanted to get back to his writings, like a shipwreck clinging to the remains of his ship. He wanted to throw himself into his work, but his mind seemed numb, and the voice of love dictated nothing to him. How could he go on, now? The whole form of everything he had imagined was crumbling within him. He should have been thinking about something completely different, but what, he wondered desperately?

Meanwhile he continued on his way. He walked quickly, head lowered, his face half-hidden by the veil of his cap, straight to the river. In front of him a wide square opened up, full of the carts and stalls of greengrocers, and surrounded by the tumbledown walls of houses as tall as towers. Here again, though, stone and brick predominated over wood, unlike the buildings in his own city of Florence. The square blocks of the buildings, with their orderly rows of openings screened by cloth coverings, rose to a height of several storeys. At ground level the doors of countless shops, coach-houses and stables opened up, all mixed together in an inextricable and foul-smelling tangle. It seemed as if there wasn't a single superintendent in any of the streets to impose order, or perhaps that a drunk had been left in charge of the task.

Dante constantly had to push his way through crowds of people, some of them actually lying in the street, and among the stalls sticking out of the shops, invading the pavement cluttered with all the filth generally found in a food market. He was surprised by what he saw: until that moment he had believed that Rome was merely a huge graveyard of memories, with very few inhabitants. But then all its few inhabitants must have arranged to meet in that square and in the narrow streets around it, so great was the swarming crowd of people jostling and cursing and calling out to each other. Or fighting, in sudden street brawls that broke out for reasons not readily understood.

A numb rage rose up within him. Where was the people that could have been crowning the emperors? He looked at the faces that crowded around him, in search of a trace of the splendour he had read about in his beloved authors, and saw nothing but feral mugs similar to – or perhaps even worse than – the ones that had come from the countryside of Tuscany to bring their rural savagery to his city. It seemed that the same leprosy that had corroded the marble of the Baths and the Forum had also attacked the living body of the city; and, as time passed – now tearing away a cornice and now a capital, breaking a column here and bringing down an arch there, drying up an aqueduct, shattering a rampart – that same plague was spreading across the faces, blinding an eye, disfiguring a lip, stiffening an arm. Never in his life had he seen so many cripples, limbless people, beggars sitting under the porticos of the residences of the senior prelates and cardinals like a besieging army.

For a moment he surprised himself by imagining what he would do if he had been responsible for civic order. How he would have ordered that whole rabble to be swept away with riding crops, after opening all the drains of the fountains to flood the city and sweep everything away, everything. Perhaps the truth was that this city was too majestic, too full of memories and pomp, still to be inhabited. And after its first sacking, its citizens would have done better to imitate those of Aquileia when it was laid waste by Attila, and go far away, to found the city of men elsewhere, after abandoning the city of gods and heroes.

As these thoughts filled his mind, Dante was aware of a hand gripping him by the elbow, trying to hold him back. He gave a start and looked round to see who it was. From one of the arches of the building a half-naked arm stretched out to clutch at him.

'Messere, why in such a hurry? Wouldn't you like to rest your feet for a moment? You're drenched with rain, and there's fire and wine inside for you. You'll have plenty of time for your devotions, with the other pilgrims.'

He instinctively tried to break free. But the grip that held him there was firm. His movement served only to pull from the shadows of the doorway a half-dressed woman, whose brightly coloured clothes were open to her chest, showing a large section of her breasts. A face humbled by the marks of age and vice, which heavy make-up tried in vain to conceal.

'Come, what are you afraid of?' the woman went on, still trying to hold him back with all her strength. 'A nice handsome man like you? Don't you want to quench your thirst a bit, recover from the efforts of your journey?'

'Leave me be, whore!' Dante cried, recognising the sort of woman he was dealing with. He went on vigorously shaking his arm, but still couldn't break free. Then a second woman's voice from within joined the cries of the hag.

'Leave him alone with his thoughts, Maria. He's not the kind of man to have dealings with us.'

Dante immediately stopped struggling, struck by the familiar Florentine accent that had uttered those words. But, above all, it was the voice that he thought he recognised.

'Pietra . . . is that you?' he stammered, his mouth wide with astonishment. A second woman had appeared in the doorway, younger than the first, her raven hair loose over her thin shoulders, her green eyes bright in a face as thin as a cat's. 'It's you!' he repeated, mystified. 'What on earth are you doing here in Rome?'

The young woman burst out laughing. That harsh, vulgar laughter that the poet knew well. Laughter that had never been an act of homage to the gods of joy, but that was born in the taverns and alleyways of his city. Laughter that was intended to sound voluptuous, but came out only as a groan of humiliation.

'They're all coming to Rome, after the Jubilee. Gentlemen, and poets. Why not whores? And what about you, Prior? Have you left the clean bed of that holy wife of yours to creep under someone else's covers?'

'No . . . what do you mean?' he replied, finally breaking away from her grip. 'And I'm no longer a prior, I'm the ambassador of the Commune.'

The young woman laughed again, her laughter still more forced and husky. 'Yeah, I know. If you had any idea of the things people say between the sheets. But this is no place for diplomatic missions. People only come here if they're after something: a scrap of bread or a bit of love.'

'I'm not looking for either of those,' Dante exclaimed, huddling into his clothes as if to defend himself from everything around him.

Pietra seemed to be studying him. In that position, with her eyes half-closed and her lips pursed, she looked even more like a wild cat. Dante was distinctly aware of the subtle smell that she gave off, that mixture of humanity and cheap perfume that always went with her.

'So, aren't you coming in?' she asked indifferently.

'No!'

'Fine. Then off you go, you're keeping my customers away.'

Dante set off again with a nervous twitch. But after a

few paces he stopped. He stood motionless for a long moment, trying to overcome the desire that had suddenly awoken within him. Then he turned, seeing once again those eyes that seemed to burn their way into him. 'Who's been talking to you about me?'

'People. Merchants.'

Dante turned back. If Pietra had met someone who had just arrived, he might learn what had happened in his city after his departure. He quickly turned round again, but not before he had spotted a flash of satisfaction in the girl's eyes.

'Changed your mind?' she asked brazenly.

'It's not that . . . I want to know what's being said.'

'In Florence?' she said. Her face was cold, hostile. Unexpectedly she gripped him by the hand. Dante felt the woman's strong fingers clutching his and pulling them against his body. With a start he became aware of the bony curve of her hip, under the cloth of her tunic. Then Pietra leaned towards his face. He felt a damp warmth in his ear, a mixture of breath and words. 'Come inside, then,' she said, touching his neck with the tip of her tongue.

Shivering, he followed her into the shop, and then up a wooden staircase that led to a small room almost entirely occupied by a rough board bedstead. Ignoring the stale air that took the breath away, the girl turned towards him, with the superior air of a queen showing off her apartments. 'It's no worse than the rooms at Monna Lagia's brothel, Paradise – what do you think?' she cackled as she slumped onto the straw mattress and then gathered herself up in a corner, with her back against the wall and her arms around her knees.

The poet went and joined her on that poor bed, covered with canvas that bore the unmistakeable traces of many other men who had gone before him. He felt those green eyes coldly exploring his face.

'So? Tell me what you know about Florence,' Dante exploded, irritated.

'You're still fond of that city of scandals?'

'What are people saying?'

'That things are about to get better.'

Better? What did they mean by that? It sounded as if they trusted him, and trusted his diplomatic mission.

'Maybe it's better if you don't go back.'

'What? And why?'

Pietra shrugged. 'That's what they say.'

Dante bit his lips uneasily. But then he shrugged as well. Who knew what Pietra had worked out, who knew whom she had met.

'But who's Beatrice?' she asked all of a sudden.

Dante gave a start. 'What?'

'Beatrice, the girl you wrote about. The Portinari woman.'

'What do you know about her?'

Pietra burst out laughing, in her harsh, coarse laughter.

She laughed with her mouth open, without restraint, to hurt him. 'Do you think it's only your clever friends who are enjoying themselves behind your back? In Florence, in Monna Lagia's house, there was one girl who knew how to read. And sometimes in the morning we sat down around her to listen to a book.'

'Books, in Lagia's house?' he replied disdainfully.

'Words travel – sometimes they go a long way. And you always say too many of them. That stuff you wrote, is it true?'

'What?'

'The dream, the heart devoured, the god of love. Does that woman really make the air tremble when she walks?'

Dante closed his eyes tight, trying to drive away the sudden ache that raged in his temples. He took his head in his hands. 'It's a poetic image . . .' he murmured between clenched teeth. Then his fury took hold of him as the pain intensified. Why the hell did he have to explain anything to a whore? 'How could you understand?'

Instead of replying, the girl brought her hands to her knees and gripped the hems of her dress, lifting it along her body until she slipped it off her head. Then she stayed like that, naked on the bed, still clutching her tunic in her hand.

There had been no feeling in the gesture, just the ostentation of her body, thin and worn by the harshness of life. And yet still triumphant in its own way.

'Do you have that pain of yours again?' she said, noticing the grimace with which he had reclosed his eyelids. Still with his eyes closed, he became aware of her hand brushing his brow, then Pietra drew him to her, gently, pressing his face against her belly. Dante felt the girl's soft skin against his cheek, along with the strong, wild smell that rose from the soft down between her legs.

A swirl of images came alive in his mind, as he struggled against the girl's hands, which were now trying to free him from his clothes. Suddenly the indignity of the situation swept over him in all its horror. He wrenched himself away from her grip, but his strength seemed strangely unequal to the silken fury with which she was guiding him inside her, with the consummate mastery of an ancient trade.

Then, with all the desperation of a love too long denied, his strength suddenly subsided. He cried out that he loved her, and while his climax confused all his emotions, he still had the sensation of distant, angry laughter.

'You don't love me, Dante. You don't love anyone.'

12

15th November, early hours of the morning

DANTE PROPPED himself up on one elbow, exhausted. Not the faintest ray of light filtered through the little window: only the constant sound of the steadily falling rain.

He leaned forward slightly, just enough to see towards the east the faint glimmer of dawn just breaking. Pietra was sleeping next to him, curled up like a cat, her head hidden by one arm.

He pressed himself towards the woman, seeking in the warmth of her body a spark of the attraction that he had been unable to resist only a few hours before. But he felt nothing – even the perfume that he had found so intoxicating seemed to have disappeared. He shifted again and rested, eyes closed, against the wall behind him.

He felt drained. How was it possible that he felt nothing now, as if all the excitement that had swept him away with its invincible frenzy had vanished with the seed from his body? He recalled the song of his friend Cavalcanti,

his idea of love as a blind instinct, a passion that undermines and destroys the will of the rational soul. He thought
again of how he had fought against his ideas, in the days
when he still believed that love was an awakening of the
noblest part of man, a call from God through the voice
of the creature closest to him: woman. When in fact it
was merely the convulsion of the body, and the moisture
of the cloths in which they fought out their nocturnal
struggle. He reached a hand out towards Pietra's body,
which lay abandoned beside him, and gripped her arm,
clutching it tightly. He wanted to feel again the consistency
of her flesh, grasp in its yieldingness the secret of that
strength that defeated him every time.

Beneath his grip Pietra moved slightly, giving a grunt,
then half-opened her eyes, still gluey with sleep. He
shifted towards her, but the woman didn't seem to recognise him. She turned an empty and indifferent gaze upon
him. Serene.

Then he was filled with fury. He was sure that in her
sleep Pietra had left that pigsty, and was still travelling the
path that her irrational soul – the one that governs dreams
– had chosen. A path that he would never be called to
travel. He tightened his grip, resisting the temptation
to strike her. He wanted to break her dream, to inflict
pain upon her. Just as she had given him one more push
along the path of death.

But at that moment he became aware of hasty footsteps

outside the door, and then of the door creaking open. In a moment he saw the bed surrounded by armed men, and even before he could work out what was happening, iron-gloved hands gripped him, dragging him away and forcing him to his feet.

'Are you Messer Dante Alighieri, the Florentine?' the man who seemed to be the head of the group asked brusquely. There must have been at least five of them holding him there. Pietra had given a brief shriek, and now she too was awake, trapped in the bed, her face pale with terror.

He groped around, seeking an explanation for this aggression in the men's uniforms. On their tabards he could make out the double wave of the Caetani. Guards from the Castello, like the ones under the Decurion's orders. He quickly glanced around in the hope of seeing Caffaro. But a sixth man had appeared in the doorway, wearing the black and white habit of the Dominicans.

'Are you Alighieri?' the monk repeated icily.

'Yes. What do you want from me?'

'The Roman Inquisition wants to interrogate you,' was the man's only reply. Then he nodded to the other men, who were still holding Dante in their grip. 'Give him time to get dressed. Let there be no trace upon him of the lewd acts to which he has recently yielded.'

He felt the men's grip loosening, although their eyes remained intent upon his movements. Only then did he realise that he was completely naked, and he was seized with shame. He angrily picked his clothes up from the floor and quickly began to cover himself, under the amused eyes of the guards. Now he suddenly felt all the humiliation of the naked body, and thought that perhaps it was one of the torments destined for the souls of the damned.

A COVERED cart waited for him outside. He was pushed violently inside, among the curious and poisonous glances of the passers-by who filled the street, even at that hour of the day. He couldn't make out the scornful words they were exchanging, alternating with fearful glances at the armed men. 'Clear off, you lot!' he heard one of the guards shouting, as he kicked away someone who had got too close. 'Or you too will be coming to the Chancellery ball.'

The man hastily ran away, as the cart bounced off along the cobblestones. As the vehicle slipped around the bend in the road, Dante just had time to see Pietra, who had appeared half-naked at the door and was looking towards him. He thought she was saying something to him, but perhaps it was only his imagination.

The cart travelled a short distance. From the corner in which he was confined, among the massive bodies of the guards, he had no way of knowing where they were taking him. He was only aware of the constant bends in the road, and the fact that on several occasions their progress was obstructed, as if the cart was having difficulty getting down the alleyways, and sometimes having to slow down almost to a stop.

Eventually he noticed that the wheels were running along a more regular stretch of road, and a moment later he felt the vehicle coming to a standstill. He was dragged to the ground, as roughly as he had been loaded on board.

He was no longer out of doors, but in a wide space surrounded on all four sides by a colonnade. It looked like the internal courtyard of a large building.

The monk had moved quickly towards the colonnade, going past it and disappearing into the shadow of the portico. The guards followed him, dragging the poet with them towards a flight of steps that led to the upper floor, and from there to a corridor lit by narrow rectangular openings set along the wall at regular intervals.

At the end of the corridor an open door led into a new space, a completely bare hall, not especially big. Against the end wall stood a long throne that occupied the whole of that side of the room, held off the ground by a high platform. Sitting behind this bench the poet saw five or six monks, whom he recognised from their robes as belonging to the orders of the Dominicans and the Franciscans. Only one of them wore a normal habit, and no emblems, but a small golden crucifix on a chain around his neck. Another cross, this one huge and made of wood, hung from their shoulders.

A violent shove from behind hurled him to the ground, forcing him to genuflect before the monks. But the pressure eased, and he got back to his feet.

'What do you want from me? I'm the ambassador of Florence!' he cried out.

The monks reacted to the shout only with a quick exchange of glances. Then the man in the cassock pointed his finger straight at him. 'Before this court the attributes of the world are of little value. It is not for your secular functions that you have been summoned here to exonerate yourself, but for the poisonous plant that you have cultivated in your soul, watering it with the evil water of your disbelief, your arrogance and your lust.'

'What are you talking about? What are you accusing me of?' the poet replied.

The man clutched the bundle of papers that he had been holding under the table, and spread them out disdainfully before the poet's eyes. 'In our hands is a copy of the papers that are so dear to you. What did you mean with your verses, Messer Alighieri? Where is this forest of death of which you speak? And what are the three wild beasts who bar your way?'

'It is the tale of the bewilderment of the soul, in the forest of sin. And the beasts are an allegory of the dark forces that lead our honest consciences astray,' Dante replied, puzzled by what he had heard.

'And why did you choose the three noblest animals as

a sign of perversion? Symbols that immediately call to mind the kingdoms of France and Rome, rather than abject habits? Or is it not perhaps the case that you wish to allude to the majesty of Rome and the excellence of the sovereigns, with your defamations?'

'No,' he replied. But he had not been able to conceal a tremor in his voice. 'I concede that the ravenous she-wolf might have been mistaken for an allegory of the misgovernment of the Church, and the lion seen as an emblem of the King of France. That is not what they signify.'

'And why have you written this fable, far from the common experience of the ordinary people? In their simplicity they have an image of the living and the dead that is closer to the font of all Knowledge, the uncontaminated voice of the fathers of our Faith. What have you sought to add to their words?'

'One writes that which cannot be said. Because the words bound to the pen and, governed by the right metre, acquire a majestic order of their own, which alone makes them worthy of transcribing the truth. With the seal of the ordering mind, only then do they reveal all the most intimate secrets of nature; they become the mirror of the voice of God.'

'Blasphemer! You too, a layman, want to ape the word of God! As if you were one of His prophets, illuminated by his terrible grace. In what abyss of the spirit have you harboured such arrogance?' cried the inquisitor, clutching the crucifix that hung from his neck as if it were an anchor. 'What terrible lesson have you witnessed, without remorse, without fear of punishment, without holding yourself in abomination? What dark masters have you met on that road to perdition of which you speak in the *incipit*, and on which you wish to be followed by your wretched readers? What have you *done*, Messer Alighieri, to trouble the authority of the ancients and the mercy of the Sainted Women? You, a miserable grain in the infinite sands of God – you would have as your advocate no less a figure than the Mother of the Saviour! As if you had formed a pact with the great Power himself. At least the inveterate Jews believe with their foolish obstinacy that God might have chosen one people among all the others to sit on his right hand; but you believe that God wants to choose one sole man, you! The dark followers of Mohammed also humble themselves before the words of their book, but you claim to have written them yourself.'

Dante shook his head. 'It is just a poetic fiction, written to redeem man from the plague of sin, to which our human weakness condemns us.'

'Our weakness . . . condemns us? Are you trying to claim that man is irredeemably sinful? That a luminous God like Christ could not have produced an imperfect creature, and that creation is clearly the work of a malign god, to whose ills our flesh is heir?' the other man continued. Dante noticed a sudden honeyed, mischievous tone to his words. The bastard was putting into his words the articles of faith of the Cathar heretics, hoping that Dante would fall into the trap. He clenched his fists, while he thought very carefully about the words he would have to use in his reply.

'What do you believe, Messer Alighieri?' the other man urged. The monks witnessed the dialogue impassively.

The poet suddenly raised his head. 'I believe in the revealed truths, as the Church in its age-old wisdom has received and ordered them. And the poem that you have stolen from me is only the poetic transfiguration of the journey that the soul must take to reach its salvation, meditating on sin and its punishments, and on goodness and its glory. The form is that of a journey through the realms of the hereafter, because it is there that the hand of God most powerfully raises people up or casts them down.'

The inquisitors darted him a rapid glance, then their leader leaned forward from the throne once more. 'And why have you written this tale in the vulgar tongue, and in a truthful tone? Do you perhaps wish to appeal directly to the unlearned, playing with their naïvety and pretending that this journey really happened? In such a way as to corrupt minds responsive to the suggestions of evil? And imply that you believe yourself to be capable of violating the laws of God? You want to be a new Apollonius of Tyana, a second Simon Magus?'

'I want my words to be understood, in a language no

less noble than that of the Church Fathers, if it is used well. I want my work to be a monument in poetry!'

'And of course you would be capable of using it in the best possible way? And why, if it is the glory of letters that impels you, and not an insane craving to make yourself a prophet, why do you impoverish your spirit with a fairytale for children? A journey to hell! Not even at fairs in front of churches, not even the worst mountebanks would think of producing such a spectacle today, silly and boorish. Unless all your work is a monstrous deception!'

'What? What deception?' Dante replied in a choked voice.

'A hidden theme! In which, thanks to the meanings secreted in the scripture a very different, diabolical message is entrusted to these pages, concealed in the allegories and the allusions with which you have stuffed your verses. Like that accursed dog that is supposed to come down and deal with the Roman wolf! Who are you alluding to, Messer Alighieri? Are you predicting a return of the Emperor or, worse, one of his brigands, like Colonna? And why do you choose as your guide the pagan Virgil, an initiate in the magic arts, to escort you upon an undertaking that should in fact be witnessed by the paternal assistance of a saint or a Doctor of the Church?'

'I thought of Virgil because ... because ...' the poet began to explain, but the words died in his throat, suffocated by the immensity of what he wanted to say. He took a deep breath and started again. 'Because in the darkness of evil, reason alone can console us! And Virgil is the man who, throughout all the centuries, best represents through his symbols the force of the human mind. But when the journey is on the threshold of the light, a different spirit will act as my companion!'

'A different one? And who might that be?'

Dante hesitated for a moment. He clenched his fists uneasily. 'I don't know – yet. Perhaps St Bernard . . .'

At that name the inquisitor looked away, silently consulting his colleagues. 'Why St Bernard?' he continued a moment later, suspiciously. 'Why not Peter, or John? Why the man who gave his name to the Order of the Temple, and bestowed its rule upon it? Is he the one you want to celebrate, hiding behind his sanctity?'

Dante didn't reply. Again he clenched his fists, then proudly raised his head. Suddenly the fear he had felt until a moment before seemed to have melted away like snow in the sun. He felt everything sliding away from him, dragging with it his plans and dreams. All that remained was the duty that had been entrusted to him: he would obey until the last.

'I am Dante Alighieri, ambassador of Florence. And I have come to negotiate with the Pope over the fate of my homeland, not about allegories and poetic images. Consign to the flames those pages that concern you so, for my plans have changed.'

GIULIO LEONI

Puzzled, the inquisitor sat back, as a murmur ran all the way along the bench of monks. The man bit his lips, then an expression of triumph slowly spread across his face. 'So you acknowledge the insolence and insanity of what you have set down on paper?'

Dante agreed with an abrupt nod of his head. 'A different man wrote those lines. Nothing of him survives.'

Again the men on the bench exchanged a glance of perplexity. 'So the weight of our accusations has illuminated you?' the inquisitor suggested after a moment. Dante could clearly see the man's unease, the distrust that still lay unchanged behind his smug expression.

Again he agreed in silence.

'So you disown these blasphemous pages?'

Dante hesitated for a moment, then shrugged indifferently. But that gesture must have been enough for the inquisitors, because he saw their leader nodding to the guard to leave. He felt himself being pushed forward, while his mind was still aflame.

DANTE WENT back down the stairs, accompanied by two silent monks who left him at the door. At that moment, almost to greet his liberation, a blue flash rent the clouds, and the rain, after a violent explosion of thunder, began to fall with even greater intensity.

He took a few dazed steps, then stopped in the middle

397

of the square with his feet in a puddle that had formed among the remains of the ancient paving stones. He no longer even felt the icy streams that passed over his skin, running down the collar of his robe.

A new flash of lightning struck a short distance away, followed closely by a roar of thunder. He raised his head towards the leaden sky, shielding his eyes with the back of his hand. Was there something up there, beyond the pall of vapour that was dissolving in that deluge? Was that thunder really the voice of God?

No, there was nothing above him. And there was nothing inside him. He no longer felt anything. Perhaps Christ was really an impostor, and the Earth just an insignificant grain of sand, thrown to spin in the void like a plaything of older, different gods. And there wasn't even a soul, just a lump of passions, dragged along by the blind torment of lust.

He thought of the pain of his ancient masters, the ones before him who had reached this same threshold, from which he was now retreating in horror. And instead they had gone beyond it, and present glory still sang their despair. He was a coward, that was what he was. He had taken his eyes off the truth, shielding himself with a legend.

Under the violent downpour the outlines of the things around him, walls and streets, were becoming increasingly vague. For a moment he thought he recognised among the leaden filaments the features of Guido Cavalcanti: it must have been fever that was guiding Dante's distorted senses, but it really did look like him, with his mocking features – having emerged from the shadow of death not with the worn-out features of his final days, but triumphant, as in the time of his earthly glory. The poet held a hand out to him, trying to grasp his body in the water.

'At last you have understood,' he heard his friend's voice gurgling in his ear, as if from below the surface of a sea. 'At last you're coming back among the Fedeli d'Amore, whom you abandoned. Too late to hold you in my arms . . .'

Guido disappeared, his face growing less distinct beyond the veil of water. Dante moved, trying not to lose sight of him. He splashed his way through the puddle, then, carried along by his own impetus, found himself under the porch of a church, with no idea how he had got there. He still felt his temples burning with fever, but his shelter had suddenly stopped the hammering of the rain over his head. He brightened a little.

The thunderclaps came thick and fast, but his mind was far away. Was what had appeared to him really Guido's ghost? Or perhaps his mind was confused, and the dream, which sinks its claws into the concupiscible soul when the rational soul flees in sleep, had taken control of him?

It was as if Guido had been trying to tell him something,

something that was hidden beneath his words. An image, like the one that our mind draws in sleep.

But he wasn't sleeping! And yet he would have sworn that he had really seen Guido, he could have read every unspoken word in his ironic smile, remembered every joke, every woman upon whom he had turned his haughty disdain . . . Then a light still more violent than the lightning flashes had entered him, lighting him up from within. The dream images were summed up by the vague picture that he had carried within him since the day of the autopsy. There – if Guido had been trying to tell him something, that was it! He had to find Giotto.

ASKING DIRECTIONS from passers-by, Dante had at last found the Via dei Colorari. He entered the alleyway, with its half-dozen workshops. In front of one of them was a boy sitting with a stone mortar gripped between his legs, busy crushing a reddish powder in the shelter of an awning that protected him from the rain.

'Do you know where Giotto's house is?' Dante asked him.

'The Florentine painter?' the boy replied, without taking his eyes off his work. 'End of the corridor, top of the stairs.'

The alleyway ended with a two-storey building, cut in the middle by a steep flight of stairs that must once have led to a third level that had now disappeared. But before it ended in the void, what must originally have been a window had been turned into a door. Dante knocked firmly.

A grunt came from within, followed by a curse. 'I'm working, go away!'

'Open up, it's Dante!'

A moment's silence followed, interrupted only by the clatter of someone moving objects out of his way. Then the door opened, and the massive figure of the painter appeared. 'Oh, Dante! You've come to—'

Without giving him time to finish his sentence, the poet pushed his way in, roughly shoving his friend out of his way. He found himself in a room that was huge, but so cluttered with tools, buckets of powder, rolls of paper, as to make it almost unusable. The wooden floorboards sagged dangerously in the middle beneath the weight, making the whole space look like a kind of big bowl on the point of overflowing.

'It was you!'

'What do you mean?'

'The face on Pope Joan's sarcophagus. You painted it!'

Giotto stared at his friend expressionlessly. He seemed to be working out whether it was worth confessing. In the end he smiled vaguely, nodding and narrowing his eyes as if watching the scene play out inside him. 'How did you find out?'

'You gave her Vana's face, you sly dog!'

Laughter rose from the painter's belly, exploding in mocking guffaws. 'The most beautiful singer in Florence, with whom I was once in love. She has stayed in my mind as if she were still alive. And in my blood.'

Dante looked away for a moment. The other man must have spotted his unease.

'And in yours, friend,' he insisted, 'given that you remembered her features straight away.'

The painter bit his lips, looking from Dante to an object in the corner, hidden by a canvas. Then, chuckling again, he took the poet's hand and pulled him over there. 'Look!' he exclaimed conspiratorially.

He firmly pulled the canvas away. Dante goggled in amazement. On an easel there stood a painted canvas, as big as an altarpiece.

With the back of his fingers he stroked the painted cheek, as moved as if he were stroking living flesh. 'Doesn't it look as if she's about to start singing? I'm really clever, my friend,' said Giotto. But there wasn't the usual impudence of his cleverness in his voice. Instead there was bitterness over beauty that had been lost, and of which this simulacrum was only a pale shadow. 'And those cursed friars who won't pay me!' he shouted with a sudden change of mood.

Dante wasn't paying him any attention. His satisfaction at having his hypothesis confirmed had disappeared, erased by what the memory of Vana del Moggio had unleashed in his breast.

'Who commissioned you to do this?' he asked after a moment, stirring himself.

'A man. But I didn't see his face, if that's what you want to know. I was just looking at his bag of coins,' Giotto added with a chuckle. But then, seeing the poet's grim expression: 'I thought it was someone like myself who was tired of seeing nothing but saints and madonnas!'

'And when did he give you the job?'

'He came to collect it with two servants, and I didn't recognise his face even then. I thought it was a joke, like the time I painted donkey's ears on the coat of arms of the Tornaquirici . . . But where are you going?'

HE STARTED wandering, gripped by his own thoughts. And as the Decurion had said of the common people, Dante too found himself going down towards ever lower levels of the city. As he approached the river, the labyrinth of alleyways that led from the Campo Marzio to the Castello became increasingly crowded. Little groups of pilgrims pressed in on Dante from every side, forcing him to press himself more closely against the walls of the poor dwellings to avoid being trampled. More than once he had been forced to pick up the hem of his robes to avoid the muddy shoes of the poorest people, or the wheels of the carriage of some nobleman who had ventured to the vault of the bridge, unaware of the maze of alleys leading to the river. Even though the Jubilee was over now, the mass of people flooding into Rome to pray over Peter's tomb and beg for grace or plead for absolution for their own sins was still impressive. Some of them marched on obstinately with nothing but the clothes they were wearing. Others dragged bundles and bags holding their possessions, getting in the way of the people who came after them. And where the roads came together, the different groups clashed like the wash of the sea, rushing and gurgling until the larger or more determined group prevailed, elbowing their way through and throwing back their adversaries in this race for the salvation of the soul.

Chants and cries rose up from the seething mass, psalms bellowed in Latin distorted by the infinite regional accents, which wounded the poet's ears like lance-blows. A violent fury rose up within him at the sound of those barbaric noises, which transformed the noble tongue of his forefathers into an accumulation of barely comprehensible grunts. A great tapestry, woven of silk and gold, chewed by dogs.

After only just avoiding being thrown against the stone corner of a house that for some reason protruded beyond the edge of the street, he found himself at last on a straight stretch of road, which he began to descend. In front of him a vista opened up, unimpeded by the city walls: he glimpsed the straight outline of the bridge, and beyond the shore of the Tiber the Castello, whose impassive shadow seemed to survey the tumult going on at its feet.

For a moment he stopped, to get his breath back. But immediately the jostle of the crowd behind him gripped him like an enormous hand and forced him to keep on walking to avoid being trampled. So he found himself almost being dragged along, by people speeding up as the road descended, heedless of the weaker or the older among them. The Jews, he reflected, must have moved like that on their flight from Egypt, when they saw the shores of the Red Sea, and the waters opening up in front of their feet.

But just as those ancient tribes had thrown themselves forward, pursued by Pharaoh's armies, so the Romans around him were advancing, trying to repel the assault of a crowd of street-sellers standing on either side of the street, coming towards them like a pack of wolves, attempting to insinuate their way through the crowd with their trays full of loaves, pieces of meat and indistinguishable fish, kegs of water and wine. Each one of them was heading towards those pilgrims who, to their expert eye, seemed most exhausted, trying to hold them back for long enough to strike a quick deal before passing on to the next wave. Little handcarts had been set up along the roadside and all the way up to the carriageway of the bridge, full of gewgaws, bits of clothing, crosses of all kinds, from metal to the humblest wood. Dozens of hands stretched out from behind these makeshift stalls, offering merchandise with loud cries.

Dante tried to free himself, staring straight ahead and mechanically shaking his head. He had barely sidestepped a person who was trying to put something that looked like a sacred image into his hand when he felt someone grabbing him firmly by his robe and dragging him sideways, towards a nook in the wall. The road there had reached its lowest point, just before it climbed back up to the bridge. He felt his feet slipping on the muddy bottom of the river bank and, to keep from losing his balance, leaned against the edge of the cart parked next to it.

'Stop, Messer!' The words echoed in his ears. He turned suddenly, ready to repel the umpteenth assault. He saw a middle-aged man carefully examining his robes, whose hem he clutched in his hand. 'Lovely clothes you have, a noble Lombard, without a doubt. Come, I have something that is bound to interest you.'

Only then did Dante glance at what lay on the cart that he was leaning against. He saw a display of objects of every shape and size, most of them metal and terracotta pots, little alabaster amphorae, statuettes, both whole and broken, pieces of coloured marble, some human heads of different sizes and the body of a horse carved from a kind of green stone, missing all four of its legs.

'Your noble features reveal your true nature,' he heard the man saying. 'I'm sure you won't want to come back from the city without a tangible memory of its past greatness! I can offer you objects that were clutched by the hands of the ancient Romans. Look at these ampullas!' he cried, holding under his nose a little container that seemed to be made of alabaster. 'Sniff it! Don't you think you can still smell the perfume of the precious aromas that it once held, for the delight of the noble matrons who could enjoy such precious balms? Don't you think you can still feel the touch of their delicious fingers on the handle?' he added with a sly smile.

Dante took the object that had been thrust into his hand and turned it round in his fingers. After studying it for a moment he handed it crossly back. The fingers of the great Romans? The lowliest workshop in his own Florence could have made better. And it wasn't even a perfume container, just the imitation of a lachrymal vase made in some humble chalky substance that was trying to imitate alabaster. Beneath his fingers he could still feel the irritating stickiness of the ink that had been used to mask it. He glanced quickly at the other objects – just as plainly fake as the one he was holding. How dare this individual so much as think of cheating a man who had come from a place where Roman antiquities were well known and well loved? How dare he . . .

At that moment his eye fell on one of the objects on

the cart, half-hidden by a horrible head of a bearded emperor. He gave a start.

'That one!' he cried in a strangled voice, reaching out a hand and picking up an opaque glass pot. The same unusual shape, the same size as the mysterious ampulla found in the she-Pope's grave. The same dog's-head stopper. 'Where did you get this?'

He feverishly turned the vessel around in his hand, beneath the man's satisfied gaze.

'I knew something would meet with the favour of a connoisseur like yourself. An ancient piece of glassware, found among the ruins of the Forum. Perhaps a pot in which Romulus himself drew water from the Veian spring . . .'

'Shut up, scoundrel! Where did you get this pot?' the poet cried, abruptly withdrawing the hand that gripped the object, and stretching the other towards the salesman's throat. The man tried to stammer something as he glanced round for someone who might come to his aid. He was probably relying on one of the trinket-sellers, but the general confusion and their hidden spot acted in Dante's favour. The poet moved menacingly closer.

The man tried timidly once more, invoking another mysterious origin, then gave up. 'It was Mastro Antonio who made it, the glass-maker with a workshop down by the Campo dei Fiori – but it's the same as the real ones . . .'

Dante let him go. There was something in his frightened face that made him believe the truth of his confession. He quickly looked in his bag for a coin, then turned away, clutching his treasure in his hand and plunging back into the stream of pilgrims.

As he ran quickly towards the square, he went on turning the glass pot around in his hands. He had no doubt: it was identical to the mysterious eternal ampulla found in the she-Pope's grave. Who was this Mastro Antonio, and what did he have to do with that business?

He was still ruminating on his doubts when in the distance he spotted a low building behind which rose a chimney with a cloud of thick, whitish smoke emerging from it. Having crossed the threshold, Dante found himself in an overheated room, at the end of which was the flaming mouth of a furnace. Inside it there burned an intense fire of big oak logs, surrounded by a kind of small brick wall supporting a large metal crucible. From this receptacle emanated a greenish luminescence, along with constant eruptions of little beads of incandescent material, which fell back down all over the floor. Ignoring this burning rain, a man was busy stirring the crucible with a metal pole.

'Are you Mastro Antonio?' the poet asked. 'Are you the man who made this?'

At first the man didn't deign to notice him, and went on with his work. Then, when he seemed satisfied with what he was doing, he removed the metal bar, dragging out a long filament of luminous material and rolling it onto the bar.

'What do you want, Messere?'

'This jar! Did you make it?'

The man glanced at the object that Dante held out to him, then looked up at him suspiciously. 'Perhaps. Why do you ask, stranger?'

'It's important, bad things are attached to your work. But perhaps good could come out of it, too, if you answer my question.'

The man didn't appear to understand. He seemed intimidated by the figure of the poet, by his clothes, by his decisive manner. As if he were a man of great authority, even though his features firmly revealed him as a stranger to the city.

'I don't think I've done anything bad. The person who gave me the job didn't forbid me from making any more of them . . .' he continued hesitantly.

'Someone commissioned you to make this pot? Who was it?'

'I don't know – a stranger. I never saw his face, he wore a hood. He paid me well . . .'

Dante clenched his fists with rage. Another ghost, certainly the same stranger who had commissioned the portrait from Giotto. But why – why?

The man had followed his movements with trepidation.

He seemed impressed by the poet's outburst of rage. 'I didn't think it was important, I swear. I only made another two or three, to sell to the pilgrims . . . I thought it was a nice shape.'

'Another two or three? But how many were you commissioned to make?'

'Twelve. All of them like the one you've brought me. I had to make copies that were as exact as possible. "Mastro Antonio," he said to me, "I know the only glass-maker in Rome who could satisfy me is you," and he gave me this jar to copy.'

'And you did it?'

'No – not exactly . . .'

'What do you mean?'

'You see, the object was too complex to be replicated precisely,' the man replied in a forced voice, as if it cost him an effort to admit his mistake. 'The lower part was more or less as you see, but its stopper – it was irreducible. That jar had a monster on its stopper . . .'

'A monster?'

'Yes, a strange beast that I'd never seen – a head, an incredible head . . . I tried, ten times, but without a result, the melted glass refused to take that shape. In the end I was forced to give up, and I made the stopper that you see . . .'

'And what did the man who gave you the job say?'

'At first he completely lost his temper,' the man replied,

shivering as if he still had the image of that rage in front of his eyes. 'Then he calmed down, and I heard him murmuring something to himself . . .'

'What?' the poet asked apprehensively.

'Something like "The gods won't care about form . . ." or something of the kind. He picked up the jars I'd made and disappeared, after paying me the agreed sum. Is there anything else you want me to do for you?' he concluded hopefully.

But Dante had already left.

13

15th November, after midday

HE HAD headed for the Florentine legation. He needed time now – perhaps he would somehow be able to pursue the trail of the crime. Outside the door was a group of mules, and some men busy fixing their loads onto the pack-saddles. One of them glanced distractedly at Dante and then, after recognising the poet, started running towards him with an anxious expression on his face.

'Messer Alighieri, at last! I've been looking for you for more than a day. Where did you get to?'

Ignoring the question, Dante approached the mounts, quickly examining the sacks fastened to the saddles. Then he turned to the man who had followed him. 'These are our bags. What are you doing, Messer Corazza? Who told you to leave?'

The other ambassador, Maso Minerbetti, appeared from behind one of the mules. 'Haven't you heard? About what has happened in Florence?'

'What has happened?' Dante asked immediately, in alarm.

'A courier has arrived from the city. Messer Corso Donati and his men have defeated the Priory, and the White party is in flight, or in hiding.'

'And that damned Frenchman, Charles de Valois! Wasn't he supposed to come with his army to pacify the factions? Weren't his lances supposed to stop this very thing happening?' Dante cried, turning pale. Then a flash of rage revived him. He had grabbed Corazza by the chest, his face right up against the other man's. He could smell the fear in his breath. 'Damned idiots! I spent days in the Council beseeching them not to open the gates to the Frenchman. A man doubly bound to Boniface, ready to sell everything, just to have the support of the Pope in his race for the imperial throne. And he's the man to whom they opened the gates of the city!'

'Maybe they thought they were doing the right thing . . .' Minerbetti suggested timidly.

Dante turned on him like a snake. 'The right thing! They've handed the sheepfold over to the wolf. And now you say that the Donati have the Commune in their fists?'

Corazza da Signa, finding himself free from the poet's grip, had taken two quick steps backwards. He stood with a cunning expression on his face. 'I would advise you to moderate your tone, Messer Alighieri! You were able to enjoy

GIULIO LEONI

the fervency of the White party when Cerchi's men, your faction, were still in charge. But now that Donati's supporters rule the city, it's time to lower your crest. There is already talk of looting and pillaging, and if you are keen to save your house and property, hurry to tie on your bags and move with us.'

The poet shook his head nervously. 'No, you leave if you want to. I still have to finish my work.'

'But the mission has come to an end,' the other man replied spitefully. 'And, it would seem, without success. Boniface didn't even listen to you. The new rulers want us to give an account of what happened. And you – having claimed leadership over the rest of us, and made things and broken them again – you of all people are the one awaited most eagerly.'

'Come, Messer Alighieri. Come with us,' Minerbetti said in a benevolent voice, stepping towards him. 'With an act of submission, and perhaps a small offering to the Baptistery, you will see that Donati will show understanding towards your past hostility. Isn't your wife basically one of them?'

'And should I shield myself with my wife's clothes to hide what I've been doing in broad daylight? No, I'll stay. If the mission to Boniface has failed, it remains for me to accomplish another one, equally important to my conscience. You do what you like, and what your standards dictate.'

415

Corazza had listened, trying to decipher the poet's allusion. Then, with a shrug, he went on his way again. 'So you admit you failed completely. And now you want to wash your hands of it, like Pontius Pilate? And send us on ahead to face the music?' he added defiantly.

Dante turned threateningly towards him, forcing him to step hastily backwards. 'Just clear off,' he hissed. 'And tell the new rulers of my city that everything possible was done. Taking account of the iniquities of Boniface, the shortness of time, the fallacy of human judgement.'

The pain behind his eye had started tormenting him again. The wretched outlines of his two companions danced before his eyes, while the fading light of sunset wounded him with its bloody glare. He could still hear Corazza's voice barking something.

'Why such arrogance? Couldn't you have bowed down before Boniface and kissed that damned hand of his? Your father, Alighieri, was very accommodating when the Ghibellines routed us at Montaperti!'

'What do you mean?'

'Oh, for heaven's sake! Even in Vacchereccia everyone knew that he made a pact with the Ghibellines of Farinata degli Uberti, and that he saved his goods and his house in exchange for his submission. And he might also have helped them out with some loans, given that he was a money-lender even then—'

The man might have been about to add something, but

the word was cut short in his mouth by the unexpected slap that Dante landed on his face. Corazza started backwards, trying to keep his balance, but the blow had been so violent that it forced him to clutch the bridle of the mule he was loading. Stung by the sudden tug on its bit, the animal emitted a whinny of pain, rearing and kicking out. Corazza slipped again, landing on all fours.

In that convulsive movement the jar had slipped from Dante's hand, shattering on the ground. He stared at its shards for a moment, then turned back on the fallen man. 'That's the posture that suits you, animal that you are!' the poet roared, giving Corazza a kick in the kidneys and sending him sprawling along the pavement. From there the man tried to get back up, aching and dirty with the mud of the street, while Maso Minerbetti had prudently taken shelter behind the other mule. Dante leaped over to the supine man, towering over him with his fist raised as if preparing to strike him again. Corazza was whining like a whipped dog, alternating groans and cries of fear.

Meanwhile people had gathered all around, attracted by the noise of the fight. A group of working people, some of them clutching the tools of their trade, was growing by the instant. As if an invisible herald had started running along the alleys, the people who came running had formed an almost perfect circle around them. In that makeshift amphitheatre, laughter and scornful jokes directed at them, along with ostentatious and insolent comments turned in general against the miserable pilgrims who had invaded Rome.

Dante looked round. Then he bent quickly over the terrified Corazza, who was protecting the back of his neck with his hands, and gripped him by the collar, forcing him to his feet.

'Stand up and stop whinging,' the poet whispered between his teeth. 'We're the ambassadors of the noble city of Florence, we mustn't provide a spectacle for the Roman plebs,' he added, brushing the most obvious traces of mud from the other man's robes, with swift blows of his hand.

'My Florence isn't yours,' Corazza replied fiercely, pressing his hand to his reddened cheek. 'The White party has been defeated. Cerchi and all his associates are being thrown out of the city.'

'If only two dogs had been left in that great pot, fighting over a bone, it wouldn't have been more bitter than the parties fighting there! It's your envy, a yearning for possessions and a hatred of merit that has burst the city like a watermelon, and is preparing its ruin,' he spat in Corazza's face by way of reply. As he spoke he had looked up, to include Maso Minerbetti in his invective.

Minerbetti went on carefully watching from behind the shelter of his mule, without giving any sign of coming closer. 'It's now that the minor guilds must free themselves from the oppression of the major,' was all he said. 'And if the dominion of the Donati achieves that, let it come!'

Dante lowered his arms, among the jokes of the onlookers who went on bawling at them. All of a sudden he felt drained of energy: what better allegory could a poet have found to sing the ruin of his city? If three of them had been unable to speak with a single voice, what would happen when the Hundred of the Council were to deliberate? And would there still be a Council where he could raise his voice on his return?

He was about to voice all his discomfort when he was interrupted by a hubbub coming from the nearby alleyway. At that very moment he saw a procession of praying men emerging into the square, wearing the sack-cloth of penitence, guided by a small group of monks carrying a large wooden cross on their shoulders. The crowd behind them walked with their arms raised to the sky, shouting something in a confused babble. Only occasionally was it possible to make out a few words of the prayer that seemed to have been born between the walls of Babylon, and which only God himself would have been able to listen to.

The procession passed between the poet and the other two Florentines, separating them. The circle of the spectators had also broken up, and a good proportion of the people who had come running to see the spectacle came and stood beside the newcomers, joining mockingly in their song with an idiotic mumble.

But they didn't seem to be aware of what was happening around them. In fact, they seemed to be flattered by the apparent fervour with which the Roman people welcomed them. They responded by making even more noise with their songs.

Dante cast one last glance at the other two Florentines, who were escaping amongst the crowd. He felt exhausted; he just wanted to reach his lodgings and throw himself down on his bed. Get back to his papers, forget everything.

He hesitated for a moment, then returned to the deserted legation and sat down on a bale of cloth, taking his head in his hands. All around were the obvious signs of hurried escape – papers left on the ground, abandoned luggage. The remains of a shipwreck caught in an aimless drift. Everything was collapsing. The orderly building of knowledge and studies, the faith that had inspired him, the conviction that he was part of a universe that was not the result of blind chance, but ordered by God for his glory – all dissipated in dust. The rumours coming from Florence only added to the landslide that had already destroyed his inner core.

HE COULDN'T have said how much time he had stayed in that position, his mind scattered in his own thoughts. He felt the gentle touch of a hand shaking him.

He turned round with a start and saw Senator Spada. Beside him was Kansbar, with his usual enigmatic expression. The Roman's noble face bore his normal cordial smile.

'I'm happy to see you, Messer Alighieri. I was about to

go to the sea with the ambassador, to show him that Rome is prepared for the venture that will bind us together. There we will tighten the knots of our new alliance.'

'The new alliance . . .?' said Dante.

But the other man dismissed the subject with a wave of his hand. 'I thought you might be here, and I was right. Join us, it's good that Florence should know how the preparations are proceeding. When you get back to your city, you too can be a herald, and encourage your fellow-citizens to unite with us.'

'To the sea?' Dante asked, puzzled. 'You're ready to embark?'

'No. The fleet is still being fitted out. But in an outpost towards the Tyrrhenian Sea the Christian forces are already on alert. Where ancient Ostia once stood,' he replied, gesturing vaguely towards the horizon.

Dante hesitated for a long moment. Perhaps he should refuse, and set off for Florence along with the others. And if he accepted the invitation, would that assure him of the protection of the senator if the situation in his city deteriorated? Or didn't it rather mean handing himself into Boniface's man, and giving up all hope? He decided to tempt fate and moved towards the door.

Outside the legation a covered wagon waited, pulled by a pair of big bay horses. Around them, a small group of men on horseback clutched the reins of their animals, as if they too were about to get moving. The senator pushed aside the canvas curtain that covered the vehicle and invited the others to climb inside.

Kansbar hoisted himself up with an agile leap, followed by Dante. When the senator had taken his place next to them, he issued an abrupt order and the little convoy set off.

They headed towards the river, following the river bank past the island to the Monte dei Cocci. Here the cart and its escort crossed a little wooden bridge that had been built beside the remains of an old stone bridge, then they passed alongside the walls to the Porta Portese. From there they climbed the road in the direction of the distant sea.

Around them, a bleak expanse of uncultivated fields and scrubland extended as far as the eye could see. Suddenly Dante was aware that the cart's wheels were passing over regular cobblestones again.

'We're on the old Via Portuense, Messer Alighieri,' the senator said. 'From here we will travel southwards for a stretch, before turning towards our destination.'

The road slipped between the remains of ancient buildings, little votive shrines, graves. For a stretch they ran alongside the ruins of a big arched building.

'That was once the castle of the Magliana, Messer Alighieri. Before it was destroyed by the attack of the Saracens.'

Dante poked his head out of the carriage to get a better look at the ruins. The traces of the ancient wall were half-submerged by brambles that had seized it in their green grip, almost hiding it from view. All around, flocks of sheep browsed on the grass.

Since leaving, they had been accompanied by a rumble of distant thunder, growing in intensity. As he went on studying the panorama, he felt on his head the first drops of rain, which immediately turned into a violent shower. He hurried to close the curtains of the carriage, while the cries of the carters reached them from outside as they spurred on their horses.

'It's the rainy season, Messer Alighieri. Rome is famous for its autumn storms. But don't be afraid, when we've reached the Fortress we'll be able to dry ourselves and get something to eat.'

'The Fortress?'

'We'll be there very soon, an outpost on the coast. Just beyond the Gregorian village, near the ruins of the Roman city. You'll be surprised by what you see, I'm sure of it. You'll be able to collect material for that poem that only you can write.'

Their march continued under the drumming rain for about ten miles. The countryside around the cart and its escort had become more even. The fields had made way for an irregular succession of tufa hillocks, with the road passing through natural gorges, or channels opened up by the hands of men in ancient times. 'We've reached the Malegrotte, Senator,' he heard a voice saying from outside.

Saturniano Spada came out from under the cover and looked around. He gave a brief order to the driver, then went back inside, shaking the rain from his clothes. 'The roads are turning to mud. But we should get on, before they become impassable,' he said to the other occupants.

'This also happens in the Holy Land. You'll have to make sure that the carriages aren't too heavy, so that you're not forced to leave them in the desert,' Kansbar observed. 'That was the mistake that is said to have put paid to Richard the Lionheart's venture on the Third Crusade.'

The senator shook his head. 'What made things easy for the infidels, and determined their success, was the insane rivalry between the Christian princes, and their skewed intentions. But that's not going to happen this time. One is the plan, one the guide, one the will. What do you think, Messer Alighieri?'

It was Dante's turn to lift the curtain and glance outside. They had abandoned the paved road, and the wheels of the cart were now running over a dirt patch of beaten earth, slightly raised above the marshy ground that extended all around. As far as he could see, a flat surface ran all the way to the horizon, bristling with tufts of reeds and other marshy grasses. He wondered if the terrain that awaited the venture across the sea was equally desolate. Here and there, sparse groups of stunted trees broke the monotony of the landscape, along with the occasional hump that rose a few yards above the stagnant waters.

The senator was still waiting for his reply. Dante looked inside himself for words that he could say to be polite to his host, but without sounding too hypocritically enthusiastic. After the first, another nine expeditions against the infidels had followed over the course of two centuries. And apart from that one, none of them had had the success that had been hoped for. A useless waste of lives and money destroyed for that dream – dominion over the Holy City – which kept reappearing in the East like the mirages that are said to appear among the sands.

'*God wills it . . .*' he murmured thoughtfully, remembering the words that the crusaders had written on their banners each time they went into battle. Those banners that had then been eroded in the dust, along with the bones of the men who once had held them.

'Of course God wills it!' the senator echoed. 'But not in the wretched sense in which the first supporters of the venture meant it, imagining a God keeping watch over his capital like a boss keeping an eye on his tenant farmers. What we are preparing is certainly part of a superhuman order, and our efforts – weak in their base humanity – will also be invincible, because foreseen and preordained by His higher will! That is what I want to be the matter of your song, more than the smallness of our valour.'

By way of reply, Dante merely nodded his agreement. His feeling of exhaustion was becoming increasingly intense, penetrating his bones, as bitter as the taste of salt that came in through the carriage window. Perhaps there really was no god jealously keeping guard over the stones of Jerusalem. Perhaps the city was just a spot on the Earth destined to pass from hand to hand, according to the power of whoever held his sword over it. A fortress on the road to the East, born to restore and tax the caravans that ventured from the Mediterranean to mysterious Asia. A return journey for the great Romans, in their final assault on Asia, in the footsteps of Alexander the Great; a boundary marker between the powerful Egyptians and the treacherous Persians; a city of everyone and no one, built – not coincidentally – by a people from everywhere and nowhere . . .

What need was there to attempt this desperate venture again? And why was Boniface taking the trouble to ensure that it succeeded, acceding to the senator's extravagance? Especially now that, with the celebration of the Jubilee, Rome had been definitively elevated to the heart of Christendom, with the pilgrimage to Peter's tomb having equal status with the one at the Holy Sepulchre?

Perhaps, in his crazed arrogance, that old hypocrite really did crave to have his name linked with the liberation of the Holy Land. Dante immediately banished the thought from his mind. However treacherous he might have been, Boniface was as cunning as a snake, and would never sacrifice an ounce of his wealth over something that didn't provide a real advantage to his power and that of his family.

Would the recapture of Jerusalem not essentially be a way of boosting the French nobility, who were bound to his enemy, Philip the Fair, or the Italian barons, friends of the Emperor?

Unless . . . unless the old crook had another plan in mind. The poet couldn't suppress a smile at this new thought. If Boniface really did succeed in crushing the Turk with the help of the terrible Mongols of Ghazan Khan, perhaps Jerusalem wasn't his true objective!

He gave his companions a sidelong glance. They were both absorbed in their thoughts, staring off somewhere beyond the window. The senator in particular seemed lost in his inner vision. And what if the true project, once the Turkish threat had been eliminated, were to terrorise the Patriarchate of Constantinople, bringing war to its borders and forcing it to come back under the protective wings of Rome? That might be Boniface's dream, to be the one who resolved the Eastern Schism.

It wasn't impossible. Attacked by the infidel Turks, the Eastern Church had become increasingly close to the Emperor of Byzantium, becoming his loyal handmaiden in exchange for his protection. But if it was now being threatened by an ally of Rome, and Rome extended a benevolent hand, promising safety in exchange for submission, would that not be the greatest victory for Boniface? Vastly greater than the mere surrender of the King of France, which would have opened his coffers to the wealth of the whole of eastern Europe. In 1204, in only three days, a marauding gang of Venetians and Franks had looted enough from the houses and churches of Constantinople to cover their cities with gold. How much would they get from Constantinople's eternal submission?

He stared at the senator again, his noble features outlined against the dark background of the carriage. How could such a man have blindly served a simoniac pope? His pagan disbelief, his devotion to the cult of ancient Rome, shouldn't they have protected him from the temptation to become Boniface's accomplice? Was there something going on that he didn't understand?

And yet this man somehow inspired a profound feeling of trust in Dante. He knew that, behind Spada's formal deference to Boniface, there was something that drew him to the senator. If things really did deteriorate in Florence, Saturniano Spada was the man to protect him in his exile.

OUTSIDE, AS far as the eye could see, there was no trace of a human presence. No settlement, not even a wretched cabin or a thread of smoke rising into the cloud-heavy sky. The wind blew implacably from the west, bringing with it a smell of brackish damp. Dante huddled in his robes, withdrawing into his corner and resting his head on his rolled-up cloak so as to soften the irritating jolts from the wheels.

He was growing increasingly unhappy about having accepted this invitation. Whatever lay behind this crusade, he was sure this wasn't the place for him: in Rome he had left all his work dramatically unfinished – the failed embassy, his writings, still incomplete. Fundamentally he felt he was neglecting both of his duties: his public one towards his city and his private one towards the Muses. The first bound up with the world, and the fates of men; the second and more important designed to give him the fame he had dreamed of, since he had seen the celebrations in St John's church at which the learned men of Florence were awarded their prizes.

He too wanted the poetic crown. And he wanted his compatriots to bow before his gifts as ruler of the common good. When he returned with news of Boniface's capitulation, a herald would have preceded his carriage along the Via Cassia, announcing to the people of Tuscany that the poet brought from Rome the restored safety of his city. The women would line the roadside as he passed, scattering petals on the ancient paving stones, after appearing at their windows in all their bright finery. And the men and boys would run alongside his carriage singing, waving olive branches to shade his passage, across the whole of the territory of the Republic, all the way to the Porta Romana, where the rulers of the Commune would welcome him and lead him in procession inside the Baptistery. And there he would see someone waiting for him, a shadowy figure of a woman, her face hidden behind a veil, the woman he had always dreamed of, and then that veil would be lifted, slowly revealing the features of the women he had loved – Beatrice, and Pietra, and Fiamma – and he would run to kiss them, and only then would he recognise the tormented features of the widow's daughter, her eyes wide with reproach. But there was something that held him back, something that obstructed his triumphal journey: the tormented face of the girl, mixed in among the bodies of the women buried at the Muro Torto, who rose from their graves waving the scraps of flesh and rags that still enwrapped their bones . . .

He suddenly opened his eyes, shaken from the torpor into which he had fallen by a jolt more violent than the others. He felt dazed; fragments of his last vision still crowded into his mind as a sense of sudden anxiety took hold of him. He quickly looked around, blushing, as if worried that his travelling companions might have caught something of his vain dreams of glory, and then his sense of guilt. But the others were still looking outside, as if curious about the void all around them.

'Here we are at Gregoriopolis!' the senator exclaimed at that moment, pointing to a cluster of dilapidated shacks that lined the road, surrounded by a wall that had collapsed in several places.

'It looks deserted, like everything else,' the poet observed.

'It is, Messer Alighieri, and it has been for many years.

It was a fortified village, erected by Pope Gregory the Great as an outpost in the marshes, and an advance stronghold in case of attack from the sea. But it has always been difficult to ensure that it was inhabited, in this malarial zone. And since its devastation by Saracen pirates, it has been unoccupied. Now it is merely a ghost, but its towers can still look daunting from a long way offshore.'

'There's a ghostly guard watching over Rome?'

'Ghosts and the mud and water of the marshes. It was from here, our forefathers believed, that souls embarked for the islands of the dead. It is said that at night horrible cries sometimes split the silence, and sudden flames light up the darkness.'

'And is it true?' the poet asked, suddenly animated again.

'It's what people who venture to these parts say. And perhaps you will bear witness to it as well, when we get to the castle.'

'A port of embarkation for the lands of the dead . . . at the mouth of the Tiber,' the poet repeated to himself. 'And who provides the transport for these souls? What is the nature of the boat that conveys them? And where do the souls cross from, and where do they stay before the journey?'

The senator exploded with ironic laughter. 'Messer Alighieri, it seems that this fairy-tale has truly struck your imagination! Very well, remember to set light to your poetic imagination when you tell of the embarkation for the crusade. Because it is from here that it will take place.'

'Here?' exclaimed the poet, looking around in disbelief.

'From Trajan's port. That's where the fleet is being fitted out.'

'The ancient port of Rome? I thought it had been abandoned centuries ago, buried by the course of the Tiber.' He had read of that marvel somewhere, a perfect hexagon of stone and precious marble, once capable of holding the entire imperial fleet.

The senator shook his head. 'It's true, like the whole city of Ostia, which followed it into oblivion. But its marble quays are still there, as perfect and efficient as the day they were made by their master-craftsmen. And the slipways and reservoirs are still there, too. Places sheltered from the prying eyes of the Turk's spies, who are swarming around the papal court, mingling among the merchants and pilgrims. The buildings around the quays, which once provided rest for the crews who sailed to the most distant lands, have been turned into lodgings for the workforce. And as for the wood and all the other equipment, they are transported along the nearby river, among the infinite quantities of merchandise that ply the Tiber every day. Don't you think such foresight will ensure the certain success of this venture, after the others that have failed?'

The temperature inside the carriage had fallen steadily with the setting of the sun. Dante felt a shiver running down his spine, and could barely suppress a sneeze. Over the past hour his headache had become steadily worse, and he felt as if the first symptoms of fever were manifesting themselves. He stirred himself, clenching his teeth and choking back the pain that was already eating away behind his eye-sockets.

'I think . . .' he murmured. Then he cleared his throat and continued in a louder voice. 'I think that God will not abandon those who fight in his name. And if other attempts were not blessed with good fortune, it happened because, in the souls of those heroes, more earthly passions supplanted the first meaning of their duty.'

The senator glanced at him wryly. 'And yet, Messer Alighieri, history should have much to teach you. Rome dominated those lands for centuries, not with the comfort of the gods, but with the force of her sword. Our venture will succeed precisely because it is based upon swords and reason. And not on the vain voices of prophets who vanished into dust centuries ago.'

The poet shrugged. He was about to reply when they were interrupted by a new cry from outside.

'Senator, we're in sight of the Fortress!'

At that moment the carriage was crossing a narrow wooden pontoon that straddled a muddy stream. Dante held open the curtain, looking out for the destination that the voice had announced. The castle seemed to have appeared from nowhere, like one of the ghosts that the senator had talked about. In the thickening darkness he glimpsed the brown outline of four towers rising towards the sky, connected by a wall made of scraps of stone and brick. The building seemed to have been built at various different periods, perhaps starting with one of the corner towers, and had gone up without any sense of harmony, as if impelled by the urgency of the moment. But even so, it gave the idea of a little stronghold that could not readily be taken by storm, and would thus be easily able to repel a treacherous attack by small pirate armies.

'At last!' the senator exclaimed. 'Here's the castle.'

As THE carriage wheels rolled noisily over the planks of the drawbridge, Dante watched the strange spectacle that appeared in front of him. The whole courtyard of the building was full of soldiers, camped around countless little campfires. Dozens of horses were tethered among them, and whinnies rose from the row of stables that entirely occupied one of the long sides. On the other side, against the surrounding wall, rose a stocky, massive building topped by a crenellated keep.

At a guess, he put the number of men encamped inside at about a hundred. Their coats of arms, in a great variety of colours, made them look more like a company of adventurers than a regular unit. He would have expected to see the red and white of the crusader uniform, but their cross was hardly to be seen, although the black and white cross of the Teutonic knights was also apparent here and there. The cramped nature of the space made them look like a tiny army: how could so few of them defeat a whole nation of pagans?

Unless these men were merely an advance party of the actual army. But if that was the case, where were all the others? From the senator's words Dante thought he had understood that everything was now ready for the embarkation. Nor had he mentioned the involvement of any other nations, because all the glory was to belong to Rome. He looked around for some sign that might help him understand, before addressing his doubts directly to Saturniano.

From the top of the tower hung a rain-drenched banner that he couldn't quite make out. But he did recognise a pair of pennants that someone had put up next to the fires. One showed a column on a red field, the other a flourish of gold lilies on a blue field.

Dante suddenly turned towards the senator. But before he could ask for confirmation of what he had seen, the other man had jumped to the ground and invited the poet to follow him.

'Aren't those the devices of Colonna?' he asked from the carriage, pointing to the pennants. 'And the lilies of France?'

'Yes, Messer Alighieri. I see that you know your army insignias.'

'But I don't understand their presence in Boniface's camp. I thought they were both diehard enemies of his.'

The senator smiled, with a fleeting glance at the Persian.

Kansbar had remained silent, and was staring at the poet as if curious about his reactions.

'I understand your perplexity, Messer Alighieri,' Saturniano said at last, 'but this in itself should give you a measure of the excellence of the venture, and material for your poem. Those who are enemies in this world will extend the hand of friendship in the next, as your poet Virgil has it: " . . *and the herds will not fear the great lions; and the serpent will perish, and the deceitful poisonous herbs; Assyrian balsam will spring up everywhere . . .*"

'The Colonna and Caetani have made peace?'

'When what awaits us is completed, even the bloodiest of their disputes will be like a breath of wind in a storm. But come, let us refresh ourselves in the rooms of the castle. There's someone I want you to meet.'

DANTE FOLLOWED the senator and Kansbar to the upper floor of the castle. There, at the end of the outside steps, a door led into a wide room with a dark beamed ceiling. The smooth stone walls were decorated only with the marble coats of arms of those who had administered the castle over the years. A fire raged in the big fireplace that occupied the whole of the end wall. In front of it, on a wooden chair, a man sat, his legs outstretched until they almost touched the flames.

At the sound of their footsteps the stranger had leaped

to his feet, his face tense and his hand wrapped around the pommel of his sword, as if he were preparing to repel an attack.

'Calm yourself, Giacomo!' exclaimed the senator, stepping forward and raising his hands in a sign of peace. 'Or my guests will really think your nickname, Sciarra – it means "quarrel" in Calabrian, Dante – is well deserved!'

The poet too had stepped uncertainly forward. He stared at the stranger, a young man with an athletic physique, who couldn't have been more than thirty. The other man seemed to have noticed Dante, too. The poet saw the other man's eyes, filled with repressed rage, studying him carefully. Then both men were sure they had met before.

'Messer Colonna, this is Maestro Dante Alighieri, the Florentine philosopher and poet. He is going to be a companion in our venture.'

'A companion? I hope he can do better than I saw at the marshes by the Colosseum,' the young man said, doing nothing to hide the contempt in his voice.

Dante flushed, then clenching his fists summoned all the coldness he could muster. 'The fortunes of war are changeable. Never measure a man on the basis of a single encounter.'

He had spoken the words calmly. But inside he still burned with fury, feeling the other man's ironic expression running over his skin like a burning iron. He would have given his arm to be back in the marshes and show this impudent person what steel Florentines were made of.

But the man seemed to have lost all interest in him. 'Poet and philosopher?' was all he said. 'Yes, I think I've heard of you. Aren't you at the court of Boniface, as ambassador? And aren't you the one they say belonged to the Fedeli d'Amore, in your youth? You've come a long way, now that you're a servant of Guelph merchants!'

Dante shrugged grimly. Rather than replying, he turned to the senator. 'And this is the new alliance that you alluded to?'

'You see some elements of it. But soon you will know everything. Meanwhile let's sit down at the table prepared for us, to set ourselves up for what awaits us.'

A table had been laid by the fire. Dante sat down, trying to dry his frozen bones, in the hope that this salutary warmth might help him overcome the unease to which he was prey.

The meal was consumed in silence, as if everything to be said had been said. Or perhaps it was the presence of Colonna, who had for some reason made the senator and the Persian taciturn. The young man had barely looked up from the plate; only every now and again had he glanced suspiciously towards the poet. Suddenly the senator broke the silence.

'Sciarra, Messer Alighieri has joined us as an observer.

With his fine voice he will sing of our venture, making it echo down the centuries.'

By way of reply Colonna merely shrugged disdainfully. 'What have you told him about our plans?' he hissed malevolently.

'Everything he needs to know.'

The young man gave the poet another sideways glance, then shrugged once more. 'Do what you like.'

'I'm surprised to find you here, Messer Colonna,' said the poet. 'You, a fervent Ghibelline. Involved in a priestly venture,' he added poisonously. Then, before giving him time to reply, he turned to Saturniano Spada. 'And you, Senator. If you don't believe in Revelation, why do you want to take the Christian banners across the sea? Instead you should be glad that pagan arrogance has shattered a pointless hope, wiping out with fire and iron the traces of that divine presence which, as you claim, is only the fruit of men's credulity.'

Sciarra Colonna laughed loudly. 'You're better with words than you are with a sword! Answer the Florentine, Senator. What are we going to do, in the Holy Land?' he asked ironically.

The senator hesitated for a moment, as if struck by the observation. Then a subtle smile appeared on his lips. 'You have read the first Caesar, I'm sure. Why do you think he took his legions to Gaul? Poor land, inhabited by fierce and uncivilised barbarians, who had nothing to give the great city of Rome except their muscles in the occasional game at the arena. With no cities that weren't mere accumulations of shacks, with no customs but the rough habits of primitive tribes, with no treasures that weren't piles of junk that could at best have adorned the women of the slums. Without a thought in their heads that might have inspired greater ones, as was the practice in the East. An expedition into the darkness – so dark that they risked losing their way for ever.'

Dante reflected for a moment on these considerations. 'Because there are men who realise their fate in conquest. And Gaius Julius was one of those. And maybe also because the foundation of the Empire was set out in the great design of Providence, and was instilled by Providence in the heart of the Roman.'

The senator shook his head. 'For the only reason to set off for foreign lands, Messer Alighieri: to come back.'

'Come back?'

'To Rome. Triumphant.'

The poet meditatively pinched his lower lip. 'So he was already imagining the future, the triumph and the empire that would follow from it, as he and his legions passed through the forests of ancient France? Is that what you think?'

'I'm sure of it. As I'm sure that it's the final effect that generates its causes. The things of the future call the things of the past to arrange themselves in an orderly fashion, so as to turn into action that which is only possible. As the great Aristotle teaches, within the oak lies the happiness of the acorn.'

'So Rome is the ultimate destination of the crusade?'

'Yes. It is there that the seed we are currently scattering will be harvested. A third empire will rise on the seven hills, after the empire of the Caesars and that of the Germans.'

Dante was about to reply when the senator turned abruptly to the Persian, who had until then listened in silence to the exchange. 'But if the seed does not die, it does not bring forth fruit. Kansbar, midnight approaches. Seek again in the earth for the signs of what awaits you, I implore you.'

The Persian replied with a nod. Then he looked under his robes and took out a small, dark leather bag. He untied its laces and reached inside with his hand. He held his hand out in front of him, still clenched, murmuring an incomprehensible invocation, then suddenly opened his fingers.

A rain of little objects fell to the ground and bounced off the stone. They looked like pebbles, irregular in shape.

'This is the chart of Fortune!' the senator exclaimed, leaning anxiously forward. 'What do the Mothers say? What the Daughters?'

The Persian in turn leaned forward to get a better view. Dante too had come closer, curious to see what was happening. At last he saw an example of the ancient art that he had only ever heard of.

'Read, Senator,' said Kansbar. 'Now you have learned everything I have been able to teach you. Geomancy no longer has any secrets for you.' The senator exchanged a quick glance with the Persian, then stretched out his hand towards the pebbles. He began to run his index finger from one to the other, as if he was trying to write on the floor the network of imaginary relationships that the stones had assumed.

His face suddenly darkened. The Persian, too, seemed uneasy.

Sciarra had been following their movements with a grimace of forbearance. He exploded with laughter, dispersing the stones with a kick. 'It won't be these rocks that decide our plan, but the edge of our sword!'

The senator suddenly got back to his feet, his face still grim. But he didn't seem to be struck by Colonna's rude gesture: he went on staring at the ground, as if in search of a new plan.

'Yes, you may be right,' the senator murmured, inviting the others to take their leave. Just then a soldier announced that the rooms had been prepared. 'Your room has been made ready in the tower, Messer Alighieri. Follow my man, we will meet again at dawn.'

Dante headed towards the stairs leading to the central tower. Reaching a doorway, he was invited to step inside.

Then the door closed behind him, with the unusual sound of a bolt being drawn.

The little stone-walled room was furnished only with a chest with a straw mattress on top of it, and a table with a stool. A felt blanket lay folded on the makeshift bed, the only shelter against the night-time damp that entered through the uncovered window. However, someone had troubled himself to leave some goose-feather quills lined up beside a little ink-bottle. And, most importantly, there was a small number of precious sheets of linen paper of the best quality, the like of which he had rarely come across, even in the best *scriptoria* of Florence.

It must have been the senator who had taken the trouble. It looked like a tacit invitation to begin the work they expected of him, the celebration of the crusade.

But what could he write? To be the Orpheus of these new Argonauts. Start with the point of departure, a city enclosed in ancient walls that encircled nothing but desolation and death? A city that was the mirror of what he saw at the centre of his vision of hell, and which was in fact real – more real than the city of Dis imagined by his master . . . Perhaps Virgil really was a magician, he really had used his magic arts to read the future, he really had foreseen how the Age of Gold that he had hoped for would finally plummet into the abyss of evil, corroded by perfidy, as its walls would be by time? There, that was what he would write, he said, picking up his quill and starting to write down the first lines that came seething into his mind. The city of Dis, the end of his poem. Because it was impossible to leave the depths, to see the stars and ascend to heaven.

That was where his work would end, in darkness and in fire. In that deep trough to which everything falls, because it is man's nature, as the Decurion had said. And neither wisdom nor knowledge nor faith could defeat that desperate will to fall, which ruins everyone.

And he too fell, still lining up his verses one after the other, going down the paper as his poem went down into the depths of the Earth. Certainly this would be the end: an encounter. But not with God, who had now vanished from his horizon. In the company of Virgil, the one who knew everything, he would pass through the gates of the city of iron, and there he would meet his fate.

The lines went on taking shape under his pen, with a fury and fluency that he hadn't felt for years: they spilled into his mind already composed. The rhymes interwove, guided by a supernatural force; they sang in his head with the melodious voice of the sirens. The great pool where everything ends up shone beneath his eyes with the light of poetry, rendered yet more bitter by its beauty.

And so, as the night progressed, line after line – as if on an interminable staircase – with his mind excited by fever, Dante wrote his celebration of hell.

*

16th November, shortly after midnight

HE LOOKED up from the paper, exhausted by all his efforts. He barely had the strength to turn the pages face down, to defeat the temptation to reread what the Furies had dictated to him.

He sat motionless, staring distraught at the pages. He felt as if he had diluted the whole of himself in words, as if his soul no longer existed.

But his senses must have been alert, because at that moment he heard footsteps outside, and a hand touching the latch. Then he heard a faint metallic sound, barely perceptible.

He got slowly to his feet, trying to overcome a feeling of vertigo. He reached his hand out, to be certain of what he had sensed, and tried to lift the latch. There must have been an obstacle on the other side, as if someone had deliberately blocked the doorway to limit his movements.

Now he was sure that someone wanted to hide from him what was happening in the castle. But who? He immediately ruled out the senator: if Saturniano Spada had wanted to keep him in the dark about his plans, he certainly wouldn't have insisted on Dante accompanying him on this inspection of the crusader forces. And the Persian didn't appear to be the author of this outrage, either. Which left only Sciarra Colonna.

He thought again of the man's reaction when he had

recognised him. Of his disdainful irony, which had made Dante furious. But had prevented him from noticing something that he now realised in the cold light of day – that Colonna's attitude really concealed his concern at seeing the poet there. As if the fact of knowing Dante was at Boniface's court was already a threat to him, and yet Colonna had shown that he knew Dante's works, and should also have known his feelings about the simoniac Pope: he was sure that the echo of his speeches in the Council had reached as far as Rome. Dante was certainly not an enemy of his.

So what was it that he was not supposed to see, here in the castle? He started running through all the strange things he had noticed. But the only things that came to mind were the most obvious ones: Boniface's enemies associated with a venture led precisely by the Pope's trusted man, and the small number of soldiers. Certainly, he had been given explanations for both of these things, but it was not enough to satisfy him.

Measured footsteps approached outside. He heard them stopping briefly outside his door, then the sound resumed, moving away. It must have been the night-sentry on his patrol. So he was being guarded as well as locked up!

He was seized by the desire to escape that place, which now felt suddenly hostile. He quickly picked up his papers and stowed them away in the inside pocket of his cloak.

Then he went to the loophole window, trying to lean out as far as possible. His body just fitted through the narrow passageway. From that position he could make out part of the courtyard, where the fires had now gone out and the dark shapes of the men had fallen asleep under their blankets.

Forty feet below he saw the tiles of the roof of the castle lodgings. Not far from the window ran a gutter for the rainwater. If he could get to it from there, he would be able to get to the ground, and maybe discover what it was that they were trying to hide from him. But getting to it looked dangerous: only a narrow cornice separated him from a disastrous fall, and he wasn't sure about the solidity of the bricks from which it had been built.

He was measuring the leap that would have been required to reach his goal when he was drawn by a movement in the courtyard. A shadow was wandering furtively among the tents, covered by a whitish cloak that flapped in the wind. Dante's heart skipped a beat.

He had thought he recognised the agile movements of Fiamma. But if it was Fiamma, why had the senator not told him she was there? And what was she doing in the middle of the soldiers' tents? For a moment he clutched at the possibility that it might be someone else, perhaps a courtesan in search of customers.

The woman seemed to be looking for something. He saw her taking a few more quick steps. Then a second shadow appeared behind her, this one taller and solidly built. A man, who had gripped her by one arm and pulled her to him.

There seemed to be a quick exchange of words between the two of them, but all he could hear were some muffled and incomprehensible fragments. Then all of a sudden the woman started wriggling vigorously, trying to free herself from the grip with which the man was pulling her by her wrists, in an attempt to kiss her.

In their silent struggle the hood hiding her head had slipped to her shoulders. With a shiver, Dante recognised the cascade of Fiamma's raven hair, gleaming in the moonlight.

A painful vice clamped his innards, and he was filled with rage. He was sure the man was none other than Sciarra Colonna. Whatever the link between them, it was plain that the woman was trying to escape some sort of rough and indecent violence. Without any further hesitation, he pushed himself out of the loophole, dropping onto the cornice and then clinging to the wall until he reached the drainpipe. The frenzy that had taken hold of him made him fearless: he clutched the terracotta pipe without even thinking of testing its solidity, and started sliding towards the roof below, kicking at the wall to slow his descent.

Moments later he leaped onto the roof and turned towards the two shadows. The man and the woman didn't seem to have noticed anything; Sciarra was still holding onto the girl's wrists and laughing his vulgar laugh. Dante had already put his hand on his dagger, and was preparing to perform his final leap to the courtyard level, when the laughter was broken by a cry of pain. Fiamma had plunged her teeth into the man's hand and had managed to free herself. Dante saw her springing back and disappearing behind the corner of the wall.

Sciarra Colonna had brought his injured hand to his mouth and was swallowing back a curse. 'Damned whore!' were the words that reached Dante's ears. 'You mad whore!'

Meanwhile Dante had swung his legs over the edge of the stable roof and was now dangling in mid-air. With one last bound he landed on the flagstones, just in time to see Colonna heading off in the opposite direction to Fiamma, and passing through the door that led to the tower of the keep.

He ran after Sciarra, ready to attack. The other man was younger and stronger than he was, but such was his fury at what he had seen, so violent his desire for revenge, that he didn't assess the risk for even a moment.

But once he reached the door through which the man had passed, his rage suddenly subsided. It was as if his will were broken: what did he want to avenge himself for, on a man who had saved his life? Was his mean envy not simply that of a frustrated lover, who had discovered that the object of his love might have relationships unknown to him?

The idea that Fiamma might have chosen a pair of wide shoulders over the blade of his intellect was what hurt him the most. *Damned whore*, Colonna had called her. If only he could have said as much, he thought angrily, putting his dagger back in his secret pocket.

All around, the most absolute peace still reigned, as if no one had noticed what had happened. From the tents came only the occasional murmur, and every now and again a louder snore. Gripped by sudden doubt, Dante cautiously approached the closest tent and peered through the opening.

It was empty. Just as many of the others were, he was stunned to discover after a quick and silent exploration. Where were the men who should have occupied them? Had they gone to the embarkation point, to join the others who, according to the senator, were already supposed to be meeting up there? And why?

This mysterious place was awakening an increasingly intense curiosity in him. He looked quickly around. There were only two sentries, leaning on their lances, who merely cast him a distracted glance before returning to their half-sleep.

Perhaps they had noticed him when he arrived along with the senator. Or else these men felt entirely calm in the shelter of the marshland. Taking advantage of the lack of any reaction, Dante moved towards the castle door, feigning an air of indifference.

As he prepared a justification for his nocturnal sortie, he was startled to discover that the door wasn't guarded, and the drawbridge was lowered. He kept going, stepping across the boarding at a leisurely pace. Perhaps his confidence was down to the presence of the other men outside the wall, whom the senator had mentioned. But as he left the castle he saw no sign of any other encampments anywhere in the vicinity.

Trajan's port couldn't be far off, but where? The clouds had opened a little, and the moonlight fell on a desolate panorama, without reference points of any kind. Dante had only a vague idea of where the coast might be, somewhere towards the west. There was a path which led in that direction, towards some dark masses that he could see in the distance – walls, apparently, and little humps and hills that largely hid them from view. He decided to head in that direction.

He had walked perhaps a thousand paces when he suddenly felt a paved road under his feet. There were fragments of wall here and there, growing taller as he walked, and then the remains of increasingly grand buildings. The road seemed to have turned into the main street of an ancient city, with its squares surrounded by columns, some of them still standing, but most of them ruined on the ground. And statues that still raised their arms to the sky, and the remains of fountains and arches. Suddenly he found himself looking at the curve of a large building supported by solid pillars; he followed its perimeter until he emerged into a clearing of shrubs and trees.

He had stepped into the orchestra of a big theatre. Behind him, the stage still stood as imposingly as ever: the façade of an imperial palace, carved with blind windows and bristling with columns, before which dramas of men and gods must once have been played out.

In one of the doors on the stage he thought he could see a light burning. He cautiously approached, his hand gripping the handle of his dagger. When he appeared in the doorway his fears subsided.

The little room had been turned into a family's lodging. There were a man and a woman there, sitting at a rough table, and children running around among their legs, ignoring the ancient glory that gave them their roof. Seeing him, the man leaped to his feet in alarm, but Dante immediately calmed him, spreading his arms in a sign of peace.

'I'm a stranger, looking for the ancient Roman port.'

The man went on staring at him suspiciously, while the woman had hurried to gather the children together behind the table.

The other man waited a long while before replying, as if he thought there was something strange about the poet's appearance. At last he decided to speak. 'There is no port over there,' he said in a barbarian and almost incomprehensible accent.

'No port?' Dante said, perplexed. 'I mean the place where the fleet's being fitted out, in ancient Ostia.'

'There is nothing, sir, beyond that hill. Just the marshland, which they say goes all the way to the sea. But I've never seen it. Where the living disappear. Do not go beyond the hill, sir, the Christian lands end here,' the man continued, hunching his shoulders as if he felt cold. 'Beyond the trench of Galeria there is nothing but Pope Gregory's village. But it was abandoned after the plague, and even the soldiers have fled the Fortress,' he added, crossing himself quickly.

'But there's a port somewhere hereabouts. The port of the ancient Emperor Trajan! You must have heard it mentioned!' the poet replied, irritated by the peasant's reticence.

'No port. Just the Devil's Pond, at the end of the river.'

'The Devil's Pond? What's that?'

'A star-shaped lake. It's where the stone that decorated Lucifer's head is said to have fallen.'

'A lake? Can you show me how to get there?'

'You have to pass by the river. It's night, it's an accursed place,' the man replied, shaking his head.

Dante fished in his pocket and took out a silver coin. The man's eyes gleamed. 'It's for you if you take me there,' the poet said, making the coin jump in the palm of his hand.

The man hesitated for another moment, then suddenly seemed to make up his mind. 'Come,' he said, 'we'll go in my boat.'

He threw his cloak over his shoulders, then set off along a path among the ruins, ignoring the confused pleas of his wife, who was trying in vain to hold him back.

The river lay about a hundred yards away. The man invited him to board a little boat, which seemed to be carved from a tree-trunk, from banks that were so low that they dangerously touched the waters of the rain-swollen river. Then, pushing hard on a pole, the man began to row against the current, staying close to the banks.

The shrubs and reeds brushed their heads as they carried on along their route. Eventually the poet saw the river forking. The oarsman doubled his efforts and began to cross the river, heading towards the branch on the other side. As he proceeded, the current became more violent, and the eddies threatened to capsize the boat. But the man must have been intimately acquainted with the river and its perils, because slowly but surely, with every stroke of the oar, he gained a few feet in the direction that he wanted to travel, until he finally pulled into the branch of the river.

The appearance of this new stretch of river was most

curious, Dante thought. Narrower and less impetuous than the other, it descended towards the sea at a regular rate that seemed as if it might not have been the work of nature. Perhaps it had once been an artificial canal, dug to connect the Tiber to the port. In which case the thing that he was looking for couldn't be far away.

The boat approached the shore again. 'There's nothing but the city of the dead over there,' said the boatman, greedily holding out his hand towards the poet, who was leaping to land.

Dante showed him the coin again, then clenched his fist. 'Wait for me here. It will be yours only on my return.'

Then he started scrambling up the steep slope, trying to reach a low stonework plinth that he had glimpsed among the bushes. The ridge of the hill was also covered with stone, as if it had once been a ramp to the top that even carts could climb. As if to confirm the peasant's assurance, as he climbed up the exhausting slope he saw the paving of the road crumbling under his feet. The stones became more sparse, and spaces of rough grass opened among them until they obliterated whole stretches of it completely.

There was a grove of pine trees at the top. He could have moved freely among the trees all the way to the sea that glittered some miles away, half-hidden by dense marsh vegetation. A hundred yards away there were still shape-less remains of buildings, and a big patch of dark green, to which the road descended, losing itself among the first puddles of stagnant water.

Pushing his way through a mass of bushes, he went on walking towards the place where the buildings could be glimpsed among the pines. At last he reached what seemed to be the start of a covered colonnade, supported by two long rows of Corinthian columns.

The roof was broken at several points, eroded by time and the mass of climbing plants that fell through the barrel-vaults, obscuring the view. From beyond the barrier came the croaking of frogs, so intense in comparison with the silence of a moment before that it was almost deafening. He moved the foliage aside.

In front of his eyes an expanse of still water appeared, perfectly hexagonal in shape, almost completely covered by a greenish slime of algae and aquatic plants. A huge basin, lined with colonnades like the one he had just walked along. And, like it, it was submerged in vegetation and had at several points collapsed. Sloping from the quays of the old port he could still see the beginnings of the ramps for the launch of triremes, the remains of warehouses, the remnants of the lighthouse at the entrance to the canal.

For a moment his view of the ruin was obliterated by the *virtus imaginativa* described by the great Boethius: the ghosts of ships now lost in the abyss re-emerged from time with all the splendour of their sails and masts; a roar of voices drowned out the croaking of the frogs; the sharp smell of goods and spices reached his nostrils. Dante saw the greatness of what had once been the gate to the Empire, a colossal work in which the memory of other great events was reflected: Carthage with its port in flames, Babylon with its truncated towers rising in search of the gods. A confused hum filled his head, and he felt his knees giving way under his weight. He fell to his knees defeated by weariness, but even more by the violence of his dream.

He couldn't have said how much time had passed. The clouds had started piling up above him, the sky was closing in. The rain had begun falling again. He shook himself and struggled to his feet. The vision had disappeared, and the ancient greatness had vanished under the weight of time, bringing back the expanse of water in its current appearance. He looked around for the slipways where the crusader fleet was being prepared.

But there was nothing, just some time-worn stonework and fragments of marble. Not a trace of the venture they had claimed was under way. His mind ran frantically through a forest of hypotheses. Scattered elements began to fit together in his memory, and then all of a sudden he understood.

It was all fake. An illusion, a canvas background like the stage of a fairground theatre. He had failed to see what had always been right before his eyes.

He glanced around one last time, discouraged. The rain had started falling again, chilly and dense, wrinkling the water in the basin. What had until a moment before been a still mirror, in which the outline of the quays was reflected like a frame, now seemed merely a big muddy puddle, stripped of all nobility.

He took his head in his hands, trying to get rid of the pain that had begun to assail him once more. He was alone, at least fifteen miles from the city, with no way of getting back there in time. Before . . .

Before what? In his feverish imagination the details of the mystery were falling into place, in an apparently logical sequence. But it was a meaningless order – he now had proof of it in this desolate spot. He had been pursuing the trail of a religious obsession, a crazy vendetta. But the cruel slaughter of those innocent women seemed to be only the visible part of a secret plot . . . like everything in this damned city! Where ports didn't receive the ships they should have done, and even the relic of the she-Pope was only one more macabre masquerade.

He had to inform the senator, as quickly as possible. The only man who seemed still to have enough power to take the situation in hand, to foil the threat that was in preparation, whatever it might be. Now Dante was sorry that he had crept from the Fortress like a thief; he had to get back down there as quickly as possible, tell the senator that his good faith had been deceived, that none of his orders had been executed. That his men were waiting pointlessly for an embarkation that would never take place.

Someone had siphoned off the funding for the venture, sold to whom knows who the wood that was meant for the fleet. Someone close to the senator, someone he trusted. And now he himself was the predestined victim, the one who had to be made to disappear, to avoid this colossal swindle coming to light. Perhaps his murderer was already preparing to strike, hidden among the soldiers camping at the castle, his blade already gripped in his fist. So Senator Saturniano would pay with his life for his dreams of redeeming Rome, for his crazed desire to take the place of Providence and rebuild a grandeur brought low by the will of God.

He slumped onto the broken trunk of a column, ignoring the rain that drenched his clothes as it slipped down his back. He shook his head, thinking sadly of the pain that lay in wait for the senator's daughter when her father was ruined. That noble voice, destined by nature to fly like an eagle in the crystal sky of the wise spirits, and which would be sadly extinguished in the shadow of some convent somewhere, walled up alive to pay for her father's shame.

A fit of rage seemed to reinvigorate him. Perhaps there was still time to warn Spada.

He set off again, along the road down which he had already walked, trying to get his bearings in the forest of marshy paths, until he reached the point where he had stepped off the boat.

The man was still there waiting for him. Dante threw him the coin, which the other man caught greedily.

THE FORTRESS seemed strangely silent. Only a single brazier burned on one of its towers, spreading a faint reddish light all around. On the moat, the drawbridge had fallen, and the gate was wide open, with no apparent guards. Dante ran the last few steps, his feet bouncing on the boards like the drums of an attacking army, and emerged breathlessly into the courtyard.

He looked all around, in search of the little army that had until only a few hours before filled that space with shouted orders and the clangour of men-at-arms. There was no one, as if the desolation of the port had extended all the way here, like a plague.

The rain had turned the ill-paved courtyard into a slippery quagmire; as he struggled to stay upright, Dante became aware of a sound coming from above. At the top of a narrow stone staircase that climbed towards the terraces, a door had creaked open and a head had poked out.

'What are you looking for, stranger?' he heard a voice shout, in the barely decipherable barbarian speech that he had by now learned to associate with these parts.

'The men of the crusade. Senator Spada! Where are they?'

'Crusade? Don't know what you're talking about,' replied the man, who had by now opened the door a little further to reveal a long lance. 'If you're a pilgrim, Rome's a long way away: you'll have to set off right now – there's nowhere for you to stay here, tonight. This is the land of the Colonna, they don't want tramps in their houses!'

The man had become threatening, now that he was sure Dante was alone. But the poet paid him no attention, bewildered as he was from the exertion of running through the marshes, and by his surprise at what he had just found. 'Senator Spada! Where has he gone?' he repeated, exhausted.

The rain had started falling even harder, but he couldn't even feel it any more. The other man took another step forward, waving his lance again. Now Dante could see him clearly, an old man with long grey hair and an unkempt beard, in the rough clothes of country people. But still strong in the arm and solid on his feet.

'They've all gone to Rome. You go too, or I'll make you regret it!'

'To Rome?' Dante murmured, baffled. 'But why . . . hasn't he gone to inspect the port?'

'They're all on the way to Rome, I tell you. Be off!'

'I need a horse, I'll pay you for it.'

'There are no horses here. Be off, I said!'

As he spoke there was a flash of lightning nearby, which flooded the courtyard with dazzling light for a moment. Immediately afterwards a loud thunderclap pierced the air and reverberated through the space. A frightened whinny followed the report, giving the lie to the man's words. Dante suddenly turned towards a gate on the opposite side of the courtyard, from where the sound seemed to have come. Immediately another whinny, louder this time, confirmed that the man was lying. Without waiting any longer, he moved quickly in that direction.

He was already at the gate, and trying frantically to untie the rope that held it shut, when behind him he heard the excited footsteps of the man, who had come down the steps and was now heading towards him with his lance lowered.

'Be off! Thief!' the man shouted again, then ran straight for him. Dante was still trying to open the gate. He had just enough time to dart sideways, avoiding the tip of the lance, which brushed past his thigh and embedded itself violently in the wood. Dante gripped the pole with all his might, trying to keep it in its harmless position. Then he delivered a kick to the man's belly, bending him double and making him roar with pain.

'I need this animal,' he shouted firmly. Pulling out the lance, he broke it in two on his knee and threw the pieces far away. Then, after another glance at the man, who still stood there panting, he started working on the rope again, finally managing to open the gate. In the stable, on the stale straw, there was only one gaunt bay, busy chewing on a scrap of hay in a sack.

Dante looked around. There was no trace of a saddle, only some old harnesses hanging from a bit of wood. Over the horse he threw a blanket that lay in a corner and, after freeing it from its feed-bag, he was about to put in the bit when he felt himself being hurled to the ground by a violent blow.

He tried to struggle back to his feet, but the old man had leaped on his back and was trying to suffocate him against the straw. His mouth, wide open as he gasped for air, filled up with a mixture of straw and horse-dung. With a desperate lurch Dante managed to swing round, and struggled to free himself from the grip that the other man had on his throat. The old man's nails tore at his skin, while with his vision blurred, the poet went on struggling desperately to free himself. By biting the man's ear, Dante managed to force him to relax his grip, then, still clutching him, he rolled through the door once more in a tangle of arms and legs.

As soon as he was outside, the lashing rain revived him, along with the painful harshness of the cobbles against his knees. He blindly gripped the throat of his adversary; who cried out like a flayed animal. He beat the old man violently against the stones, until he heard his moans growing fainter and no longer felt any consistency in his muscles. Only then, with a sudden movement of horror, did he let go of the man's throat, leaving him as inert as a wet rag beneath his fingers.

He got back up, panting and shivering violently. The blind beast that had awoken within him howled and slashed, searing him with pain. He couldn't bring himself to look again at that lifeless body, as he leaped on the horse and sped towards the road to Rome.

14

16th November, morning

H E TRAVELLED the miles to the city in a state of stunned intoxication, as his fever rose and he began trembling uncontrollably. The horse panted and whinnied under the constant kicks of his heels, hampered by the rain and the puddles that blocked its way with mounting frequency.

At last, as in a dream, just past the low hills of the last stretch of the Portuense district, Dante saw in the distance the walls of Rome and the Porta Portese. On the other side of the river he could make out the rain-drenched apex of the white marble pyramid, like a milestone put there by the hand of some god, he thought, taking in a great lungful of air and rainwater. Constant coughing was tearing his chest apart, and an increasingly violent feeling of exhaustion drained his breath.

A dark cloud-bank hung above the walls. When he drew near, a sharp smell of burning stung his nostrils. The big gate was locked, and there was no sign of anyone on the guards' communication trench. He met some men coming away very quickly, weighed down with bundles. As they ran, they constantly darted anxious glances towards an invisible danger.

'The river! It's rising!' he heard them shouting, and immediately they turned again towards the far-off menace. In their haste a small service-passage cut into the oak door had been left open. He leapt from his horse, passed through the door and plunged into the maze of alleyways.

He looked around in bewilderment.

The whole area seemed to be in flames, with columns of dark smoke rising high into the sky, heedless of the rain. At one point in particular the pyre seemed invincible. He began to worry that it might be the widow's house, and that his papers were going up in flames along with his lodgings. Stirred by a sudden frenzy, he ran in that direction.

When he had run about a hundred yards he stopped in front of the cause of the flames: the fire was devouring the synagogue, fought in vain by a small crowd that had created a long chain of buckets all the way to the bank of the Tiber. When he arrived, the men and women in the chain were giving up, vanquished by the heat and their desperation over the outcome of their efforts. Among them he recognised the dead girl's young brother.

'What's happened?' he shouted, trying to make himself heard among the swirls of sharp-smelling smoke that threatened to suffocate him.

'All hell has broken loose, Messer Alighieri,' the boy replied, while with the back of his hand he tried to wipe away the tears that filled his eyes. 'A gang attacked the district and set fire to the homes of the Jews. Then they attacked the synagogue!'

'Who are they? Boniface's men?'

'No, they're ordinary people, they've come from the Ponte dell'Isola. We don't know why they're doing it, they're shouting that all idols must be destroyed . . .'

'And where's the rabbi?'

'Mastro Manoello has locked himself in his house – perhaps he's trying to hide the vestments and the Torah rolls. He ordered the community to flee to the other side of the river, towards the Torre Argentina. There are already some co-religionists over there, they might be able to take in the fugitives. There won't be any Jews on this bank of the Tiber for a long time to come . . .'

'You should flee too, but try to be quick about it,' Dante shouted, as he too retreated, vanquished by the heat. 'The river is breaking its banks everywhere, and this time it could drag even the bridges to the island away from their foundations. Or perhaps the island itself will slip its moorings and resume its course towards the mouth of the river, which it interrupted centuries ago.'

Meanwhile the internal structure of the little dome that topped the synagogue flared up still more intensely, throwing into the sky a cloud of incandescent sparks, like a candle flame just before it gives its last light. Then the joists gave, and the whole mass collapsed in on itself, leaving behind only an empty tower, consumed from within.

'Help me save the rabbi, Messere!' the boy begged him, gripping Dante's hand and dragging him towards a small house that leaned against the wall of the synagogue, and which had so far been miraculously spared by the flames.

The door was barred. Dante knocked desperately on it several times, and then, seeing that no reply was coming from inside, he brought the worn-out door down with a firm blow of his shoulder.

What met his eyes was incredible. Manoello was standing in the middle of the little room, in the solemn robes that the poet had seen him wearing on the Campidoglio, his hands raised to the sky as he intoned a chant in his unfamiliar language. At his feet was a motionless human form, as if frozen in the sleep of death.

A strange, blackish creature. Dante thought it must be one of the victims charred by the flames, to whom the rabbi was delivering the rites of the dead.

The rabbi had interrupted his chant. Dante saw him bending over the damp mass that represented the head, and tracing incomprehensible signs upon it.

'Live!' he heard him cry. Then the rabbi fell to his knees until his forehead was touching the muddy mass, and repeated again, 'Live! Live!' in a melancholy voice.

Puzzled, Dante followed his movements. He went over to the man and gripped him by a shoulder.

'Manoello, what are you doing?' he exclaimed. 'You've got to get to safety, the fire is at the gates!'

'He will live – it's written in the book . . . He will come to help us . . .'

Dante shook him again, more violently this time. 'The synagogue is in flames, soon this house will burn as well. You have to join your people, they need your leadership. Escape to the other side of the Tiber – you have to go with them!'

The rabbi paced agitatedly around the little room, which was already filled with smoke from the fire. Suddenly he brought his hands to his mouth and bit them hard. 'My faith is weak, it is not enough to bring the golem to life! God is punishing me, and with me my people.'

THE ASHES mixed with rain had turned into a sticky morass, which ran down the walls of the humble shacks piled together in the streets. Dante and the boy hurled themselves towards the river, as the flaming structure of the synagogue finally collapsed behind them, sending out a great blast of embers and fragments of flaming beams.

'Go to your mother, boy,' the poet said. 'She needs you even more now.'

'And what will you do, Ambassador?'

'I . . . I don't know. Yet. But first I have to find Senator Spada. Warn him about what's happening. Someone's scheming . . .'

Dante thought furiously about what was to be done. As the boy ran off, he suddenly saw a tall figure wrapped from head to toe in a cloak, pressing a flap of it to his mouth against the smoke.

'Messer Martino!' he called out as he recognised him. 'Are you here too?'

'I was looking for you, Alighieri.'

'For me?'

'I have a message for you. The last one before I leave the city.'

'You're going? You too?'

The other man gestured vaguely with his hand. 'Venice already knows what it needs to regulate its government. A courier came this morning with orders for me. And news of other parts of Italy.' A shiver suddenly ran down the poet's spine. But before he could say anything, the other man went on. 'He passed through Florence, as you may imagine.'

'What's happening in my city?'

'Just what you feared. With the help of the French, Corso Donati has overturned the White party, and now his men are in charge and taking their revenge. They are running through the houses of their enemies, plundering all their goods.'

'My wife . . . my children . . .' Dante murmured.

'They're still safe, for the time being. The vendettas started with the poorest and those least able to defend themselves. Charles de Valois is pretending to arbitrate among the factions, maintaining a minimum of order. But it's only a matter of time, and soon he will cast aside his mask, setting trials and banishments in motion. Geri Spini, Betto Brunelleschi, the Buondalmonti, the Agli and the Tornaquinci are sharpening their claws. Come back straight away, and try to defend what's yours. The White party lacks leadership; Vieri dei Cerchi, its head, is a faint-heart who will only try for a compromise, just to save himself and his properties. Be careful, Messer Alighieri,' Martino went on. He had suddenly abandoned his habitual calm. There was a melancholy tone to his voice now, and for the first time he seemed sincere. 'Boniface is preparing to strike you, too. Flee! He still doesn't know that his plans in Florence have come into effect, the papal couriers are still on their way there. But in a few hours, when the news has reached him and he feels safe, he will cast his mask aside and Rome will become your prison. Flee, I implore you!'

'I can't, Martino,' the poet murmured. 'My work is not complete.'

'Your work? You can write your poems anywhere. Every city in Italy will be proud to take you in, if you only ask. Come to Venice with me, I'll protect you against the banners of the Republic.'

Dante shook his head. 'It's not my poems I was thinking about. But the justice that was asked of me, which I did not provide. And then I have to tell the senator about the conspiracy that's going on behind his back: he's an honest man, and he must know . . .'

'A conspiracy . . . behind his back?' the old man repeated doubtfully.

'The crusade that was being prepared – there's something he doesn't know. Something that may ruin him.'

'Senator Spada knows everything,' the Venetian declared unexpectedly.

Dante stared at him in bafflement. 'Everything? Even what's happening at Trajan's port?'

'Nothing can ruin him. Except what he himself is hatching,' the old man replied enigmatically. 'Flee, I beg you!'

'I have made a pact with him. I can't abandon him,' Dante murmured. But as he uttered those words he was aware that he was lying, to himself first and foremost. It was Fiamma who chained him to Rome, and the desire to see her once again.

'You've made your decision – let it be for the best. Many things divide us,' the old man said, stepping forward and gripping the poet's arms. 'But maybe there's something else that unites us even more strongly: the love of knowledge. And if I had a great deal of life still ahead of me, I'm sure our paths would cross again. And just as two wayfarers on an unfamiliar road would exchange the little they have in their knapsacks, that would be enough to illuminate the darkness of the desert for a night. But now almost a century weighs upon my shoulders. I have seen the glory of the Emperor Frederick, and I won't see what you will be able to add to his glory.'

Filled with emotion, Dante threw himself into the arms that the other man held out to him. Then the old man gently pulled away and disappeared beyond the corner of the street.

Flee. But where to? If what Martino had said was true, his city was waiting for him, only to throw him in irons. And Boniface would nail those irons shut with all the force of his hostility. Perhaps only Saturniano Spada would be able to help him, if he really was still alive. But could he trust the senator, Boniface's man? For how long would he be able to withstand his boss's will?

He thought again of the man's noble features, of his measured words. Could the senator be merely a dissembler, ready to betray him? And what other hopes were left to him?

He quickly decided on a course of action: he would try to reach the senator before he received his orders from Boniface, to ask him for a pass as far as Viterbo. From there he would enter Tuscany, and then in Siena he would seek shelter and wait to see how things turned out.

But where could he find Spada? Certainly the critical situation in the city would call for a meeting of the Senate, and the senator couldn't miss that. He could go and look for Spada at the Campidoglio, he said to himself, as he headed resolutely for the Ponte dell'Isola.

Under the pelting rain he set off towards the bridge. But as he emerged along the river, an unsettling spectacle awaited him: the waters of the Tiber had risen, submerging the banks and licking at the doorways of the buildings that stood almost on the water's edge. The last arch of the Ponte Cestio was now under water, and the muddy floods had reached the closed door of the watchmen's tower. Wading up to his ankles in the water, Dante headed towards the door, trying to attract the attention of the guards, who had taken refuge under the canopy.

'Open up! I must pass, I am the ambassador of Florence,' he yelled in as loud a voice as he could muster.

'Caetani rules here!' one of the men called from above, leaning slightly over the edge. 'The pass is closed.'

'I have an urgent message for Senator Spada. Open up, or his punishment will fall upon you.'

The senator's name must have had some effect, because a few moments later he heard a sound of chains and the shutter rose just enough to let him through. In the arch that passed through the whole length of the tower, there were three men, weapons in their hands, their chests bearing the waves of the papal insignia. They peered at Dante suspiciously and then, seeing that he was unarmed, stepped aside.

'You did well,' the poet exclaimed. 'Where is the senator? At the Campidoglio?'

The three men glanced dubiously at one another, then the oldest of them threw out his arms. 'What do we know, stranger? We received the order to let him pass, perhaps to make sure that all that rabble from Trastevere didn't come pouring in from the other side of the city. We've already sent back a gang of Jews who wanted to get through, but you strike me as a good Christian. They say an army of Ghibellines smashed their way through at Porta San Paolo, and that there's fighting down by the Colosseum. We're staying here, waiting for more orders from the Castello.'

'Let's hope they get there before the Tiber does!' another, younger man exclaimed, pointing to a flood of water that was already pouring in through the gap.

'I'm not staying here to provide work for the Hoods,' the third man said angrily. 'And you,' he added roughly, 'get a move on!'

Dante slipped under the barrier, which immediately fell back behind him with a mighty splash.

'You're not trying to stop the Tiber with those planks?' the poet asked as he passed along the covered passage.

'Nothing stops the river, stranger,' the old man replied lugubriously behind him.

ON THE other side of the island the Caetani Tower seemed to have been abandoned. Dante crossed the second bridge without encountering a single obstacle. But when he was on the opposite bank he suddenly realised how little he knew the city: he desperately tried to reconstruct a map in his mind, connecting the different places that he still had in his memory. But in his imagination he only managed to draw up a kind of disjointed tapestry, in which the mass of buildings mixed together in an indecipherable chaos. Where, in relation to where he was now, were the Campidoglio, the Colosseum? The Castel Sant'Angelo, and the big columns that he had seen? He remembered only that to reach the Senate he had passed through a densely populated area, and then climbed up the slopes of a pleasant hill, rich in tilled fields and beautiful buildings. He had walked along a winding road, which wrapped in an embrace the big rock of the Capitoline Hill.

'Which way to the Campidoglio?' he called to someone who was passing, buried under a huge bundle of rags. The man stared at him suspiciously for a moment at the sound of his foreign accent, then seemed to accept that he was only one pilgrim among many. 'Take the road towards the

Teatro di Marcello, then turn left. You'll reach the steps of the Ara Coeli, and you'll see it from there. But take care,' he added, as the poet set off in the direction that he had indicated. 'The Tiber is rising, don't go towards the Campo Marzio!'

He followed the man's directions, walking along the Tarpeian Rock. At the top of the hill there were clear signs of a battle: some carts lay upside down in the middle of the road, surrounded by men in armour who seemed to be waiting for something. Here and there one could see the banners of the papacy, along with the yellow and red flags of the Senate. At the foot of the steps leading to the Ara Coeli there were more traces of fighting and, at the top, in front of the church, more soldiers who appeared to be guarding the hill.

He stopped an officer who was dashing down the hill, asking him for news of Senator Spada.

'There's no one at the Palace. The Senate is dissolved!'

'Saturniano Spada? Where is he?' the poet asked, distraught.

'The Curia has ordered all the senators to go to their own houses. He must be at his villa.'

'His villa . . . How can I get there?'

The official shrugged and started running again towards who knows what destination. Dante looked around. There was a thin horse wandering slowly among the remains of the carts. It was limping, with a visible wound in one hoof, drenched in congealed blood. It must have escaped from somewhere, perhaps a caravan of pilgrims, judging by its battered saddle and its worn bridle. But at that moment it seemed to the poet to be the most precious of treasures. He bounded over to it and grabbed it by the tufts of its mane, trying to hold it back. Then, ignoring its whinny of pain, he grabbed the animal's neck and leaped into the saddle.

He spurred the animal hard and hurtled off along the road in front of him, heading towards a crossroads near a ruined apartment block from which he could finally see Trajan's Column, and the start of the road that would bring him to the senator's house.

Down below, at the foot of the column, the fighting was still going on. A dozen men, armed with sticks and other makeshift weapons, had surrounded three or four members of Boniface's guard, and were forcing them against the wall of a house, ignoring their cries for help and mercy.

Dante gave them a wide berth, passing along an alley to the side that seemed deserted, then after a few yards he turned back into the straight road that headed as far as the eye could see towards the Porta Flaminia. He galloped off in that direction, shouting to clear his path through the pedestrians and carts that were flowing tumultuously in the other direction. The end of the road was already under at least six inches of yellowish water, in which the hooves of his mount sent up great sprays of water and threatened to slip with every step.

He travelled several hundred yards and the road suddenly widened, leading into a square with a second column on the left, as big as the one at the Forum. He turned in the other direction, looking out along the road that crossed at that point, and saw the shoulder of the hill upon which the senator's house stood. He turned towards it with a tug on the reins.

LEAVING THE Via Lata, he had begun to ride along the side of the hill that overlooked the Campo Marzio.

At last his destination appeared just past a patch of little fruit trees. He had almost reached the wall surrounding the villa when he felt the horse tottering beneath him with a muffled whinny. The animal came to an abrupt standstill, ignoring the kicks of the poet's heels, then its back legs suddenly collapsed. Dante barely managed to cling to the horse's neck as it fell to the ground, before jumping just far enough not to be crushed by the carcase of the animal, which had fainted with exhaustion.

He struggled back to his feet, trying to conquer his feeling of dizziness. Then he dragged himself, limping, towards the door of the villa.

There was no one there. He ran across the courtyard until he reached the *impluvium*. As he did so, he called in a loud voice, but the sumptuously painted walls returned only the echo of his own voice. He entered the first room, and then the next ones, getting deeper and deeper inside the house. He vaguely remembered the arrangements of the rooms, which followed one another in an endless enfilade.

Around him the furniture of the rooms changed as he approached the apartments of the senator and his daughter; the light that fell from the windows became less intense, protected by precious curtains.

Suddenly he had the feeling that he was lost. He crossed a smaller courtyard, its walls covered with precious onyx, which he didn't seem to remember, and from which another series of rooms opened up. He frantically passed from one to the other, still to no avail. The last door opened onto a bigger room whose walls bore a fresco of a delicate flight of birds that seemed to be exchanging loving kisses through their conjoined beaks. Or perhaps they were engaged in a deadly struggle, he reflected uneasily.

In the middle of the room stood a large stone throne. And on that throne, in precious vestments, Fiamma sat motionlessly, her head covered by a strange kind of mitre. She was staring straight at the door, but she didn't react when he came in, as if she hadn't seen him. Her gaze was dreamy and vacant.

Dante stopped, startled, as a memory passed through his mind. The woman was wearing the same costume he had seen in the little picture at the tavern, encrusted with precious stones. The same one worn by the veiled woman who had officiated at the underground ritual. He thought he could still hear the tinkle of the sistra, the murmur of voices that had accompanied her on her procession through the underground labyrinth. Her headgear was also identical, a big silver circle with two curved crescent moons. And she was holding something on her knees, just as the woman in the picture had held her son.

It was a milky glass jar, of the purest alabaster consistency, similar in shape to the ampulla in the she-Pope's sarcophagus. But there was something different about this one, which added to the purity of the moulding. The upper part wasn't the simple stopper made by Mastro Antonio, but an elaborate sculpture that represented an extraordinary demoniac being, a perverse imitation of the face of a man, as if some diabolical hand had tried to pervert the features carved from the primal clay in the image of God, to make it an obscene object of mockery.

Suddenly he recalled the story of the glass-maker, the strange commission that he had received from his mysterious client. Was this the stopper that had so disturbed him? 'What is it?' he murmured, reaching his hand out towards the jar.

It was only at that moment that the woman appeared to become aware of his presence. 'You are here – you have come. You know the task that awaits you. Is your voice ready to relate what will happen? The return . . .'

'There will be no crusade,' said the poet, trying to speak as gently as possible so as not to increase the girl's unease. But she pressed the jar to her breast and started caressing it with her hand, as she would have done to a child. She seemed to have returned to her strange indifference, her ear listening to inaudible voices.

'What is it?' the poet repeated, stepping closer until he was almost touching the young woman. From that distance he was clearly aware of the intoxicating perfume of her hair that fell in tendrils from the straps of her mitre; he could see the traces of the oil that drenched it, dripping along her delicate cheeks and down towards her slender neck.

'This will be the grave of the base part of me,' she replied unexpectedly. 'When the soul is freed from the body, and goes to justice, lighter than a feather. Then the Mother will delight in me, and I will dwell in her rooms for ever.'

'The mother? The Virgin Mary?'

A smile appeared on Fiamma's lips. 'The Great Mother of all. The goddess Isis, the goddess with a thousand faces, who speaks within me.'

Then she began to say something, in a voice that grew gradually louder, as if she were trying to be heard by someone who was getting further and further away.

Dante listened to the words that flowed from the young

woman's lips, like a ceremonial chant. Every now and again Fiamma abandoned herself to words and whole sentences in that ancient language, as if the poet were able to understand her. Or perhaps she didn't care, in fact, instead addressing the mysterious goddess to whom she was referring, concerned only with her and her judgement. She went on staring into the void with her glassy gaze, the gaze of madness.

He had seen that opaque light before. In the ecstasy of impassioned monks, in the convulsions of those possessed by demons. In the eyes of a forger being dragged to the pyre. Now her face shone with pure beauty, a soul burned out in worship of a far-off goddess, whom the centuries had submerged in the sands of the desert. And superimposed over that angelic face was the memory of the obscene tangle of spellbound bodies in that underground hall, excited by her chant. The face of a woman who seemed to have descended from the sky, and was in fact climbing up from the abyss.

He felt uneasy. He let his arms dangle along his sides and said nothing. Fiamma had stopped speaking, and was still stroking her jar with trepidation. 'I will not die!' she exclaimed suddenly, throwing her head back and spraying a new breath of perfume through the air.

Dante fell at her feet and hugged her knees. 'Your father has been betrayed, I must warn him,' he cried desperately. 'Where is he?'

'I will not die!' the girl said again, leaping to her feet. She stared at the little window as if in search of something. 'It's time! My father awaits me.'

She abruptly freed herself from his grip. She made for the door, brushing past Dante, who was too stunned to stop her.

ONLY AFTER she had disappeared across the threshold did he find the strength to follow her. In the next room two doors opened: he hesitated for a moment, then passed through one of them, thinking he was following the sound of distant footsteps. But beyond the doorway he saw no one, only other doors and other rooms, all deserted.

He was alone. He had to find the way out, but he couldn't remember the labyrinthine route that had brought him to this room: he took a step towards another door, but then turned back, uncertainly. For a long moment he thought of yielding to the weariness of his bones, and slumping to the ground right there, waiting to see what happened, no longer thinking of anything.

He took his head in his hands, completely drained. He had failed in everything. He called to mind the faces of his fellow-citizens, who had trusted in him to repel the Pope's designs on Florence. What would he say, when he returned within the walls of his city, with nothing to show for it? Pursued by Boniface's interdict, suspected by the

Inquisition? And what would he say to the widow, who hoped he would bring justice for her murdered daughter?

Stirring himself, he forced himself to continue walking. Somehow or other he would get out of there, he said to himself, as he faced the door once more and entered the adjoining room. He must have been in a kind of antechamber to Fiamma's apartments: in the dark he glimpsed a series of bed rolls lined up on the floor, perhaps the beds of her handmaidens. He quickly stepped over them one by one, making for the new door that he could see on the opposite side.

He had almost reached the other side when he suddenly stopped, his legs straddling one of the rolls. His attention had been caught by a crunching sound under his feet, as if he had trodden on something that shattered beneath his weight. It seemed to be fragments of glass.

Then he saw it. What he had taken for a sleeping bag was a human body, completely covered by a bloodstained silk cloak. Through the thin veil he could just make out the features of the face, as if it were a shroud. The outline of the nose was especially strong and marked. He quickly bent down, took and lifted a flap of the cloth. Kansbar's face appeared, its features frozen in death. The whole of the lower part of the face was a mask of blood that had spilled copiously from his mouth and then coagulated on the curls of his beard, while his noble brow and his still-open eyes, pupils dilated, seemed strangely immune to the horror that had struck him. That empty gaze still contained all the amazement with which the Persian must have faced his death.

Dante finished pulling away the cloak, which bore the bloody imprint of the man's face, a kind of obscene Veronica. The handle of a dagger protruded from his chest, plunged in almost to the hilt, piercing the lung until the man drowned in his own blood.

He let go of the cloak, while a new cold feeling came over him. It was as if, overcoming the dismay that had crushed his vegetable soul, the irrational part of him, the spirit of reason had finally prevailed. He gripped the handle and pulled it from the wound, then in the faint light brought it up to his eyes: a long, thin weapon like the tongue of a snake, forged in a Damascus steel with so strong and compact a grain that blood slipped along its surface without coagulating, like oil on glass. Almost a pin, a murderous version of the wooden ones that he had seen so often decorating the tresses of the women of Florence. He noticed only a few clotted lumps: the metal was cold, but the Persian could not have been killed more than an hour before.

He bent down, running his hands over the corpse in search of some clue that might give him an explanation of that death. The man still wore his purse tied to his belt. The poet quickly rummaged inside it, without finding anything apart from a few coins and the brass key that activated the marvellous mechanism. Was this what Kansbar had been killed for? To steal a treasure from him? He went on searching the body; the ebony box had fallen not far from him, hidden by the nearest of the beds. It seemed to have suffered some damage at one corner, probably from the effects of its fall. One of the pointers had come loose, but otherwise it appeared to be entirely unharmed. It couldn't possibly have escaped the murderer, so there must have been another motive.

He shivered as he thought back to the reason for his coming. Perhaps the man's death was also linked to the dark conspiracy behind the fake crusade. Perhaps Kansbar too had discovered that nothing had in fact been prepared in terms of the agreement. And he had been eliminated to keep him from revealing the betrayal to his master, who sat in Persia faithfully waiting for the signal to attack alongside the Christian forces. An attack that would never happen, given that there was no trace at Trajan's port of the fleet that was supposed to carry it out.

That meant that the senator too was now in mortal danger. And his daughter, lost in her religious delirium, but still trusting in the enterprise.

The savage face of Sciarra Colonna appeared before his eyes. Had his sneer been the last thing those lifeless eyes had seen? Sciarra, the quarrelsome one, who had only been pretending to make himself available to the plans of the senator and Boniface, while instead pursuing his own secret plan of revenge. Or did he only have his eyes on the chest of gold? And in order to get hold of it, he needed the whole project to collapse in the convulsions of a struggle of all against all, to hide his crimes in the forest of wickedness into which all of Rome had fallen, like a tree hidden in the depths of a wood?

That was why he had killed the Mongols' ambassador, to make the alliance collapse in suspicion and rage. And then he would eliminate Saturniano Spada, who still trusted in him. And Fiamma! Would she too soon be joining the chorus of murdered women?

His eyes filled with tears, as he desperately clenched his fists. He thought again of his naïve determination, of that religious folly that he had suddenly discovered. Of his blind trust in that ancient error. Who would defend her, who would drag her from the sword of betrayal? Or the flames of the pyre, if the Inquisition discovered her ideas?

He had to follow her and stop her before it was too late. But he couldn't tear himself away from the corpse of the Persian. There was something in that image that continued to speak to his soul, but he was unable to understand its words. He was like a traveller in a distant land, listening to the voices of the unfamiliar city in which he has set foot and recognising only the feelings, the joy, the rage or the song, without understanding them.

Yes, it was strange. The man had been struck from in front, with a weapon unlike the ones normally used by men-at-arms, which are broader and more solid. And he had made no attempt to defend himself, Dante thought, noticing his short scimitar still hidden away in the sheath in the silk belt wrapped around his waist.

Not from behind, but by stealth. And by someone Kansbar trusted, someone from whom he feared nothing. Otherwise it would have taken only a bare hand to grip the blade and ward off the blow, perhaps suffering some injuries in self-defence, but certainly not that fatal gash. But his hands appeared intact, with no trace of cuts or scratches. He had faced death impassively.

Or in disbelief. And now at last that voice that screamed within him became comprehensible. And cried out the name of Fiamma.

A VIOLENT feeling of dizziness took over him, as his eyes filled with tears. Then, with the comfort of a friendly voice suddenly breaking the silence, the words of an ancient echoed in his mind:

> *Ipse ignotus, egens, Libyae deserta peragro.*
> *Europa atque Asia pulsus.*

The lament of Aeneas in exile, banished from Europe and from Asia, lost in the desert. The comfort of Virgil's poetry gave Dante courage. His master, the poet dear to all noble souls. And his verses were there, written by his divine hand, in that house!

Suddenly a new energy warmed his limbs. Where was Saturniano's library? Before leaving that house for ever he wanted to see those rolls again, brush with his fingers the ancient papyrus written in his master's hand. He leaped to his feet and left the room.

He started wandering through the deserted rooms, moving around at random, with no preconceived plan. He came and went frantically from the various rooms, but the room full of books seemed to have disappeared. Then at last, at the end of a corridor that he didn't remember ever walking down before, he found the door that led to the library.

From that point he believed he remembered the way to the front door, he thought with relief. As he walked he couldn't overcome the temptation to cast one last glance at the treasures lined up on the shelves. And it was then that he saw something unexpected. In the space between two piles of rolls there were three more jars of alabaster glass, just like the one he had seen in Fiamma's hands.

The same refined manufacture, the same delicacy in the outlines of the carving on their lids. Only the design of these was different: different monsters, different incongruous forms. Three demons stared at him from the shadow of the wardrobe.

With trepidation he picked up one of them and took out its stopper, overcoming his repulsion at the obscene shape that seemed to come alive beneath his fingers. The container was empty: only a faint hint of unfamiliar perfumes emanated from inside it.

Why were they of such importance to Fiamma? And why had the senator, as everything seemed to indicate, commissioned numerous copies of them? The lamp that lit the tomb of the she-Pope was of the same kind, too. Had Kansbar brought its secret back from the East where, according to Manoello, he had gone after the sack of Jerusalem? And was it to preserve that secret that the Persian had been killed?

There was something next to the third jar. It looked like another roll of papyrus. Seized by sudden curiosity, Dante began to unroll it.

In front of his eyes a series of signs appeared, tiny and indecipherable. Some showed recognisable objects – eyes, animals, little human figures, boats plying the waves, jars . . . But some didn't seem to refer to anything familiar. The little signs, written in dark-coloured ink that had faded with time, framed larger figures, drawn with more resolute colours: red, green, blue. The last of these showed scenes from a far-off life, half-naked men busying themselves with strange occupations: some seemed to be praying in chorus, others dragged big chests, with human faces drawn on them. Still others crowded around prostrate bodies, brandishing tools that looked like small scythes, while behind them creatures of superhuman size seemed to be observing their movements with watchful eyes set in the extraordinary heads of birds and dogs.

He looked with greater attention: one of the small figures was shown leaning over the chest of a body, busy . . . extracting its innards. That was what it was doing, cleansing the bodies to embalm them! The roll illustrated the rituals with which the ancient Egyptians obtained their mysterious mummies. And that indecipherable script doubtless described the complex procedures with which the bodies of the pharaohs were said to have been preserved intact until the Christian era.

Then he noticed a little door in the corner. He blindly grabbed the latch and pulled it towards him. In front of him he saw the top of a big stone staircase that disappeared, after a few steps, into the darkness below.

He looked quickly around. On the desk there was an oil lamp. From the purse at his belt he took the waxed cloth bag in which he kept his tinderbox and began quickly striking the flint. Luckily the wax had protected the tinder from the rain: after a few strikes he saw the first sparks flying and the wick coming alight.

Holding the lantern in front of him, he set off down the steep staircase; there must have been another building under the villa, so vast was the room in which he found himself at the end of his descent. An older building, whose large arches now served as foundation.

The big space was half-empty, apart from a few wooden chests and what looked like a large stone tub in the middle. A strong smell took his breath away. He was enwrapped in an aroma that he had never smelled before, a mixture of corruption and opulence, like the breath of a vast animal hidden somewhere in the shadows.

He approached the basin. It was full of a whitish material that looked like salt. On the chests next to it were other glass jars – imitations, yet again, of the precious jars hidden in the library. But these seemed to contain something; through the milky glass he could just make out the vague shapes of dark masses.

He was about to open one when his attention was drawn by something that seemed to protrude from the saline mass. He reached out his hand and picked up the object, drawing it towards him.

The object resisted his efforts, as if the mass in which it was immersed held it in a tight grip. He gave a harder tug. He felt something yielding and starting to move.

With a cry of horror Dante let go of the thing he had been gripping. The fingers of a hand, followed by the arm, had emerged from the salt, like a swimmer surfacing from a dive in the depths of the ocean. Then all of a sudden a head appeared, reduced to a skeletal mask, the dark cavities of its eye-sockets disappearing into the skull. Still attached to the wrinkled skin that still covered part of the forehead was a long hank of hair, which the salt had turned the colour of flax.

He felt his knees giving way and slipped to the ground. Panting, with his heart thumping in his throat, he felt as if all his spirits were in conflict with one another, ready to free themselves from the servitude of his body.

Then he slowly recovered, as his mind finally began to connect all the scattered shadows in which he had been flailing around until that moment. How many more corpses, how many horrors lay hidden in that tub?

He picked up one of the jars and threw it to the ground. Among the glass fragments he saw a brownish mass spreading like a snake on the floor. Biting his lips, he recognised the intestines of one of those unfortunate women, which the murderer's hand had dragged from its belly, still palpitating with its last sparks of life.

He stared again at the horror in the tub. A test, that was what it was. Like the others. A test to produce at last that sinful perfection that was described in the demons' papyruses – the perfect mummy that was supposed to deceive everyone, even the Inquisition. How many lives had been lost for that terrible masquerade with the fake Pope Joan?

The senator's plan seemed clear to him now, in all its folly. His words were acquiring a premonitory meaning.

Preparing the second coming of the ancient religion, to rebuild upon it the grandeur of Rome, shaken to its foundation by the message of Christ.

Was that his plan? To elevate his daughter to the status of revealed priestess of ancient Isis? To exploit her naïvety after taking her to the brink of madness, offer her to the Roman people as a guide, after demonstrating that a woman had already reached the summit of the priesthood once before. Or perhaps to present her to her followers as a reincarnation of Isis herself, to stir up around her the superstition of the mob and build his own dominion upon it.

He couldn't believe what he found himself thinking. Only the blindest folly could have come up with such a plan. How did Saturniano Spada imagine he could rise up against the weapons of the Pope, against his fortresses scattered around the city, the ramparts of his impregnable Castello? Did he really think that a convulsive stirring of popular credulity could defeat centuries of deep faith, and the thought of the great minds who had believed in the existence of a divine order, a meaning to history?

He looked around again, seeking the signs of that madness. How many innocents had paid for it? And how many more would be dragged to their ruin, when the hand of Boniface consigned to the flames of the Inquisition all the poor wretches who were trying to climb this pointless stairway to heaven?

Saturniano would pay the penalty for his crimes. But

what about his daughter, that young mind full of dreams? Even if she had lost the way of salvation, did her youth – her grace – not make her innocent?

He suddenly shook away that thought. He had to save Fiamma, if he still had time; the girl had said her father was waiting for her: where? He wanted to run in search of her, but outside those walls lay the vast desert of Rome: had she returned to the temple of her faith? And how would he find her? Or was the machination happening somewhere else, perhaps in the apartments of St John, or inside the Vatican itself?

Without thinking any further, he leaped towards the stairs and ran through the endless rooms of the villa, until he emerged into the peristyle of the *impluvium*. Here the violent downpour brought him back to his senses: wherever they were, he was sure he would find them somewhere in the centre of the city, near the Campo Marzio.

He ran desperately towards the Via Lata, down the slopes of the hill. From there he could see the water spurting violently below the barred Porta Flaminia, a sign that the countryside beyond it was flooded and the waters were pressing against the Aurelian walls. His feet splashed in the puddles of water that were building up, and streams of mud were being dragged by the increasingly heavy rain.

It seemed as if the whole of the Pincian Hill was dis-integrating in a great mass of mud and detritus, ready to engulf the centre of the city and wipe it away, like one last great barbarian invasion.

From below Dante heard the sound of shouting and the clash of weapons. The whole city was in tumult, and in places he could see columns of smoke rising to the sky, in spite of the rain.

16th November, afternoon

THE ROAD was blocked by a group of armed men piling up chests and looted goods from nearby shops around a wagon overturned in the narrow street. Dante paused apprehensively, trying to spot which insignia they were wearing. But a ragged banner hanging nearby had been so drenched by the rain that it was unrecognisable. For a moment he thought they might be Colonna's men, having come from Castel da Guido to accomplish their real mission.

'Florentine!' he heard someone shout from the barricade.

Then he saw a man detaching himself from the group and running towards him, sword in hand. He recognised the Decurion and stopped uncertainly. The man was on top of him, with his sword to his throat, staring at him suspiciously.

'What are you doing here? Have your fellow-citizens got a hand in this revolt?'

Dante firmly pushed the blade aside. 'What revolt?

Florence sent me to negotiate peace, not war. What's happening?'

In the face of Dante's resolute reaction, the man suddenly seemed less sure of himself. He lowered his weapon, then pointed it to some vague spot beyond the barricade. 'Rome seems to have gone mad! It must be those vagabond pilgrims who are causing uproar. News is coming in of assaults and fires all over the place; the Pope has locked himself away in the Castello and called for reinforcements from the city walls. The senatorial guard is rallied around the Ara Coeli, we've alerted the militia. All the gates are shut, no one can go in or out. You'd be best off getting out of here, like your colleagues, if you really aren't involved in this devilry. Because the devil himself is behind this business!'

'The devil?'

'A group of lunatics that we've repelled a few streets away from here. They attacked us, singing hymns to the new goddess – may the plague take them! What new goddess? There's no one here but Christ and Boniface. Do they mean the Madonna?' he added, as if gripped by sudden doubt. 'And this accursed rain! Couldn't they have their rebellion in the spring, the way they usually do?'

'Master Hemp!' Dante cried, gripping him by his chest. 'Where is the centre of the revolt?'

'Near the river, towards the Ponte del Castello. That's where we're hearing about news of the fiercest clashes, but there isn't a soul who knows what's going on!'

Dante thought furiously. Suddenly his legs felt cold, and he looked down at the ground. The narrow street seemed to have been transformed into a torrent, where the first little whirlpools were already forming on the surface. The phenomenon must have been noticed by the other men, too, because he heard a chorus of shouts rising up among the soldiers.

'The river! It's broken its banks!'

The Decurion turned towards the Tiber, with an anxious expression on his face. 'The autumn floods. That's all we need,' he murmured, biting his lips. 'But at least the water will flush away that crowd of vagabonds. It isn't the first time that the river will have stopped some hothead from getting carried away. When people need to get themselves and their children to safety, they stop thinking about rebellion,' he concluded cynically.

At that moment Dante saw a breathless man running down a side-street. The soldier quickly glanced around the faces of his companions, then leaped towards the Decurion. 'Master Hemp, the river's flooding the districts of the city!'

'I can see that for myself, you idiot!' the Decurion replied scornfully, stamping his foot on the ground and splashing the water that already rose to his calves. 'We'll keep this position for a bit longer, then we'll head towards the Pincian Hill, leaving the Tiber to finish its work.'

'Decurion, the situation is serious. I've come from the river, the flood-wave's coming in! And the storm in the night must have torn some trees from the lands upriver, because tree-trunks are building up at the bend in the river by the Castello. The river isn't getting through. The port has already been filled with water, everybody's leaving the Campo Marzio!'

The Decurion furiously grabbed the man by the collar and shook him. 'What tree-trunks? What are you saying?'

'At the Ponte del Castello. All the arches are blocked now – I'm telling you, this time the whole of Rome's going under!'

Master Hemp pushed the man away and then turned towards the Tiber. 'I'm going to see for myself, you pack of craven idiots.'

'I'll come with you,' Dante said firmly, setting off on his heels.

By now the water was nearly up to their waists. It was impossible to get any further, but on their right, in between two buildings whose doors had already been ripped away by the flood, a wide stretch of the river could be seen. As the soldier had said, an impressive number of tree-trunks had built up against the arches of the bridge, completely blocking them. And more were coming in with the rushing current, to add to the blockade. The whole port of Ripetta had disappeared under the floods, and the water was cascading furiously through the openings between the hovels on the banks.

Dante saw the Decurion gripping his head between

his hands. For the first time the man seemed to have lost his armour of indifference, as if he had only now become aware of the enormity of what was about to happen. His coarse features bore a look of terror.

The poet took his arm and forced him to keep walking. Once his moment of hesitation had passed, the man started walking forward. They walked through the water that was surging in still faster now, a mass of mud that seemed to grab their clothes to drag them down, pulling at the stragglers fleeing in the opposite direction, shouting and wailing, towards the safety of the higher ground. By now the water had reached the base of the walls around the Castello, spouting through the arches of the Ponte dell'Angelo, which now resembled the feet of some marine animal emerging from the depths.

From this point the signs of the disaster were clearly visible. Pushing against the pillars of the bridge there was now a great mass of tree-trunks and foliage, animal carcases and the remains of boats of various sizes, which the raging flood had smashed and dragged with it. Dante could also see a big mill-wheel, which had come to rest against the bank and seemed to want to go on turning under the pressure of the current.

'What the devil . . . How is it possible . . . ?' he heard the Decurion muttering. 'The river must have dragged down a whole forest . . .'

'The trees weren't pulled down,' Dante replied, still

studying the terrifying spectacle through narrowed eyes. 'Look at those tree-trunks – the clean cut at either end. That is the wood that Senator Spada collected to build his fleet. Someone must have pushed it all into the river!'

'What bastard would have done that? I'll have all the mountain wood-cutters hanged . . . I'll strangle them with my own hands . . .' the Decurion had started cursing, as he realised that the poet was right. 'Rome has never seen a spectacle like the one I will prepare – I'll have them nailed to the gates of the city walls . . .'

'That's if Rome still exists after this deluge. Look!' Dante cried, pointing towards a spot in the distance, upriver from where they stood. Towards the north, where the bed of the Tiber curved close to the walls, a dark shadow had appeared, leaping towards them like a vast school of dolphins. A new mass of tree-trunks was coming, it too destined to smash against the barrier.

'We're lost . . .' was all the Decurion had the strength to murmur, pale as a corpse. Dante too was distressed by what he saw, and by the thought of what was on the brink of happening. He was about to turn and try to flee when his attention was drawn by something on the opposite bank. Below the ramparts of the Castello, on the edge of the moat that was about to be joined by the waves of the river, a group of armed men had appeared.

For a moment he had a sense that the little troop of perhaps a hundred soldiers was about to attack the walls of the fortress. But the venture seemed far beyond their capacity. The disaster had plunged them into madness, along with everyone else, if they thought they could assault the ramparts. There was no apparent sign of a siege engine, a battering ram or a catapult. The little dark figures seemed so tiny in comparison to the vast fortified tambour that they looked like a clutch of dolls thrown distractedly onto the shore by the hand of a god playing some mysterious game.

Banners flapped above their heads, but at this distance he couldn't make them out. 'Colonna's men!' he heard the Decurion say, his eyesight apparently keener than the poet's.

'Colonna's men? Them?'

'They've come back from the countryside, like sewer rats!'

Suddenly he remembered the little army that he had seen at the fortress in Ostia. So this was the true destination of the crusade! Then, as his mind tried furiously to find a meaning in all that had been revealed over the past few hours, his attention was drawn by a little boat in the middle of the river, which was trying to get to the opposite shore, propelled by four oars that flew like wings across the surface of the water. Standing up, as if defying the advancing tide of tree-trunks, was a tall, white figure, wearing a very striking piece of headgear. A goddess from the Underworld, plying the waters that separate the living from the dead.

The image of Fiamma exploded inside him. He was seized by a frenzied desire to join her. He looked desperately around in search of some way of crossing the river. He thought of running to the bridge, in the hope that the ancient structure might resist the pressure of the water just long enough to let him cross. But even then, in the time it took to make the journey, he would lose all trace of the woman.

Then he saw a little boat bobbing in their direction. On it were two men, wearing the scarlet uniform that he knew so well. The two members of the confraternity seemed to be busy scouring the waves in search of booty.

'Order those men to come over here,' he called to the Decurion. The man hesitated for a moment, perplexed. At first he seemed about to raise an objection, but the poet's firm tone cut him short. He gestured imperiously towards the boat, shouting at the oarsmen to turn towards them.

'Do you want that boat to take us to safety?' he asked Dante, as the two men drew nearer.

'I want to get to the other side of the river!'

'To do what?' the other man replied in surprise. 'Soon everything will be under water, all the way to the fields of the Vatican. And don't you see Colonna's men? Surely you don't want to end up in their clutches? Or are you in league with them?' he added, suspiciously.

Dante merely shrugged indifferently by way of reply.

All his attention was focused on the slender white figure standing on the boat, which had now passed the middle of the river and was about to reach the opposite shore.

BY NOW the Red Hoods' boat was only a few yards away from them. The two men on board bowed deferentially towards the Decurion, reserving only a suspicious glance for the poet. Without adding anything else, Dante moved towards them, disappearing up to his chest in the muddy water until he gripped the edge of the boat with one hand.

'Take me to the other side!' he ordered imperiously.

One of the two men in the prow glanced towards the Decurion as if asking for an explanation of this request. But, seeing that the man merely shrugged, he got to his feet and planted his oar firmly in the muddy bottom.

'You are mad, stranger. Don't you see the tree-trunks coming down on the current? In a few minutes they'll be on top of us!'

Instead of replying, Dante clutched the boat, pushed himself up on his elbows and hoisted himself in. His movement made the boat rock violently, and it leaned over under his weight until it nearly capsized. Taken by surprise, the standing man lost his balance. He staggered as he tried to clutch his oar, then fell with a splash into the water as the poet slipped to his seat. 'A gold florin if you ferry me over,' he called to the other man, rattling his purse.

A flash of greed lit up the Red Hood's face, more powerful than the apprehension with which he studied the dark, approaching mass. He bit his lips as he assessed the risk, without making his mind up.

Dante looked frantically in his purse, rummaging among his poor copper coins in search of the only florin in his possession. Then he took out the gold coin and held it out to the man.

'Look at John the Baptist! You won't see another one like that for as long as you live.'

Meanwhile he searched in his pocket for the handle of his dagger, ready to use it if the man didn't accept the deal. But, after one last hesitation, he darted forward and took the coin, putting it under his tunic. Then, with a nod of agreement, he made for the bows of the boat, standing up and pushing the oar against the river bed. Behind him his companion had surfaced from his dive, and followed the last phase of the negotiation with his head sticking out of the water. Dante heard him shouting to attract their attention. The man expressed himself in a dialect that the poet barely understood – just enough to know that he, too, wanted to join in the task.

By way of reply, his companion stretched out the oar and brought it down hard on his head. The man went down with a gurgle, while the Red Hood turned to the poet with a savage smile, revealing a set of broken teeth. 'There's no time to lose, Messere. Stay where you are, and leave it to me.'

Dante clenched his fists as the boat moved beneath him, impelled by the oar. As soon as it had left the shore, he felt beneath the small of his back the force of the current, which was suddenly growing more intense.

The oarsman rowed hard, his back to the prow, ignoring the rain, which was now coming down so hard that it filled the bottom of the boat. Dante, who could already feel the water at his ankles, was about to draw attention to the danger, when he noticed that the man was staring at him suspiciously from under his hood.

They were almost at the middle of the river when the man's voice reached him between splashes. 'A florin isn't enough,' he heard him shouting as he drew his oar from the water and held it in mid-air, with the tip pointing towards Dante. 'It's dangerous, as you can see. I want more!'

'How much?'

'Everything!' the man cried, as he suddenly lifted his oar and brought it down hard where the poet was sitting.

Dante rolled swiftly to one side. The oar brushed his head and crashed loudly against the edge of the boat, close to the rowlock. The Red Hood immediately picked it up, but before he could strike again, the poet had grabbed it, and held onto it with the force of desperation. Then he suddenly pushed the oar away from him as hard as he could.

The other man was caught by surprise and reacted a moment too late, falling back until his legs hit the side of the boat. As he tried to regain his equilibrium he let go of the oar, his hands groping uselessly for something to hold onto. The poet took advantage of this to strike him in the chest, prodding him with the tip of the oar, which he was still clutching. The man toppled backwards and fell right into the whirling waters.

For a few moments Dante saw his hand groping around near the boat, trying in vain to grab at the slippery hull. Then the current grabbed him and dragged him towards a whirlpool, where his cries for help finally faded away.

The poet got up from the bottom of the boat, panting with exertion and spluttering with water. But before he regained control of himself completely, the vessel was violently shaken by a blow.

He turned towards the river with a start. A new mass of floating tree-trunks was coming towards him. Trying desperately to keep his balance, he stood up and started pushing the oar, trying to propel the boat towards a spot where the current seemed free of tree-trunks.

Luck more than skill was on his side, he said to himself, as he breathlessly saw the opposite shore approaching. He was looking for a good place to disembark when a fresh impact knocked him over and left him with his legs in the air.

A huge tree-trunk had struck the bow and shifted the boat from its trajectory, pushing it further towards the bank. He desperately clutched the tufts of reeds that sprouted from the waves, pulling on them with all his might to bring the boat closer.

He felt the skin of his hands being pierced by the sharp-edged reeds, but, heedless of the pain, he went on pulling, stroke by stroke, until the boat touched something solid on the bottom. At that point the water didn't seem to be deep, and with a leap he threw himself into the icy water, plunging in up to the waist.

For a long moment he felt imprisoned in the mud, while a new flood-wave rose around him. Then, with a tug, he managed to free his ankles and kept on walking.

HE HAD landed upriver of the Castello. From that point he could see the top of the pyramid of Remus, and further on the ramparts of the castle, now surrounded by water like a vast galley. The clamour and shouts of a battle reached his ears: still clutching the vegetation, he managed to get through what was left of a mill that the floods had dragged away, and got out. A troop of soldiers had clustered around the pyramid and were sheltering behind its bulk from the arrows and stones being fired from the terraces of the castle.

In the midst of them he recognised with a shiver the tall outline of the senator, wrapped in his red robes and, beside him, his daughter in her strange costume. They both contemplated the battle with the composed posture of a Roman statue, as if the convulsion of the struggle had nothing to do with them.

Dante ran forward, ignoring the projectiles that were hissing over his head, in the direction of the pyramid. With one final spurt he finally managed to reach her. He got his breath back, then approached the senator from behind, touching him on the shoulder. The man turned slowly, then a flicker in his eyes seemed to draw him out of his indifference, as if that touch had brought him back to reality.

'Messer Alighieri, at last! I was afraid you had left us, when you disappeared from the castle . . .' he said reproachfully. 'But I knew you would come,' he added immediately, after shaking his head. 'That you would be with me in this venture. At last. I need your song!'

For a moment Dante looked up towards the terraces, from which the rain of stones continued uninterruptedly. At that moment a rock crashed into the pyramid, tearing away a great travertine slab, which smashed a short distance away from them. Overcoming his fear, the poet stared at the senator again. 'Your venture is a murderous one. How do you expect it to feed the voice of poetry, which is more than anything a voice of love?'

He had spoken with anger. But the emotion faded as he saw the man's daughter, now pressing herself against her father, her face serene, lit by the incredible grace that he had seen before.

'Murderous?' the senator asked, aggrieved. His surprise seemed genuine.

'I saw it in your house. The remains of those innocent girls that you sacrificed for your hoax. For your madness. You were the one who faked the remains of the fake she-Pope, to confuse the common people and incite rebellion. But what do you expect to achieve by throwing Peter's city into a state of despair?'

'Peter's throne! That's where I will put my daughter.'

Dante opened his eyes wide. The sound of those words whirled in his head with a roar that had suddenly erased all the other sounds of battle.

'You're mad! The College of Cardinals will never recognise a woman as Bishop of Rome. Our faith itself denies it! The peoples of the world, their princes. The Emperor and the kings of Europe. Which of them would ever support so diabolical a project? Who will link his name to an act so heretical that it will make that name notorious for centuries? Your venture will end in blood and dust, just as it began.'

'When Boniface is vanquished, his cardinals in flight, the people of Rome themselves will acclaim her as their leader. And the troops of the Roman families loyal to me

– the ones you can see, and others who will come from the countryside – will be her first supporters. And the Council that will be held in the city, inspired by its veneration of the Great Mother, will put its seal on the new truth of faith. With the protection of the goddess, my daughter will reign. And her world will be a new one – of justice and love, the one that has already been sung of by Virgil, and which your voice will answer, with all the power of a crash of thunder. Rome will return to its ancient grandeur, its temples will be restored, the outrage of false prophecies and false doctrines erased!'

Dante had listened aghast. He stared once again at Fiamma and at the ceremonial robes she was wearing. Not those of a Christian bishop, but the more ancient robes that he had seen depicted on the papyrus in the room of death. He imagined her clutching a sistrum, as she advanced in procession amongst her cheering worshippers, among songs that rose up in an incomprehensible language. 'You don't just want your daughter on Peter's throne,' he stammered. 'That would be simply an act of madness, the agitation of a mind blinded by demons. You wanted your daughter to become God himself!'

The senator nodded. A resolute light shone in his eyes, the gleam of someone who sees with certainty the things to come, as if the veil of the future had been rent in front of him. The same light that Dante had seen shining in the eyes of men who had been sent to the pyre. He shook himself, dragged into the present by the crash of a new rock hurtling against the pyramid.

'But Boniface is far from falling,' he shouted, raising his arm towards the Castello, whose great bulk loomed above them. 'His fortress is impregnable, you are leading your own flesh and blood, your own accomplices, to ruin. What you are trying to do is quite hopeless!'

'Give my plan time to proceed, Messer Alighieri. And watch what is preordained,' the senator replied, pointing to the muddy waters of the Tiber, which had reached the base of the rampart walls. 'While we have been speaking, while the defenders of the castle have carried on with their vain attempt to repel us, the flood-wave has entered the false grave of the she-Pope, far beneath the foundations of the corner keep. And it is pressing with all its vast strength, dragging away the earth that supports it, and preparing its ruin.'

'So that's why you pushed the tree-trunks into the current upriver. So that when they crashed against the Ponte dell'Angelo, the level of the river would rise right here!'

'Yes, it was all planned. I told you that November was the preordained month: because at that time of year Latium is drenched in rain, and the river that usually receives it floods.'

'But this way you have decreed the devastation of the whole city.'

The senator was impassive. Dante was about to return to the task, when a cry from the man's daughter stopped him. 'Look, Father! The walls!'

On the smooth brick surface of the surrounding wall, where it entered the corner of the keep, a thin line had appeared, darker than the rest, and marked by puffs of red dust. The bricks were parting as the line grew, becoming a distinct crack. Then, with a roar, an entire section of the wall collapsed, dragging with it the bodies of some screaming men and one of the catapults, which crashed to the ground in a pile of shattered fragments.

The collapse was met with a cry of jubilation from the ranks of the besieging forces. The senator had called out too, pressing his daughter enthusiastically to him. Then the man released himself from the embrace and pointed his sword towards the breach.

'The road to victory is open. Let us enter Boniface's lair, and let our new age begin,' Saturniano cried.

Colonna's men had enthusiastically headed for the walls, taking advantage of the break in the stone-throwing caused by the bewilderment of the men on the terraces over what had happened. The senator had set off as well, after giving his daughter one last look of affection. Fiamma had watched after him, eyes bright, and then, after standing still for a moment, she too had thrown herself among the advancing men, showing no fear.

Dante had gripped the girl's hand, trying to hold her back.

But she pulled herself away from him and started to run. With a few leaps he saw her reach the front line of the fighters, beside her father, who had now got to the breach. Without thinking, the poet too hurled himself forward, forcing his way through the mass of shouting soldiers.

The gap that had opened up in the wall was only a few yards wide, just enough to let a few men in at once. He found himself being squashed by the mass of people, forced onwards by their armour and the poles of their lances. For a moment he thought he would be crushed to death, but then the momentum of the crowd dragged him through the crack along with everyone else. He collided painfully against the broken wall, with a blow to the forehead that left him almost dazed, then found himself back on the ramp that descended steeply towards the internal courtyard. In front of him, the mass of the cylinder of volcanic rock reached the sky, as heedless as a Titan of the blows with which the attackers had begun hammering at the great arched gate leading into the fortress.

He glimpsed the senator and his daughter in front of the gate. The man was urging the attackers to hurry up, striking with his sword at the great oak panels, which groaned and shattered under the blows, but continued to resist the assault.

'Hurry up. Hurry up!' the poet heard him cry. 'Don't be afraid of anything. In a few moments the waters will erode the foundations of the tambour, too. It will open up before us like the gates of Paradise!'

The men continued their attack. But at that moment a boulder fell from above, bouncing near the gate and crushing some of the men who were trying to force down the gate. For a moment the poet thought the senator's prophecy was coming true, and that the central bulk of the Castello, eroded by the water, was beginning to fall.

But then, looking up, he saw that the defenders up above, having recovered from their initial surprise, had started to target them with their projectiles. He saw the trapdoors opening, and a second boulder fell, followed by another hail of arrows. The soldiers who had stayed on the surrounding wall were returning to action as well, and had started firing arrows at the attacking men.

The senator continued urging on the attackers. The gates seemed to be starting to give, and one of the boards had already been pulled away. The blows were concentrated on the bolts.

Meanwhile a breathless man joined the group from the hole in the wall. He looked rapidly among the fighting men, then ran over to Sciarra Colonna. 'I'm coming from the island! The tree-trunks are giving way – it looks as if the waterway is opening up again.'

Agitated, Colonna turned to the senator. 'You said the Castle would fall!'

'Keep striking the gate, and have faith in me,' Saturniano

Spada replied imperturbably. 'Look at the river – see if it isn't moving as I predicted.'

A muddy torrent had started flooding through the breach in the walls, submerging the courtyard below, which began to turn into a muddy trench. A new boulder landed close to them, this time throwing up a wave of mud.

Pressed onwards by the projectiles above them, and by the river that rose beneath their feet, the attackers had redoubled their efforts. At last one of the hinges of the gate gave and then, beneath the pressure of the hands of hundreds of shouting men, the whole gate leaned and fell inside with a crash.

In the dark gap that had opened up, Dante saw the vague shadows of men retreating at a great rate, and the beginning of a vast vaulted ramp that climbed with a curve towards the top of the castle, following the circular mass of the tambour.

'Keep going!' cried the senator, rushing inside, followed by Colonna and the men who were closest to the entrance. Dante joined Fiamma, who was running undaunted beside them in her white robes, her eyes bright with excitement.

He remembered the first time he had seen her, still fresh with the excitement of hunting. It was as if the girl was on a hunt, although this time it was her own life that was at stake. Her lips were parted and she was breathing heavily, her forehead pearly with sweat, beneath her sumptuous crown. He ran in front of her to protect her with his own body against the rain of arrows that was flying down the tunnel. He picked up an abandoned shield and lifted it up in front of him. He felt he had to protect her from this madness: it wasn't possible that she should be a willing accomplice in her father's venture; she must have been dragged into it, blinded by her youth.

He took her by the hand and began to follow the mass of fighters who were climbing like men possessed. Someone had lit a torch, and flashes of light darted here and there, lighting up the walls of the gloomy passageway, as the defenders retreated in the darkness, still firing at them as they did. Dante heard the hiss of the arrows passing over their heads, and the dull thud of the ones that crashed against the rock. And the cries of the men who were hit and rolled back, trampled by the men who came running behind them.

He had been in the middle of fighting before, but he had never seen battles being fought with so much improvisation, and with such crazed ardour. Everyone around him seemed to be devoured by blind hatred, a desire for destruction that was utterly heedless of the risks.

He too climbed blindly, overwhelmed by what was happening around him. Suddenly he found himself crashing against the backs of the people in front of him, who had abruptly come to a standstill.

He heard cries of fury coming from the ramp. He craned his neck to see what was happening, and saw that an insurmountable chasm had opened up in front of him. Perhaps an ancient well, dug at the time of the castle's first construction, or a means of defence when the mausoleum had been turned into a fortress. One of the men at the front had toppled into the abyss, and his desperate cry had come to an end only after an interminable fall.

'They've opened the trapdoor in the passageway,' the senator cried. 'Bring the ladders, quickly!'

Dante was knocked violently against the stone wall, pushed aside by men who came from behind him, carrying long poles and planks.

The poet let the men pass. Within moments they had thrown a gangway over the gaping hole, and already the first men were hurling themselves across it. On the other side Dante could see the defenders, barricaded behind the structure of the bridge that had been raised, and reloading their crossbows. When the first two attackers had almost reached the opposite side, a new flight of arrows fell upon them, piercing the most exposed.

Dante heard the dry thud of an arrow striking his shield, passing halfway through it and stopping only a few inches from his head. He fell to his knees, dragging Fiamma with him and forcing her to take shelter with him behind his shield. The girl resisted, trying to stay upright to see what was happening in the battle. She seemed to be increasingly intoxicated by the conflict, ignoring the danger, as if certain that her gods were beside her.

The first to have ventured across the gangway had been struck point-blank by a new flight of arrows, and had fallen howling down below. A new unit had immediately come forward to take their place, but by now the defenders had sprung from their hiding places and had thrown themselves frantically at the end of the gangway, pushing it back with all their might.

The boards were heavy with the weight of the men running across them, and resisted the defenders' efforts. But, helped on by the force of desperation, they went on shaking it, trying to drag the planks away with their bare hands and using the poles of their lances as levers. The cluster of humanity standing on it began to stagger, shouting with pain and fury.

Amongst contradictory orders and frantic shouts, the men closer to the other side of the gap began to retreat, terrified at the thought of their imminent deaths, while behind the poet the others were pressing forward, trying to find a way out. Dante rose from his hiding place, without thinking of his own safety, guessing at the disaster that was taking place in front of him. The men on the gangway, who were by now out of their minds with panic, were fighting amongst themselves as if the enemy had joined their number, and no longer recognised their companions' faces in the men who had been fighting beside them only a moment before.

'Stop!' he cried, running towards the gangway. 'Calm yourselves, or you're done for.'

The spectre of the battle of Montaperti had appeared in his mind, as he had heard it related a thousand times by the old men of Florence: when, at the sign of the traitor Bocca degli Abati, the Ghibellines who had managed to slip behind the Florentine lines had leaped from their hiding places to slaughter the enemy. And how each man, blinded by the sun and dust, had failed to recognise his fellow, and they had all abandoned themselves to a horrible slaughter, pointless and directionless, in which flight and attack were no longer recognisable except for the bloody footprints of the fatally wounded. Now that scene, which he had known only in words, appeared before his eyes, and at last he understood the terrible impotence that some-times blinds the mind in the fury of battle.

The flash of that far-off memory had lasted only a moment, but within that brief space of time the tragedy had occurred. Dante just had time to reach the edge of the abyss to witness the last shake of the end of the gangway, which fell far below, dragging its cargo of screaming humanity with it. As they plunged, he saw the last of the men stretching out his arms in a desperate attempt to clutch onto something. He leaped towards the man, grip-ping his wrist and holding it tightly. With a violent effort he managed to hold the man's weight, just enough to let him turn in the void and grab the stone edge with his other hand.

Only then did he see that the face looking at him from

the chasm below, as contorted as the face of a corpse rising from the grave, was that of Sciarra Colonna. There was nothing of his old arrogance in that face, purple with exertion, its eyes dilated with terror. Tugging hard, Dante helped the man back onto the floor of the tunnel, as their eyes met again.

'I'm repaying my debt from the marshes,' the poet panted, as the other man struggled back to his feet. An unreal silence had fallen around them, after the screams of terror and jubilation of the attackers. Sciarra Colonna gave him an icy sneer, then turned his gaze on the surviving men. With a grimace he seemed to assess the effects of the fall, then turned to the senator, who was also standing at the edge of the chasm. 'You promised the fortress would fall, and instead you dragged us into a trap!'

Colonna bared his teeth like a caged animal. His men stared at him uncertainly, leaning against the stone walls in search of some means of escape, waiting for orders. The man spat on the ground, as a new hail of arrows fell all around them, but without doing any damage. It seemed that the defenders of the castle, satisfied with their success, weren't paying too much attention to their aim.

'Come on!' the young man shouted after a moment. 'The venture has failed, we were mad to listen to this traitor,' he added, slapping the senator's face with his iron-gloved hand. He seemed to be preparing to strike him again when Dante stopped him, holding Colonna by the wrist. Perhaps Sciarra felt in his grip the same strength that he had felt when he had saved Dante from death, because he lowered his head as if he didn't dare meet the poet's eyes. Then he tugged his arm away, retreating quickly and leading the flight of his men, who began following him back down the ramp.

'Where are you off to, coward?' Dante called after him, taking a step in Colonna's direction. But the mass of retreating fugitives had interposed themselves between them. He only managed to hurl one last poisonous curse after him, before seeing him disappear around the bend in the stone passageway.

AN UNREAL silence weighed all around. Dante gripped Fiamma's hand, pulling her with him. Then he gestured to the senator, showing him the way down as well. But the man seemed not to see him.

His face was drenched in blood, which poured copiously from his eyebrow, split by Colonna's blow. He slowly brought his hand to his cheek, pulling it back streaked with scarlet. Big drops of blood had fallen at his feet, staining the stone of the tunnel.

'Saturniano Spada,' Dante said. 'This is where your desire to break the laws of God has brought you. There is a justice in things. Now you'll have to face it.'

The senator stared with fascination at the bloodstains.

He pointed at them with his index finger. 'That's the plan for the future,' he murmured.

Dante lowered his eyes to the spot that Saturniano was pointing to. At first he didn't understand what the senator was trying to say. That spatter of stains was the visible sign of his failure. And what future could there be for him? Wandering into exile, followed by shame and persecution by Boniface? Or handing himself over to the executioner's axe?

Then, suddenly, he understood. Those stains were just a map, a series of points drawn from Colonna's body and marking out his fate.

'There is no future in what you're reading,' Dante said, gripping the senator by a shoulder. 'Your plan failed. And I understood too late why you opened the gates to hell,' he went on bitterly.

The man suddenly glanced towards him. 'So you know,' he said, with despair in his voice. 'My dream! The salvation of the new Rome.'

Dante shook him furiously. 'Deposing Boniface! If that had been it, you would have had the comfort and assistance of all the good men in Italy. But wiping out Revelation, and restoring false and lying gods. Making her think she was worthy to sit on Peter's throne – and wiping it out, in fact, to impose in its place the girdle of Isis, in the place of the blood-drenched cross of Christ!'

The senator's eyes burned with mad light. 'Yes . . .' he murmured. 'And you will sing all of this . . .'

'The murder of so many innocent women, just to reach the false relic of the she-Pope. To make the mob expect a female saviour, a leader of the Christian people like one who had been before!'

The senator nodded again. 'Yes . . . and you will say it, in your ornate language?' he pleaded, raising his arms towards the poet.

'No.'

The senator's hands fell back along his hips, as if the whole of his body had been drained of energy. Then all of a sudden the poet saw his right hand darting up, gripping a shining blade that seemed to have appeared out of nowhere. He saw the senator bringing it to his throat and then, before he had time to react, slicing his throat clean across. A spurt of blood gushed from the wound, drenching Dante's face and covering the stains on the stone. The man fell to the ground with a groan, as the poet tried in vain to hold him.

He let the man's head fall back, among the rivulets of his own blood. Then he turned in search of the senator's daughter. Fiamma had watched the scene wide-eyed, as still as a statue. Further up, at the bend in the ramp, the defenders of the barricade were preparing to climb over it. Others were operating the drawbridge, and in a moment they would be on top of them. There was only another moment left in which to try and escape. But the girl stood dazed, looking at her father's body. Her crown had slipped from her head, falling into the blood. Then Dante saw her draw from beneath her robes a small bronze instrument and slowly start to wave it around.

A metallic tinkle wafted through the air, like a subtle perfume.

THE GIRL had started softly tidying her hair with her fingers; it was curled in the style of a classical statue, held tightly at the brow by a scarlet ribbon. Her hair shone as if a balm had been poured over it. She went on mechanically doing what she was doing: she seemed to be staring at her image in the clear bronze back of her little instrument, as if gauging with her blank gaze the results of her efforts. But she was not really staring at her image: her eye wandered beyond the reflection to something hidden at a secret distance, which she alone could recognise.

'Listen to me, I beg you!' the poet exclaimed.

'My temple – that's where I have to get back to. That's where I will meet the goddess, and when we meet again it will be in her arms,' Fiamma said, glancing once more at the senator's body. 'She will seek his soul, which wanders in the dark dimension, and she will bring it back together with his body, as she did with her lover Osiris.' Beside her feet lay the crown. She picked it up, ignoring its weight, and put it back on her head.

She waved the sistrum again, then pricked her ears as if she were trying to call the attention of Isis and waiting to hear the goddess's voice.

'After death you will know the judgement of the true God, incarnated in Christ,' the poet whispered in her ear. 'And his will be the thundering voice uttering the final sermon, deciding between the good and the bad. He and his angels, and not the ghosts of African gods who are dead and lying beneath the sands of the desert. We must flee. Or it will be too late!'

As he spoke he heard his own voice resounding in his ears, his words uttered with pain. But as if someone else were saying them. What God was he talking about? Was there still a God watching over the fates of men, like a benevolent father? Had there ever been? Or was creation merely a blind, mute abyss, in which a wretched Earth orbited like dust amongst other dust, a cosmos made of the names of ancient gods, dead just as they were?

She didn't reply, merely leaving her hand in Dante's. The poet moved towards the end of the ramp, dragging the girl along in water up to her knees, in the hope that it might still be possible to turn back.

It was then that he was seized by desperation. The water was now almost as deep as they were tall, and must have completely submerged the entrance. Every escape route was blocked – they were prisoners in the Castello, which was now once more the ancient tomb of its origins.

Without noticing, he had let go of Fiamma's hand. The girl, still tinkling her sistrum, took another few steps forward, plunging into the flood. She seemed oblivious to the coldness of the water, lost in her dream.

Dante was about to hold her back when a deep rumble came from the bend of the underwater ramp. The water was seething violently, as if a huge sea creature were coming towards them up the tunnel. The foam rose, submerging Fiamma almost up to the chest.

'Turn back!' cried Dante, gripping her by a wrist once more. 'The flood is rising again.'

At that moment, in a great whirlpool, the water seemed to subside. As he stretched forward to grab the girl's hand as she was dragged away, in his mind the frightened words of Colonna's man came back to him in a flash: the barrier to the island must have given, and the current of the river was resuming its course.

With his right hand he clutched at a piece of rock protruding from the wall to avoid being dragged away, while with his other hand he tried to grip the girl's wrist. He felt her damp skin slipping between his fingers. He gripped her tightly, with the strength that comes from desperation, calling to Fiamma to hold on. But he felt her hand slipping from his grip, and he was left holding nothing but water. He thought he heard the girl shouting something, but her words were lost in the noise of the water flowing violently away.

For a moment he saw again the whiteness of Fiamma's body disappearing into the swirling waters as they withdrew, the waves pulling her crown from her head. That headgear floated on the surface of the water for another moment and swirled around in an eddy, before it too was dragged away.

Weeping, Dante fell to his knees. Like the sighs of Orpheus at the gate of Hades, his own sighs echoed in vain, in the tunnel where a goddess had appeared for a moment, and had now disappeared again behind her mysterious veils.

Following the surge of the subsiding waters, Dante struggled back down the big tunnel. In front of him the seething liquid mass disappeared with the roar of a huge wounded animal; it must have sounded like the whale that swallowed the prophet Jonah, he thought, as he looked around for the path that was gradually becoming passable, in the hope of finding Fiamma's body. Perhaps the waters had spared her, perhaps her terrible trust in immortality really had summoned a goddess to protect her.

But he found no sign of her, all the way to the entrance arch. The portal opened only a few feet above the water, just enough to let a human body pass through. He stopped hesitantly. He had never been a good swimmer, and even as a boy he had avoided the swimming competitions in the Arno. But the voices of the Castello soldiers, who were also making their way towards the exit, were close behind him now. Sighing deeply, he threw himself into the cold, fetid water and desperately began to swim.

He reached the gap, gripped the remains of the door to get his breath back and then, with one decisive push, slipped beneath the narrow arch, emerging into the open.

The light outside was painful to his eyes, blinding him for a moment. When he could finally see again, he thought he was dreaming. He seemed to be in the middle of a dead sea, with islands in the distance, topped with buildings.

Around him there was nothing but water in every direction, and piles of tree-trunks, uprooted shrubs, detritus of every kind. Above his head towered the mass of the Castello. For a moment he thought of swimming in that direction, in search of safety, but the violent current gripped him, dragging him towards the open water. He tried to resist, swimming clumsily, but ended up with his head beneath the surface of the water, his mouth filled with that revolting mud. Then, as if his movements had called it from the abyss, a kind of aquatic monster appeared with a gurgle beside him, making him quake with fear, before he realised that it was only the swollen carcase of a drowned sheep. Terror was taking hold of him; he felt his strength draining away, while his clothes, weighed down with water, drew him ineluctably towards the bottom.

He felt a painful blow against his back, which dragged him once again below the water. He just managed to surface, panting and spitting out the water that he had swallowed, beside a boat half-filled with water. He saw a rowlock just in front of his eyes and grabbed it. Summoning up his last energies, he managed to hoist himself onto the vessel, then lay prone inside it, letting the boat pull him where it would.

As he desperately tried to recover his strength, he felt the dinghy slipping away through the whirls and eddies of the river, bumping and jolting violently as if it threatened to capsize at any moment. The current seemed extraordinarily fast, as if a dyke had abruptly broken downriver from the Castello and the whole mass of water had found a sudden outlet. He heard the roar of distant cataracts, as if a waterfall had somehow been dug in the river bed.

Then a violent knock brought the boat to a standstill, throwing him into the prow. The boat had stopped almost level with the Ponte Cestio, stuck in the roots of a big tree-trunk, which had itself come to rest against the base of the guards' tower. Dante struggled up from the waterlogged bottom of the boat, looking around in search of a way of reaching the shore.

Someone called to him from the parapet of the bridge.

Dante looked up: it was the widow's young son, holding out an arm and inviting him to take it. He clutched that hand.

STUNNED, HE climbed from the boat, and in the same condition leaned on the boy's shoulder, staggering behind him towards the house. The flood-water was gradually subsiding, and his feet sank into the mud-filled street as if into a bog. At last they went inside; Dante barely had the strength to slump onto a wooden bench, and fell into a kind of faint that swept his senses away.

He woke to the pleasant feeling of a fire burning in the hearth nearby.

'What will you do now, Messere?' the boy asked, solic-itously holding out a cup of hot wine. Dante tried to take it in both trembling hands. He felt the boy putting a dry blanket around his shoulders. The warmth around his body, along with the liquid descending into his stomach, slowly revived him. Gradually the tremor in his muscles faded away.

His mind grew clearer. And, with the return of consciousness, despair took hold of him. Several times he opened his mouth to say something, but his words died on his lips as if a demon within him were amusing himself by holding them back. 'In Siena, I'll try to rejoin my party,' he finally managed to stammer. 'They will have taken refuge there, if the situation has worsened. I have a few friends among them. Perhaps,' he added, with a bitter expression.

He turned his head, but could no longer see the boy. He sighed. The boy too had abandoned him. Besides, what had he done for the boy, or for his old mother? What good would it have done them to know the name of the murderer of their daughter and sister? A murderer who had escaped justice, whom he himself might even have helped to escape.

At that moment he saw the boy coming back into the room. He was holding the carved wooden cylinder, which he held carefully out to the poet. 'I thought this might be something valuable. I hid it when the district came under attack. While you were looking for my sister's murderer. Did you find him?' the boy asked, his voice filled with hope.

'Yes. But he won't be punished. His name will remain unknown.'

The boy nodded sadly. Then he lifted his head. 'It doesn't matter, God knows it. My mother will be able to die now. She will see Ninfa again in heaven, because that's where the innocent go, isn't it?'

'Yes. That's where they go,' Dante replied mechanically, without taking the cylinder that the boy held out to him. Was he still worthy to touch the work of that great man? If only God would speak to him again. If only there was a way to turn back, if only he could find it . . .

He drew from within his robes the pages that he had written at the castle in Ostia, reduced by the river to an almost shapeless mass, and opened them delicately one by one. The water had washed away the ink, turning the lines into an indecipherable string of ghosts. He slowly began to tear the paper into tiny fragments, beneath the surprised eyes of the boy, and threw them away. There must be a way. For the humble, and for everyone. He would find it.

He reached out his hand towards the cylinder that the boy was still holding out to him. His fingers gripped the container, so hard that it creaked.

'That's where the innocent go,' he repeated, raising his eyes to the stars.

GLOSSARY

Aeneas – the Trojan hero (son of Aphrodite and Anchises) in Greco-Roman mythology whose journey from Troy, leading to the founding of Rome and the Roman race, was recounted in Virgil's *Aeneid* (see below)

Beatrice – the woman in Dante's *Divine Comedy* who takes over from Virgil as guide; also referred to in the novel as the 'Portinari woman' because her real name was Bice dei Portinari; Dante fell in love with her at a young age, continuing to dedicate work to her after her death at the age of twenty-four in 1290 (she had married the banker Simone dei Bardi three years earlier)

Boniface VIII (c.1235–1303) – Pope of the Roman Catholic Church, 1294–1303; born Benedetto Caetani, he was elected Pope after Celestine V renounced the papacy, and pushed papal supremacy to the limit, leading to conflict with Philip IV of France, and with Dante himself, who depicted Boniface in the *Inferno* as being destined for a circle of Hell

Caetani – an Italian noble family with close links to the papacy, especially after the election of Benedetto Caetani as Boniface VIII; their struggles with the Colonna family (see below) were to lead to frequent clashes in Rome and the Campagna

Campaldino – a battle on the banks of the River Arno, on 11th June, 1289, in which Dante fought for the victorious Guelphs (led by Florence; see below) against the Ghibellines (led by the commune of Arezzo)

Campidoglio – the Capitoline Hill in Rome, the smallest of Rome's seven hills, but the religious and political seat of the city since its foundation more than two millennia ago

Castello Sant'Angelo – a massive circular tomb on the right bank of the Tiber, commissioned by the Roman Emperor Hadrian (76–138) as the mausoleum for himself and his family; it subsequently functioned as a papal fortress and prison, and is now a museum

Guido Cavalcanti (c.1255–1300) – a poet and a member of a prominent Florentine Guelph family, whom Dante had to exile for factionalism, despite being a friend; in his poetry Cavalcanti explored the philosophy of love, and he led a secret sect of poets known as the Fedeli d'Amore

(The Faithful of Love), which Dante was eventually invited to join

Cerchi and Donati – two leading Florentine families whose disputes eventually led to virtual civil war between the 'White' faction of the Guelphs (led by the Cerchi, a banking family) and the 'Black' faction (led by the Donati); the Blacks were ultimately victorious, leading to exile for numerous Whites, including Dante, as Prior of the Republic of Florence

Colonna – a powerful Italian noble family in medieval Rome, supporters of the pro-Emperor Ghibelline faction; Sciarra Colonna was vehemently opposed to Pope Boniface VIII, who was captured in his palace at Anagni (and allegedly slapped by Sciarra Colonna) in 1303 – an event recorded by Dante in his *Divine Comedy*

Curia – the papal court at the Vatican, through which the Roman Catholic Church is governed

Frederick II of Swabia (1194–1250) – Holy Roman Emperor 1220–50; pretender to the title of King of the Romans from 1212 and unopposed monarch of Italy from 1215; as one of the foremost Christian monarchs in Europe during the Middle Ages, he was widely respected and was known by the title *Stupor mundi* ('the wonder of the world'), but was frequently at war with the papacy and was excommunicated four times

Giotto di Bondone (c.1266/7–1337) – the Florentine painter who is generally seen as one of the first great artists of the Italian Renaissance; he worked in most of the major artistic centres of Italy, especially in Florence, Padua and Assisi, and on the Navicella mosaic in St Peter's, Rome

Guelphs and Ghibellines – of these two rival factions in thirteenth-century Italy, the Guelphs (to whom Dante belonged, and who subsequently split into the Whites and Blacks – see above) supported the Pope and consisted of middle-class merchants and shopkeepers, while the Ghibellines supported the Holy Roman Emperor and comprised an alliance of the feudal nobility and leading merchants

guild – in thirteenth-century Italy there were numerous guilds or professional and trade associations, which set the standards for the profession in question and granted protection and privileges to their members; in the novel the Apothecaries' and Cloth Merchants' Guilds are both mentioned

Inquisition – throughout Europe from c.1184 a series of Roman Catholic bodies were known as the 'Inquisition', charged with suppressing heresy, as a response to the threat posed by large popular movements such as those of the Cathars and Waldensians in France and northern Italy

Pope Joan – an English woman who, according to legend, became Pope (as Johanna) in around 855–7, but was allegedly stoned to death after she subsequently gave birth to a child during a papal procession in Rome

Jubilee – this refers to the holy year of 'great remissions and indulgences for sins', beginning on 22nd February, 1300, convoked by Pope Boniface III – a tradition that continued in the Catholic Church every twenty-five or fifty years; it promised a universal pardon to those who visited the basilicas of St Peter and St Paul in Rome, and Dante is reputed by some people to have done so in 1300

Leonine City – the part of Rome on the right bank of the Tiber around which Pope Leo IV commissioned the Leonine Wall during the ninth century; it includes, but is not limited to, the Vatican City

Monna Lagia – a brothel-keeper in Florence, possibly named after the one mentioned in poems by Dante and Cavalcanti

Nero – Roman Emperor, AD 54–68, whose rule is often associated with extravagance and tyranny; he was an early persecutor of Christians and was said to have 'fiddled while Rome burned' during the Great Fire of AD 64; his Domus Aurea ('Golden House') was an extravagant villa built on the Esquiline Hill after the Fire

The Pantheon – a circular pagan temple in Rome, replaced by the Emperor Hadrian in 118–25 and containing the largest unreinforced concrete dome in the world until the twentieth century, which is exactly as high as it is wide; the light effects through the oculus and the building's perfect proportions remain a source of wonder today

Philip IV of France ('the Fair') (1268–1314) – King of France, 1285–1314; he battled frequently with Boniface VIII over the Pope's attempts to tax the French clergy, leading eventually to the 'Babylonish captivity' of the papacy and its move to Avignon for seventy years

Pietra – Italian for 'stone': in 1296 a series of Dante's verses were written to one Donna Pietra, who may have been named for her stony indifference to him; it was possibly a reference to Pietra degli Scrovigni, the daughter of a Paduan money-lender assigned to the circle of usurers in Dante's *Inferno*

La Serenissima – literally, 'the Most Serene Republic' in Venetian, a term widely used to refer to the Republic of Venice

Trajan – Emperor of Rome, AD 98–117, known for his extensive public-building programme, which reshaped the city and left numerous landmarks, including Trajan's Market (a 'mall' incorporating offices and shops), Trajan's Forum and Column (of which only the column, celebrating the Emperor's victories, now remains) and Trajan's Baths (a massive bathing and leisure complex)

Trastevere – a district of Rome on the west bank of the Tiber (its name means 'beyond the Tiber'), south of the Vatican City; this former working-class area has retained its medieval character better than most other districts and is known as a bohemian neighbourhood

Virgil (70–19 BC) – born Publius Virgilius Maro, he was a classical Roman poet, best known for his *Eclogues*, *Georgics* and the *Aeneid*, the last of which followed the epic model of Homer's *Iliad* and *Odyssey* and related the travels of Aeneas (see above) in his search for a new homeland and the founding of Rome; in *The Divine Comedy* Dante made Virgil his guide in Hell and much of Purgatory

TRANSLATOR'S NOTE

READERS OF Giulio Leoni's earlier novels about Dante Alighieri (1265–1351) will be aware that the author interweaves his tales with historical fact and quotations from the poet's works.

In order to understand *The Crusade of Darkness*, a little background to the politics of the period might be useful. At this time Northern Italy was dominated by the conflict between the Guelphs – supporters of the Pope, broadly speaking – and the Ghibellines – supporters of the Holy Roman Emperor. If only it were that simple, however: relations between the two factions were often based on personal disputes and family rivalries. And just to make matters more complicated, Florence was, at the time when this novel is set, divided between the 'White Guelphs', led by Vieri dei Cerchi, and the 'Black Guelphs', led by Corso Donati. Dante was a supporter of the Whites, who sought greater freedom from Rome.

In 1301, Dante was sent as a delegate to Rome, to investigate the intentions of Pope Boniface VIII, who was planning to invade Florence. Boniface – Benedetto Caetani, a member of a noble Roman family – was notorious for his desire to expand the power of the papacy, and would later – after receiving a slap from Sciarra Colonna at the town of Anagni – issue the papal bull *Unam Sanctam*, which decreed that the power of the Pope should exceed that of the Emperor. He was also responsible, as *The Crusade of Darkness* suggests, for the ruthless destruction of the rebel fortress at Palestrina, and the slaughter of its inhabitants.

Once negotiations were completed Dante was kept in Rome at Boniface's 'suggestion': meanwhile the Black party in Florence, supported by Charles de Valois, brother of the French King Philip the Fair, destroyed much of the city and took the opportunity to kill many members of the White faction. Dante was condemned to exile by the new rulers of Florence both as a supporter of the Whites, and as an absconder for having stayed in Rome. In Dante's *Inferno*, Pope Boniface is singled out for special punishment, and sent to Hell for simony (the buying and selling of pardons and favours), even though the Pope was still alive when the poem was written.

There are, as ever, many other allusions to Dante's great work in Giulio Leoni's novel. Gianni Schicchi de' Cavalcanti, for example (p. 334), was a Florentine notorious for faking the will of a member of the Donati family to his own advantage (Canto XXX, lines 22–45). He is now remembered chiefly as the subject of the Puccini opera of the same name.

Most allusions, however, are to politicians: Farinata degli Uberti (p. 416) was a leader of the Ghibelline faction in Florentine politics, which took control of the city in 1260. The Ghibellines' rivals, the Guelphs, regained control of Florence in 1265 and destroyed the properties of the Uberti family to make way for what is now the Piazza della Signoria. After his death, Farinata's body and that of his wife were exhumed and burned on grounds of heresy. In Canto X of the *Inferno* (lines 22–51) Farinata prophesies Dante's exile from Florence.

In Canto XXXII of the *Inferno*, Bocca degli Abati (p. 521) is one of the Traitors whose souls are trapped in the frozen Lake of Cocytus, which fills the bottom of the pit in the innermost of hell. A Ghibelline who remained in Florence after the Guelphs had assumed power in the city, Bocca fought on the Guelph side at the crucial Battle of Montaperti, but at a key moment hacked off the hand of the Guelph standard-bearer, causing confusion among the Guelphs and their ultimate defeat. Tegghiaio Aldobrandi, mentioned at the very beginning of the novel, was a Guelph politician whose careful diplomacy helped to maintain peace in Florence (Canto XVI, 32–33), but whose shade ends up among the Sodomites in the seventh circle of Hell. And Mosca de' Lamberti (Canto VI, line 80 and XXVIII, 106–111) is a Ghibelline held to be responsible for the sorrows of

Florence: his soul, its hands severed and bleeding, suffers its ghastly torment among the Sowers of Discord in the Eighth Circle of Dante's Hell.

I have quoted from various works by Dante and Virgil in the following translations: Virgil's *Aeneid*, translated by John Dryden; Dante's *Inferno* in the translation by Henry Wadsworth Longfellow; and Dante's *Vita Nuova*, the poet's account of his love for Beatrice, translated by Charles Eliot Norton.

www.vintage-books.co.uk